Always, Janie

Meghan Sorley

Nimble Scribbler
Press

Printed in the United States of America

First Edition, August 2025

Book Design by Lizatroyabeth

ISBN 979-8-9987390-0-2 (paperback).
ISBN 979-8-9987390-2-6 (ebook).
ISBN979-8-9987390-1-9 (hardcover).

Published by Nimble Scribbler Press
www.nimblescribblerpress.com

For Mom and Liz. I call upon your wit
every day and grieve you as often.

Part I

Summer 1990

...the most natural, and, consequently, the truest and most intense of the human affections are those which arise in the heart as if by electric sympathy – in a word, that the brightest and most enduring of the psychal fetters are those which are riveted by a glance.
- Edgar Allan Poe, *The Spectacles*

Chapter One

If you were to ask her, Janie Harris would tell you she's nothing like those kids always dreaming of their ticket out of town. It's everywhere in the halls, the kids who already know they're too big for Clayton, dead set on their great escape through college or enlistment. Janie has never understood it. Of course she has dreams too. Heaps of them. She dreams of a summer job out by the lake. Of the sweet inky aroma of her favorite comic fresh off the presses. Of summer's promise of pocket money to buy said comic, and breathing room enough to read it without her mother finding out. Little does she know that by summer's end, what began as serendipitous reverie will cut a swath a thousand miles wide and a decade long clean through the life she's known. Till then, she'll hold tight to the notion it's better to be restless than rudderless. Not so much because she feels it in her bones, but because she has never encountered anything or anyone that could usurp her fear of the unknown.

Funnily enough, the same could not be said for her father when he was fourteen. Even less so at eighteen, when he swore that he had kicked the last of this town off his boots for good.

Though on days like today, you'd never know such murmurings rumble in the bellies of the too big for Clayton kids as they hurry alongside their parents to the fairgrounds. Driving through town, the lamp posts are adorned in centennial banners whose reds, blues and gold lettering catch in the midday sun just so. Heat radiates from the asphalt, and it's only June. The scent of kettle corn carried on a wave of hickory from the pit masters competition washes over the festivities. Hopped up on funnel cake and slushies, farm kids and townie kids clamor alike for a chance to be carried skyward on the Ferris wheel. At least half the town is here, and a good measure more will arrive by sundown. Clayton is the little town that could, and did, for that matter.

Just the same, come tomorrow, anyone in town will tell you plain as day that no one moves to Clayton for the scenery or proximity to industrial agriculture. Instead, they marry in and over time acquiesce to the immutable rhythm of small-town life. Each generation disrupts the comfortable stasis of the previous. Children lurching their parents forward, and grandparents easing into the lull of their golden years. That charming paradox of perpetual renewal and steadfast tradition are what drew Janie Harris' parents back to Clayton.

Reluctantly joining the ranks of Clayton's prodigal children who have found their way home with fresh blood in tow, Ray Harris returned home with his wife Helene a matter of weeks before welcoming Janie's older sister Kate. Once brimming with disdain, time softened Ray's memories of a life he had outgrown. Clayton had become a safe harbor to moor himself to when the life he thought he wanted left him unfulfilled. The impending birth of their first child further compelled him to set right the wrongs of his childhood. Despite it all, somehow there's comfort in the devil you know.

Ray Harris cannot be counted among those who lose their grip yet manage to steer into the apex, course corrected they continue in the safety of the middle. He's never known the middle, not in the turbulence of childhood or the excesses of adulthood. Hundreds of miles away, he and Helene found themselves fitting snugly into the well-worn grooves of everything he loathed about his father. Accordingly, it came as no surprise he wouldn't seek salvation in the middle either. In returning to Clayton, they held their reclaimed faith tightly to the point of piety, at times even encroaching upon zealotry.

As time passed, their view of the world became wicked. Culpability shifted from their shoulders to the boogeyman that robbed them of their youth. Ray and Helene devoted themselves to insulating their children from the sorrows of life outside. Church was not merely a place to spend Sunday mornings, fellowship was an enclave anchored by shared values.

Firmly believing in the devil's capacity for finding work for idle hands, Helene splits her time between working the counter at the post office and administrative tasks at church. She shoehorns her three children into the spaces between, without so much as missing a meal or a single parent-teacher conference. The Harris household is well synchronized, and deviation from the routine cannot and will not be tolerated. With Ray commuting to Modesto, household responsibilities rest upon Helene, who revels in being the family linchpin. Nothing happens at work, at church or under her roof without Helene knowing about it. Always keenly aware of how she's perceived, always nursing an insatiable thirst for affirmation of her worth.

As a result, Kathryn, Janine, and little Mathew Harris gaze ahead with certainty, liberated from the restlessness that plagues many of their classmates, trusting in a sort of spiritual bliss to lead them to their calling. Though, at times, Janie suspects their mother intercepts those divine signals and disseminates them at will.

Kate is very much her mother's daughter, what with her slender frame, sandy hair, and serious disposition. Janie, on the other hand, is cut from the same cloth as her father. They share an affinity for junk food and an umber glare that always foreshadows a good sulk. Ray should've seen that much like himself; Janie would not go quietly into the thick of adolescence.

After taping a polaroid of her and Matty from the centennial fair to the vanity, Janie adjusts a photo of her and Yaya. The gappy grin suggests she was about seven or so, not much older than Matty. She traces the paper's edge, if only he had gotten to know her, or even remembered the lightness of their parents when she was still here. Passed years now, Janie's Yaya left an indelible mark upon her. She was Janie's glimpse into before, the teller of tales that her parents preferred to forget, and most importantly, she was Janie's confidant.

Eschewing convention in favor of discovery, even trips to the park with Yaya were destined for adventure. Having emigrated from Greece when she was young, her family settled in Clayton. While faithful to their traditions, she eagerly embraced their new homeland but married an American boy with Greek lineage as a compromise.

Yaya regaled Janie with stories of Ray's adventures after wanderlust and resentment carried him off to the Rockies, and of how it took him going all the way to Colorado to meet a good girl from the Central Valley. When Janie asked why he left, the explanation was simple. *He was meant to meet your mother there, just as your sister was meant to bring him home. No one outfoxes the Moirai, not even your father.* Too young at the time, Janie came to understand she was speaking of fate, as she often did in her unvarnished way.

What Yaya could never share were the spaces in between the adventures and the homecoming. The secondhand heartache Ray related in brief calls as he and Helene resisted the call home. With each year, it took more and more to sustain the euphoria of autonomy they'd come to crave. In the throes of self-discovery Helene's grandfather, whom she adored, fell ill. It wasn't enough to draw her home. She sent a card and reasoned he would understand her plight. A year later when her mother called to tell her she was sick, again Helene told herself there was time. She would get home when she could, but with all their plans and friends, time passed and took her mother along with it.

Kissing her fingers and placing them upon Yaya's cheek, Janie feels the photo paper growing soft to the touch. Turning out the light, she thinks of all that is to come this summer. If only Yaya were here to see it.

The last day of school couldn't arrive soon enough, classrooms have begun taking on a tepid quality as a heat wave lumbers through the valley. Trying to keep her distance from herself, Janie futilely fans the warm air as she waits for Matty. They walk home together twice a week when their mother has an afternoon shift. Lucas informally escorts them home, meandering on his bike and hopping curbs along the way.

Unlike most days when Matty tells tales of new bugs, today is special. Today is the last day of first grade, a two-year effort. Proud, he's bursting at the seams to show them a small model of the Hubble telescope Mrs. Roberts gave him. Hurrying them along, he repeats her instructions to keep it to himself until he's away from the other kids. Holding up the model for Lucas and Janie to admire, he grows weary of waiting for them to guess how many miles it's traveled since it launched in April. Running ahead, he chatters on about showing Kate when she comes home from college next week.

Blaming the heat, Lucas breaks tradition and walks his bike. Janie notices but doesn't particularly care enough to comment. Her only wish is to plant herself in front of the fan.

Clamping and releasing the front brake, Lucas' bike squeaks and skids in an infinite loop.

"Lucas!" Janie groans in exasperation.

Never one to be picky when it comes to getting someone's ear, he pays no mind to her annoyance. "I saw you in the Guidance Office last week. You get your work permit?"

"Yeah, how'd you know?"

"Ya know I TA in the office, right? Had to file a bunch and saw yours."

Giving him a low effort scowl, Janie sighs. "Well if you knew then why'd you ask?"

"Dunno, didn't want to sound like a creep I guess," as he blushes.

"Too late." She nudges him, laughing off the awkwardness. "I'm workin' at the diner over in McCreary this summer. How bout you?"

"My Dad got me a job cutting bait out by the lake, same as last summer."

Janie crinkles her nose at the thought of it. "Your Dad works for the Department of Fish and Game. Couldn't he find you a job in his office?"

Lucas laughs, "It's not that bad." After a pause, "Okay, it ain't roses but they feed me lunch and I can save all the money I make. Besides, who wants to be trapped in some office when I can spend the day on the lake while getting paid?"

"To each their own, I guess. I'll stick to the diner, thanks."

"I'm gonna drive out with my Dad every day." Fidgeting with his brakes again, "So if you want a ride there's room." Lucas slows to a near halt approaching her driveway.

"Ah thanks anyway, I'm riding with a few girls from my youth group," she says with a noted lack of enthusiasm.

"Sure?" Then, thinking better of pushing, "If you change your mind just meet outside my house by 7:30."

"I kinda have to go with them, was the only way my Mom agreed to work out of town."

Lucas hops on his bike. "Alright Janie, be good then. Maybe I'll bring you some fish guts by the diner."

"Gross Lucas, gross." Watching him ride away, "Bye!"

Without looking back, Lucas raises his hand in a sort of wave. By now Matty's hopping up and down the porch steps, his dark curly locks rising and falling in time. With a sigh, Janie heads in to make them a snack. After asking Matty what he wants, she mouths his reply in sync. "Cheese sammich," *hop, hop, huff*, "And milk."

Chapter Two

With a week gap between the end of school and starting work at the diner, Janie pays heed to Helene's credo. *Never let a minute go to waste.* Days are spent lending a hand at church, helping Matty excavate faux fossils their father buried during the rainy season, and lastly shopping, given that an inch growth spurt has rendered last summer's shorts indecent according to her mother.

Despite her griping, Janie's thankful for new stuff to wear. She only knows one of the three girls she'll be riding with, the others are too cool for most of the youth group. It isn't that she wants to fit in, just that she doesn't want to stand out. No one wants to be the chicken with disparate head feathers. Wendy, the eldest by a year and driver, is known for dispersing small crumbs of gossip. Monica and Krissa are harmless on their own but gallingly two-faced if it means avoiding scrutiny from Wendy. This and a dozen other things rattle around Janie's mind as she wills herself to sleep.

Tired but undeterred, Janie launches into her day certain this is a glimpse into the freedom of adulthood. She recalls how the older siblings of church friends changed after summer jobs. There was an air about them suggesting something transformative had taken place, something about interloping in the adult world had assuaged their plaintive angst. Of course, that wasn't always the case. Some were homesick, yearning for the cocoon of adolescence. Janie hopes some of whatever the first phenomenon is rubs off on her.

As is their morning ritual, Janie helps Matty dress before heading downstairs for breakfast. While she awaits her ride to conquer the world one bussed table at a time, he fuels up to hang out with kids from the children's ministry. Helene double-checks Janie's backpack to ensure she hasn't for-

gotten anything, simultaneously going through the tenants of good customer service. Helene fusses ceaselessly till Janie's so nervous she volunteers
to wait on the porch.

Gripping Janie's shoulders, Helene looks her in the eyes, "Stay with the
girls from your youth group."

Janie trails off, "I will," pulling the door shut behind her.

Though she sees Janie waiting on the front steps, Wendy honks anyway.
Krissa and Monica greet her excitedly, while Wendy manages a smirk meant
to acknowledge existence but little more. The drive is peppered with talk of
who else is working in McCreary this summer, who they wish was working
there and tailored questions to keep Wendy's interest.

Orientation is far less strict than implied. It's them and two girls from the
next town over. They're each handed a waist apron and two forest green
tees with the diner's logo and phone number. The rest of their uniform is
dictated by the rules of teenage fashion conformity, medium rinse denim
shorts, and white scrunch socks finished with white Keds or chucks.

One of the older waitresses, who reeks of maple syrup and menthol,
cautions against going crazy with perfume and smelly lotions so it doesn't
offend the customers. They get a tour of the diner, the rules on comped
meals, timekeeping and a breakdown of their responsibilities. Janie tries to
conduct herself matter of fact, inside she beams with importance.

Her mind leaps to scenarios of chatting with customers about grown up
things like traveling the world or which Broadway plays to catch should
one find themselves in New York. I mean, what worldly grown up hasn't
been? Course, the farthest she's gone is a youth retreat in Idaho. And even
though she's not allowed to watch many mainstream films or listen to
non-Christian music, none of this sways her. She is confident that given the
opportunity, she could wing it. There was a Christian Destinations special
on the *700 Club,* and the girl with the locker above hers always taped up
recent playbills. Piece of cake really. Scrubbing sticky handprints from a
booth window for the tenth time as customers avoid eye contact levels out
her feelings of unlimited social trajectory.

When the clock strikes *why for the love of God can't you people teach your kids how to eat with utensils*, they've made it through the first week. A routine establishes, like school, except they get paid and can have as much free soda and fries as they can handle. Given they see each other six days a week between work and church, drive-time conversation dries up. To keep it fresh, they take turns bringing mix tapes. The soundtrack defaults to Crystal Lewis, but Krissa and Monica break it up with The Winans and First Call. Janie rocks the boat buying an Amy Grant tape with her first paycheck. A verse into *Faithless Heart*, Wendy ejects the tape with a decree that it's not real praise music, just a pop imposter. Monica seizes the opportunity to bust out her 4Him tape, collectively swooning as Janie quietly tucks away poor Amy.

Janie spends her break at the market across the road despite the lure of free soda. She's resolved to go her own way with the girls. Three's a clique and four's one too many it seems. She takes her break after the lunch rush, eagerly trading the smell of a flat-top grill for the fragrance of walnut firewood bundles baking in the sun. The market is small with narrow stout aisles crammed full of the fun stuff you suddenly wish you had packed when you get to the lake.

The best part of the whole place is a news rack along the back wall, well stocked with essentials like the *Farmers' Almanac*, magazines and puzzle books. Not to mention a decent comic selection. However, she's not there for some casual perusing, this is a mission. She's there for her favorite comic, *Fright Night*. Never having seen the film, she's followed the comic for the past two years with the help of Lucas stowing issues away for her.

Thumbing through *Spider-Man* and the like, she absentmindedly contemplates what shenanigans the Anti-Monster Society will get up to this time around. Crouching down, she spots a bundle of new issues. Nibbling her thumbnail, Janie pulls back the corners in the bundle with her other hand. Disappointment grows as she thumbs past Marvel after Marvel. Then, without salutation, it's hiding mid-stack. As she reaches to pull it free, she hesitates for fear of trespass.

A voice from behind whispers, "Go for it."

Janie bumps her head rocking back from a crouching position, landing firmly on her ass. All grace abandoned, she sits stunned.

The owner of the erstwhile disembodied voice pulls the comic free. She turns to Janie, still finding her feet. "Was this the one?"

Nodding, "Yeah, I've been waiting for the new issue." Desperately wanting to reach for it, Janie shoves her hand in her pocket instead.

Not noticing the tremor, the girl replies, "Me too."

"Yeah, that's fine." *It's not fine.* Hiding her disappointment, Janie shrugs. "Go ahead and have it then."

Swatting Janie's arm as she turns to walk away, "Wait, I have an idea." Smiling, "I'm Lydia."

"Janie." She shakes her hand, trying not to stare at the comic.

"So, since there's only one copy, what do ya say we share it?"

"Share it?" Janie raises an eyebrow at this strange girl wanting to walk away with her comic without feeling bad about startling her into submission.

She smirks at Janie's skepticism, "I come to town every Monday with the camp leader for supplies, we could read it together. I'm usually just bored in the truck anyway."

Janie finds this irrationally appealing and is too enthralled to wonder why. "Sure, why not." Pivoting to find her north, the ceiling and track lighting bare no clues. She motions in the general direction of the diner. "I work over at the diner, usually take my break after lunch."

Her name called from a couple aisles over, Lydia shrugs. "That's my ride."

Meandering to the register, Janie buys her Bubble Up and hovers near the door, taking stock of Lydia while she waits for her to pay. Every movement of Lydia's lean frame is fluid, like she should be playing tennis or something instead of reading horror comics. Stopping by the camp truck, Lydia extends the comic as an olive branch. "Do you wanna hold on to it? I've got my hands full trying to finish reading *Villette* before camp is over."

Suppressing a hasty yes, Janie pushes it back. "You keep it. I'm not really allowed to have them in the house. Saves me having to smuggle it home."

Lydia laughs, leaning into the cab to toss it on the seat. She can stall no more when the camp leader whistles from inside. "I have to help load the truck. I'll see you next week."

"Yeah, my break is probably way over." Walking towards the road, Janie does a half turn to wave bye.

In the home stretch of cleaning a corner booth, it dawns on Janie that Lucas will be expecting some reading material the next time she sees him. With no desire to explain a weekly reading date with a stranger, she'll go with sold-out instead. The ride home passes with ease, Janie's thoughts are elsewhere. So much so, the girls burst out in laughter when Janie finally looks up to see they're outside her house. Barely out of the car, Janie says "See you tomorrow" to the ghost of the Camry rounding the corner.

The unmistakable aroma of her mother's moussaka welcomes her. After tossing her bag on the couch, she hurries to wash up. Eyeing the creamy goodness as she kisses her mother's cheek, she sets the table.

Without turning from the sink, her mother asks, "Was that Wendy speeding off like that?"

"Was she speeding?" Janie asks in a non-committal, please don't get me involved tone of voice.

Turning, Helene stares her down before returning to the dishes. There's comfort in knowing her mother will complain intermittently about it through the evening, but not utter an actual word to Wendy's mother when they see each other.

Putting the afternoon aside, Janie loses herself in her favorite dish. Diving in for seconds before anyone else has made a dent, she slows to quell her mother's critical eye.

"This tastes just like Yaya's moussaka," Janie coos as she eats.

Ray counters, "Your Yaya used to put ground lamb in with the meat."

"I could eat this every day." Janie laughs as she bumps elbows with Matty.

Helene quips, "If you keep going back for seconds, you'll end up looking like Yaya too."

Ray shoots a glare at Helene but says nothing. Janie tries to laugh it off and explain how much she runs around the diner all day, but the conversation has moved on. She picks at her food until everyone is ready to leave the table, the allure is gone.

Chapter Three

S tronger after surviving July Fourth crowds at the diner, the girls suspect summer will be a breeze from here on out. With all the hustle, Janie nearly forgets Lydia until the camp truck pulls into the lot. Butterflies race up, leaving her flush. With the lunch rush running long, she ramps up the sweetness when asking for her break.

Lydia's nowhere to be seen, Janie walks around the truck, checking for the worn camp logo.

"Hey Janie!" comes an increasingly familiar voice from the concrete dock backing up to the market.

Turning, Janie makes her way over and plops down next to her. "How was it?"

"Haven't read it yet." Again, Lydia observes Janie's skepticism. "I said we'd read it together, remember?"

Janie can't help but smile at this peculiar creature whom she feels as though she's known for ages yet hardly recognized from across the lot. "I've got fifteen minutes, kinda busy today."

Only getting through a few pages, the be all end all of comics can't compete with Janie's need to know more about Lydia. Though she's never had a job, she already has that air of confidence which thus far eludes Janie. When Janie's alarm sounds adamantly, *Time to go, she* ignores it for just a moment longer.

Without a word, Lydia presses the button to silence the alarm. A charge cascades up Janie's arm.

"I used to have that watch, mine was yellow though." Lydia adjusts the band to where it was. "You should probably get back, don't want ya getting in trouble on my account."

"Yeah" is all Janie manages, brushing away the dust as she stands. "How long are you usually here while they shop?"

"Depends, I guess about half an hour." Nodding towards the clerk stacking firewood, she whispers, "I think my camp leader Tricia, has a thing for him."

He catches them looking over and abruptly heads inside.

"I'm gonna take my lunch late on Mondays, if you still wanna meet up." Janie already wishes it was next Monday.

"I'd like that. Bye Janie," Lydia lingers by the door before heading in with another smirk for the beet-necked clerk doing his best to keep it business-like as he rings up the camp order.

Janie's rendezvous doesn't go unnoticed by her car mates, she derails their cloying inquiries with scraps of innocuous gossip overheard in the diner. Mrs. Maple, as they've come to call her, is trying to quit smoking on doctor's orders. However, Janie caught her out back sneaking a smoke. This spurns a long discussion of why she always smells of syrup.

"What if it's a tumor or something?" Krissa suggests. Continuing, "Haven't you seen those shows where the animals can smell when people are sick?"

Unable to contain her laughter, Monica blurts, "What? Krissa that's ridiculous, you need to start wearing a mask in the cleaning closet."

Janie half listens and laughs along. Krissa becomes more serious, "No, for real. My cousin swears that my uncle smelled funny before he was diagnosed."

Monica continues to snicker. "Are you sure he didn't always smell funny?"

"Real nice Monica. All I'm gonna say is I've been to your house," Krissa retorts, her freckled face growing flush.

Monica's pitch rising, "What's that supposed to mean?"

"Oh my gosh you guys!" Exasperated, Wendy stares Krissa down in the rearview, then Monica in the passenger seat. "She's the one who fills all the syrup things every morning, it's on her shoes and she dries her hands on her apron after rinsing the syrup off."

Krissa spies the rearview and whispers, "You saw the show, didn't you?"

Janie nods.

Monica giggles as she turns the radio up, singing along with her arm hanging out the window. Krissa slumps in a snit, staring out the window defeated. Ordinarily, Janie would have laughed at their bickering, but today she's relieved the discord was sufficient to shift the spotlight.

The thought of them asking about Lydia feels dangerous, though there isn't much to tell. She hasn't done anything wrong, nonetheless, she feels guilty. Lydia silencing her alarm circles the forefront of her thoughts. The resonance of the tame gesture is dazzlingly unnerving.

Days begin to blur as they all lead to Monday. By Sunday Janie goes through the motions in church, at home and what feels like the longest drive of the week on Monday morning. After a few weeks, it goes without saying, when that truck pulls in across the street, she's going to drop whatever she's doing and run off for lunch. Mrs. Maple dampens the clucking as a couple of the girls watch from the counter when Janie crosses the street. She gets midway through the "If you've got time to lean" speech before they disperse to their stations.

Knowing they're gossiping, Janie can't be bothered to care until those few steps from the car to the front door. Always wondering if today will be the day one of them mentions her friend to their mother. In the moment, it couldn't possibly matter less, nothing does. Not even the random lycan like storyline they're now two-thirds through.

Last week, Janie noticed that Lydia reread the same section from the week before, she didn't mind. She liked the way her inflection shifted ever so slightly for each character. Even more, Janie loved the way Lydia's attention never wandered. She supposes it's not so different from Lucas giving her his undivided attention as she recounts something that happened at the diner. Sometimes it was annoying that he hung on every word when the story wasn't that good. With Lydia it was the same but different, Janie wanted her to notice. She wanted her full attention, even when she was rambling, or not saying anything, now that she thought about it.

By the edge of August, they have dragged out the issue for as long as they could. Lydia gives it to Janie to stow with her friend, sure that her brother has a copy back home. While they wait two weeks for the next issue, they pass the time sitting on the dock sharing tales of camp and table service.

Everything with Lydia is easier than with the girls in her youth group, or at school, for that matter. She can talk to her about anything and nothing at all, without ever wanting to be anywhere but there with her. Lydia knows heaps more about music and TV shows than Janie but never crows about it. Instead, she brings her Walkman and shares her favorite bands. When the battery gets low, they rock out to KXDR.

Janie's world expands exponentially to the backbeat of "Policy of Truth" and "Cities in Dust." Besieged by the restlessness she found trite in others, the surety that once comforted now stifles her every move. Thoughts all lead to the inevitable truth that she's running out of Mondays and not quite sure what to do about that. Shoulder to shoulder, their legs dangling over the dock, Janie trembles in anticipation of her alarm going off.

Trying to find the words, she falters. "So, you excited about the August issue? Seth said it'd be here Wednesday."

"Yeah, I think we read the last issue to death." Nervously, Lydia turns to Janie. "Listen Janie, I..."

"I asked him to pull it when it comes in, but I won't read it till I see you." Wishing she hadn't, she couldn't stop herself. A wave of fear swells at the thought of what Lydia might have said, leaving her begging for her alarm to sound.

Lydia takes in Janie's clock-watching, then looks away to the camp truck, "That's nice of him." Getting up from the dock, "I should probably get inside, see if Tricia needs a hand."

Janie's heart sinks with disappointment and reluctant relief. "Yeah, I should get back too. Been kinda busy today."

In unison, they turn to the empty lot with Monica and Krissa leaning on the counter, undeterred by discovery. Lydia, looking at Janie blankly, sighs and waves goodbye. Standing idle for a beat, Janie squares away her thoughts. A willful blankness claims the day, no one or nothing can draw her out. Not the coy remarks from the girls or the weeknight takeout dinner. She runs out the clock on the day, stalled at a murky impasse.

Seth breaks the news that it's the last issue per the distribution rep. *Just when you think it can't get any lousier. What else?* She wonders how they'll tie up the loose ends in a single issue, but feels no real desire to find out without Lydia. As the week grows thin, a fear that Lydia won't show next Monday anchors itself.

Awake as the house grows quiet on Sunday night, Janie keeps coming back to a memory. In high school, Kate committed her only major transgression against their parents' rules. She covertly dated a boy she knew they wouldn't have approved of. He was popular and doted on Kate, but not of their faith. The relationship fell flat after someone from church saw them together while she was supposed to be at a friend's house. Janie spied from the stairs as their mother lambasted Kate, their father looking on in silent agreement. Though Kate and Janie didn't share the kind of bond she had with Matty, Janie was pained watching her vehemently deny the relationship. She wasn't fighting for the relationship so much as grappling to maintain her mother's favor.

Done sparring, their mother went in for the kill reading a verse from Timothy. *Now flee from youthful lusts and pursue righteousness, faith, love and peace, with those who call on the Lord from a pure heart.* Kate never spoke to the boy again. In time, the terse truce melted, and she was again the golden child.

Though she never spoke of it, Janie had seen them. That was perhaps the only time she envied her sister. There isn't anyone among her peers who makes her light up, nor anyone who seems better for knowing her. Except maybe Lucas, doesn't count though since he's a weirdo anyway. Curiously, Lydia elicits a certain blissfulness.

Drifting from dread to solace, maybe it's best if life returns to what it was. Whatever this is with Lydia and wherever it's headed will probably be met with more than Timothy's strongly worded thoughts on teenage lust, given her parents' firm belief that any step away from God's plan is the first step on a path to spiritual rot.

Janie oversleeps and hurries out the door carrying her shoes. Tying her laces in the backseat, she avoids their glances and feigns contempt for her alarm. The diner's busier than usual, leaving no time to count down. With noon come and gone, the day's given up till the most joyful sound Janie's heard in a week rattles into the grocery parking. With one last wipe, she deems the booth clean enough. The comic tucked under her shirt, she casually heads out, pushing a reluctant cinnamon strand behind her ear only for it to fall across her eyes again. Her nerves fire wildly turning toward the dock, ready to make up for last week. *Where is she?*

Glancing back at the diner, Mrs. Maple is shooing Krissa. *Dang. Give it a minute, then call it done.* Fanning herself as she squints at nothing in particular, she refuses to think of what done means. The merciless afternoon glare mellows, Janie follows the shifting light.

"Seth said he saw you walk by." Handing her a Bubble Up, Lydia sits, leaving some space. "I didn't think you were gonna show."

"Sorry about being weird last week." Shielding her brow, she can't quite read Lydia's face. "Thanks for the soda, hotter than a kiln out here." Noticing Lydia's bare feet, "I guess that's how I didn't hear ya coming."

"Soaked my shoes, Tricia made me leave em' in the truck bed to dry." Picking up the comic and pretending to examine the page corners, "So you resisted reading it?"

"Did Seth tell you it's the last issue?" Looking down, only half talking about the comic, "It's going to be kinda sad reading it, knowing that's it."

Folding the cover, Lydia waits for Janie to look over. Taking her in, there's something endearing about the way Janie undoes her hair and messily pulls it back again whenever she's antsy. The way her eyes brighten when she's brave enough to meet her gaze. "Well, then I guess we'll just take our time."

Janie smiles but says nothing.

"Is everything alright? You still wanna read together?" Lydia asks.

"I'm fine, guess I just don't want summer to end."

"It's not over yet," Lydia scoots closer until they're shoulder to shoulder, then begins reading.

Tricia takes longer than usual. Janie seizes the opportunity to defy her alarm till they see Seth and Tricia carrying out the camp supplies. Janie hurries back knowing she cannot go back to before, nor does she want to.

Cleaning duties for the rest of her shift are the toll for tardiness. The frenetic milieu of the diner as folks march in escaping the heat falls into the background. Somehow between packing up a catered picnic order in the morning and wiping up after the bussers, her paradigm has shifted. The sustained threat of gossip becoming a problem at home pales in comparison to the sense of loss stalking her all week, the gravity of which Janie only came to understand once it lifted.

The girls pay no mind to Janie on the ride home with news of Wendy being asked out by Tommy Daily, who fronts the church youth band. Feebly dismissive of Krissa and Monica's adulation, Wendy deftly brings the conversation back to the subject at every opportunity.

"Hold on you guys, I want to hear this." Wendy turns the radio up, and they listen as though it hasn't played on rotation all summer. "Did you hear when Tommy played 'Spinnin' Around' at the Independence Day festival? I heard that DC Talk's manager has been going to small worship shows, so they're adding it to their set." Without missing a beat, she turns the volume back down to better hear them compete for her attention. Janie nods in agreement when Krissa loops her in before returning to gazing out the window. She catches Wendy's glare in the rearview during the lulls, meeting it with her own. The world, or hers at least, has gotten a little bigger since the morning ride and the weight of Wendy's opinion has grown lighter.

August may have eased in lazily with a dry heat spell, but overnight it gives way to a sweltering stickiness that will bring an uncharacteristically humid end to the summer. Janie and Lydia finish the comic over two weeks. Loose ends clue them in that someone forgot to tell the writers this was the end. They stave off disappointment with speculation of a revival. Despite their devotion to Charley and his endless quest to get Ed to cool it with his pernicious hijinks, the end of summer is edging toward a more nail-biting cliffhanger.

Chapter Four

A solitary Monday is all that remains of August before Labor Day calls the whole summer good. Janie bemoans her lack of forthrightness, devoting her spare time to spinning over barfing extraneous comic factoids. Who knows what Lydia was about to say, but it felt like everything would change when she said it. *Why can't things stay the same for a while?*

Her sulkiness gains momentum as the week groans on. Helene reminds her that summer's almost over and she doesn't have to go back next year. "Mrs. Whitley mentioned Monica was concerned you don't socialize much with the girls at the diner. Do you not get on well with them? Doesn't Lucas work at the docks? You could eat lunch with him instead, just so long as you stay clear of those camp kids. They're all shipped off by their families in the city to play *Lord of the Flies* for the summer." Helene awaits an explanation she will, regardless of its content, refute as an overreaction or counter by suggesting Janie try harder.

An icy chill descends Janie's spine anticipating a retelling of what Monica shared with her mother. She forges on while the little voice in the back of her mind shrieks *This is it! This is it!* Turns out, her being antisocial is the sum of it.

"Monica is so annoying. She's always kissing Wendy's backside. Plus, Lucas and I take our breaks at different times. And I don't know any camp kids anyhow." Visualizing working at the church alongside her mother next summer is sobering. "But the diner's pretty great though! I've met a bunch of people over the summer and I'm learning lots of different stuff."

Janie pushes her bean bag chair under the window to corral the languid breeze over her. Leary of anyone coming up the stairs, the radio plays on low as an interlude to her uneasiness. Her taut nerves slacken knowing Amy's cued up and ready to go if the stairs so much as creak. Light flints break through a canopy of leaves just beyond her window, dancing on the wall like calm waters in the afternoon sun. Lulled into the gray space between the here and now and the recent then, her mind wanders through the summer. Fragments big and small, the seemingly insignificant and the imperceptibly monumental. From fretting over slouchy socks, the perils of spontaneity, and falling on her ass at the market, to the moment she no longer stowed away things to tell Lucas but filtered what she couldn't tell him without telling him about Lydia.

She's seen Lucas, whom she's known since first grade, a total of five times over the summer. Guiltily, Janie concedes she doesn't miss him as much as someone with whom she's spent a collective five hours in the company of. The gap widens between what she wants to be true and what she knows deep down is true.

Helene prepares a large batch of kataifi under the guise of a church potluck to cheer Janie up in the one way that always works. She only makes it once a year, leaving Janie and Ray to pine for it in the interim. Janie nibbles. Ray is charged with getting to the root of the issue when Helene's threshold for trying to reach Janie is spent. With Kate it's different, be it symbiotic or complementary personalities, they're attuned.

Lucas, being the savvy collector he is, manages to track down the *Fright Night* graphic novel he and Janie read a while back. Not seeing the allure, he impresses himself nonetheless. A little worse for wear since they last met, it costs him his *Justice League Quarterly* and a few lame issues he had lying around. All told, it was worth it.

He'd trade his whole collection to see her light up for something he's done. They exchange tourist tales over pizza, laughing at how some involve the same families. Lousy fishermen are her favorite regulars at the diner. She's come to believe there's a direct correlation between how much tackle is scattered about their person and their ineptitude as anglers. Janie doesn't share anything about Lydia, nor does she tell him why she wants the book. Knowing that a preoccupied Janie is not to be prodded, he lets her keep her secret. He's assured it's not for another guy since it's not God approved reading material, and so far as he knows, he's the only heathen in her inner circle.

Janie hides the book in plain sight, wagering her mother is wrapped up with Kate and still sour about dessert. Tucked between two novels from her summer reading list, her arm obscures the spine. Thumbing through it on her bed, a knock sends her scrambling.

Sitting next to her, Ray sighs. "Honey, your mother's a little concerned something's bothering you. Anything I can do?"

Relieved, Janie reaches for a reason. "Oh, it's nothing. I'm just trying to finish all the reading for school."

Ray examines the books. "Glad I never had to read these. I'd been bored to tears." Placing the books down, he holds a moment longer. "Are you sure that's it? Your Mom said you haven't been eating much. That's not like you, Janie."

Wishing she'd just choked down the kataifi, Janie smiles her best you caught me dad smile. "Well, I'm trying to watch it a bit. I think Mom was right about all those second helpings."

Aghast, he leans down to look her in the eyes. "Nonsense, don't you listen to any of that. You're half Greek and we're sturdy people. You may have your mother's laugh but you have Yaya's wit. You also have her kind brown eyes that keep nothing to themselves. God gave you the best of her. You're beautiful. Don't ever doubt it." He pats her leg, satisfied he's resolved the issue. "Get some sleep kiddo."

"Thanks Dad!"

Hearing his descent on the stairs, Janie hops up. Creased and crumpled, it's nothing a stack of books can't press out. A tinge of guilt for exploiting her father's sensitivity about his mother hovers as she nods off.

Janie crams the book into her locker, enjoying the light vibe of their last week. Postulating what they'll buy with their minimum wage bounties, they theorize who will be so jealous that they just can't hardly wait to show them. The permanent fixtures look on bemused, and if truth be told, a little envious. Morning creeps toward noon, Janie digs for what she wants to say. She's got nothing, and switches to hoping Lydia might suggest keeping in touch. They could be pen pals, nothing wrong with that except that it doesn't feel like enough.

Noon. Half past noon. One o'clock. Nothing. Janie stays close to the front cleaning tables to maintain her view, cleaning some twice. When she goes in for her third sweep, Mrs. Maple pipes up, "Girl you're going to wipe a hole through those tabletops. That booth in the back had two moppits hopped up on jam, you can wipe your little heart out."

Janie's unmasked by eagle eye Maple. "Okay, I was just going to..."

"Get on it, that's the only place we can put groups out of the way." Shaking her head as Janie heads over, "Jiminy Christmas you girls."

Fresh out of booths and tables, she moves to the last frontier with a view, the counter. Halfheartedly wiping down laminated menus, she resents the clock's ticking toward the end of her shift. A familiar rattle sends Janie into the kitchen, tossing her dishrag, she beelines for her locker as she calls out that she's on break. Dumbfounded, Krissa and Monica eye the clock. Despite her disapproval, her legs bound into a light jog across the road. Tricia's already inside when Janie comes in for a landing next to the firewood.

Her gears grind to a halt realizing the girl tagging along isn't Lydia, not soon enough to avoid startling her. Clamminess adorns Janie's flush face as she walks it off into the store, earning a sneer from the imposter on her way by.

Surveying the cooler, Janie reads the sodas like runes withholding the key to Lydia's whereabouts. The only revelation is the cold hard truth, she's about to be out a buck for a lonely bottle of Bubble Up.

After loitering long enough for the gawkers to disperse, Janie gives up. To her dismay, they're still looking, miming their way through straightening up the counter. It's going to be a long drive home. Mrs. Maple calls her over to help collect empty condiments from the tables. She shoves the sweaty comic into her apron, hoping the ink doesn't smudge.

Monica's the first to instigate, smirking at Wendy as she cranes her neck to the backseat. "Hey Janie, so we're just wondering why you buy soda at the market when we get free soda at work?"

Krissa glares at her as if to say, we agreed not to bring this up. "Maybe she wants some fresh air is all."

"Shut up Krissa!" Monica snipes. "No, seriously. Are you sweet on someone over there?"

Krissa is held silent by Wendy's stare down in the rearview. Janie pretends not to notice. Instead, fixing a blank stare on Monica. "I know that, but it tastes better in the bottle. And the diner doesn't have Bubble Up."

"Okaaay, we have Sprite you know. I dunno, seems kinda lame to rush over for the same thing. I mean if that's really why." Monica turns forward, checking in with Wendy for approval. "You know we're not supposed to hang out with those camp kids, right? My Mom says they're all a bunch of pagans and beatniks." Satisfied she's had the final word, a smug gotcha smirk settles in.

Krissa draws a deep yielding breath. Janie pats her hand reassuringly. She'll take it from here. "For one, Sprite and Bubble Up are not the same thing. Pretty different actually, but I wouldn't expect someone who drinks RC Cola to be able to tell the difference. Also, I don't know what camp kids you're referring to." Leaning back to let it go, Janie decides better of it. They're not done, so why stop. "Oh, and when you tell your Mom about this, tell her I said hi."

Monica whips her head around, then lays it on thick. "Get over yourself, I haven't told my mother anything."

Janie laughs. "Whatever."

Monica huffs, incredulous Janie would dare confront her.

Krissa endeavors to lighten the mood. "I almost forgot, Marilyn gave me a cut of her tips cuz I filled in for Leo bussing tables." She holds up a wad of crumpled singles. "See? You guys wanna go for pizza?"

Wendy talks over Krissa. "Come off it Janie! I think we're all getting a little sick of your attitude."

"My attitude?"

"We may only have a week left, but you're welcome to find another ride if you hate it with us so much." Wendy stares into the rearview until Janie looks away, thereby submitting.

Shut down at every turn, Janie cannot maneuver through dinner talk when all she wants is to go to her room. Drifting from wounded to mad, she settles into the big letdown resigned to run down the clock on this awful summer.

She's tired of the drive, the tourists and most of all, the inane notion that schlepping dirty dishes around the diner was going to somehow transform her into someone else. Her lukewarm demeanor wicks the fun out of any razzing in the car, they mostly listen to the radio while Krissa cracks little smiles when she and Janie run out of stuff to stare at on the roadside.

To show their appreciation, the owners treat each of them to a small bonus, a sweatshirt and their choice of dessert. Farewells till next year are exchanged, and they're sent on their way an hour early to stay ahead of the weather. Blue skies suggesting otherwise, the girls hit the road before they figure it out and call them back.

Turning onto the interstate, clouds rolling into the valley paint the horizon graphite. The light falls flat along with their plans to stop at the lake. Rain overwhelms the parched wiper blades.

Helene breaks precedent allowing the TV on at the dinner table. She's spent weeks preparing for the Labor Day festivities, her first effort as co-chair of the event committee. All but Janie collectively sigh as the usually blasé meteorologist gleefully reports the weather system will linger in the valley through Labor Day.

Spurned, Helene shuts the set off. "I don't know what he's so chipper about. What kind of person extracts joy from ruining people's holiday?"

"The kind of person who's been repeating sunny and clear for going on two months straight." Ray hooks his arm around Helene's waist on her march to her seat. Stealing some of his calm, she pats his hand before sitting down.

Janie wears her best neutral expression, inside she hopes it floods. She's free from obligation to attend the parade, to mingle with youth group kids, and to smile when she wants to cry.

After dinner, Ray nods as Helene drones on between phone calls with frantic committee members. Satisfied with the state of events, Janie takes to her room with her mother's words trailing behind. "Well, it's official. We're rained out!"

Ray and Helene are out of the house before Janie or Matty wake up. Kate's busy packing, desperate for the weekend to reach its end. There's oatmeal on the stove and juice on the table. Kate makes a display of her adulthood, leaning against the counter with a cup of coffee and toast. Eating away from the table is a faux pas in the Harris household. Kate has mastered the art of pedestrian rebellion. Matty shovels his oats, bursting at the seams to dredge through the muck in search of all matter of unearthed creatures.

Come Sunday, Kate's keeper of the crock-pot. Fulfilling the cycle of catch and release, Matty and Janie spend the morning distributing his bounty of earthworms in the yard. Bored in her room, Janie sets out to wander downtown.

Her poncho is no match for water spraying off the tires, its soaked sleeves cling to her. Determined not to go back to school with road rash, Janie walks her bike after skidding out in a puddle.

"You look like a wet cat all hunched up!" Even without the snark, Janie would know those squeaking brakes anywhere.

Feigning a scowl, "Feel like one too."

Lucas catches up and hops off his bike. "Where ya headed?"

"Nowhere I guess," kicking at a puddle. "What's the good word with you?"

Shrugging. "Nothin'." Lucas hesitates then takes a drag of damp air. "So did your friend like the book?"

Janie replies flatly, "Fell through guess you could say." Thinking better of sounding ungrateful, "It's alright, I'm gonna read it again."

"I kinda wish I'd never seen the movies, cause then I might love it like you do."

"You wanna read it again when I'm done?"

"Nah, you go head." Lucas slows to a stop. His bill dripping, he shakes his hat off and molds it back into place. "I'm gonna kill some time at Manny's Music, you wanna come?"

Shielding her eyes from the obnoxious drizzle, Janie pans around before resting her eyes on Lucas. "No, think I'm gonna just ride around. You're gonna have to ask your Dad for another hat, that one's getting pretty warped."

"Nah, it'll flatten out. Alright then, don't get all shriveled up." He rides off with a wave of his hat.

Ducking into Leeds' Books when the rain picks up, Janie digs into the periodicals to read as many off limits magazines as possible. Kate can keep her kitchen subversion, Janie's defiance takes the form of ravenous pop culture consumption. Maybe not ravenous, but eager anyway. Her conclusion, *Tiger Beat's* way over-hyped. Only a quarter past four, she sets out for home amidst an eerie quiet. The heavens are about to let loose again. Skimming puddles, she pushes her bike along.

Stopping in her tracks beneath the Lyric marquee, she beholds a sight most unexpected. Laid out before her are the camp truck and three Camp Mariposa vans sticking into the street like dirty piano keys. Paying her muttering pride no mind, her heart leaps. Lucas must have ended up here too. "Of course." Grumbling, she locks her bike next to his.

Peeking into the lobby, it's empty save for a suspicious usher staring back. Indifferent, Janie eyes the box office. *Duck Tales* is a safe bet in case her mother finds the ticket. She's already seen it with Matty, but hey why not dump a few more bucks into this money pit of a...whatever it is.

Crossing the lobby, Janie spots a camper dipping into *Young Guns*. Falling in, she grabs a corner seat for a better vantage point. The camp kids are loosely grouped in the center. Even in the dark they're easy to spot with their matching shirts. Janie imagines them as her mother sees them, shipwrecked wild things fleeing the great storm, then snickers at the ridiculousness of it all. Slouching, she barely misses Lucas with his friend Ben. Or is it Bill? She can never remember, but he looks more like a Ben. So, Ben it is.

Scanning the theater, a wave of foolishness washes over her. Already stood up once, she's now compounded her humiliation with a wasted trip to the movies. May as well join Lucas and Ben, on second thought, that sounds worse than being alone.

The lobby is bustling as theaters let out. Dodging a cross-section of those in need of the facilities and those aiming to beat the rain, Janie stops short of colliding with Lydia.

"Hi," Lydia says softly.

"Hi," Janie replies, locking eyes. "I thought you'd gone home."

Looking to escape the sea of theatergoers flowing around them, Lydia asks, "Do you wanna go for a walk?"

"Yes."

"Where to?" Lydia asks, leading them through the lobby doors.

"Dunno." Looking in each direction for a sign, nothing avails itself. "I have my bike."

Accustomed to riding Matty on the handlebars, Lydia weighs a smidge more. A modest steering challenge, no biggie till she catches Lydia white-knuckling the bars. Unlike Matty, Lydia's far more interesting than the road. *Focus Janie, focus.* They reach the sidewalk's end, the playground by the muddy little league field is as good a place as any to stop.

The air takes on a chill as the breeze comes up. Goosebumps cascade over Lydia's sun-kissed arms, her camp shirt sopping. Dragging their feet, they skim the dugout puddles beneath their swings, neither saying much. In her peripherals, Janie sees Lydia rub her arms. Digging her heels into the edge, Janie slows to a stop. Pulling the heavy blue-hued poncho over her head, she holds it up, "Here, take it."

Lydia shakes her head, "Oh that's okay."

"I've got a sweatshirt. Go on, it's damp but the lining's dry." Not waiting for a reply, Janie tosses it over.

"Thanks."

Seizing the lull, Janie fears it might burst out of her. "So, where were you last week?"

Sheepish, Lydia pulls her dirty blonde hair back before speaking. "Yeah, sorry about that."

Janie says nothing, unsure if this is the only explanation she'll get.

"Me and my cabin mate tipped our kayak that morning, she got her foot stuck. She's fine but they made us hang out in the nurse's cabin all afternoon, so that's why I didn't come to town. Mostly just read and ate up the leftover snacks."

Relief abounds. Despite the gross squishy feeling of soaked socks, she could jump up and down. Playing it cool, she twists the chains on the swing, sending it into a subtle sway. "Finish your book?"

"Have a few chapters left. I'll read them on the drive down." Lydia rifles through her shoulder bag. "I have the last issue, you wanna take it?"

"That's okay, keep it." Janie pivots to face Lydia, twisting her fingers till her knuckles give all they've got to give. "I brought something for you to the market, but now it's at home."

Lydia folds the comic, tucking it under her bag. "You could send it to me if you want."

"Yeah, I think I could do that." Janie lifts her feet, letting gravity drag the swing to and fro.

Again, rummaging through her bag, Lydia withdraws a pen. She flips pages and tears away an ad, avoiding Janie's gaze in case this constitutes desecrating a sacred text. Using her bag as a shield, she writes out her address. Janie hangs on each pen stroke, resisting the urge to push back a stray strand of hair that's given way under the weight of the drizzle.

As Lydia hands Janie the folded paper, Lydia leans in and kisses her. A simple lingering peck, hinting at something more. "Here ya go."

After a summer spent searching in vain for the catalyst that would change everything, here it was the whole time hidden in hazel eyes.

Janie pockets the paper, kicking off into an arc before leaping and sticking the landing. Sweeping her arm to the side, she half bows much to Lydia's amusement. Wishing she could stretch this evening out forever, her faithful watch alerts it's time to head back.

Ambling along to spite the swelling rain, they manage a comfortable silence until Lydia begins to giggle.

"What's so funny?"

"Nothin', just you and that watch I guess."

Janie shrugs. "I tend to get sidetracked is all."

Resting her hand over Janie's as she pushes the bike along, Lydia smirks. "It's alright, I like weird." Lydia sways into Janie's shoulder and back again.

Janie summons the courage to kiss her while they're still on their own. *That was so dumb, someone could've seen.* Janie doesn't care. All she can think of is the rain bringing out the scent of chamomile in Lydia's hair, and how she tasted of apple Jolly Ranchers. "You going to camp next year?"

"I think this year's it for me. I qualify for a junior counselor position, but missed the deadline to apply."

Janie nods along.

"I'll have my permit next Spring. I could come see you when I get my license."

"I'd like that." Janie looks ahead smiling.

"Till then we could talk on the phone and write each other."

Sighing, Janie shakes her head. "My Mom will never let me talk on the phone with someone she doesn't know, but we could write each other."

"Letters it is, like Victorian pen pals. Miss Florence Hartley herself wouldn't suspect a thing."

"I don't know who that is, but pen pals sounds alright to me."

Camp kids are spilling out of the theater as they approach. A spent counselor futilely wrangles them only for them to split off again. Slowing to a full stop, Lydia pulls her arms free to lift the poncho over her head.

Janie insists, "No, keep it."

Lydia flattens it, running her thumb across the fabric. "Looks like they're gonna do a head count, I better get over there." She draws a deep breath, then squeezes Janie's hand and pushes off. "Wait for me."

"I will," Janie says, almost to herself.

Janie watches, hoping for one more glimpse. Lydia steals a last peek over her shoulder before disappearing into a sea of burgundy windbreakers. Greedily, Janie dawdles a spell longer searching for the poncho. Preoccupied, she misses Lucas till he bumps his bike into hers. Looking over his shoulder to see what she's looking at, "I can't believe you didn't see me coming right at ya. What are ya looking at?"

"Nothin'. Those camps kids are swarming like ants." Janie turns away.

"Headed home?"

"Yeah."

"I'll walk you."

"What about Ben? I saw you guys in the theater."

Laughing, he looks around then back at Janie. "His name's Bill. You always call him Ben."

"Well, he looks more like a Ben, I guess." Janie chuckles. "Like he even knows my name."

"Why do you say that? You should've sat with us."

"Yeah and watch him stick licked sour patch kids to the seat, no thanks. Besides, he's your friend Lucas, not mine."

"Yeah, he hates them lemon ones. He knows you. I talk about you all the time." Lucas stops short, shifting his feet uncomfortably.

Reflexively glancing up at his admission, her eyes return to the road with an unspoken mutual desire to let it go. "Anyway, I'll probably never call him Ben again. Satisfied?"

"Yes ma'am."

Adrenaline settling, Janie enjoys the easiness of hanging out with Lucas. She can be herself without him getting the wrong idea.

Coasting with one foot on the peddle, Lucas takes her in. "You look happy, it's nice to see."

Scoffing, Janie weakly objects. "What's that supposed to mean?"

"You've been walking around like your dog died lately, and tonight it's like someone got you a bucket of puppies."

"That sounds messy. Just glad summer's over is all."

"Yeah, me too. I mean sorta." He paces himself, not wanting the conversation to die off. "You ready for school? I kinda like we're starting half an hour earlier, more daylight after."

"I'm not of one mind or another about it, but yeah I like starting earlier too I guess."

Poised to continue down his usual list of Lucas questions, they fall silent as they hear her screen door swing open and snap furiously shut. Helene, with a magazine overhead deflecting the rain, launches down the steps toward the front gate.

"Where have you been?" Impatiently, she eyes them both.

Fumbling for words, Janie stammers "At the movies."

"Janine Harris, are you actually going to stand here and lie to my face?"

Janie meekly replies, "I'm not lying."

For the first time in recent memory, Janie feels the sting of her mother's palm across her cheek. Helene looks as surprised to have done it as Janie looks having been the recipient. "Kate saw you with that girl. Too busy to notice your own sister when you walked by the shop!"

Janie massages her cheek, staring at her mother in stunned disbelief.

"Oh, you thought I didn't know about her? Mrs. Whitley mentioned you ignoring your friends for some girl from that summer camp. Monica told her all about how you run off to the market every chance you get."

Burning with embarrassment, Janie feels hot tears streaking down her cheeks. She stays quiet, desperate to go inside. Lucas speaks as she lifts the latch. "She was with me Mrs. Harris. We went to see *Young Guns*, it was my idea though."

Janie stops, turning askew. Determined not to give her tears an audience, she wicks them away with the cuff of her shirt.

Helene's glare fixes on Lucas. Hand on her hip, she dares him to continue. "She was with you?"

"Yes ma'am. Been stuck inside all weekend, bout to get cabin fever. Me and a couple kids from school talked Janie into going. We were all foolin' around when the movie let out. Maybe Kate saw one of them with us."

Locking eyes with Janie, Helene sternly asks, "This true?"

Janie nods, leery of looking at Lucas.

Skeptical, Helene opens the gate and steps back enough for Janie to squeeze through. "Go home Lucas," Helene snipes.

"You got it. Night Mrs. Harris, Janie." He peddles off into the dark, betrayed only by the squeal of his slick worn brakes.

Chapter Five

Tenth grade reveals all its mysteries in a matter of days. If Janie's being honest, it's not quite all it was built up to be. Everything seems the same, the faces in the hall haven't changed much save for a little more acne on some and a little less on others. Teachers reciting the same spiels is the sort of thing you don't figure out till your second go round.

Lucas misses the first few days, a bummer for him but a nice deferral for Janie. Things are eerily quiet at home. Janie helps Matty settle into first grade, easing the stress of a new classroom with a new teacher. Luckily, his teacher was also Janie's teacher and she allows Janie to sit at the back of the class each morning.

Janie plots to mail the book to Lydia. Wednesday rewards her perseverance when Helene takes a day off to attend a church function. Janie stalks the parking lot for ten minutes before dipping in, their old mail carrier is working the counter. He's the grumpy old man caricature manifest, complete with errant hairs breaking free from the pack to stand guard in his ears.

"Hi, Mr. Nakamura! Can I have a large envelope and some stamps please?"

"How many?" Looking down at her expectantly.

"Just one."

"What are you mailing?" He asks, sighing through the question.

"Why?" Janie counters suspiciously.

"One stamp's not enough to mail anything in a big envelope. So how many?"

"Oh," Janie thinks about how much the book weighs.

"Well?"

Panicking, "Five stamps and one envelope." She stares him down to denote this is her final offer.

He raises an eyebrow and grabs an envelope. Looking through the drawer for stamps until he sighs again, lamenting, "I'm out of loose stamps, hold on."

Not wanting to irritate him enough to complain to her mother, Janie tries some small talk. Turns out, a summer at the diner is finally good for something. "Is that a pin of Hawaii on your collar?"

Pushing the envelope and bent stamps across the counter, he looks further put upon. "Yes. Dollar eighty-four."

Handing over the money, the tide is turning. "Here ya go. Man, I wanna go there some day."

Palming the change down onto the counter, "I bet they can't wait."

Janie grumbles across the lobby. *Can't wait. Geezer.*

Carefully unwrapping the torn page with Lydia's address, it's soft from two weeks in her pocket. Though an inkling of creepy shame wells, she sniffs it anyway. There's a faint air of bubblegum with subtle acrid notes of sweat and cheap ink. Guarding the paper with her arm, she hastily writes the address and seals it. Lastly, she adds her return address, her pen dithering every other letter. Each pause brings her no closer to knowing how she'll explain getting mail from Lydia. She'd rather figure it out than think about not having to. Stealthily, she drops it in the drive-up mailbox. Her mom says they always fill up faster, which she figures makes hers less likely to stand out.

"Janie!"

Turning, Mrs. Kean's waving at her, Janie shoves the paper in her pocket. *Where did she come from? Shit! How long's she been standing there?*

"Hi hon, where's your Mom?" She navigates the fractured asphalt in chunky heels with all the grace she can muster.

"Oh, she's over at the church, it's her day off here." Janie turns to go.

Fidgeting with her hair, it's plain to see she's unaware of the ladies getting together. "Isn't that nice."

Unsure of what else to do, Janie turns to leave. "Bye, Mrs. Kean!"

"Whatcha mailing?"

Frozen, Janie turns to Mrs. Kean patiently awaiting an answer. "I, um, what's that?"

"I said, whatcha mailing there?" The strained smile in Mrs. Kean's eyes is sinking below the horizon.

"Sorry, didn't hear ya. Yeah, I was, well, it's just a copy of Christian Teen I was sending to Kate. They had an article on her college." A burst of pride at her resourcefulness gives Janie butterflies. She's intrepid in the face of nosy Mrs. Kean.

Curiosity sated, "Janie that's just so sweet. You're a good sister. I wish my girls were close like that. I don't know why you're not more involved at church."

"Yeah, school keeps me pretty busy. Okay, bye Mrs. Kean!"

"Bye hon, say hi to your Mom!"

Wearing her yard clothes, Janie cuts every corner she can find. Sweeping the path, she catches Lucas walking his bike past the house. He waves but doesn't stop.

"Hold on," she runs over to the gate.

Slowing at the gate, he looks rough. "Hey Janie."

"Wow, you look bad. Where ya been?"

"Thanks." Sniffling, he clears his throat. "Been sick, I'll be back at school tomorrow." He digs in his pocket for tissue, discreetly wiping his nose. "See ya at school."

Leaning on the fence, she watches him go. "Wait, Lucas hold on."

"Yeah?"

"I just wanted to say thank you." Her eyes speak to the gratitude for which she lacks the words.

"It's alright. Everything okay now?"

Rolling her eyes, "Who knows. Better than it would've been." Pulling at a weed wound around the fence post, she looks up. "So, the girl, well, my sister didn't see what she thought she saw."

"You don't owe me nothing. Have your secret." Smiling, he bounces the front end of his bike. "Hell, I got secrets too."

Janie laughs, again grateful. "Yeah?"

"Yeah." Stifling a cough, he plants the front end of the bike. "Alright Janie I gotta go. Be good."

"Tryin'." She gives a quick wave and gets back to work.

Days pass, with each Janie wonders if Lydia's written yet. She eases into the rhythm of another school year. When night falls and she's alone with her thoughts, the possibility of what next sits like a tightrope daring her to walk it. Taut with the promise of all she's pined for, she drifts off praying for the courage to step out onto it.

A week gone, nothing yet. Walking home from school, her mind wanders as Matty speaks at length of the virtues of scratch-made play-dough. Janie nods along. *Should've put a note in it.* She imagines the envelope trashed. *What if her address got messed up?* Her mother always complains about the sorting machines catching the corners of big envelopes if someone's too lazy to hand-sort them. *Just a quick note.* Reasoning she'll drop it off before school, Janie suggests they pick up the pace so they can make play-dough after homework.

She's home early. After a quick shout of hello, she and Matty part ways at the top of the stairs. Tossing her backpack onto the bed topples a stack of laundry. Janie's stomach flips hearing the dryer buzz downstairs. The hamper's empty. Searching the stack for the pants she wore to the post office, they're not there. *Shit! Where are they?* Looking under her bed, it bares only fresh vacuum lines.

Run walking to the laundry room, she hopes against hope to see her dirty laundry still dirty. The washer is mid-cycle with dark clothes, her heart sinks. Defeated, she's startled to see her mother in the doorway holding the paper up to her eye line.

"Looking for this?"

Janie nods, hopeful she might fish it out of the trash after her tongue lashing.

"Is this who you were mailing the package to?" Helene looks ten feet tall, her shoulders rigid and voice demanding contrition.

"It was a big envelope not a package. How do you know about that?" More defiant than intended, Janie stands her ground for the time being.

"Mrs. Kean was singing your praises at prayer group. I checked with Kate, she didn't get anything from you!" Exasperated, she shakes the paper. "Is this the girl from the summer?"

All Janie manages is a nod. *Stop nodding like a dang bobblehead.*

"This is deviant behavior." Angrily waiting for a reply, she presses through clenched teeth. "Answer me Janie!"

"Okay." Janie's face burns with humiliation, suspecting her life is about to implode.

"Okay? That's it? You're going to destroy your soul and you say okay?" On the verge of tears, Helene draws a breath to compose herself.

Tears streak Janie's face, she'd give anything if her mother would move just enough to let her by. "I don't know what you want me to say."

Helene's eyes grow wide, she bears down in her efforts to elicit something reminiscent of penance. Matty bursts past, stopping when he sees Janie crying. He grabs her hand, asking, "You wanna go play Janie?"

Smiling at him then looking to her mother, Helene steps aside.

Her appetite waning, Janie takes the stairs in pairs to gain enough momentum to carry her through the kitchen and out the door. To her surprise, Ray's still at the table eating breakfast. Catching a side glare from Helene, who's making Matty's lunch, Janie ignores it as she leans in to hug her father. "Morning Dad! Why are you still here?"

Ray tenses as she kisses his cheek and hugs him, he pats her arm. "Have a seat."

Backpack slung over one shoulder, she presses onto the door. "I'm gonna be late."

"Janie, sit down." He wipes his mouth and folds the napkin on his plate. "I want you to know we're not going to give up on you."

Looking to her mother, Helene keeps her back to them. "I don't know what Mom told you, but I can explain."

"That's enough. Morality isn't some game of semantics." Ray refuses to look at her, fixing on something beyond her shoulder.

Sliding her chair back with a shove, Janie's blindsided. "Dad! I haven't done anything wrong."

Janie follows her father's gaze when something slams down on the counter. Helene looks through her to Ray.

Ray calmly pushes his plate aside. "Starting today you'll be dropped off and picked up."

"What?"

He continues without breaking stride. "Next week you'll begin counseling with Pastor Mike." His eyes begin to well. He looks away, sparing himself the hurt in her face. "This isn't just about you. This is an indignity to us all."

Speechless, Janie watches him carry his plate to the sink. Helene rubs his back to comfort him. Matty smiles at her, even without understanding, he looks at her with pity.

"Get your stuff. I'll drop you off." Ray grabs his keys and kisses Helene goodbye.

"Can I come?" Matty asks, gulping the milk in his cereal.

"Mom's gonna take you kiddo."

Janie mouths bye to Matty, boring a hole into her mother's back the whole way out the door.

To feel farther away from her father, Janie practically hangs out the window.

"Your mother's cutting her hours at the post office so she can pick you up every day." Ray shares his attention between her and the road. "Are you listening?"

"I heard you."

"Do you realize the sacrifices your mother's making?" Ray implores her to see his perspective, which is ultimately Helene's perspective.

"This is for her, and you know it," Janie says, getting out of the car without looking back.

The ride home from school is silent. Helene walks Janie into the house, checking the answering machine, she doles out instructions. "Leave your house key on the table. There's homework for you in the den."

Fighting the urge to cry or scream, Janie watches her mother leave to pick up Matty. Tossing the key onto the dining table, she returns to place it near the centerpiece lest she incur another wrath.

Neatly stacked on the desk is a bible, legal pad and a Bic pen. The first page lists a series of passages with instructions to read a passage per day and write a summary. Staring at the notepad, she slumps in the chair. All the anger and hurt she's feeling sinks too. What fills the void is neither joy nor sadness, it's surrender without relief or any assurance thereof, a mother-daughter Alford doctrine.

Yaya used to say *never take your medicine on an empty stomach*. Maybe a quick snack while she's out. Raiding her father's bologna stash feels fair, considering his actions deprived her of enjoying breakfast. When he realizes he's having PB&J for lunch tomorrow, perhaps he'll reflect upon his harshness. Giving the wrapper a good shove in the bin, she returns to her task. Laying her palm into the bread until she hears the delectable crunch of Fritos beneath, a car door shuts in the distance. Taunting the clock, she drags her feet to the den.

The first passage is John: 3:16-24. *How original.* A dab of mayo drops onto the page, wiping at it spreads the grease stain. Sliding her arm over it and pretending to write sufficiently gratifies Helene from the doorway. Eventually, Janie hunkers down to reword the passage, refusing to oblige the spirit of the exercise by interpreting it in any way that relates to her circumstance. Scanning the list, she'll be deep in Leviticus territory come a month or so. With a hushed groan, she pushes the pad and good book to the corner of the desk.

Chapter Six

Gossip spreads expeditiously and with greater fervor than the gospel, as evidenced by the avoidance Janie and Helene face entering the church. Mrs. Kean whom only a week ago lavished her with praise, looks to Helene with that same pained smile and eyes dripping with pity. She avoids Janie altogether as though meeting her eyes would brand her complicit, and obviously at once render her a pillar of salt. Helene hangs her head. Her hand firmly on Janie's back, she ushers her through the barrage of phony commiseration. For a split second, Janie feels something approaching empathy for her mother's plight.

Pastor Mike waits, tending to church matters while never losing sight of their approach. Janie remembers him from his youth pastor days, though she wasn't old enough to attend the teen group he ministered to, she remembers how some of the older girls cooed over his blue eyes. *Looks more like a TV dad these days.*

"You must be Janie. Welcome!" His voice is kind and even, almost casual. When he shakes her hand, his hands are warm and envelop her with a quick squeeze before releasing.

Shifty eyed, Janie sheepishly replies, "Thank you."

Turning to speak with Helene, he looks back at Janie every so often with a warm smile to keep her included. "So, we'll meet every Thursday at four going forward."

"Absolutely, thank you Pastor Mike!" Helene fawns over him like he's just dragged Janie and half a dozen kittens out of a burning building.

"Janie's in good hands." He turns to Janie with his most modest crinkly-eyed smile. She nearly closes her eyes to keep them from rolling. His hand on her shoulder, he leads them to his office. Pausing in perfect time, he turns back to Helene. "I almost forgot, Helene I just wanted to thank you for all your hard work pulling together the Labor Day Worship Celebration."

Flustered and flattered, Helene beams. "Oh, just doing my part."

Flashing another smile, they resume their walk. Janie locks eyes with the choir director, who's following their path until the pastor looks over.

Fifteen minutes from now, Helene will learn she's being replaced as head of the events committee under the guise of unburdening her from church affairs during her family's time of trial. The demotion is presented as an act of solicitude instead of culling. Helene feigns gratitude in equal measure, embracing each of the three messengers for their sacrifice in shouldering the load.

Pastor Mike's office is modern and welcoming, everything in its place with a few personal touches. The faint scent of aftershave and citrus furniture polish hangs in the air. Janie sits in a chair across from his desk, only realizing he hasn't followed as she scoots in.

Seated in an armchair adjacent to the small sofa, he pats the sofa cushion. "Have a seat." Again, the smile and crinkly eyes. "I like to keep things informal, ya know?"

Forcing a blip of a smile, Janie relocates.

"First, I want you to know I'm here for you." Leaning forward, resting his arms on his knees. "You're safe here, we'll get through this. Okay?"

Janie nods, unmoved but acquiesced.

"Great, let's get started." Sitting back, he reads through a small leather-bound pocketbook.

The session is focused on getting to know Janie. Lydia nor anything that led her here is discussed, only her life in general. He shares struggles from his teen days, digging deeper to show interest when he notices something sparks a light.

To become an island in a sea of people is lonelier than being alone. Helene speaks to Janie infrequently, and almost not at all once Ray's home. Matty is Janie's only anchor to life at home before all this. He doesn't look at her differently, nor does he ask why everyone else seems to.

The spurning doesn't end at home. Seeds of gossip planted over the summer have taken root, rendering her a pariah amongst the kids from her congregation. Solace sought in non-church friends wanes each time she begs off an invite. Unwilling to explain why she's unable to attend, she offers flimsy excuses. Even to Lucas, she doesn't dare confide. She's caught between embarrassment and a concrete fear of being dismissed as something other by them too.

Helene's so successful in her campaign to set right the order of her house, Janie no longer resists through word or posture. She does what's expected without complaint. Playing outside with Matty is the only time she doesn't feel surveilled. This is the new normal.

Keeping to herself at school, friends and fading friendships drift in and out at lunch. Lucas is the only constant. Ready, if only she'd say the word, he'd give the hypocrites a piece of his mind. While Janie pretends not to notice the whispering during lunch, Lucas pretends he doesn't glower at them in the halls. Watchful eyes abound, Janie learns to guard what she says even in passing. In her third session, Pastor Mike brings up something overheard and taken out of context as an example of the insidious way evil attempts to besmirch those on the path.

In a strange paradox, counseling with Pastor Mike is effortless the first few sessions. So long as she nods and shares knowing smiles at the appropriate cues, he's content to carry the momentum of the session with anecdote upon anecdote. He's yet to mention Lydia. Instead, his focus is relating the passages she's working through at home to contemporary culture. Each moral comes full circle, ending on a sanguine note. It would be inspirational, were she not certain she'll be the baddie in the retelling of this parable to some downtrodden soul whose life is upended because some nosy bitty couldn't tend to her own business instead of cornering people by mailboxes.

He has a penchant for films and TV shows, most of which she's not allowed to watch. While her role is primarily that of coal shoveler to the machine that drives his ego, it's a far cry better than the depthless heap of concessions she shovels elsewhere.

Janie builds an immunity to the distance. Indifference prevails except for snubs from people she considered friends a mere month ago. Walking to meet her mother, Krissa looks right through her as she passes. Helene waits for her alone each session unless she wakes up on the tenacious side of the bed, intent to reclaim her rank only to be met with insouciance.

In a month's time, the family drifts from the front of the church to the mid-right mire to languish with backsliders unable to accept their fate. Nourished by hope they'll eventually be rid of their scarlet stigma and welcomed back into the fold.

Each passage is a prelude to their next session, this week's a double header of old and new. Savoring her latest triumph in the bologna war, Janie loses her appetite turning to Leviticus: 18:22. The Old Testament has never been among her favorites for spiritual inspiration. From what Janie can tell, they were a capricious lot who could have benefited from Mathew's perspective earlier on. Though her second passage, James 1:14-15, doesn't exactly make her feel all warm and fuzzy about the New Testament either.

Fighting back tears, she writes out the summary of her condemnation. Though she hasn't done much of anything with anyone, after the summer it would be a betrayal to profess otherwise. If a sin of the heart is enough to defile one's soul, as she's heard on end each Sunday, then her intentions have already laid ruin enough.

Distractions ease her nerves in the days leading up to her session with Pastor Mike. If he stays on trend, this is the week she's been dreading, no more coasting.

Entering his office, she notices the chair is cluttered with a bag and a pile of books.

Pastor Mike waves her over to the couch, she sits at the other end. Motioning to the books, "We're going to begin working through those texts. They're all individuals who've recovered from journeys like yours."

Half smiling and looking down, here it comes. Janie tucks her hands under her legs.

"So Janie, I think we've reached a point where we can be honest with one another. Right?"

Janie nods, again half smiling.

"You don't need to be afraid, think of me as a guide not a judge. Okay?"

Like the last few ticks of the rollercoaster before the drop, "Okay."

"The scripture provides us with everything we need to get back on track when we've gone off course." He leans a little further to reach her eye level. "Why don't you grab that book on the top there."

He has her read from it throughout the session, pausing to explain the already explained. He ends their session by praying over her, laying hands upon her bowed head. Their sessions follow this trajectory for the next few weeks, working through the salient points of the books. He never refers to Lydia by name, only referencing abstractions which exist to lead us astray. Emphasizing how imperative it is to see through their disguises.

By mid-October, Pastor Mike is increasingly dedicated to the power of laying hands in their sessions. He's taken to staying close instead of retreating to his end of the sofa. They've stopped discussing Janie's summaries, their sessions shift to his books and walking through prayers he believes possess curative potential.

Halloween drives home Janie's standing. Despite the church rejecting the greater idea of Halloween, there are always parallel festivities. Watching her parents take Matty trunk-or-treating alone is another reminder this won't blow over. Matty, who did alright, futilely offers to share until their mother catches wind of it.

Desperate to get out of the house, Janie hits the yard early to rake leaves and weed the flower beds. Lucas arrives a sight for sore eyes, sneaking up in near silence.

"I was hoping you'd be outside."

"You finally get new brakes?" Janie glances over her shoulder, a cursory check for her mother.

"Yeah, neighbor complained to my Dad when he was leaving for work." He mashes the handles, impressed with the silence. "How'd you do on candy?"

"Didn't go. I'm too old anyhow. Matty did alright though."

"Thought so." Swinging his backpack around, he retrieves a crumpled paper sack and hands it over the fence. "Here."

Laughing, Janie looks inside. "What's all this?"

Putting his backpack on, he hops onto his bike. "Olivia cleaned up, went with our cousin to some fancy development."

"Lucas, did you take all her candy?"

"It's my job, she's got plenty. No such thing as too old for candy." Balanced on the pedals, he fights a wobble. "Alright, see you."

Janie transports the contraband under her yard coat, distributing it amongst her Sunday shoes and pocketed cardigans. After two weeks of nibbling, she finds the leftovers replaced with an updated list of passages. Having eaten the best of it and given that she harbors no expectation of privacy, her mother did her a favor by disposing of the ant bait.

A week out from her birthday, Matty's hints for a bowling alley party go unheard. During dinner he strategically waits until his mother has a mouth full of food. "Janie, where do you want to have your party this year?"

Janie stops chewing and looks to both ends of the table. "Don't know."

Sipping his juice, he wipes his mouth with the back of his hand to save time. "How about the bowling alley?"

Swallowing hard, Helene's disappointed at Ray staying quiet, leaving her to settle it. "Matty honey, we're not doing a party this year."

"What? Why?" Head cocked, he looks to his father who never looks up from his plate.

Helene looks to Janie before continuing. "Well honey, there's no sense in planning something that no one will come to."

Janie gives Matty a little smile and pushes her food around her plate until they're allowed to leave the table.

Carrying the dishes to the sink, Ray hesitates before retreating to the den to watch TV. The kitchen table covered in Helene's orphaned letters, she goes over each with a magnifying glass to discern any legible addresses. Stalled on a water-stained envelope, she gives up after the light on the stairs goes off.

Quietly changing in the dark, Helene climbs into bed with Ray facing the window.

"When will it be enough?" Ray asks, keeping his back to her.

"It was a small mercy. You should see the way they look at her." Helene sits up in bed, ready to hash it out.

"The way they look at her or you?" Ray rolls over to face her.

Growing incredulous, "Like you were any help. You're not the one who has to show your face there every week. I'm being punished for seeking guidance and she acts like she's the victim."

"She's a good girl. She knows she did wrong."

"Does she?" Scooting down, she pummels her pillow.

Sighing heavily, Ray turns back over.

Without conceding his point, Helene makes amends with a mea culpa moussaka. While there's no cake or candles, Janie settles for an exuberant happy birthday from Matty, complete with a drawing of them wearing party hats. Trying to pretend everything's okay, she would have succeeded were it any other day. Her present of sorts from her parents is a break from passages study. Not knowing if she could stomach writing another word about what thou shalt not do or with whom thou shalt not do it, it's a pretty good gift all things considered.

Waiting outside first period, Lucas pulls Janie aside to present her with a cupcake. All the hurt pooled scarcely beneath the surface threatens to spill out as she wells up and hugs him tightly. Quietly and mostly into his shoulder, "Thank you."

He holds her and tries to lighten the mood. "Don't get too excited, my Mom made them."

Janie dabs at fledgling tears, she smiles and takes a big bite. "Want some?"

"No thanks. I think I ate like six last night." The bell rings, he looks off to his class down the hall. "I better go before they close the doors. See you at lunch?"

Unbothered by her teacher waiting, "Yeah."

Janie fights off tears during first period, the battle carries on until lunch. In the last couple of months she's gotten good at being neutral regarding her needs. Shifting her effort into getting by as though she were holding a storm door closed, borrowing strength from another day because she knows eventually the storm will relent. The sun will show itself. A new day will spell an end to this dark time, and life will right itself. Lucas is the only person outside of Matty who hasn't treated her like some damaged thing. Today is a break in the clouds. Janie knows it's just that: temporary. An aberration from what is.

Unprepared for her session with Pastor Mike, Janie tamps down every bit of emotion beyond his reach. Pity once easing into apathy tracks toward contempt watching her mother rub elbows with folks who'd prefer she kept her elbows to herself.

Ten minutes late and giddily apologetic, Pastor Mike catches them off guard. "So sorry to keep you ladies waiting."

Smiling and putting her arm around Janie's shoulder, Helene waves it off, "No need to apologize!"

"That's very kind. Janie, all set?"

It's not lost on Helene she's disappeared from his line of sight. Fidgeting with her purse, she feigns interest in this month's book club selection.

"Have a seat." Pastor Mike fumbles through his bag, his back to her. "How was your birthday?"

Taken aback that he knew, Janie forces a cheery "It was nice."

He holds up a small cardboard jewelry box. "This is for you."

Staring at him, she opens the box. Inside is a small gold cross on a thin chain. Before she can thank him, he takes the box and removes the chain.

"We encourage families not to celebrate with members going through counseling, helps the light of the path shine brighter." He unclasps it and scoots to put it on.

Uncomfortable, Janie shifts to face him. "It's okay, I can do it"

Pushing her hair aside, "It's hard to reach. I'll do it." He pauses until she puts her hands down. Her posture stiffened, he's undeterred and continues. "You're making a lot of progress Janie. That should be celebrated." Ignoring her rigidity, he lingers to slide the cross around. Patting her shoulder, "There." He fixes her hair back into place. "This will keep me with you whenever you need to draw strength."

Not wanting to touch the necklace, Janie looks down at her lap. Only after he moves back does she cease to hold her breath. Knowing what's expected, she thanks him without looking up.

With three-quarters of the session to go, Janie's mind races with uneasiness at his growing boldness, his intent to be familiar with her. While he goes on as usual with his book references and pop culture analogies, something has changed in the way he looks at her. No longer is it enough to smile and nod appropriately when cued, in those moments he studies her more appraisingly. The need for admiration has been surpassed by entitlement to veneration.

Janie quickens her pace down the hall after the session, maintaining a few steps ahead until she reaches her mother. Though she feels the weight of the choir director watching, as she always seems to, Janie keeps going without acknowledging her. Helene's eyes zone in on the necklace, dart to Pastor Mike and back to the necklace.

Eager to leave, Janie hopes to curtail any pleasantries. "Can we go?"

Put off by Janie's curtness in front of the Pastor, Helene tries to catch up. "Let me put my book away." Still glancing at the cross then back at Janie, she fumbles with her book while Pastor Mike looks on.

Waiting until Helene says goodbye, he lets her pivot and gain a few steps before calling out, "One more thing."

Helene turns apprehensively. "Did we forget something?"

"No, not at all." He smiles and pauses another moment to maintain the cadence. "I was wondering if you'd be interested in heading the ladies' Christmas planning brunch?"

Making no attempt to hide her flattery, Helene retracts the few steps she and Janie have made. "Of course! It would be an honor!"

Janie looks to her mother then back to her feet, refusing to look at him.

"Wonderful!" he replies in matched delight. "Coordinate with Maureen in accounting for whatever resources you need."

He waves, pausing until Helene nudges Janie to return the gesture. Without saying a word, a sense of hopefulness springs forth from Helene. She walks taller, no longer afraid to meet the gaze of others as they leave. Noting who looks through her, she bides her time until evidence of her return to the fold reaches them, imagining their chagrin at having disregarded the person entrusted with heading the Christmas planning brunch.

Janie sits quietly, an unacknowledged countdown until she can remove his presence from her neck. At least for the week anyway.

Feeling more emotionally charitable, Helene studies Janie's solemn air as they wait at the rail crossing. "Everything okay?"

Nodding, Janie's under no impression the query is imbued with an expectation of candor. Helene readily accepts the nod as affirmation of Janie's okayness, despite an inkling to the contrary.

"You must be making progress honey!" Helene fills the space with her aspirations. "He must be so proud of us for all our hard work. Don't ya think?" Leaving no room for reply, she continues her analysis of the fortuitous turn of events. "I always say hard work pays off, and you know what? It does."

Chapter Seven

Lying in bed, Janie swings the chain as a pendulum overhead. How can a symbol of salvation inspire such foreboding? The unshakable feeling that this is the start of something awful fosters a sense of urgency to bring these sessions to an end.

Things return to normal leading up to Thanksgiving. Nonetheless, the timer ticks away, growing louder as each Thursday afternoon draws near. Their dynamic lacks the authenticity of previous sessions, as though they're both humoring one another. Janie can tell Pastor Mike is trying to reinforce his role as mentor. Knowing her mother is blind with giddiness, Janie tries to move past her birthday. Crossing paths with the choir director in the hall, she slows as though she might say something to Janie until she sees Pastor Mike exiting his office.

Helene no longer waits meekly in the pew. Instead, she can be heard laughing with those who only a month ago were content to deny her existence. She smiles from a distance, waving to Janie and the pastor. Saccharine apologies and half hugs abound as she says her goodbyes.

Janie's reception at school takes a turn as word spreads. Kids from her congregation are either politely indifferent or gallingly genial. She feels no less surveilled. There will be no mending of fences with her non-church friends. The teenage radar system is buggy and prone to overcrowding. If you fly stealth long enough, people forget you were ever there in the first place.

Lucas is wholly unimpressed with the turning tide. He helplessly watches Janie accept their hellos and small talk with pity.

Krissa plops down with her lunch in a failed attempt at a casual drop in. "Feel like I haven't seen you guys in forever!"

Lucas curtly replies, "Really? Cause we've seen you plenty."

Krissa disregards Lucas and shifts towards Janie. "I got a new 4Him tape. Maybe you and your Mom could come by, we could listen."

Janie replies, struggling to look at her. "Yeah, I'll talk to my Mom."

"Yeah, cause my Mom had some ideas for the Christmas planning, ya know."

"Okay, I'll tell her." Janie shifts in her seat, wanting nothing more than to liberate Krissa of her clever smile.

Lucas stares stone-faced, fully intent on wearing away whatever claim she's got to Janie as an extension of her mother.

Unnerved and contented at having accomplished her mission, she mouths *oh hey* at no one. "Gotta go. See you at church. Let me know."

Janie nods, avoiding the sight of Lucas making gagging and barfing sounds. Looking over, she smirks. "Stop it!"

"Sorry, was gagging on all that bullshit," Lucas declares loud enough for Krissa to hear.

Shushing him, Janie looks around hoping no one heard.

"She's so fake. Who cares? I said it, not you. They can't blame you for what I said."

"Oh yes they can."

"Janie, I don't get it." His voice lowered, he speaks earnestly. "They're not your friends."

Endeared, Janie pushes over her freshly opened bag of salt and vinegar chips. "I know, but it follows me home either way, so it's easier to just pretend. Cause if she runs home caterwauling about me being mean, her mother and the other bitches of Bisquick are gonna get me in trouble."

Crunching on chips, Lucas grumbles, "Well doesn't mean I gotta be nice to them."

"Sure doesn't, just don't gettem going okay?" Janie pleads in a light-hearted nudge.

"I won't," nudging her back.

Thursday afternoon arrives, Helene unapologetically ditches Janie, hurrying off to make sure no one's overstepping what was decided at the planning brunch. From the instant Janie told her about Krissa, she's been keeping an eye on Mrs. Langley. Blustering to Ray, "I mean really, what kind of woman uses her daughter as a ladder."

Pastor Mike only comes as far as the hall leading to the offices. "Janie...ready?"

Instinctively looking for her mother, Janie senses a shift. "Coming." She grabs her bag and hurries, unsure of where her mother wandered off to.

He walks ahead, holding the door open without looking at her. "After you."

Janie notices two chairs facing one another in the center of the room. Pretending otherwise, she heads to her usual spot on the couch.

"Grab a chair. We'll be working through an exercise today. Did you bring your notebook?" Pastor Mike asks, gathering some notes and a pen from his desk.

"Mmhmm."

"What's that?" He asks firmly, sitting down across from her knee to knee.

"Yes." Restlessly adjusting her position, uneasy at the sudden shift from brotherly advisor to stern leader.

"Go ahead and read back this week's passage."

"K. It's from Proverbs. Trust in the Lord with all your heart and lean not on your own understanding." She pauses for confirmation that she should continue. "In all your ways submit to him, and he will make your paths straight."

"What do you think it means to trust in the Lord Janie?" Shifting his weight, he shuffles his notes.

"I guess to use the bible as a guide." She fidgets, fighting a nervous giggle at the thought of him explaining straight paths.

"That's part of it yeah, but what else?"

Uneasy, she looks to her notepad. "Dunno."

"Dunno?" Sighing. "Okay, for the sake of brevity I'll explain." His face betrays a mix of amusement and disappointment. "It's about trusting in God's plan, as well as trusting in his proxies. Do you know what a proxy is?"

Janie shakes her head.

"Someone ordained to guide others to God's plan, someone like me. Understand?" He places his notes on the desk.

Apprehensively, "I think so."

Placing his palms firmly on her knees, her legs tense beneath his fingers. "Your lack of trust in the Lord has left you vulnerable and lured you into same-sex attraction."

Janie struggles to organize her thoughts, his hands moving further along the tops of her thighs. She freezes, her mind and body united in a standoff.

"You must trust in me." Looking at her intently, demanding eye contact. "Tell me you trust me." He places his hands on her hips, leans in and kisses her.

The warmth of his breath threatens her gag reflex. Panic rings in her ears, she resists the urge to vomit. Swallowing hard, her eyes go wide as she stares at him in disbelief.

Returning to his seat, he pats her knee. "See the love that's right in front of you when you trust in the Lord?" He follows her gaze to the door and back. "Okay, let's get back on track." He carries on matter of fact, pleased with the success of his first exercise. "Let's move to the couch. These chairs are kinda hard, huh?"

Cornered by an invisible wall, Janie moves from the chair without losing sight of him.

Giving her a wider breadth on the couch, Pastor Mike no longer looks at Janie. "Let's discuss Peter's thoughts on the unrighteous, shall we?"

Staring into nothing, Janie doesn't hear a word. He makes no pause for acknowledgement, instead he reads to fill the space. Rotating through scribbled notes, anything to avoid Janie's impassive expression.

He plants a fatherly hand on her shoulder to keep her from sprinting down the hall. "Have you given any thought to joining the choir?" His voice again pleasant and pastoral.

Counting every step, she gives whatever answer will end the conversation. "I'll think about it."

Closing in on the end of the hall, he maintains his grip. "You let me know. I'll make sure you get a good placement."

"Okay." She pulls free. Again, Janie locks eyes with the choir director until Pastor Mike slows to speak with her.

"Emily you're doing a wonderful job directing, you really shine. I might have a recruit for you." Crinkling his nose and squinting, he points out Janie.

"Thank you. I'm sure she'll fit right in." Dismissively, she turns back to a bin of decorations.

Janie crowds her mother, willing her to wrap up her conversation. Intently watching his approach, she steps a smidge closer. Helene feels Janie butted up against her but says nothing.

Pastor Mike broadcasts his praise. "Helene, this is all fantastic! I'm so glad I reached out to you." He extends his hand, avoiding Janie altogether.

Stepping aside to shake his hand, "I'm just glad to be of service."

"I know you guys have to run, so I'll be quick." Pushing his hands into his pockets, he pauses for effect. "I thought you might like to introduce the Christmas pageant. What do ya think?"

"Of course!"

"Wonderful! Rehearsals start Saturday. Janie, maybe you'd like to join your Mom? We could use all hands on deck with decorating."

"She'd love to," Helene replies enthusiastically.

Pastor Mike forces a laugh as Janie refuses to mirror his tempo, he lights it back up for Helene. "Awesome!"

Janie resists all attempts at conversation on the way home. Helene scolds her for taking this opportunity for granted, more out of obligation than genuine letdown. Bypassing Matty, Janie hurries to brush her teeth.

Having regained her footing, Helene doles out suggestions more akin to mandates. Not a soul dares remind her she's only the emcee. Janie sorts ornaments by color, a tedious task that proves futile after the tenth or so ornament rolls away from its own kind.

Emily greets Helene, "Would you mind if I borrowed Janie to steady to ladder?"

Looking to the ladder then back to Janie, "Absolutely." Helene looks down at Janie's color wheel of ornaments, giving her a nod to go on.

Janie plants her feet wide, gripping the ladder from the side.

Emily climbs a few rungs, hanging a sack of decorations eye level with Janie. Acutely aware of everyone within earshot, she times her retrieval of décor for the gaps between people passing by. "I just love these little doves." Trailing off, she watches another passerby. "Has he touched you?"

Janie, whom up until now was only half paying attention, whips her head around unsure if she heard right. "He kissed me at our last session."

Emily, looking at her gravely, adjusts the ribbon on a small carved dove. "You need to find a way to end the counseling. Do whatever it takes."

Handing her the next dove, Janie nods. "Did he kiss you too?"

Taking the dove, she stalls to adjust the fixed ribbon. "He did a lot more than that, and he will with you too."

Janie forgets herself, letting go of the ladder. "Did you tell anyone?"

Emily ascends once Janie reaffirms her grip. "He was my youth pastor. No one would've believed me. I was in his group for kissin' on boys, which was really just one boy with a reputation."

"Shit." Covering her mouth, Janie swiftly stops the wobble. "Sorry."

"Be careful." Looking up to see Helene walking over, Emily hugs Janie. "Thank you so much, what a Godsend you were!"

Helene smiles along. "Janie, those ornaments are rolling away over there."

With one last look, Janie says goodbye. Taking every word to heart, she's emboldened in her mission to get out from under this.

The tick of the countdown bangs like a drum, Janie racks her brain for solutions. *I could fake being sick*. It would only buy a week. Not enough, but better than nothing. *Think bigger dang it.*

While Ray works a rare Saturday, Janie convinces her mother to take them to Dunn's Family Books to pick up some of Pastor Mike's suggestions. Matty objects, sunny Saturdays are best spent at the park, not shopping.

Finishing the dishes, Helene calls her marching orders from the foot of the stairs. "Matty three toys max. Janie, don't forget your book money."

Rolling her eyes, Janie stuffs the twenty her dad gave her into her pocket.

Halfway through the door, Helene stops Matty. "You can't bring those."

Looking down at his stego and t-rex, he whines, "Why?"

"It's complicated. Go get one of your cars." Taking them, she hands them to Janie with a glare. Whispering, "You know he can't bring those in there."

One of the committee ladies runs the store. What with her fawning over Helene, Janie can't get a word in edgewise till someone comes in looking for a monogrammed bible.

Holding up a book that resembles one from their sessions, Janie chirps, "Pastor Mike and I worked from this book a lot. Think I'll get it."

"You worked from that book?"

"Mmhmm."

"Why would he have you read about divorce? Your father and I aren't getting divorced." Helene scoffs, returning to her browsing.

Janie looks at the cover then at four other blue books with clouds. She finds the right one and holds it up. "Grabbed the wrong one. Here it is!"

Her mother has moved on. Janie trails behind, watching Matty's car race from one display to the next. "Well, you know what Mathew said about stumbling." She chuckles. *Pretty sly trotting that one out there.*

"Mathew didn't say that, James did. And he was talking about sin not reading comprehension Janie." Helene reaches down, taking Matty's car as they approach the display of Lladro angels.

Deflated, Janie tucks her book of blue skies under her arm. Grateful she's spending her father's money instead of her own.

Since Saturday was a wash, she'll focus on her father today. Things between them are not like they were, but they're not too bad either. Janie chooses to see this as a bridge to somewhere.

Ray is on his second helping by the time Janie and Matty make their way downstairs. Janie leans in to hug him, feeling him tense she corrects to a pat on the back before taking her seat.

Looking up from his eggs, Ray smiles at them. "Mornin'."

"Mornin' Dad," Matty declares, filling his plate with pancakes.

"Good morning!" Janie says cheerily.

"Slow down son, they're not going anywhere." Ray teases Matty as he stuffs a large pancake wedge into his mouth.

Janie waits for her mother to join them, hoping for a nod of approval when her father does his flick of the eye check in before answering. "Dad, I was thinkin' maybe we could all go do something today?"

As expected, he looks to her mother then back to his plate. "Can't kiddo." Taking another bite of egg and bacon, he takes his time chewing before continuing. "I have a fellowship meeting after services. Speaking of which, finish up or we'll be late."

Their position near the front of the church reclaimed, Helene glows with gratification. Pastor Mike delivers a phoned in sermon. Janie flips through the book of Psalms until a gently pointed elbow leaves her vacantly looking ahead.

Monday morning brings a throbbing headache Janie might assume was the banging of the countdown were it not for the stuffiness and fever tagging along. Helene sympathetically insists Janie go to class anyway, she cannot afford a day off since Mr. Nakamura called out. Janie asks to stay home on her own, Helene refuses to even consider it.

Puffy eyed and boogery, Janie blows through a dozen tissues on the drive to school. Using the visor mirror, she does one last sweep for stragglers.

Checking her watch, a tinge of guilt compels Helene to offer a compromise of sorts. "You can always go to the nurse's office to laydown till class is done."

Until this morning, if all else failed, feigning illness was Janie's ace in the hole. *So much for that.* The last three periods slip away sulking in the nurse's office. If looking and sounding like the undead couldn't buy enough trust to stay home, then she has gained nowhere near the ground she assumed.

Janie prepares for Thursday by studying the most repulsive people at school, noting their most off-putting traits. To start, she brushes her teeth for the last time Tuesday morning. The cold abandons her Wednesday, leaving a crackly cough in its wake. She challenges Matty to backyard races. A coughing fit stymies her desired level of muskiness. However, she has faith that skipping her shower combined with the sorcery of hormones will yield an acceptable level of funk by the session.

No one at school seems to notice, not even Lucas. She chalks it up to him having caught her cold. Still stuffed up, she's unable to measure the success of her endeavor until after school. Helene sniffs around her, a stifled laugh and a perplexed stare follow. She rests easy, her work is done.

Helene gives Janie an arm's length walking in. The decorations are a sight to behold. Everyone's buzzing with excitement as they round out the final days of prep. Emily works with the choir off in the distance. Janie hears her mother telling the soundboard tech she needs more volume in the mic. She takes in the scene with wonderment despite herself. The dedication and collective jubilation are most evident in the Christmas season. It's in those few weeks Janie understands the allure, the sense of purpose that drives everyone, and paradoxically the desire to belong to this fickle bunch.

Pastor Mike's stealth arrival startles Janie. "All set?"

Janie gathers herself and follows. He stares when she passes him, just as her mother had. Assured of her repellent, she plants herself on the couch and grabs her notebook.

Sitting next to her, he pushes her bag aside. Leaning close, he takes the notebook from her hand. "You trust me, right?"

Janie scoots against the arm of the couch. "Wait." She pushes his hands away as he paws at her.

Straining to settle her hands, he's freakishly calm. "You have to trust in the process." Putting his knee against her legs, he'll use his weight if his words cannot convince her.

Fire alarms ring out in her mind. *Scream!* The voice in her head screams, but she doesn't. Panic threatens to pound right through her chest. He's still talking, she hears nothing over the voice in her head wailing for her to do something. Anything. Despite incessantly slapping his hands away, the distinct feeling of his index finger hooking her belt shatters her into abject silence.

Triumph assumed, he relaxes a little. A knowing smile crests. Janie wrestles loose, turning away. "It's my time of the month!"

His smile twists into disgust, he recoils. "Keep your voice down!"

A coughing fit strikes, refusing to abate until it gags her. Janie fumbles with her buckle, watching his every move.

Sorting himself out, he shuffles his notes again. Clearing his throat as though about to begin a sermon, he pretends to gather what he wants to say from his notes. "So, let's get started."

Knees pulled up to her chest, Janie rests her weight on the arm of the couch. Her head turned away, another coughing fit rises through her lungs. Though she doesn't notice when exactly, at some point he trails off and they sit in silence.

An indeterminate span of time hinting at eternity elapses. The weight of the silence, which he takes as an expression of her defiance, is more than he can stand. "We're going to wrap up early. I have a responsibility to the choir, you understand."

Lurching through the door, Janie knocks it back into his face. Catching it, his pace quickens to stay in step with her. He eases into the contented smile he wears like a uniform. Pastor Malcolm and Pastor Ignacio, engrossed in conversation, nearly collide with her.

Patting her shoulder, Pastor Ignacio frets. "Almost got you, are you alright dear?"

Distracted, Janie cranes to see Pastor Mike and his plaster smile a stone's throw behind them. "Yes sir, I'm fine."

Pastor Malcom joins in. "How are you feeling Janie? Better?"

Wishing he were referring to her cold, knowing full well he isn't, she replies, "Much!"

Pastor Ignacio shakes Pastor Mike's hand. "God has blessed you brother! Such a gift with the youth."

He emotes an award worthy display of modesty. "No sir, the credit goes to the kids. I just give them the tools."

Pastor Malcom gives Janie a parting fatherly pat on the shoulder. "Listen to this man, child. He's got the light."

Pastor Mike's unable to keep up in the last stretch. She scans for her mother without breaking pace. *Of all times to be off mucking about.* Emily pauses mid-critique, tracking Janie's hurried search. Janie avoids eye contact for fear she'll burst into tears at the recognition of the one person who knows.

On her second pass, Janie spots her mother in the sound booth. Knocking on the door frame, she doesn't wait for an acknowledgment. "Mom, I'm done. Let's go."

Perturbed by Janie's demands, Helene returns to persuading the sound tech to make her voice sound less tinny.

Exasperated, Janie interrupts. "I don't feel well. Can we please go?"

Finishing her note, Helene hands it to the sound tech. "I'm so sorry. We'll talk more tomorrow."

He lets out a meditative exhale reading her notes.

Helene walks past Janie, determined to make her catch up. "Well let's go then since your cold's more important than the audio for the play."

They bicker quietly in their slog to the door. Almost there, the sound of jangling keys grows ever closer.

"Ladies! Hold up a moment!" Pastor Mike's eyes dart to Janie, glaring at him. "Would you mind if we break till the start of the year? Taking the family to Branson after Christmas."

Wrapped up in worrying he heard her chiding Janie, Helene fails to notice his unease. "That sounds wonderful! Enjoy them while they're little. When it's still easy."

Laughing along, he shakes his head. "Isn't that the truth. The oldest starts high school next year."

"Oh, I remember when she was just a little thing." Helene looks off sentimentally till Janie ruins the moment coughing. "Anyway. Give those kiddos a squeeze for me."

Within reach of the door, Janie pushes out into the dark parking lot. The damp air triggers another fit.

Helene grabs cough drops from the glove box. "Here. If that doesn't clear up by the weekend, I'll make an appointment with Dr. Milstein."

Sullenly unwrapping the drop, Janie sighs. "Fine."

"Fine? Honestly Janie?" Shoving a Kleenex at her, she shakes it. "You've got something," pointing, "There, on your cuff."

Attacking a glob of phlegm with the tissue, she crumples it into a fist. "Perfect."

Chapter Eight

After a course of antibiotics supplemented with copious cough syrup consumption, Janie's back at it the week of Christmas. Leveraging her mother's guilt over downplaying her illness and sympathizing with her countless pageant responsibilities, Janie's allowed to stay home on her own over break. Though she suspects Mrs. Parlow next door may be keeping an eye on her from a distance. Either that or she's having senior moments because she's already checked her mail three times.

Janie's first gift of the season is finding out Kate's not coming home for Christmas. Without a doubt, if she were, their mother wouldn't cut Janie a single break. Busy with rehearsals, Helene wishes Kate were here to help. As a supportive sister, Janie talks up Kate managing her university's production. Even going so far as to remind her mother how important Christmas production ticket sales are to the chapel's spring budget.

With Matty at the children's ministry, the house is quiet. Almost too quiet. It's been months since she's been anywhere alone. Though there are no stated restrictions on where she can go, her fear of losing this hard won autonomy is lock and key enough. At this point she'll take her victories wherever she can get them, however small they may be. While going into town has the potential to get her in trouble over some misstep in front of the wrong person, home is her oyster. She's free to wear pants or not, to eat the salad her mother left in the fridge or steal her father's cold cuts, she could even take her lunch up to her room if she wanted to. Really, the possibilities are endless.

After a day on the couch watching reruns in old sweatpants, the thrill is gone.

The clamor of Matty running through the house yelling that he's got to pee is a welcome shift from the restless glum settling over her like an itchy wool blanket. The commotion breaks Janie's rumination over a scene from a movie she'd never heard of and wouldn't watch again, but just so happened to land on flipping channels if her mother were to ask. Yet it reminds her of Lydia and how much she wishes she were here. Not that Lydia's ever far from her mind except during sessions with Pastor Mike. No matter how many ridiculous things she must fill her mind with before walking through those doors, she'll do it. Anything less would pollute the one place in her world which remains beautiful.

Relieved, Matty joins them. "Phew!"

"You make it?" Janie laughs at his exaggerated exhaustion.

"It was close!" His laugh has a whistle thanks to a couple baby teeth that cut out early.

Watching his mother unpack groceries, Matty figures they may as well go play if they're never going to eat. "Wanna play catch?"

"Wait. Jackets, zipped up." Helene calls to Janie at the stairs. "How's your cough?"

"Way better. We won't run around."

Even with a coat, the cold is bitterly damp. The baseball always feels harder when it's cold. Matty tells tales of the kids from ministry, Janie pities their teachers and mothers. The worst of them go to school at the church, a small blessing he only sees them at church.

Her mind wanders, tossing the ball back and forth. Not because she's bored, simply because it's easy. Easy is a nice change from constant vigilance.

Eating dinner when the sky's gone dark is Janie's least favorite part of winter. Not like in summer when you can still go outside for a spell, still feel like there's life left in the day. Summer ended and took Lydia with it a mere four months ago, or three months and three weeks if you want to get technical about it. Either way, feels like a lifetime.

Matty has everyone laughing about Michael A. farting during silent prayer. Rules or not, Helene can't bring herself to give him a hard time for potty talk at the table. Ray contentedly listens as she describes their first full run through. Conversation flows around Janie until her mother notices she's not wearing the cross.

"I snagged it on my sweater." Janie dives into her food, hoping the tide will turn back towards that one soprano girl who can't seem to hit her cue.

"You can always wear your Yaya's cross," Ray remarks offhandedly.

"Your mother was Greek Orthodox," Helene quips, turning back to Janie. "Remind me to take it to the jeweler before your next session."

Janie nods. A stinging reminder this is but a brief sojourn from sparring with Pastor Mike.

"What difference does it make Helene? I was Greek Orthodox before I converted. A cross is a cross." Ray's paying attention now, she's treaded into Yaya territory.

"It was a gift." Helene sidesteps Yaya.

"Seems like something that should be left to us," Ray declares with little conviction.

"Honey, I think he was just offering encouragement."

Ray nods, refusing to contest or concede.

"Anyway. Janie I'll need you to get dinner going tomorrow. Matty and I'll be late, last rehearsal." She beams with pride.

Janie agrees, scooping another helping. "You got it."

Helene follows the spoon's journey from the Pyrex but says nothing in trade for Janie's cooperation.

The night proves too cold for even the clouds, Janie spies a few stars strutting in the shadow of the slivered moon. Lying with her head hanging over the edge of her bed, a tangent of light piercing her window hits the dangling necklace. Twisting the cross in her fingers, she stretches the chain like a web between her hands waiting for the weakest link to show itself. She lets it run through her fingers until it slips to the floor.

Janie struggles to remember how long Lydia said until her birthday, or how she looked when she said it. Has Lydia forgotten her already? After all, she hasn't written back. Happens all the time at school. Sometimes, Friday to Thursday is the high school equivalent of May to September.

Janie thinks of their goodbye, as she often does, absently curious if Lydia wears her poncho. Shaking her belly with both hands, she wonders if she isn't getting a little fat. *Might have to let Lydia keep it if you don't cool it with the snacks.*

Maybe Lydia will do like she said, come up to see her when she gets her license. They could go for a drive and Janie could show her around the valley.

What would she show her? Dead fields of yellow weeds so withered from the heat they can't even command the dust to the ground. Sweltering livestock wallowing in an abhorrent concoction of dirt, feed and their own muck. The stench of it rising from the field to the road and down your throat displacing every last breath of decent air with its own foul essence.

Spring is green fields speckled with whatever wildflowers migrating birds gifted them, water flows through the canals glistening under the midday sun and a constant breeze lifts away the ugliness of everything hidden from the road. Summer in the valley forsakes them all.

She'll take her to the lake instead. Maybe Lucas could come, he might take a shine to her with all the stuff she knows about comics and movies. And when the time comes for Lydia to head home, she could go with her. The prospect sits perched upon her tongue like the name of a song beyond your grasp but close enough to hum the tune. The practical voice, always there in the recesses, levels the lovely chimera.

Holed up in the den no more, Manny's is the spot. Blustery weather cannot keep people from their Christmas shopping. Hell, a plague of locusts couldn't slow their march. Watching folks honk and hiss at one another over parking spots a matter of breaths after wishing others a Christmas blessing, leaves Janie thankful she's on her bike. She locks it up next to Lucas' at the light post.

If you've never been to Manny's Music before, it probably looks like any other store on the row. A little more expensive than the mall, some stuff looks like it's been on the shelf for a while because it has, and the walls are adorned with witty handwritten signs.

For the acquainted, there's a divine order to the store. The front is tuned to the season with everything you need for that poor soul who mentioned they really love that one thing. The middle is for buyers who know what they want, know what it's worth, and have the cash to buy it. Then there's the back, a mess of overstock, beat up merchandise waiting to be marked down and listening booths. A haven for the broke and musically thirsty.

Lucas is lost in an old copy of *Heavy Metal* magazine at a corner station. Not one to crowd or be crowded, Janie goes for the opposite end. Static is all the headphones have left to give. Exposed wires reach for the input, holding on by the sinew of some hastily applied electrical tape. Shuffling over to the station next to Lucas, he gives her a little smile.

The store's busy, but no one pays any mind to the back. All the sample tracks have been swapped since summer. Janie gives the Ramones' "Merry Christmas" a whirl, but it reminds her of the pageant. "Achin' to Be" has legs though. Waiting for her to finish, Lucas pretends to inspect the demo menu he's already memorized.

Janie sets the headphones on the cradle, holding up a cassette of *Don't Tell a Soul*. "Hi, didn't want to bother you. These guys are awesome. What are you listening to?"

"Bunch of different stuff, mostly country. You out shopping?"

"Nah. Just getting out of the house. How's the new guy?" They look to the skinny clerk with ripped off sleeves, and a murkily dyed shag.

"Can you tell he picked the music?" Lucas laughs, dropping his gaze to avoid the clerk. "I hope Manny comes back soon. Can't get this guy to order comics."

"Lucas do you really need more comics?" Studying him, Janie works through what to say.

"Always."

Pushing their bikes, they meander towards the pizza place they always end up at. With Christmas only a few days out, Janie knows she's halfway to the counseling couch. Having gone nowhere, she's held onto most of her summer money and treats them to pizza. Lucas puts up the requisite protest. Truth be told, he's still a little light in the wallet after tracking down the last covers of *Spider-Man #1*.

"Thanks for pizza, I'll getcha next time."

"Please, I totally owe you." Janie crumples the edges of her paper plate as she rotates it. "My Mom's the emcee at our church pageant."

Snickering, "Really?"

Nervous, she tears into the plate's edge. "I know, but it looks alright."

Watching her fidget, Lucas gives the teasing a rest. "She making you go?"

"Kinda."

"That sucks. My Mom makes my Dad go to her office party. He says the booze isn't even worth it." He flushes, remembering she comes from a dry family.

"Yeah." Chewing through another bite, twisting away at the crust. "You wanna go?"

"To the play?"

"Yeah. It's Saturday night." She takes a long sip of her soda. "Maybe we could go together."

"Like together?" He's stopped chewing.

"Yeah. I mean if you want to."

He stares at her for a moment, taking it all in. "Yeah, that'd be cool."

They finish their pizza drifting from one thing to the next, never landing on anything too serious.

Helene's in a good place the day before the pageant. Rehearsals have gone off without a hitch, and she fits into the dress she didn't fit into last Christmas. All that remains is getting Matty a red tie for the pageant. Janie nonchalantly takes the lead through Sears, steering them into the cosmetics department.

Janie grabs a few things here and there, Helene takes the bait. "Makeup?"

Feigning interest in the benefits described on the box, she pauses. "Ehh, thinking about getting a couple things to wear to the pageant."

"Really?" Helene raises an eyebrow but stops short of discouraging her. "Well, let's have a look."

Matty sighs dramatically, crouching with his stego next to the display.

"Those aren't the right shade, you'll look anemic." Helene handily grabs foundation and a tinted lip balm. "Gotta keep it simple or your father will have a fit."

Janie adds a clear mascara to the heap. In line she offers to take them, but Helene waves her hand. "I'll get them."

Walking to the car, Helene hands the bag off to Janie so she can unwrap Matty's GI Joe.

Spit it out already. "Lucas is taking me to the pageant."

"Taking you?"

"He's my date."

"I don't know how your father will feel about that," Helene cautions.

"Kate started dating when she was fifteen." Knowing full well they're going through the motions, Janie plays her part close to the cuff.

"Right, that's right," Helene trails off. Pulling into traffic, it's hard to hide her grin. "Your Dad likes Lucas."

The pageant's a success for Janie and her mother. Mostly, it's like any other time she and Lucas have hung out, except they sat a little closer and her family was there. Helene buys Lucas a small trinket for Christmas, which Janie delivers upon emerging from her turkey casserole coma.

Inviting Lucas to the New Year's carnival seals the deal. Though he's not particularly religious, he does worship at the altar of free ride tickets and games. Matty attaches himself like a prosthetic limb for the entirety of the carnival till Helene calls his day done.

They wander the booths hopped up on peppermint tiger tails, for a while she forgets her motives. Lucas puts his arm around her on the squat Ferris wheel, reckoning he'd go around and around all night to stay there with Janie. Seeing the approving smiles of girls who acted like she should be quarantined, deepens her commitment to see this through. Playing it up, she rests her head on his shoulder here and there.

Lucas drives them home in his father's truck. Though they talk about the same stuff, there's a quiet confidence in his way. The nerves that once beleaguered him are all but gone, having recalibrated to beset him whenever Ray speaks. Walking her to the door, making no attempt to kiss her, he waits until she's inside.

Her parents stop speaking in the den. Pausing in anticipation of being summoned, Janie takes to the stairs when nothing comes. A few steps in, she hears her father. "Have a good time?"

Popping into the den, she holds up an oversized blue bunny Lucas won at the shooting booth. "It was good."

"I see." Ray smiles and goes back to the Dick Clark special.

Waiting a moment longer, Janie turns to leave. "Night."

"Janie..." Helene, leaning against Ray, turns to her.

"Yeah?"

"Your Dad and I talked. We think you should start the New Year fresh. We'll let Pastor Mike share his gift with someone else in need."

Wanting to jump for joy, Janie replies earnestly, "I won't let you guys down."

"Goodnight honey!"

Listening to a national broadcast from Times Square on low, the pride of a goal accomplished fades. She did what Emily said, what she had to do. Rationalizing no one's been hurt does little to lessen the guilt of using Lucas as a means to her own end. She drafts a truce between her head and her heart, promising to end it if he gets too serious.

Chapter Nine

In a month's time, Lucas is an honorary member of the Harris household. Helene puts him to work reaching upper cabinets and takes to doting on him like one of her kids. At first, Janie reaps the benefits of redemption. Benefits which exceed restrictions placed on her sister when she began dating.

Her bedroom remains untouched while she's at school, save for the usual laundry sweep. Lucas is allowed over on weeknights, they're even allowed to study in her room. Neither Ray nor Helene has raised a single issue with Lucas not being of their faith. No one has. The air of gratification at being such a clever girl starts to come apart with each boundary she matter-of-factly oversteps.

Crashed out studying for spring midterms, Janie awakens to her mother knocking on her cracked bedroom door. Unaware her mother even understood the concept of knocking, Janie fumbles to turn the barely audible radio off as her eyes adjust.

"Honey, can I come in?" Though she doesn't wait for an answer, it's better than a bed check.

Janie pushes her book aside, reaching to nudge Lucas awake on the floor. "Sorry, fell asleep."

Helene looks at him the way she does Matty when he falls asleep in odd places. "Falls asleep anywhere, doesn't he?"

Dumbfounded, Janie scares him awake brusquely shaking his shoulder.

"Lucas, honey. It's almost nine. Your folks are probably wondering where you are." Helene looks at Janie expecting her to say something. She doesn't. "You okay to drive?"

"Yeah, thanks Mrs. Harris." Sleepily shoving everything into his bag, he gives Janie a sumo hug. "Pick you up at eight?"

Janie nods, "Mmhmm."

Helene pulls the door closed behind them, then pops her head back in. "Need anything?"

Yeah, a barf bag. Janie shakes her head.

An epiphany whiplashes Janie as she groggily fights the outlet plugging in her night light. They find who she is so loathsome, they would turn a blind eye to their moral code so long as it serves to confirm her rejection of Lydia. Better to risk having a whore for a daughter than a homo.

Lucas revels in their relationship, chaste as it may be. Yearning for boredom, Janie's wish is granted when he picks up an afternoon job at Luigi's. After a few weeks of her mother talking about Lucas on end, Janie figures she'd rather spend time with the actual Lucas than talking about her mother's weird Lucas projection. The only drag of having a boyfriend who drives and slings pizza, is that he's still a boy. What is it her father always says when they complain? *When you're parched, a drop of dew is better than a cup of nothing. Right, a friend is a friend.*

Lucas accompanies Janie to the Easter luncheon without objection. For the cost of resting his eyes and making a tent of his hands, he gets a tasty buffet and the joy of trash talking uptight goody goodies like Krissa under his breath.

Pastor Mike makes his rounds after the service, altering his path to Janie's table. Lucas puts his arm around Janie as she scoots closer to him on the pastor's approach. He doesn't know the details of her counseling, nor does he care to. He knows Janie so nothing else matters. Locking eyes, Lucas holds steady until Pastor Mike looks away.

With a hand on Helene's shoulder, he reaches out to shake Ray's hand. "Good to see you Ray! Helene, another wonderful event!"

Ray shakes his hand firmly. Wait for it. There it is. Her dad's trademark grin, the one where his eyes drift to something else before his smile retreats to a neutral state. Best to leave the conversation to Helene.

"I had a lot of help!" Helene gushes.

"Well, we couldn't have done it without you!" Looking to Janie with his most pastoral expression, "Hi Janie!"

Sheepish, she forces a smile through a stiffened jaw. "Hi."

"You know I have a couple sessions open this month. Sometimes it's the closure that keeps you." He leans on the back of Ray's chair, giving her a little wink.

Janie's eyes dart to her mother. Having no desire to revisit the events which brought them to counseling, Helene jumps in. "That's very generous! We think it's best Janie have her fresh start, and we owe it all to you!"

"Of course." The twinkle abandons his eyes, leaving only a facade of teeth. "I'm here if you need me."

Janie looks up long enough to appease her mother. Her appetite annihilated, she rakes the food around her plate. Lucas, her hero in chinos, puts an end to her dilemma one forkful at a time.

Helene absolves herself from the burden of further inquiry into Janie's sudden sullenness by busying herself with Matty. Ray attributes everything to the rise and fall of teenage moods, uncharted and dubious territory as any father can attest to. Lucas watches them look everywhere but in front of them as Janie withdraws to the confines of her chair.

Closing the passenger door, Lucas leans into it to compel the latch. Janie flattens her dress, turning on the radio in rhythm with the ignition. Commercials do little to lift her spirits. Giving the cassette a firm push, she waits through the click of the teeth grabbing the spool and the flat pull of the tape across the heads. A moody bass line leads the pack, but not soon enough to derail the runaway line of thought she'll be chasing down the rest of the day.

She's triumphed. The sessions are done. Yet here she sits ashamed and complicit in his sin, their sin. The public indignity for her transgression with Lydia pales in comparison to this silent degradation. No amount of doctrine or moralizing can force her to take ownership of the notion she and Lydia were guilty of deviance. Much like Emily, she's assumed both shares of blame without so much as an accusation.

Lucas calls her name from across the cab. *How long's he been watching?* Janie gives a caught smirk, pushing a stray hair from her cheek. "Yeah?"

"You okay?" He reaches for her arm, she flinches. Regret flushes her face. He withdraws, his hand landing on the stick.

"Shit. Sorry." She puts her hand over his for as long as she can bear, putting him at ease.

"He was your counselor?"

Running her hands over her face, she puts her hair up. "He's just really preachy is all. I kinda hate him." Leaning back, she turns her face to the window. "Can we talk about something else?"

"Sure." He puts his hand over hers, running his thumb over her fingers to soothe her.

Steeling her reflexes, she defies the blaring urge to pull her hand away. Wanting to want to hold his hand calls for more strength than she has today.

Chapter Ten

Summer arrives ahead of schedule, same as last year. Notwithstanding the lack of word from Lydia, there remains the promise of maybe. Maybe her letters got lost in the mail. Maybe she couldn't find a pen...for a year. Maybe she'll pull up outside the diner like Janie imagined. Or maybe, just maybe, she met someone else and moved on like a normal person. *Nah, scratch that last one.*

A seasoned veteran, Janie prepares for another summer slinging grub to tourists. Unhampered by last year's anxieties, she looks forward to helping the new girls learn the ropes. Most of all, she hopes that by serendipity or celestial alignment, she and Lydia's paths remain destined to converge at the market dock.

Choosing bait over pizza, Lucas will spend the summer on the lake. Occasionally, a tourist who lands a big one tips him on their way out. Tips hardly cover the extra gas money, but one can never undervalue bragging rights for superior knife skills in the art of cutting bait. Janie knows he mostly took the job so they could ride together.

The routine is effortless, some days the prospect of spending her future with her best friend doesn't sound so terrible. Love doesn't have to be some, be all end all, heap of happiness. Hell, there's plenty of moments she's happy with Lucas. Driving around in his dad's old truck talking about the ruin that would be leveled upon humanity if the villains from their favorite comics formed an alliance. Watching *Fright Night, An American Werewolf in London* or *Hellraiser* for the hundredth time. Eating free pizza from messed up orders and having a thumb war for the last slice. She can almost see it. Then he puts his arms around her and kisses her. Those are the days she knows the difference between almost and desire is infinite.

The diner and its keepers remain unchanged, save for Mrs. Maple upgrading her Dr. Scholl's to bright white LA Gears. *She's going to need some sneaker paint.* Krissa and Monica are lost without Wendy. They float around the small crew of waitresses like barnacles seeking an invitation to adhere themselves. Janie marvels at their ability to unify for a shared cause.

Their sisterhood goes south when Krissa scratches the hostess's fender squeezing her mother's Buick into the next spot over. Just like that she scrapes herself free of them, and again they're adrift bickering over whose fault it is.

Licking their wounds from a slow spring, only two new girls are brought on for the season. Sizing up Isabel and Amy, Janie wonders if she looked that scared at orientation. Thinking back, she was too fixed on having her *Mystic Pizza* awakening to know what she was in for. Mrs. Maple nudges Isabel under Janie's wing to get the lay of the land bussing tables. Monica and Krissa settle for Amy. If they can't find a leader, then an underling will have to do.

"So, the tables all have numbers. There's a map behind the counter." Teaching while she cleans, by the third table Isabel's a step ahead. "You done this before?"

Smirking, Isabel flips the towel for another swipe. "I worked at my auntie's place back home."

Tapping her with a stack of menus, "Coulda said something. Took me a month to figure out I was sweeping crumbs into the seat backs."

Isabel looks to a booth near the door with empty plates and toast shrapnel littering the floor. "Man, some people are straight up slobs. So, do you live here in town?"

"No, me, Krissa and Monica are from a few towns over." She points to them, chattering away at Amy behind the counter.

"They look nice." Pivoting to spectate, "Which one?"

"Clayton." Expecting the usual where's that, "It's not too big."

"We just moved to Clarksdale. We're neighbors." Isabel senses eagle eye Maple's glare, instinctively she starts wiping down the counter next to the register.

"Welcome, I guess. How'd you end up working here then?" Janie stacks menus. She need not look over to notice Mrs. Maple, her nose knows that aroma of syrup and stale Shalimar from ten feet away.

"My youth pastor suggested it." Isabel pauses when Janie goes quiet. "Don't worry, I'm not a Jesus freak or anything."

Janie replies in a hushed tone, "You gotta be careful what you say."

Krissa and Monica have worked their way closer. It's not lost on Isabel. "I see what you mean."

Isabel's proficiency doesn't go unnoticed, she leapfrogs over them to server ahead of the July 4th crowds. Amy falls in step with her mercurial mentors, her hair goes from Laura Ingalls to a scrunchy top pony with bangs sprayed into an eternally cresting wave. Janie can tell her eyebrows are Monica's handy work by the shared surrealist influence in their penciling. Isabel gets the brunt of it since they're in the same youth group. Janie envies the way Isabel's unaffected by the cliques at the diner and church.

Joining Janie and Lucas for lunch on the spur of the moment is all it takes. Never a third, always a trio. Like three peas in a pod, they spend the summer inseparable.

Leary of Isabel asking too many questions, Janie drags her along to lunch on the market dock two days a week when Lucas is off with his pops.

By August Janie cannot steer clear of feeling the fool holding vigil for a lost cause. No more sweaty legs dangling over cracked concrete or watching out for bitey ants madder than a junkyard dog. When the weather is tolerable, they walk through town on their lunch break. Janie's convinced Seth misses them loitering over at the market.

Weeks of unacknowledged hinting evolves into a more advanced form of intimation, firm prodding. Helene leaves a choir robe on Janie's bed. She pushes it aside, flopping down in its place. Tossing her sneakers, she massages her aching feet. The floor was so busy, closest they could get to a break was leaning on the counter to down a soda. Lazily pushing herself up onto an elbow, Janie studies her mother's incursion.

Bent on giving her a piece of her mind, Janie marches halfway downstairs before treading lightly back to shake the wrinkles out of the garish teal robe. She may have to wear it, but that doesn't mean she has to look at it.

Helene holds out until dessert. "Did you see the robe?"

Cautiously aloof, "Huh? Yeah, I saw it."

"So?" Helene pushes, patience frayed. "Janie, there are a lot of girls who've tried out for choir. You've been invited."

"I hate singing."

"Don't say hate," Ray cautions cheekily.

"I can't sing," Janie counters with raised eyebrows.

"Better," Ray smirks.

Ignoring their repartee, Helene's jaw tightens. "You don't know that. Emily can coach anyone." Helene pushes a slice of pie in front of her.

Exhaling dramatically, "Fine."

"We'll be practicing over in Clarksdale for the rest of the summer," Helene adds, pleased with her pie persuasion.

"Why?" Picking at her pie. "Wait, what do you mean we?"

"Emily and Pastor Mike are helping get their congregation's choir program off the ground." Collecting serving dishes, she shovels the leftovers into Tupperware. "I'm lending a hand." Gushing, "They're growing so fast, the pastor thought I could help create a little order."

The thought of croaking away in front of Isabel's youth group is preemptively mortifying.

On their lunch walk, Janie works up the courage to spill. "Listen, I gotta tell you something. Don't laugh."

Eyes wide, Isabel grins. "Oooh!" Rubbing her hands together playfully, "What?"

"My church's choir is merging with yours." Isabel looks at her, waiting. "My Mom made me join."

Still grinning, Isabel starts walking again. "I'll join too."

Relieved, Janie asks, "Can you sing?"

Isabel gasps in mock offense. "Can you?"

Janie wants to warn Isabel but can conceive of no way of telling her without giving up what landed her in his office in the first place. Between her and Emily, he'll never get near Isabel.

Driving to their first practice, Janie uses the time alone with Lucas to feel things out. "Thanks for tagging along."

Laughing as he shifts into third, "And miss you two singing? No way."

Nudging the radio knob, he knows it's her tell that she wants to talk. She asks, "You sure you're okay with me bringing Isabel around all the time?"

"Yeah. Why?"

"No. I mean, nothing." Janie flips to another station.

Glancing at her and back to the radio, "Are you okay with it?"

"Totally." She smiles at him, turning it up. "I love this song."

As it turns out, Isabel can sing. Quite beautifully, in fact. Janie, however, does not surpass her own expectations. Emily catches her mouthing the words, leaving Janie to panic she might call her out.

Pastor Mike hardly pays Janie a passing glance. His usual hubris is replaced with an acute focus on the head pastor. With two senior pastors ahead of him at their church, Janie speculates in the safety of her head that he's vying for the top spot at Isabel's church. Her pastor's a little past his prime and overwhelmed with all the commotion.

Always attentive, Lucas watches them practice while grazing the snack table. He laughs at Janie mouthing the words out of sync and laughs harder at her hitting flat notes when she does dare jump in. However, Janie's doing some watching of her own. There's a certain look which has always belonged to her, and only her, when it comes to Lucas. A look she had never given a second thought to before having to share it with someone else. *Totally not jealous. Don't be selfish.* Be it today or a year from today, the truth is indisputable. She needs to let him go.

Chapter Eleven

A season already on life support due to competing with the 75th anniversary of the National Park Service, flat lines when an algae bloom renders the lake a no man's land. Reservations vanish overnight, leaving the town once again sleepy and hurting for revenue. True to their word, Dwight and Mary let everyone at the diner stay on to finish out the season. Thanks to the girls and the diner's rainy day fund, they tackle deferred maintenance.

Mrs. Maple and her seasoned mavens continue dishing sass and grub to locals. They offer patty melts and consolation to bummed out stragglers who missed the memo. The girls of summer along with the younger wait-staff help with assembly of new booths and deep cleaning. Krissa scores a pity spot as hostess when an old elbow injury flares up in the nick of time.

Janie and Isabel land a coveted spot inside deep cleaning tables and cabinets. Meanwhile Amy and Monica work in the sweltering parking lot stripping down old booths. A year's worth of gum encrusts the table bottoms. After a day of sickeningly nondescript fruit flavors mixing with cleaning agents, Janie will go three months before she can stomach a Juicy Fruit stick. Clad in dishwashing gloves, a germ mask and an old busser shirt, Isabel's ready to clean. Once Janie scrapes each table bottom, Isabel moves in to sanitize.

Saving the worst for last, Janie stretches and contorts herself to ratchet loose a gob of gum some sadist pressed into the table mount. Sweat flows in directions which defy gravity and basic decency. Chipping away at the last bolt, she hums to tune out the girls filling shakers at the counter. *Who spends twenty minutes talking about bras? Honestly.*

Somewhere between the murmuring of the shaker twins and her own scraping, a familiar rattle beckons. Smacking her face on the table in a seamless ascent, she sets out to the market without a word. Isabel ditches her hazmat accoutrements with a knowing eye turned toward anyone who might think of taking them.

Wiping away sweat from her eyes, Janie can't make out who's in the truck with Tricia. As she has all summer, she hoped it might be Lydia driving.

Isabel half jogs to catch up. "Hey, what's up?"

Unrelenting in her pace, Janie doesn't turn to answer. "Nothin' just needed a break."

Shaking the collar of her shirt to cool herself, "God it's hot out here." Isabel squints as she tries to figure out what the hurry is. "Wonder why they're here on Tuesday instead of Monday."

Janie stops at the curb. "I dunno, had a hankering for a cream soda is all."

Not buying it, Isabel half smiles. "You pop up like a prairie dog when that truck pulls in every week."

"No I don't. Anyway, I can't look at another piece of chewed gum for at least ten minutes."

Following Janie into the store, "You should wear a mask. I sprayed some Lysol in mine, don't smell a thing anymore."

Grimacing, Janie turns, "I dunno if Lysol's any better than bad breath and fruit punch."

Grabbing sodas, they kill time trying on cheap sunglasses. Tracking Tricia in the security mirrors, Janie loses sight. *Just as well.*

Giving some serious thought to a pair of dayglow orange Clubmaster knockoffs, Janie catches a strangely familiar boy who's mostly kneecaps and Adam's apple, hovering at the edge of the aisle. She takes off the glasses.

"Are you Janie?" He asks standoffishly.

"Yeah," she replies slowly. Isabel hangs on intrigued.

He hands her a small folded envelope that has a fuzziness to it. "My sister told me to give you this."

Reflexively beaming, Janie plays it cool and wedges it in her pocket. "How'd you know it was me?"

"She described you pretty good." Proud, he stands a bit taller. "I've been trying to get assigned to the camp run all summer."

Isabel chimes in. "How'd you convince them?"

Matter of fact like, he explains, "I lied, told them the regular guy was stealing the s'mores bars."

Isabel smirks, needing to know more. "Aren't you slick. He get in trouble?"

"A little, no s'mores for the rest of camp." Unremorseful, he smiles slyly. "K. See ya."

"Wait." Janie wants to ask about Lydia then chickens out. "What'd you do with the chocolate?"

"Buried it." His laugh trails off the same way Lydia's does.

Isabel stifles her curiosity for as long as she can, which isn't long at all. "Who's the letter from?"

"An old church friend." Janie's face flushes. "Hey, don't tell anyone, k?"

Isabel throws her arm around Janie. "Not a word, swear."

Janie floats through the afternoon, wishing and willing the hands of the clock forward. Imagining the contents of the letter, she barely utters a word on the way home as Isabel and Lucas debate the merits of grooming in a full-blown zombie apocalypse. The smell of Lucas after a day of clearing dead fish from the shore is inescapable.

Faking a stomachache, Janie avoids dinner and her mother's complaints of Krissa's mother upstaging her at the planning meeting. Sent to bed with a napkin full of saltines, ginger ale and a long face, she's off the hook.

Unfolding the letter, she breathes it in expecting the same light scent of Nivea and sunscreen she remembers from the market. She's met with an odious stench the likes of which could only be cultivated by a summer spent in the pocket of an active teenage boy. After a silent heave, she sips her ginger ale. *A year of waiting and barely a dang page.*

Dear Janie,
If you're reading this, then Ethan must have found you. He's
a dork but a pretty good brother. I've been writing to you
all year. After a while, I felt like Lucy Snowe watching the
seasons change as she waited for Monsieur Paul. Probably
read enough Bronte by now to have seen this coming. Guess
I should have gotten the hint after the first couple letters.
I wanted to tell you this in person, but I had summer prac-
tice drills. I think about you all the time, even when I don't
want to. Everything changed for me last summer. I thought
maybe it had for you too.
Anyway, no point in saying what I already said, so this
is my last letter. I'm not mad, I know asking you to wait
was asking a lot. God that sounds so sappy. Think I'll quit
embarrassing myself now.
Lydia
P.S. I'm getting my license soon.

Tears give way to a full sob, muffled only by her pillow. Months of checking the mail when her mother brought it in, never once suspecting she was taking Lydia's letters. Catching her breath, Janie pushes the letter away rather than arm her sadness with bootless anger.

Blotting at her eyes, Janie won't give up the ground she's gained. Surrendering this fragile armistice to anger would unleash a beast born of indelible grievance. Corralled beneath the surface since that last day in his office, it sits waiting for her guard to fall so it can creep out into the light. It knows all that she knows, all that she feels. Even the feelings whose existence she denies, it knows them too. Feeding on them, slowly metastasizing.

Helene knocks at the door, easing through on the third knock. Janie kicks the letter under her blanket, hopeful she looks more feverish than tragic.

"Honey, I brought you some iced tea." She pushes the window open. "It's like an oven in here."

Janie rests against the wall, even in the dim glow of the bedside lamp her swollen eyes and blush cheeks push forward.

Lifting her chin to the light, Helene stops. "Oh Janie, you don't look good. I'm getting the thermometer. Don't move!"

Janie presses her face to the open window, breathing in the sweet evening air. Her weepy eyes sting against the light breeze. Taking in as much air as she can, each breath pushes her vexation further down.

"You okay kiddo?" Ray asks quietly from the doorway.

Surprised, Janie rubs away a little soot from resting against the screen. "Fine Daddy."

He sits next to her. "Maybe you should call out tomorrow. You're not lookin' so good."

"Think I overdid it is all. I'll be alright." For a moment it's almost like before. Looking into his eyes, that little twinkle's been snuffed out and they both know it. They play along like nothing has changed. What else is there, what's gone is gone.

Helene returns with the thermometer, squeezing in between them. "Now let's see." She looks at Janie as they wait. Up close, she looks less like she is under the spell of illness and more forlorn. "Hmm, it's normal. Well, your father's going to pray over you anyway." Kissing Janie's head, she leaves.

Ray takes his anointed oil from his shirt pocket and gives her a blessing. Janie's reminded of when she was little and feeling sick, his blessings always made her feel so safe. "Get some rest."

Sleep is sparse, and like many a night she watches the light change through her curtains. If only she hadn't walked across to the market. What good does it do to know? Hurray for another helping of guilt over something she cannot change. Wedging the letter under her mattress, it's a battle for another day.

Chapter Twelve

Autumn arrives quietly in October with the first cool evening of the season. Helene calls upstairs for Janie to close her window or she'll let out all the heat. Lucas is off building a battle robot with Ben for robotics club, and Isabel's celebrating her grandparents' golden anniversary. Even Matty has a friend over. Janie's left to skulk around in her room.

Rubbing away a shiver, she's inspired to dig out her warm clothes. Dragging out storage bins knocks Lydia's letter free. *Don't read it again.* Not that she's forgotten a word, she's just decided to live with it for a while. Paranoia or premonition, she shoves it under her lamp in case her mother comes barging in. Her door swings open.

"Janie bo banie, guess what?" Matty giggles, trying to catch his breath.

Fixing his disheveled hair, "I dunno. What?"

Grinning like a jack o' lantern, he looks toward the door. "It's a secret."

"Yeah?" Janie asks with a raised eyebrow.

Unaware of his volume and convinced their mom has super hearing, he cups his hand to Janie's ear. "Mom's planning your birthday party."

"That's awesome!" Janie gives him a high five.

"I know!" He jumps up and down, giving away his location. Helene calls that it's bedtime. "Don't tell, k?"

"I won't." Hugging him, "I'll walk you to bed."

Helene overhears another Matty birthday debriefing but keeps it to herself, unable to deprive him of the joy of having a secret. Janie knows the jig is up when her mother brings the cake pans down from the upper cabinets. Janie plays along, acting surprised with each Matty update.

Isabel and Lucas surprise Janie before her party. Lucas gets her a Walkman with an FM tuner, so she doesn't have to hover over her radio like a wartime cryptographer. Isabel gives her a case of used Christian rock cassettes. *It's the thought that counts. You like Petra and Stryper. Be excited dang it.*

"Open one!" Isabel urges, nearly doing it for her.

"Okay, okay gosh." Janie rambles on about liking Petra until she opens the case to find a blank cassette with Isabel's handwriting. "Oh."

"Get it?" Isabel looks at her then Lucas when it's clear she doesn't. She holds up the case. "I bought these at the Salvation Army, like a quarter each."

"Cool, why are you telling me this?"

"These are copies of music from Lucas and I." Pointing to the letters on the label, "These are initials of the real band."

Looking closer, Janie reads off the initials. "REM?"

"Well yeah, but that's cause their name is initials." Isabel hands her another tape.

"GS." Janie reads, enthused. "This is fun."

Lucas checks his watch then chimes in. "George Strait. That's from me. We gotta get in there."

Isabel has rarely been prouder. "It'll take your Mom a while to figure it out."

Helene may not know everything about her daughter, but the parts she does know, she knows well. From Yaya's sour cream chocolate cake to pickled vegetables with hummus for nibbles, Helene takes pride in her planning. When Janie catches her father going around with a platter of bite-sized bologna sandwiches, she spies her mother giving her a gotcha smile.

Working through her second slice of cake with no fear of a snarky remark, Janie counts her birthday blessings. As mad as she is at her mother, there's part of her obliged to admit she's in her element. She's found her way back to benevolence, making sure to thank and encourage the ladies from church.

Lucas and Isabel chat by the back door, he's lost in his storytelling. Janie smirks as Isabel glances over, knowing exactly which story he's telling. Come to think of it, they haven't been alone in ages. Janie doesn't mind seeing them together, knowing he doesn't mind eases her conscience. Isabel complements them. She's the graft which Janie hopes might flourish in the wake of the inevitable break.

Coming down from a sugar high, Janie second and triple guesses where to stow her gifts. Really, she's evading the one thing circling her mind all night, the Lydia situation. Wide awake, she settles into bed with her tunes and the letter. To paraphrase the great poet Neil Peart: Whether she chooses to respond or not, it's still a response. *Something like that anyway.*

Summer's long gone, perhaps Janie's silence has already soared across their divide. Surely, Ethan gave his report of their meeting when he got home. Writing to her now, no matter how heartsick, would be too little too late. Flipping the tape, there's a knock at the door.

"Janie, it's Dad." Cracking the door, flaxen light from the hall cascades through her room. "Whatcha' listen' to?"

Confident in the low light, she holds up Isabel's tape. "New Amy Grant, wanna borrow it?"

"Oh no, that's alright." Raising his hand, it's the keys to his car. "Your mom and I talked. Once you get your license, the Grand Prix's yours."

Janie's mind races. *Calm down, there could be a catch.* "Really? Thank you!"

He hangs the keys from her bulletin board. "Why don't you hold on to the spare till then. Love ya kiddo!"

As they always do this time of year, days take flight into weeks only to drag their brakes a couple weeks out from Christmas. Kate's home for the holidays with her boyfriend Greg. Helene remains convinced he's here to ask for Kate's hand in marriage.

Busy with the pageant, Helene insists they go for a welcome dinner. As has become the custom, Lucas and Isabel are uniformly invited. Slighted, Kate fumes over her mother not cooking. By dessert she resumes her mission of creating opportunities for Greg to impress her father. Already adequately impressed with himself, Greg damn near blinds everyone with all the light he shines on his finer points.

On the ride home, Lucas can hold his tongue no longer. "Is no one gonna say anything?"

Isabel and Janie burst into laughter. Lucas's annoyance persists. "Janie, don't know what you're laughing at. I think he's fixin' to be family."

"You think?" Isabel cackles. Puffing out her chest, she forces a deep voice, "Well sir, I have golfed with the dean."

"Have you met my sister?" Janie looks at them both, waiting for the realization to hit. "Yeah, God's match if I ever seen it."

Kate joins Helene's pageant whirlwind. Ray ducks out of lunch with Greg only to get roped into playing hooky for a round of golf on the frigid fairway. Janie's left home tending to a flu stricken Matty, there's no doubt it's serious business when he doesn't resist being sequestered to the couch.

Waiting on Lucas, Janie reads *The Last Battle* in the comfy chair catty corner from Matty's cocoon of blankets, tissues and humidifier. Bored with the litany of holiday cartoons she's watched a hundred times over, she collects her laundry for the sake of having something to do.

Eyeing the spare keys, she wonders if she couldn't just visit Lydia. Envisioning Isabel's tapes playing with the windows down, she might even stop at the market to get those shades since everyone down south wears sunglasses all the time. Fields, familiar faces and pestering pastors fall to the wayside in a cloud of dust. Something takes shape in the rearview. Gaining on her, a highway patrol motorcycle rises from the heat waves coming off the highway. Waiting for backup, he lectures in her mother's voice. *What will people think?* Mercifully, the buzz of the dryer yanks her back to reality.

Intent on finding the letters if they're anywhere to be found, Janie cranes her neck to peek in on the pint-sized invalid. Time check, she has a good hour before Lucas turns up.

Meticulously, she searches the floral fabric covered storage boxes lining the top of her mother's closet. Undoubtedly, her mother will know something is amiss. Janie doesn't care, she'll deny it. The attic is nothing but sealed dusty boxes. Sitting by the hatch, her feet dangle over the hall. *What if she threw them away?* As spiteful as her mother is, her sentiment towards undelivered parcels is unwavering. *But where then? Where else could she stash them?*

Stirring her Nesquik, Janie's eyes wander the kitchen. There, next to the cereal on the fridge, the orphaned mail tin. *Of course!* Rifling through the densely packed box, Janie's careful not to disturb the myriad of post its in various states of adhesion. Each mated to an envelope, each a living document recording her mother's scribbles. Smack dab in the middle is a grouping of letters, they lack the wilted quality of the others that Helene's thumbed through in countless sleuthing sessions. Pulling them free, Janie puts the tin back up on the fridge.

Matty snores his congested way through the morning, Janie fixes his blanket before settling into the comfy chair. Each letter's been opened, her face burns brighter inspecting one after another. Starting at the beginning, the postmark is a week after she sent the book. With trepidation, she inhales the letter. That sweet fragrance she remembers from the playground clings to the paper.

> *Dear Janie,*
> *How did I not know this existed? I asked my older brother Peter about it, and he never read it either. My favorite part was when they went vampire bowling. What was your favorite part? I think I already know, but let's see.*
> *I'm reading Persuasion. There are no vampires or undead but it's still pretty good. You kind of remind me of the main character Anne. You're what she calls "good company." I can send it to you to when I'm done.*
> *How's school? Have you taken photos yet? I'll send you mine, I expect one in return. If I can't talk to you or hug you, at least I can see you.*
> *I have to get ready for volleyball practice so that's all for now. Write soon!*
> *As ever your friend,*
> *Lydia*

The first few are spaced weeks apart until the start of the year when they're less frequent, each shorter than the last. Though it's missing from the envelope, Lydia made good on her photo according to her third letter.

A crack of thunder rattles the windows. *So much for driving out to Wilke's Point, road's going to be nothing but mud.* The rain's coming down in sheets like the last time they saw one another.

With each letter, she's privy to Lydia's life away from here. To her thoughts on what Charley was up to and theories on what happened to Dandridge. To her musings on characters she adores and which she detests in those stuffy old books that she likes so much. Lydia's experiences seem so divergent from her own. There's an effortless cool which might be misconstrued as bragging by a lesser person. Not from her though. Lydia's candor is devoid of conceit or meanness, a casual honesty. While Janie's spent the last year worried they'll strap rocks to her chest and try to float her in a cow pond, Lydia was a member of the homecoming court. She played varsity volleyball, they made it to CIF finals but lost to a prep school from Camarillo. On the other hand, Janie lip-synced her way through many a choir practice at varsity level, so there's that.

Each affectionate phrase levels Janie with the asperity of her mother's betrayal, at deeming herself entitled to thoughts so personal that Janie herself couldn't bear them until their absence moved her to feel their loss. Each sequential letter fosters a homely pairing of yearning and guilt. Lydia declares her feelings unfettered by fear of being rebuffed, yet slowly her words become fraught with the anxiety of unrequited devotion. Janie grows queasy. Reaching further and further, Lydia's last letter signals an inkling of withdrawal or perhaps resignation.

Dear Janie,
I think I've written you at least seven or eight times, but it feels like a hundred every time I don't hear anything back. I'm thinking this might be it for me, probably should have been it a few letters ago.
Anywho, I joined the swim team. Thank god there's only a couple months of school left, the chlorine is wrecking my hair. My little brother Ethan is going to Camp Mariposa this summer, I'm trying to convince my Mom to stay a couple extra days by the lake. Maybe we could meet up at the market and you can tell me all about your year?
Yours sincerely,
Lydia

Lucas brings pizza for lunch. "Sorry, man we got slammed. Gerry sent you some pasta salad."

Kissing his cheek, Janie fetches plates. "Mmm, anchovies. Smells good!"

Lucas sees the sadness in her eyes through her laugh. Scrunching his nose, he shakes his head. "I like Gerry an all, but I don't know how you two eat that garbage."

Janie laughs, making a show of her first bite.

Lucas peeks into the den. "Think he wants some pizza?"

"Nah, let him sleep."

After lunch they squeeze into the comfy chair to watch TV like any other lazy afternoon. Resting against him, Janie withdraws at Lucas' warmth. The very closeness that patched the emptiness now amplifies it. Absentmindedly flipping channels until Matty awakens, he demands she put cartoons back on. Janie convinces him to have a slice of pizza, closing the deal by putting *The Sword and the Stone* on.

Lucas drifts off with his arm resting over her. Massaging his hand, Janie anguishes over dragging him along on this dead end. With the volume low, the staccato of rain lulls her weary mind to sleep.

The light growing low, Janie wakes to the sound of pots sliding over stove grates. Rubbing the sleep from her eyes, she hears her mother speaking to Matty.

Janie nudges Lucas, whispering, "Lucas, wake up."

"What time is it?"

Helene chimes in. "Quarter past five. You joining us for dinner?"

Forcing his eyes open, he tries to focus. "Hi Mrs. Harris. Thanks, but I gotta get home."

Helene calls from the kitchen. "Janie, can you set the table."

Lucas pretends to crash down on Matty, teasing him about being sick and checking out his GI Joe Crimson Guard figure. Janie crams the letters under her sweatshirt, cutting through the hall to stash them in her room. Lucas is getting his coat on when she returns.

Helene looks to the stairs then to Janie. "Honey, the table. Dad and Greg are going to be home anytime now."

Kate sets a fistful of utensils and napkins on the table, giving Janie a passing glare.

Janie scowls in kind. "I know. Let me walk Lucas out."

Helene meets them at the door with Janie's coat. "Put this on. Last thing I need is you both sick."

Chuckling at her mother's hovering, Lucas ambles to his truck. "Wanna go to the movies later?"

Fixed on the letters, Janie entertains the idea long enough to fake a yawn. "Nah, think I'm staying in."

Stalling, he studies her. "Isabel was thinking about going. You sure?"

Relieved, Janie smirks. "Yeah, go on. I'll see you guys tomorrow."

"Be good." He watches her walk up the drive.

Chapter Thirteen

S kin thinned, Janie buries her head in her plate for fear of unleashing barely constrained wrath upon her mother. Suspicious when her second helping goes unnoticed, Janie chalks it up to her mother being busy heaping food onto Greg's plate. Janie and her father grimace at fit as a fiddle Greg pitifully cramming bite after bite in his gob while her sister dishes daggers for spectating.

Offering Greg the only speck of respite he might have for his whole trip, Janie hijacks the conversation. "So Dad, you, me?" Gripping an imaginary wheel, she steers hard into the turn. "Tomorrow?"

Kate groans, no one's paying attention. Taking Greg's fork, she scolds him in a hushed tone, "Just stop."

Ray amusedly nods. "Let's go at nine, beat the crowds."

Holed up with her tunes, Janie reads Lucas' copy of *Sleepwalker*. In a standoff with her notepad, it dares her to do more than ogle it. Hitting the stop button, she leaves her headphones on to dampen the aural bleed from below. Giving up on finding the right words, she longs for any words at all. *Say something, say anything.*

Dear Lydia,
Sorry I took so long to write back. Ethan gave me your letter.
You guys have the same laugh. Ask him about the supply detail,
it's a good story. If you're still reading, good. I swear I didn't
get your other letters. My Mom hid them in her orphan box.
Don't ask, she's weird. Maybe I can tell you about it someday.
There are lots of things I want to tell you someday.
Thinking about seeing you again got me through some tough
times. I think about the swings, and it makes me miss you like
crazy. I got in a lot of trouble for sending the book. Getting
caught again would be more than I can handle right now. I'm
going to tell my friend about us, maybe you can write me at his
address. I'll write more when I can.
I've been practicing driving with my Dad, and I'll have my
license by next summer. We'll see each other again, might take
a little while is all. Wait for me.
Always,
Janie

Janie heads down to breakfast early. Helene sips her coffee, nibbling on a crispy strip of bacon. Eyeing the clock, Janie worries they'll get a late start.

"You're going to stare a hole in that thing. He didn't forget."

Janie scoops scrambled eggs and butters a hot slice of toast. "I know." She grabs a piece of bacon for the walk.

"Janie, can you wait till you sit to eat?" The level of perturbed in her voice suggests she's mad about more than bacon.

In an equally annoyed sigh, Janie draws out, "Sorry."

Bellies full and skies clear, they set out for her driving lesson. Janie feels right at home in the driver's seat. Reaching for the radio dial, she hears a firm, "No" from the passenger seat. *Fair enough, still his car.* Feeling good to go on the interstate, Ray pumps non-existent brakes. Suggesting they master turn signals and full stops first. Janie ignores the erratic tapping of her father's foot.

Janie rubs the scuffed passenger rim. "Sorry about that."

Taking the keys, Ray puts his arm around her. "That's why they call it practice. You did good kiddo."

Not wanting to ask her mom, Janie leverages his pre-golf good mood. "Can you guys drop me in town?"

"Sure." He holds the door. "We're heading out, grab your bag."

Greg hurries to the sink with his plate. Kate insists on taking it, but pauses when she hears Janie and her dad. "Wait, where are you going?"

Janie looks at Helene and her sister wearing the same expression. "Meeting Isabel for some shopping."

Mirrored in manner, they return to their agenda. Like prisoners after every minute of their hour in the yard, Janie, Greg and her father shuffle out the door.

Bundled up, Isabel waits huddled outside Manny's, her already fair skin paler in the cold. Janie takes advantage of the substantial fringe on her parka hood, sneaking up on her.

Hugging Janie, there's an absence of layers. "Aren't you cold? You look cold. Want my scarf?"

Lifting her coat, Janie shakes her head. "It was Hades hot in the car."

"How bout we start at the south end and work back to Luigi's for lunch with Lucas?"

Nodding in firm agreement, Janie sweeps her arm for Isabel to lead the way.

Popping in and out of shops, they find only odds and ends. Much to Janie's pleasure, the hardware store keeps with their seasonal tradition of stocking random stuff that's more gag than gift.

Isabel holds up a pair of Blublockers. "Okay, you should totally get these for Lucas."

Inspecting them thoroughly, Janie hands them back. "Get them. You know he'll wear 'em."

"Nah, it's okay." Isabel retreats, looking for something else to keep the laughs going.

Browsing an aisle over, Janie summons the courage to do what needs to be done. "Hey, Isabel?"

"Yeah?" She rounds the aisle to lessen the feeling of being on opposite ends of a confessional.

Going through the motions of picking stuff up, the tension is a fog rising around them. *Say it.* "Do you like Lucas? I mean like, not just regular like."

"No." Flustered, she drops the chia pet she's admiring. "Sorry, I never know when to shut it."

"Listen, it's okay." Janie retrieves the box, forcing the flattened edge into a cornerish shape.

Worked up, Isabel pleads her case. "Is this cause we went to the movies? I told him."

Janie shakes her head emphatically. "I think we're mostly just good friends anyhow."

Blank, Isabel considers whether Janie's capable of entrapment.

"Me and Lucas are gonna talk about this sooner than later. When we do, he'll need you." Isabel silently dukes it out with guilt laden confusion. To let her continue borders upon cruel, amusing but cruel. Janie puts her arms out for a hug. "God's match my friend, I'm tellin' ya."

Isabel hugs her. "You sure about this?"

"Yes, now grab them glasses." Janie strolls to the checkout with a genuine Thighmaster for Kate, whose thighs are in fact smaller than Janie's. Nevertheless, she's hilariously insecure about them. Two birds, one stone. All before lunch. *Not bad, not bad at all.*

At lunch Isabel's uneasiness is palpable. When two under the table kicks get her nowhere, Janie takes the lead. Plating slices, Janie glances at Isabel, whose eyes are wide with panic. "So, Lucas?"

Weirded out by Isabel's bug eyes, Lucas looks to Janie. "Yes, Janie."

"Did Gerry buy the place from Luigi?"

Cocking his head, he sips his soda. "Nope." Smirking at Isabel battling a tendril of cheese, he settles in for a Janie goose chase. "There is no Luigi."

"So how come it's called Luigi's then?" Janie asks, determined to get to the heart of the matter.

The clock taunts him, Lucas exhales. "Cuz no one wants to buy Italian food from Gerry's." Shaking his head, he looks at Isabel siphoning the bottom of her soda. "You two thinkin' bout buyin' the place?"

Furrowing her brow at such a ridiculous question, she holds up her cup, giving it a rattle. "Refill good sir?"

Grabbing her cup then Isabel's, he climbs out of the booth. "Gladly."

Janie locks eyes with Isabel. "Pull yourself together woman!"

Leaving off their drinks, Lucas adjusts his apron. "I gotta get back."

Janie cranes to get his attention before losing him in the lunch crowd. "Wanna catch a movie tonight?"

"Yeah, sure. Isabel, you in?"

On cue and with a pizza packed cheek, she blurts, "I'm busy."

Mildly disgusted, Lucas laughs. "K." Looking to Janie, "Pick you up at seven?"

Janie gives a thumbs up she immediately regrets. Isabel works on her mountain of a bite and smiles gratefully. "I gotta pee then we should probably get."

Rounding out their shopping at Manny's, they part ways. Isabel's off to meet her mother, maybe carve out a minute or two to freak out over whatever the hell Janie's set in motion. Janie stalks the post office drive-up. Slyly shoving the letter through the slot, it banks off the lip and flutters to the ground. She shoves it through again with more moxie.

Janie helps Matty wrap his gifts before getting ready to go out. Ray and Greg admire the 5 iron Ray gifted him as an early present. Kate mopes in the den, unaccustomed to sharing her father or boyfriend's attention, least of all with each other. Janie coasts under the radar through dinner and out to Lucas waiting at the foot of the drive.

Any reservations about what comes next are alleviated when Isabel's absence is appreciable in Lucas' eyes. He steals a glance while she buckles up. "So, we saw Star Trek last night. I can see it again though if ya want to."

Appreciatively, Janie commits all these lasts to memory. "I was thinkin' maybe we might talk some instead. That okay?"

Lucas doesn't miss a beat. "Yeah, sure."

In an easy silence, they drive out to the bluffs overlooking Sunderland Park. The tension Janie feared inevitable never materializes, an air approximating mutual relief hangs brightly.

Dreaming of understanding, Janie prepares to face another side of Lucas. Ruefully wishing she'd given more thought to what she might say, Janie watches Lucas drag his palms over the seat edge. Guilt having absconded with her wit, when she says it outpaces the particulars of what she'll say. Putting her hand over his to slow the raking, "You okay?"

Gently pulling his hand free, he runs his fingers through his dark cropped hair. "Yeah. So, what'd you want to talk about?"

Get on with it. Go on. "Lucas, I think we need to end this."

Without looking over, he nods. There's a notable lack of surprise or reaction at all for that matter.

"It's just that I gotta figure some stuff out and I don't think I can do that with you." Feeling a lump in her throat, the waterworks are not far behind. "You know you mean the world to me, right?"

Eyes glistening in the umber glow of the radio, he stretches his arms to full tension against the steering wheel. "I know." Reluctantly sniffling, he runs his knuckle under his eye to intercept a defiant tear. "Figured this was coming." Turning to Janie, he hugs her tightly before kissing her cheek. Knowing it will be the last, he commits to his own collection of lasts. "I just want you in my life."

"You're not getting rid of me, not by a long shot." Janie laughs, on the precipice of crying.

"We don't have to tell your folks if it keeps your Mom off your back."

Exposed, Janie shakes her head. "Nah, you've done your time." Sinking further down in her seat, she sighs. "Besides, Isabel's kinda sweet on you."

Embarrassed, he faces forward. "She's not."

Calmly persistent, "She is. You should ask her out."

Resting against the seat, he turns toward her. "You think?" Trying to get a read, he second guesses himself. "No, no. It'd be weird."

"It's really okay." Sensing she's said enough, Janie turns to the window for a burst of frigid air.

"Ok," Lucas replies in a *we've settled this* sort of way.

There in sight of where everything changed one rainy summer evening, they look beyond the playground to the vast valley on this clear wintry night. They listen to the last half of the Christmas rock countdown till their fingers begin to tingle from the cold.

Chapter Fourteen

With Matty on the mend, Helene errs on the side of caution leaving him home one last day. Janie doesn't mind, a lightness abounds. Christmas music fills the house as they finish decorating the tree with candy canes. Matty marvels at his missing tooth measuring the exact width of a mini candy cane. Doing a jangly candy cane dance, Janie worries he may be eating more than he's hanging.

Licking the mayo knife clean, the jovial vibe of the kitchen falls flat as they hear hulk stomping up the back steps. Janie and Matty's bewilderment swiftly resolves upon their mother charging through the door. Her face is flush, her eyes narrow and fixed on Janie. For a fleeting moment, Janie frets someone has died until a familiar flash of controlled ire shows itself. This is not the face of a woman on the precipice of mourning. No ma'am. This is the face of a woman overwrought with indignation, Janie's pretty sure she knows what about too.

Janie watches in speechless dread as her mother pulls the envelope from her purse, palming it down on the table. Reeling herself in, Helene looks to Matty. "Honey, take your lunch to your room." When he opens his mouth to remind her that he isn't allowed to eat in his room, she puts her hand up. "I know, today's an exception. Go!"

Janie sits, staring at the envelope beneath her mother's tense hand. Not daring reach for it, she watches haplessly as Matty heads upstairs, knowing each step puts her closer to being read the riot act. Helene glowers, hurling unspoken accusations with her eyes. A sheepish, "How" escapes Janie's lips before she can stop it.

Trembling with anger, Helene holds her tongue for confirmation of Matty's door closing. "How? I'll tell you how!" Pausing to compose herself, "George Kilroy is the laziest excuse for a mail carrier I have ever seen.

In fact, he's so lazy that I have to clean out the bottom of the mailboxes every morning or else mail gets stuck in the seam. This morning, I found this!" She shakes the letter in front of Janie, who now also thinks George Kilroy is the laziest excuse for a mail carrier there ever was.

Sunken in her chair, Janie's fixed on the opened envelope.

"Well?" Helene demands.

"Well, what?" Janie replies dejectedly.

"And what of poor Lucas?" Helene bemoans.

Janie stares at her feet, betraying not a glimmer of guilt or shame.

Throwing her hands up, an epiphany touches down. "Of course! That little Godless liar!" Snatching the envelope, she puts the kettle on. "You've both been making fools of us all." In between the clanging of teacups and rummaging through the cabinet, her voice softens to a listless tone of resignation. "I don't know who you are anymore Janie." Mashing a tea bag into her cup, she ties off the string to the handle. "I know you're a liar... I know that much."

Coming over to plead her case, Janie leans on the counter. "I've done nothing wrong."

Refusing to look at her, Helene coldly replies "Go to your room."

Lunch untouched, no sense in wasting a perfectly good sandwich. Head hanging, Janie takes her plate and cream soda with her. Third step from the top, *the letters*, she sprints to her room. Haphazardly shoving the clutter on her desk aside, she drops to her knees and throws her bedspread out of the way to reach the letters. "Shit! Shit! Shit!" Tearing them up as fast as she can, she crams the pieces into the wastebasket. *Thump. Thump. Thump.* She can hear her mother's march up the stairs. After one last swig, she dumps what's left in the bin and frantically mashes the shreds through the fizzy syrup until the ink is sufficiently smeared.

Barging in, Helene catches Janie wiping stray shards from her fingers. "Give me the letters!"

Standing, Janie defiantly shakes her head, still trying to roll the small clumps of paper free.

Helene's eyes well with rage. Putting her hand out, she never breaks eye contact. "I said give them to me."

Through spit and tears, Janie lifts the wastebasket. "You want them?" She empties the basket onto the floor, leaving a small pool of caramel liquid and clumps of pulpy paper. "Take em'."

Helene looks at the mess in disbelief.

Fault lines trip one after another, a year and a half of pent up frustration is a heartbeat from the surface. Willful and through clenched teeth, Janie forges on. "I'd rather destroy them than have you lock them away in some old box."

Stunned, Helene regards Janie before turning on her heels and pulling the door closed behind her.

Collapsing on her bed, Janie steadies herself on her elbows. Waiting for her pounding chest to settle back into a soft thump. *What have I done? Shit!* The house is unnervingly quiet, not a peep from Matty's room either. Sitting up, elbows perched on her knees, she runs her hands through her hair. Surveying the scene, her eyes hang on the mess. As quietly as she can, she scoops it back into the bin. Grabbing a shirt from the hamper, she soaks up the puddle. Damage done, she grips the bundled fabric in her fist before chucking it in defeat.

Not wanting to feel anything at all, Janie crawls into bed. Pulling the covers overhead, she loses herself in her music. A small voice draws her back to this time and place.

"Janie? Can I come in?" Matty whispers loudly through the gap in the door, struggling to keep her dinner plate level when she opens it.

"You brought me dinner?" With all the enthusiasm she can muster.

"Mmhm."

Searching for an open surface, she sets the plate on her bed. "Thanks!"

Looking at his soulful brown eyes, she worries she's lent him some of her sadness. Matty gives her the tightest bear hug he's got. Wrapping her arms around him, she holds on till her mother's voice beckons. Fussing up his already unruly mop, Janie walks him to the door. "Go on, I'm fine."

Stomach in knots, her saliva recedes thinking of eating a meal her mother prepared. The fragrance of vanilla carpet nauseatingly mingles with the pepper gravy. Retreating to her blanket, she turns up the volume to drown out the dinner chatter below. With the performance her mother's putting on for Kate and Greg, she should be starring in the pageant instead of emceeing it. Drifting off, fading batteries drag the fantastic highs of "Valley of Lost Souls" to a low creepy crawl.

Watching the clouds roll in one thunderhead at a time, the moon is little more than a suggestion against the midnight sky. Janie doesn't notice the house easing into quiet. Hearing the door handle turn, she goes limp on her pillow.

"Janie?" Ray enquires plainly. "You awake?"

Knowing her father as she does, the rough translation is *listen up*. Leaning on her sleepy voice in a midnight call for leniency, "Yeah."

The thin metal ping of the keys against the hook tells her everything she needs to know. "You're going back to counseling tomorrow."

Alone in the dark of her room, Janie Harris comes quietly undone. A dull ache fills her chest, pushing the air out of her lungs as she wearily weeps for what has been lost and even more for what's to come.

Morning brings a return to the new normal, extinguishing any hope of returning to before. Standing by her bedroom door, Janie times her exit to avoid crossing paths with anyone. In one fell swoop, she steps out into the hall cutting Kate off at the pass and forcing her into the bathroom to avoid a collision.

Wearing her mother's bathrobe and demi-snarl, she huffs, "Watch it!"

"Sorry. Not like I did it on purpose." Seeing her sister wearing her mother's robe is too much for the hour. "Hey, why are you wearing Mom's stuff?"

In the most duh voice possible, "Laundry."

Smirking, Janie takes her laughs where she can before the hits start rolling.

Kate hurries after, checking the stairs to ensure no one is coming. "You should know, Mom's making Greg postpone his proposal until you finish treatment."

Cocking her head, Janie asks, "Wait, so you know he's gonna propose?"

Irritated, Kate shushes her. "Shut up!" Grabbing a towel from the linen closet, she pauses. "You're ruining my life. You know that don't you?"

Head hanging, Janie takes to the stairs. "I know, mine too."

Helene stays home to "Reclaim the order" of her house. Declaring it loud enough for Mrs. Parlow next door to hear, even with a shoddy hearing aid crammed in her ear. Janie picks at breakfast and retreats to her room, only to hear, "Leave the door open" when she reaches the top step. *Bet Mrs. Parlow heard that too.* Vanilla carpet, a dead cassette player and an inedible feast, she's unable to venture to the kitchen till the coast is clear. *Great.*

Helene converts the kitchen into a nerve center for the pageant, fielding phone calls and furiously taking notes. Actually, mostly making phone calls and sharing her notes. During a particularly critical exchange over whether the Christmas angel would really wear tulle, Janie sneaks down to clear the plates. Gagging silently, she puts her hand through last night's dinner and shoves it to the bottom of the trash. The pungent aroma of mayo melding with soggy chicken fried breading hangs heavily in the kitchen. Helene sniffs the air while nodding along as the beleaguered seam-stress pleads her case on the other end of the line.

Acclimated to the stench, Janie washes up oblivious to the olfactory assault she's unleashed upon her mother. Hearing the receiver settle onto the cradle, Janie closes her eyes and waits.

"You know, your father works hard to put that food you threw away on the table." Not waiting for a reply, she consults her notes for the next number to call. The phone rings as she reaches for the receiver, she grabs it on the first ring with an abrupt "Hello."

Janie doesn't turnaround, she doesn't need to. She can feel her watching. Lucas was to call this morning. Her feet drag with each leaden step, not wanting to go up and definitely not wanting to stay down.

"No, you may not." Helene lets him speak, not that anything he says will change her mind. "Lucas, you are not welcome in our home, and YOU are never to speak to our daughter again. Never!" She takes a moment to center herself. More importantly, it's time for him to hang up because God be with him if he's still on the line when she picks up. Deep breath, stay on task Helene. You're integral to the pageant. Don't let them down. They need you. "Helen? Hi, it's Helene Harris.... Great! You free to discuss the color for those songbooks?"

Strained silence sucks the air out of the car. The last light before they ascend the hill to the church stays red forever. Unaccustomed to being ignored, Helene grips the steering wheel. "Do you realize Pastor Mike is missing choir practice only days before the pageant for this?"

Fuming, Janie yearns for indifference to carry her through. "So."

"You are the maker of your own suffering Janie. You do realize that, right?" Helene implores her, "If you opened yourself to the Lord, you could be absolved of this vile attachment."

Mumbling unintelligibly, Janie angrily pushes away obstinate tears.

Straining to hear, Helene asks, "What?"

Wiping her nose, Janie puts her legs up and rests against her knees. "Nothing."

"Did you bring your choir gown?"

"Yes."

"Pastor Mike found a replacement. Let's hope it fits her." Helene frets, pulling into the first open spot.

"Yeah, you said that already." Janie lets the car door swing closed at gravity's will. Grabbing the garment bag, she keeps two steps ahead. Helene gains on her at the entrance, cutting Janie off when she stops to hold the door for an old fella.

Nearing the stage, Helene points to the pews. "Go sit down."

Trying not to think of what awaits her or what to do when the waiting is done, the long buried voice is on the verge of shrieking. *Run, Run now, Run fast.* Isabel sits down, and leans against her shoulder.

Janie looks to confirm her mother's watching. She is. *So effing what.* "You might catch my disease. Careful."

Looking at her feet, Isabel wrings her hands. "I don't care. They can kick me off choir if they don't like it."

Not terribly surprised but profoundly appreciative, Janie's expression hints at a smile. "Thank you."

"Me and Lucas'll be around." Isabel slinks away to avoid Mrs. Harris.

"You'll have nothing to do with her," Helene quietly commands. She leans closer. "Do you hear me?"

Janie shifts her weight to reset the distance, denying her mother any form of recognition. Pastor Mike's approach puts a lid on Helene's percolating.

Giving Helene a nod dripping with sympathy, he extends his arm. "After you." Planting his hand firmly on Janie's shoulder like old times, he stops just short of the hall. Making eye contact with Emily, he signals he has something to say. "Man you guys sound good! Praise be, this is going to be awesome!" Holding back, as he's always wont to do. "Isabel, you're lagging. Let's try to keep that focus hmm?" Flashing a big bogus grin, he gives the go ahead.

Once concealed by the hallway, he walks ahead into the office. Curtly dragging a chair out for her, he clears his throat and takes a seat at his desk. He pushes her letter across. "You can keep that."

Janie takes him at his word, shoving it in her pocket. Folding her hands, she rests them on his desk.

"I almost didn't agree to see you. Did you know that?" He lowers his gaze to meet hers.

Quietly, Janie replies, "No."

"Look at me." His eyes cold as deep water on a winter's night, his nostrils flare with disgust. "I've taken pity on your parents being saddled with your burden. They deserve better."

Looking to her feet, she presses her hands into her lap.

"You're a deviant. Probably too far gone if your letter's any indication." Sighing. "Look. At. Me."

Janie meets his gaze, matching his emptiness.

"That letter's proof of your sickness." Reaching across, he pushes the collar of her coat aside. "Figures. You've even made a mockery of my gift." He plants his hands on the desk. Settling back into his seat, its bones creak under his weight. A filament of temper burns in his eyes.

Unsettled and a little afraid, Janie's posture stiffens. "No, it snagged on my sweater is all. My Mom's having it mended."

Unmoved, he looks down at his hands still pressing against the desk. Breathing deeply, he exhales with a ham-handed drum roll. "Okay."

Janie watches apprehensively as he comes around to her side. Leaning against the desk, he towers above her. Just like that, an ominous sparkle returns. His gaze softens. Leaning to her, a condescending smile crests his eager face.

"Only way we're gonna pull this off is if you start taking this seriously." He traces his index finger along her crown. "Don't you want to be free of this?"

Janie pushes back from the desk with nowhere to go, he grips the armrest. Leaning so close she can feel the stray hairs of his dark manicured beard, he whispers in her ear. "You might be able to coerce some dumb boy into concealing your perversion, you're not fooling me though." Pulling back, he stares into her eyes. "I see the devil right through you."

The choir launches into a full run through down the hall. Surveying the distance to the door, her mind races to wager the odds of making it before he overtakes her.

Her body tenses to bolt. Slowly, he shakes his head. Consolingly brushing her hair behind her ear, he speaks softly. "I can restore you."

Fuck the odds. Janie pushes off only to have him grip her shoulders, driving her back into the chair. He looks through her, drifting in and out of his lecture. Subduing her physically when words fail, Janie slaps at his hands wrapping around her like deformed branches.

Knowing if he drags her off the chair, she's done for. Janie screams from the depths of her belly, a sound she's never heard before. Nothing. They cannot hear her. Only he hears her.

Eyes wide, he seethes fastening his hand over her mouth. Breathlessly, snarling, "Quiet!"

Realizing he's not getting her out of the chair, he jostles her down across the seat. No longer looking her in the eye, he mutters, "Stop fighting." His forearm pressed into her chest, she could swear the pressure's the only thing keeping her heart contained, Janie's throat burns from the slew of shallow breaths shearing across it.

Feeling her resistance wilt, he senses surrender. Feeling the tension of her belt buckle release sends Janie's mind into a schism, the visceral voice earlier beseeching her to run seizes the reins with all the fight she has left. Her heart stomps a beat so doggedly, it cracks like lightning in her ears. Biting down as hard as she can, Janie feels the flesh of his palm yield to her teeth. Screeching a shrill alto cry, he yanks his hand. Jaw clenched, Janie feels the wound tear as he heaves her off the seat in his panic. A sharp pain boomerangs around her jaw and she wonders if a tooth didn't go with him.

He stands frozen, clutching his mutilated mitt. His eyes bathed in pain and fear, he presses his shirt cuff into his palm. Taking to her feet, Janie locks her wild eyes with his. Spitting his own blood at him, it spatters the side of his face and collar. Wiping her mouth with the back of her hand, she drags it across his sweater. His midnight cable knit sucks it up lickety-split, leaving no tale of what it's seen.

Squaring off, they hold steady in a breathless standoff. Neither sure of what the other will do, Janie's muscles are electric with adrenaline. Pastor Mike relents, stepping aside. Fingers trembling, Janie grapples with her belt.

Taking a handkerchief from his pocket, he dabs at the spittle on his face. "They're sending you to bootcamp." Forcing a prideful laugh, "They're gonna sweat the disease right out of you."

Silently watching his every move, Janie grabs her things.

Applying pressure, he heaves with loathing. "You little impenitent bitch! You could've had it so easy." Turning away, he whimpers when his cufflink catches his lame hand. "Lucky's what you are, lucky I don't press charges. You rabid..."

The sight of Janie's blood-tinged smile renders him silent. Straightening the collar of her coat, she gives the hem one last tug to set it right. "Do it. Cuz the minute I hand over my clothes, we'll see who the sicko is. You pathetic prick."

Scoffing, he pulls one end of the knotted handkerchief tight with his teeth. "Watch your filthy mouth! What, are they gonna dust em' for prints? Nothing happened except an unprovoked attack by a troubled girl, that's what I'll tell them."

Impassively, Janie bares an unflinching glare. "We leave all kinds of stuff when we touch things. Ya know, skin cells, stuff like that. What do you think they'll find when they look at the scratches you left trying to drag me off that chair? With all that TV, think you woulda seen *Unsolved Mysteries* once or twice."

Hands shaking, he rummages through his desk drawers. Wrapping his hand in packaging tape, he tears the strip free with his teeth. "You think they'll take your word over mine?"

He's probably right. Don't you know by now, you're the weirdo and he's the saver of souls? C'mon Janie, get before he gets brave again. Nerves frayed, she struggles to unlock the door. Reaching over her, he flips a small flat latch beneath the knob. Janie hurls the door open, but he stops it before she can squeeze through.

"It's a done deal. They're coming on Saturday, better get packing."

Wrenching the door free, Janie pushes her way through. "You're lying."

"Am I?" Stopping her in the hall, he leans on the wall blocking her path. "After I leave you off with your cloying mother, I'll be writing your assessment. Think about that."

Janie knows better than to think he's bluffing. A spot of red peeks through the tape and cloth, a thin line trails down his pinky. Following the trajectory, a blood stain takes form on his spendy taupe oxfords. Staring down, she grimly reports, "Missed a spot" and sets off down the hall.

Skip jogging every few steps fails to close the distance, Janie's already within feet of her mother when he clears the hall. Feeling another drip give way, a droplet soaks into the carpet. Cupping his hand, Pastor Mike turns back to his office.

Helene is listening to the choir and reading a book of psalms curated by the pastors when Janie blows by. "Janie?"

Without breaking stride, she replies, "Going to the bathroom, don't feel well."

Surging through the bathroom door, she charges an empty stall not a moment too soon. Retching until her insides ache as much as her mind, she kneels at the commode with her arms draped across to cradle her head. Hearing the creak of the door, she leaps to her feet. Clenching her fists to the point of digging her nails into her palms, she holds idle. After an eternity, the lock engages next stall over. Rinsing her mouth while aggressively finger-brushing her teeth, she accidentally gags. The stall behind her goes silent mid-stream. Janie clears her throat, splashing some water on her face.

Helene's packing when Janie returns. "There she is."

Scanning the choir for Isabel, she's already gone. A feeling of being watched persists, she sees Emily gazing across in solemn commiseration. Turning away, Janie grabs her mother's bags. "This everything?"

Unprepared for her daughter's brashness, Helene senses something is off. "Now hold on a minute. Why are you out early? Aren't you going to wait for Pastor Mike?"

Grabbing a third bag and wedging it under her arm, Janie turns to leave. "He had to take a call."

Putting the car in gear, Helene sits trying to read Janie's inscrutable face. Lips tight and thin, jaw tense and eyes fixed on the distance. It dawns on her what it reminds her of, a cornered animal poised to take your face off with one errant move.

Janie whips her head around to face her mother. "What?"

Ordinarily, raising her mother's hackles would lead to a tongue lashing. However, the last few minutes have been anything but ordinary. Helene lets it go, backing out and keeping her eyes to her own business.

Counting off in her head, she's almost there, Janie beelines for the stairs. *Just keep going.* Matty ditches Kate and Greg to tag along.

"Janie bo banie, wait up," he singsongs along behind her.

Clutching the banister, she tells herself just a little longer. "Hi mister! I gotta do some stuff, but I'll be down in a few minutes. K?"

Pausing, he gives her the same sad smile from last night. "Hurry up, k? Greg and Kate are boring."

Smiling, Janie shakes on it. Little thuds of him hopping down the stairs echo her steps up.

A hot shower does little to wash away the vulgar feeling emanating from every pore. Going through the motions of Rock'em Sock'em Robots with Matty, she labors to measure her equilibrium and adjust accordingly.

Lying in bed, she waits for the tears to flow. They are conspicuously absent. Unbridled from the desire to earn a place in the life she knows, Janie decides not to. She sees only two options, an indeterminate commission to some hellhole with her parents' blessing or she can leave. As her father says when he grows weary of debate, *like it or lump it kiddo*. So it is then, she'll lump it right the frick out of town.

Counting what's left of last summer's earnings, the sum of her worth is four hundred and fifty-seven dollars. *Good seed money.* Since it's Thursday, no more laundry before the weekend. Sneakily, Janie lays out the essentials on her bed. Turning her backpack over her bottom drawer, she shakes the fall semester loose.

Trying the zipper, she must reconsider her definition of essentials. Cramming only as much as she would take for a weekend at the lake, the rest is stuffed into the bulging bottom drawer. Dropping the stocked pack into the hamper, she crumples up some jeans and tees to toss on top.

Chapter Fifteen

B one tired, heavy eyes ebb open with the first traces of dawn. Soft yellow bands cross her comforter, inching up the wall with the ascending sun. Janie surveys her room from the warmth of her bed. Blankets snug under her chin, she stretches to open the blinds. Taking it all in, there will never be another sunrise like this one. Sure, the sun will come up ad infinitum, but not from this perspective, in this bed, in this place, her home. *Their home.*

The only upside to unfathomable loss is there's no way to prepare. She lets herself drift in this life a little longer, rising when she hears the house begin to stir.

Her door ajar to monitor hall traffic, Janie takes her time getting ready. Steak frying on the griddle wafts through the house. Huddled around the dining table, pageant chatter dominates the conversation.

Helene stops speaking when Janie enters the room, considering her expression carefully. "Kate's making breakfast today."

Kate's eyes dart to Janie, who only nods.

"So anyway." Helene puts her hand to her temple. "What was I saying?"

Having commandeered Janie's seat, Greg hops up to make room.

Catching her mother up, Kate takes the last steak off the griddle. "You were sayin' the sound guy."

Eggs and toast already on the table, the steaks complete the trinity.

"Right. I asked him if he had ever done the sound in a church before. I mean honestly."

Ray on one side and Greg on the other, Janie feels her stomach sink at the sight of what would normally inspire salivatory splendor. Ray reaches across to serve his future son-in-law. Lifting a piece, he motions towards her. "Janie?"

Dilute blood gathers on the plate, drippings from the speared meat add to the shallow pool. A sickly pallor comes over Janie as the iron aroma invades her space. Shoving herself back from the table, her chair skips along the linoleum as she flees to the bathroom.

Kate and Helene share a concerned glance. Kate takes over while Helene excuses herself. Peeking, Helene doesn't wait for an invitation when she sees Janie over the commode. "Honey."

Raspy and embarrassed, Janie dismisses her. "I'm fine, I'm fine."

Kneeling, Helene rubs her back. "I know, just get it all out. You're okay."

Janie detests her mother, and even more so herself for hoping Helene doesn't leave her to relive it alone. Instinct trumps animus. Turning to hug her mother, she holds onto her like a child.

Not remembering the last time her daughter hugged her so tightly, Helene pats her back. "You're alright. Something mustn't have agreed with you." Gingerly prying herself free, she grabs a hand towel hanging within reach. She blots at Janie's face, then thinks better of it, helplessly handing her the towel. "Why don't you take a minute to get yourself together. I'll make you some oatmeal."

Alone in the bathroom, Janie sits crumpled, her back against the tub. A few minutes pass, maybe more, her feet tingle under her weight as she pushes herself up. Palms flat, she locks eyes with the vanity. Staring back, a child pleadingly waits for someone to tell her what to do. She's come to loathe this kid always hanging on the whim of others, always waiting for permission to breathe. "What are you waiting for? What? Coward!"

Leaning into the basin, the cool water tempers the heat radiating like waves off hot blacktop. Refusing to give the feeble child an audience, she remains hunched brushing her teeth. Patting her face dry, she's done all she can to abrade the acrid residue of what she can only guess was bile.

Janie slips into her seat, a bowl of oats awaits. Not hungry, she lifts her spoon to make an effort.

A cheery little voice breaks the silence. "Janie...Janie! I'm having oatmeal too. See?" He lifts his half-eaten bowl of oats and berries to show her.

Mustering a bit of cheer, Janie gives an impressed eyebrow raise. "What? Matty passed up steak?"

Chewing away on a bite of pilfered steak, he stabs at his father's plate for another. "Yeah, I wanted oats like you."

Gradually, everyone excuses themselves. Janie finishes her breakfast serenaded by the clinks and clanks of her mother doing the dishes.

Giving her room a once over, she sees nothing she cannot live without. Tying her shoes, the sound of car doors urges her to pick up the pace. Craning to see from her window, Kate and Greg are leaving. Hurrying downstairs, her folks and Matty are getting their coats on. "You guys leaving?"

Helene halts wrist deep in her sleeve. "We're going to help out." Looking to Ray, she shakes her head. "Honestly, we're so behind."

Ray nods like he's heard it all before because he has.

Hoping to track down Isabel, Janie grabs her coat. "I'll come to help with Matty."

Helene and Ray exchange a nervous glance, each challenging the other to respond.

"What?" Janie questions.

Helene bites when Ray's eyes find their way to his feet. "After this morning, well, I thought you might like to stay home and rest." Gears turning, Helene's suspicion is piqued. "Ray, why don't you stay back in case Janie needs something."

Ray sighs and starts taking his coat off.

Adamant, Janie persists. "I'm fine. I mean, unless you don't want me to come."

Not willing to die on this hill, Helene hurriedly buttons Matty's coat. "Don't be ridiculous. Okay, let's go! Kate's probably wondering where we are."

Minus the go team chant, the Harris clan disperses from their huddle at the back of the church. Greg and Ray help reinforce the sets. The sweet baby Jesus nearly suffered a concussion during last night's dress rehearsal when a failed split brace sent the star of Bethlehem swinging.

Helene corners the director to share suggestions for her lines at intermission. Kate's dispatched as her eyes and ears in wardrobe.

Trailing behind, Matty's Raphael action figure manages amazing feats of acrobatics. Janie surveys the gaggle of choir robes congregating near the stage for any sign of Isabel, steadily avoiding Emily's gaze.

"Looking for me?" Isabel asks, scanning the room with Janie.

"As a matter of fact." Motioning to the choir, Janie asks, "Where's your robe?"

Shrugging, Isabel watches them take their places on stage. "Got here this morning, found out I was cut."

"Why?" Janie laments.

"Said I was too distracted. Whatever. My church is going out on our own next month anyway." Smiling down at Matty, she looks back at Janie's miffed mug. "I'm alright. Let's raid the snack table."

Raising Raphael to the heavens, Matty leads the way. "Yesss!"

Janie lets him skip ahead. "You wanna see a movie tonight?"

Skeptical, Isabel smirks. "Your folks are gonna let you miss the pageant for a movie?"

Shrugging, "Dunno, but it's lookin' good. I'll ask my Mom."

Scattering a few nibbles on her plate, Janie grazes. Her mother, waving from the foot of the stage, calls as they approach. Hoping to capitalize on her being busy, there's nothing quite like a go away I'm busy okay fine kind of yes. "Hey mom!"

"Hold on a sec Janie." Putting her arm out for them, Helene speaks to a guy Janie's never seen before. "Neil, these are two of my kids, Janie and Matty. I think you met Kate earlier?"

"I did." He shakes each of their hands, taking an interest in Matty. "Is that a Ninja Turtle?"

"Yeah." Matty grins at Neil's good guess. "His name's Raphael."

Kneeling to eye level, an agreeable smile emerges. "Say Matty, I know he seems pretty cool, but our church teaches that magic's pretty bad stuff, ya know?"

Excited at someone taking an interest, Matty leaps at the chance to explain. "No, see they were just regular turtles then one day..."

Helene grabs Raphael, shoving him in her bag in one fluid movement as Janie pulls Matty into her bosom for a sisterly hug. Janie laughs, shaking her head at her silly brother. "He borrowed it from a friend at school."

Neil smiles along, silently judging them until Helene launches the first of a barrage of get to know you questions.

Janie observes Isabel watching Neil but cannot get a read on why. When trying to discreetly shush Matty fails, she guides him to Isabel who has already begun searching her bag for something to show him. Walking back, Pastor Mike joins them with a freshly bandaged hand.

Like a game of double dutch, Pastor Mike waits for his moment to jump in when Helene takes a breath. Switching at the last moment, he clumsily extends his left hand. "Well, hey Neil! Welcome!"

"Thank you! What happened to your hand?"

Helene echoes the concern. "Yes, that looks awful."

Actively avoiding Janie, Pastor Mike maneuvers to maintain the veneer. "Looks worse than it is, really."

The busy body in Helene must know. "But what happened? Were you bitten?"

Like someone pulled the plug, the blood drains from his face. Pastor Mike stammers, "Scuse me?"

Bewildered, Helene speaks a little slower. "Don't you volunteer out at the county shelter? Thought maybe a stray gotcha."

With an upwelling of relief, he nods. "Right, right! I'm all over the place this season." Discerning their desire for an explanation, he shifts into preacher mode. "Not much to tell. Basement window jammed in the cold." Still acting as though she isn't there, he raises his hand for inspection. "Leaned on it too hard and put my hand right through it."

Satiated, his audience grimaces with sympathy. Helene turns to Neil, "Isn't that just awful?" He nods. Then back to Pastor Mike. "I'll pray for a quick mend Pastor."

"Thanks Helene. God bless." Placing his hand in his pocket, he winces at bending his fingers in haste. "Neil, shall we?"

Any reason to dip out of twenty questions, Neil eagerly agrees. "Yes! Nice meeting you all!"

Helene turns to Janie and Isabel, cooing with sympathy. "Poor guy!"

Janie's nostrils flair, she fights an urge to hiss at her mother. Not that she's ever hissed before, but it feels right. Instead, she changes the subject. "Can I go to the movies tonight with Isabel?"

Huffing, Helene looks back and forth between them. "No. Why would you even ask me that? The pageant is tonight. Didn't I tell you that this," she points to Isabel and back at Janie, "Is not okay?"

"I'm not going to the pageant." Janie protests.

"Then you'll stay home. Alone." She hands off Raphael. "Get rid of this. I can't believe you let me buy him that. I have to get back to work."

Janie stuffs the toy in her bag, winking at Matty when her mother looks away.

Isabel steps aside to let Helene pass. Biding her time, she takes a deep breath until her cheeks can expand no further, forcing an exhale. "Wonder what he's doin' here?"

"Who? Neil?" Janie asks curiously.

Isabel replies confounded. "Yeah, he's part of Camp Jeremiah."

Eyes darting, Janie's pulse quickens. "What's that?"

"It's like a rehab or somethin', you pretty much get sent there to get straightened out." Isabel senses her change in demeanor. "My cousin was sent there when I was in 7th grade. That guy Neil came to his house for dinner, next day he was gone."

Janie presses for details. "Gone? Like never to be seen again, gone?"

A smile forms then dissipates when Isabel notes her friend is dead serious. "No, he got sober and was home after three months."

"Does he seem the same?"

"Kinda. It was weird how everyone was so nice, think it was too much for him." Isabel watches Janie hang on every word. "Anyway, he ended up getting his girlfriend pregnant and his whole family got the backslider treatment after that."

"Then what happened?" Janie asks.

"Eh, we moved for my Dad's job, and their parents signed off on a shotgun wedding. He moved up somewhere near El Dorado. My Dad called in a favor with a shipping company up there."

"That was nice of your Dad." Janie hopes tonight won't turn into some horrible guess who's coming to dinner, oh surprise, it's Neil from bible bootcamp thing.

"I'm gonna have my Mom come get me. I think your Mom's pissed at me."

"No, it's me. You still wanna go to the movies tonight? Think your Mom will let you borrow the car?"

Wide eyed, Isabel does a double take. "She'll murder you!"

Checking that Matty's busy playing, Janie counters, "Not if I get back before they do."

A little thrown by the sudden gust of gumption, Isabel cannot turn her down. "Well okay, meet me out front at 7."

Janie and Kate converge at the pews. "Mom wants me to take you guys home."

Helene sends Ray to pick up pizza, reminding him to get paper plates and utensils, a sure sign there will be no dinner guests. Janie can only assume it will go down tomorrow night once the frenzy of the pageant is put to rest. She watches the door throughout dinner just the same. Only when Matty excitedly counts the days till Santa, does the reality of what comes next set in.

In the fray of getting ready, Janie steals a moment alone with Matty under the guise of helping him find his crayons. Taking in every little Mattyism, she watches him scrounge under his bed, rising victorious having fished out his coveted worn to a nub cerulean.

"Gottem'"

Packing his coloring book, she zips his backpack. "Ready?"

Slinging the pack over his shoulder like a big kid, he looks up. "Why can't you come? It's boring when you're not there."

"I gotta sit this one out. You'll have fun, you'll see." Fussing his hair, she hesitates and gives him a big hug. "I love you Matty bo batty."

An air of worry settles over him. "Are you sad?"

Pulling away, she sniffles. "No, I'm just a little stuffy. We better get downstairs. C'mon slowpoke, shake a leg."

From the kitchen window, Janie watches them drive off. The house is dark, save for the kitchen where she waits at the dining table. Already starting to feel like a stranger, Isabel's right on time.

Janie hurries down the driveway, motioning for her to put the window down. "Just a sec."

Isabel looks on mystified as Janie tears open a trash bag in the bin, removing her backpack. She's in for a night, no doubt. Janie hops in, her pack too full to stuff down by her feet.

"What in the world?"

Tossing her bag into the backseat elicits a thud and a yelp. Crunched on the floor between the seats, Lucas swats the bag off him. Pleasantly surprised and curious how he managed to fold himself behind the seat, Janie asks, "What are you doing here?"

Scuffling with the seat as he extricates himself, "I wanted to see you. Gah, what's in there?"

"Janie, what's going on?" Isabel demands.

"Shit. Well, okay here goes." She watches Isabel's eyes flick to the rearview. "I'm pretty sure that Neil guy's here for me."

"Why would he be here for you?" Isabel asks.

Lucas rests his arms across the tops of the front seats, not wanting to miss anything.

"Remember the kid from the market?"

· "The s'mores kid?"

"Well, his sister and I got on pretty well the summer before. Lucas bailed me out on Labor Day, but I got in big trouble for a letter I wrote her." Glancing, all that's left is the truth. "So, I got sent to counseling with Pastor Mike. Turns out he's a big frickin' creep."

"I knew it!" Lucas interjects.

Isabel pulls over. "What happened?"

Wishing she'd keep driving, Janie lets it go since they're already close to town. "Last year he started getting handsy, but our sessions ended before much happened. Well, I got sent back this week for tryna' send another letter."

Lucas leans between the seats as far as his frame will allow. "How?"

Rolling her eyes, a defeated sigh escapes. "My Mom works for the post office, what can I say?"

"I knew something was up at practice. What'd he do?" Isabel nudges Lucas backward so she can lean closer.

"He went for it. I bit the crap out of his hand before he got anywhere." Emotionless in her retelling, Janie fixes on the distance beyond the windshield. "Said he was going to recommend me for some therapy camp. I'm guessin' that's where Neil comes in."

Isabel sits looking at her, mouth agape. "I dunno Janie, my cousin never said anything about that kind of stuff there."

"Isabel, I saw him go into Pastor Mike's office. I'm not waiting around to find out."

Lucas fumes, pounding the seat. "We gotta go to the cops. My Mom will go with us, I told her about that weirdo after the Easter thing."

Turning to the backseat, Janie's emphatic. "No way. They're not gonna believe me over him."

"Why wouldn't they believe you?" Lucas pleads, "Janie it's not right."

"And if you're wrong?" Janie argues. "I'll have to live with that, not you. I just need a ride to the bus station is all. I don't want to drag you guys into this anymore than I have. You're all I have."

"Where'll you go? Think Janie." Lucas tries to make her see.

"Dunno. I've got almost five hundred to hold me over. Whichever bus gets me the farthest I guess."

Lucas sinks into the backseat.

"We can do that," Isabel replies. Despite Lucas' dissent, they're interstate bound.

Janie turns the radio up to kill the quiet. Resting her head, she lets her body ebb with the rough road.

Twisting the steering wheel cover, Isabel amasses courage and draws a deep breath. "Hey Janie?"

Eyes closed, listening to the radio and the road, "Yeah?"

"For real, only answer if you want." Her eyes meet Lucas' in the rearview. "So, you're gay then?"

"Guess so." Unable to bear the thought of them looking at her like some wretched thing, maybe this was a mistake. "It might be better if you just drop me at the gas station. I can make my way from there."

Dismayed, Isabel turns the radio off. "What? No! Doesn't change anything. You're our friend. Right Lucas?"

Janie looks on, sick with guilt Lucas found out this way.

Lucas pipes up from the back. "Turn here, don't get on the freeway. We gotta go back."

Frazzled, Janie grabs her bag. "I can't do that. Isabel just drop me off."

Patting her forearm, Lucas leans over. "Relax. Just have to get somethin' from my house. It'll be quick."

Not entirely convinced, Janie studies him. "What're you getting?"

"I'm not turnin' you in DB. I got you something for Christmas." He settles into his seat.

More curious than a cat, Isabel can't help passing the time waiting on Lucas with a teensy tiny bit of prying. "Is she nice?"

Giggling at Isabel's innate inability to mind her business, Janie shifts to face her. "It's been a while, but yeah she is." A sad excuse for a chuckle trails behind. "I guess she better be. Kinda trashed my life to pass her a note."

Keeping an eye out for Lucas, Isabel runs her fingers over the wheel absentmindedly. "I don't know. I think it's kinda romantic." Her eyes twinkle with possibility.

"I think it's done now." Shifting, she's given a voice to the thought pushed down for months. "I can't change though, I know that much."

"Screw em'." As Lucas comes down the walkway, Isabel sits up and starts the car. "He's coming."

Janie scrunches forward so Lucas can squeeze into the backseat. "Let's grab food on the way. There's that Dairy Queen off the 99 over by the station."

They down their burgers on the freezing patio before they're too cold to be palpable. Happy to speak of something other than leaving, Janie picks at Lucas. "So?"

Lucas drags it out, chewing leisurely like.

Hitting his arm, Isabel laughs. "Just give it to her."

"Shush, you don't even know what I'm givin' her." He looks to Janie, "Nah, I'll give it to you at the station. You're already getting' it early, be patient now."

When delaying the inevitable wears thin, they set out for the station. Janie points to the parking lot entrance. "There's fine. I'll walk it from there." Janie gives her second goodbye hug of the night, doesn't get any easier with practice.

"You know where to find me, k?" Isabel offers, her eyes azure pools spilling over onto her cheeks.

"I know. Thank you, for everything." Janie climbs out, stepping aside to wait for Lucas.

Handing her a scuffed envelope, Lucas doesn't wait for her to ask. "There's nine hundred eighty-seven bucks in there."

Handing it back, "Lucas, no. I can't take your dirt bike money."

"Five hundred bucks is piss out there. Take it, you're gonna need it."

Acquiescing, she wells up tucking it in her pack. "I'm sorry. Shit." Gesturing upward, her hand collapses by her side. "I'm just sorry, you found out this way."

"You know I've loved you since the second grade?" Lucas confesses.

Laughing, Janie looks at him quizzically. "Second grade?"

Hardly able to believe he's telling her this, an exhale eases into a sheepish laugh. His breath frosty, Lucas pulls at his collar to keep the cold out. "Yup. Chad Dennie jumped on my lunch in the coat cubby, everyone laughed but you. You gave me half your sandwich and told him right to his face he smelled like pee. That was it. I'm easy I guess."

Crinkling her nose at the memory, "He did smell like pee."

Stretching, he shoves his hands in his pockets. "Labor Day aside, I figured out somewhere around middle school that it wasn't gonna happen. Ever."

"Middle school." Curious, Janie asks, "How so? Why on earth did you say yes when I asked you out?"

Scratching his nose, he shrugs. "From what I could tell walking to class with you, we have the same type." Letting her flounder until she buries her head in her hands, he nudges her. "Seriously though, I knew you were in a bind after Labor Day. Better me than some jerk. It was kinda fun, right?"

Throwing her arms around his neck, Janie hugs him tighter than she ever has. "I'm gonna miss you." Opening her eyes, she sees Isabel in the car watching. "You better make a move. She already has a nicer car than you, gonna be out of your league by prom. Go on then."

Putting her arms through the straps of her backpack, she aims to leave on a high note. Lucas rolls down the passenger window, waving her over. Misty eyed, he fixes his hat low. "You be good Janie Harris. I hope this ain't goodbye."

"This isn't the last of me. It's just see you later."

Patting the door like his trusted steed, Lucas points onward. Isabel's laughter trails in their wake. Watching till they hit the main road, Janie feels more loved in leaving than she has in all her labors to find a median between who she is and who she's supposed to be.

Nearly all the bays sit abandoned, Janie frets she's missed the last bus for the night. Her watch reads a quarter past nine. By her calculations, she's got an hour and a half before they get home from the pageant. The solari board is pretty dismal, looks like the long-distance routes have all gone. Mostly local shots across the valley left. Then second to the last, there it is. Albuquerque. Departing at ten thirty.

An empty schedule is about to decide your future. "What are you doing? What's in New Mexico?" She mumbles to herself and the vast hordes of no one. Pulling the folded letter from her pocket, she tries to press out the creases against her jacket.

Stepping up to the only open counter, a stout clerk accepts her challenge of who'll speak first. Raising a single bushy eyebrow, he smacks his lips and cleans his frameless lenses on a worn sweater vest before returning them to their perch upon his plump beak. All the while, uttering not a word.

Fine. "The bus to Albuquerque the last of the night?"

He rests on the counter ledge to see the schedule board and adjusts his glasses. "Looks that way."

Janie figures it's best not to scrooge the scrooge. "One regular ticket please. Thought there'd be more busses, Friday night an all." She slides a worse for wear c note across the counter.

"Hah, you're lucky there's any busses at all with them strikin'." One finger stomp at a time, he rings her up.

Waiting, she inspects her beat up letter. "Can I get a piece of tape?"

"Ehhthmm." He reaches with the tape strip stuck to his fingertip.

Lifting it off, she seals the envelope. "Thanks."

"Mmhmm." He stomps out a few more strokes, sending the printer into a tizzy till it coughs out the ticket. "Bon voyage."

Scrutinizing the ticket, she feels like Charlie in gilded awe. Sticking the ticket in the small pocket of her backpack, she picks a bench out of the thoroughfare. She's not the only one flying under the radar. A few guys living rough are catching every z they can before security sweeps through at midnight. The letter tucked away, Janie second guesses her plan to mail it from New Mexico.

Scanning the perimeter, a mailbox reveals itself off by the pay phones. Gripping the handle, her hand hovers above the bin. *Wait, write an update. There's time, just a quick note.* Eyeing the tape's edge, she looks back toward the clerk locking up. Will Return at 10:30. "Shit!" The handle slips, the bin slamming shut echoes across the station, setting off coughs and general grumbling from the camp.

Carefully, she pulls the bin open and drops the letter in. Like she told Isabel, it's mostly done anyhow. More closure than catch up will have to do for now.

Keeping company and taking notes, Janie chats with a wayward old timer on his way home. His worn wears and weathered skin suggest he's been trying to find his way home for a long time. It occurs to Janie he's probably been just about everywhere. "You ever been to Albuquerque?"

He's taken back to the last time he was home. Janie favors her some around the face. He aches for the time passed. Lord, she must have kids of her own by now. "Rode a freight train through just south of there bout ten years back. Pretty country. That where yer headed?"

Cautiously, Janie nods.

His quick laughter unleashes a sharp cough. "Don't worry, won't say a word."

"Thanks." The driver calls for boarding from the bay, Janie gets her ticket out. "That's me."

"Hey kid," he calls to her.

Stopping a few paces away, "Yeah?"

"Sit up front by the driver, there's some undesirables riding the overnight busses. Keep by the driver, you'll be alright." He gives her a fatherly nod and tucks his head against his bent arm.

"Thanks, I will." Giving the bus a cursory glance, Janie digs out the twenty from her change. She wedges the folded bill under his elbow.

Holding up the cash, he asks, "What's this?"

"It's nothin'." Janie gives a shallow wave and hurries to board.

Grabbing a window seat near the front, she breathes a sigh of relief. The engine humming, she prays for sleep to outpace her fear of what lies ahead.

Part II

Christmastime 1991

I loved her against reason, against promise, against peace, against hope, against happiness, against all discouragement that could be.
– Charles Dickens, *Great Expectations*

Chapter Sixteen

F our stops and twenty-six hours later, welcome to Albuquerque. Buttoning her coat, the air is a different kind of cold than back home. Thin enough to slip through the threads of your clothes and nip at you. Tired, stiff and unaccustomed to being out past midnight, Janie finds a nook till morning. She bear hugs her backpack using it as both a pillow and shield.

Arrivals begin trickling into the station before dawn, Janie gets her bearings via tourist brochures while fashioning the nerve to venture out. Working her way a block at a time, she wanders through small shops lining the street. Each a baby step away from the safety of the station, her tether to before. Reconciling the abstract version of what next with the tactile reality of it is proving a formidable task.

Light sleep folded into yourself on a bus may as well be no sleep at all. Janie's thoughts grow fuzzier as the day wears on. Convinced sleep deprivation is the villain keeping her from sorting herself out rather than an all-consuming fear of this strange place, she's delighted to see a vacancy sign for a small motor lodge. Giving the overhead sign a second pass, they even offer hourly rates. *Must be like those pod hotels in Japan they talked about on the evening news. Dad said before you know it, they'll start popping up in all the business parks. He may have been onto something.* Entering the lobby, Janie gets to thinking she could rent the room long enough to nap to avoid digging too deep into her funds just yet.

Having never checked into a motel before, the requirements of operating in the adult world are far more stringent than she had imagined. Credit cards, age requirements and identification may be the death knell for this plan of hers. Hungry, dog tired and holding on to her wits by a thread, Janie seeks resolution to one of the three burdens she can do something about.

Mighty Burger looks like the burger joints back home. Placing her order, she secludes herself in a corner booth as far from the counter as possible.

Her burger is a masterwork, maybe the best she's ever had or maybe she's just starving. Who's to say really. What she can say for certain is sitting here for four hours picking at the peeling laminate tabletop must be pushing some sort of vagrancy rule. Crossing the empty dining room for her third refill feels akin to crossing a rotted rope bridge. *Don't look down, don't look anywhere but ahead.* Perhaps she should order some fries as a gesture of goodwill, she's no freeloader after all.

Doing her best to look busy, Janie skims a local out-of-towner mag. Each passing hour brings her closer to buying a ticket home. The very thought of Neil barking psalms at her while she labors through push-ups and jumping jacks for hours on end is tiring in and of itself.

An unsought lunch companion brazenly seats himself across from her. Extending his callused hand, "Tanner, you?"

Suspicious, she shakes his hand. "Janie. Were you at the bus station earlier?"

Equable in manner, Tanner offers an approving snap of his fingers. "Good eye, yeah. Waiting for a friend, must've missed his bus." Lighting up, he glances towards the counter before speaking. "Just so ya know, they'll kick you out at the shift change."

On the surface, Tanner's any other college guy who wandered in off the street clad in worn out jeans, plain single pocket tee, surplus jacket and a straight edge haircut. Still, there's craftiness in his eyes. In the way he squints as he takes a drag off his cig, his eyes flick over her, sizing her up. Intuition hinting, he's anything but the average college guy.

"And how do you know that?" Janie regards him as you would an unfamiliar dog with their ears pinned back.

Waving an arc around the sparse dining area, he arches his brow. "Well, we're two blocks from the bus station, and it's the closest place to eat. Look around. Ain't no locals rushing in."

Nodding, she concedes his theory. "I'm headin' out soon anyway."

"I'm gonna guess you're not from around here. You got a place to stay darlin'?" Stretching his arms across the back of the booth, he forces his moderate frame to claim the span of the bench, brandishing a self-satisfied smirk.

The familiar urge to get out while she can nudges Janie to abandon courtesy in favor of an inexorable compulsion to put some pavement between herself and her wolfish suitor. A tray of food slaps down in front of her. It's accompanied by a wiry blond slipping in next to her, scooching her over with a gutty hip check. Addressing Tanner directly, her taut shoulders reveal her umbrage. "You're pretty thick aren't you fuck face." Looking to her watch then back at him, she shakes her head forebodingly. "Reggie's gonna be here any minute, you think he won't beat your ass right out the door?"

Smiling through a squelched fit of temper, Tanner rests against the booth. His ring finger twitches, betraying his agitation. "Janie don't mind me sitting here. Do ya darlin'?"

Wagging her finger, she leans on the table. "Quit it with that darlin' shit. You're from Oregon you asshole." Turning to Janie, she stares ardently into her eyes. "Let me tell you about Tanner here. He's a parasite who sits around the bus station, waiting on girls like you stepping off the bus all pouty eyed and looking for some prince charming to fix their shit. He'll promise you the world, and when he's done with you whatever bullshit you're runnin' from will seem like a vision of heaven."

Janie looks at Tanner wide eyed, the revelation has rendered her a dead loss. It's over.

The door chimes ominously. Janie's snarky avenger eases into a smile. "You wanna guess who that is shithead?"

Sighing, Tanner stubs his cigarette out on the tray. "You've always been a jealous bitch Cici."

A deep voice booms from behind the counter. "Thought I told you to stay out."

Tanner flips him off, arresting his fear long enough to stroll out.

Cornered in the booth, Janie's leery but grateful. Introducing herself, she regards her champion. "Thanks for whatever that was. I'm Janie."

Stealing a fry, she replies in kind. "Cicely. Don't worry, they won't bother you so long as it looks like you just ordered."

Cautious, Janie resists the desperate urge to cling to the slightest of kindnesses. "That's really nice of you, but I was gonna head out."

"Stay. No one's gonna bother you. You don't wanna spend too much time hanging out at the station, there's creeps a plenty over there." Poaching one last fry, Cicely smiles sympathetically. "Go on, dive in. I'll come round on my break in an hour."

"Cicely!" Beckons the voice from the kitchen.

"Comin'!" She bellows back. "Gotta go," she tells Janie, dropping a few ketchup packets on her tray out of habit.

Pacing herself, Janie picks at her food while reading and rereading the magazine waiting for her new friend. Not yet sold on her motives, Janie thinks of a proverb from when she was on her KJV kick. *He that hateth dissembleth with his lips, and layeth up deceit within him.* Lips, lovely as they are, shouldn't be given unearned trust. Stealing a glance towards the counter, Cicely could indeed be disemblething some bullshit just like Tanner. Too early to tell.

Tossing her visor on the bench, Cicely slides in across from Janie with a sigh. "Two hours and I'm out."

Janie forces a smile, unsure of the fleeting familiarity. "Don't take this the wrong way, but why're you being so nice to me?"

Pleased that Janie's learning, Cicely's mood settles. "Been where you're at is all, thereabouts anyway. You 18?"

Deciding whether she wants to answer, Janie doesn't get the chance.

"Thought so. There's a hostel that don't check IDs. I stayed there when I first got here."

"How do you know Tanner?" Janie asks, siphoning her soda through leftover ice.

"Oh, I had the pleasure of making his acquaintance two years ago when I moved here with my friend Amelia. Lucky for me, I grew up around a bunch of shitbags, so I saw his sorry ass comin' from a mile away. Amelia not so much." She rotates the band of her visor through her fingers pensively. "Swallowed her up. Wasn't till she got yanked again for solicitation, they gave her a choice. Rehab or jail. Her uncle drove down from St. Louis to get her last I heard."

"Shit," Janie says mostly to herself then covers her mouth. "Sorry."

"Shit, I've probably cussed more since you met me than you have your whole life."

Janie blushes, feeling her adult card slip through her fingers. "I didn't really notice."

"Alright greenhorn, what's it gonna be? You wanna give the hostel a try? I can walk you over after work."

Nodding, Janie grabs her tray to leave.

"I'm off at five. There's a drugstore a few blocks down. Good place to kill time, grab yer this and that's."

Not wanting to look any more like a puppy tied to the news stand than she already feels, Janie waits around the corner till just past five. Cicely's waiting, her uniform shirt slung over her slender shoulder and visor hooped around her arm.

Motioning to Janie's shopping bag, Cicely fishes out a pack of cigarettes from her coat. "See you found it alright." Tapping the pack against her hand, she offers Janie a smoke. Lighting up, she takes a long drag as they make their way. "This place is decent. I stayed there for six months before I turned 18. As long as you don't give them no trouble, there won't be any."

Shaking her head, Janie watches her every move. "No trouble. I just need somewhere to figure things out."

Stifling a laugh, Cicely appraises Janie. "Yeah, you don't really look like trouble. But you never know." Pointing to herself, "This right here, this is trouble."

"Well today you got me outta trouble, so thank you."

Waving her off, "It was nothin'. If you can afford it, spring for a single room."

"Single, like single bed?" Janie asks, wondering if she can afford a full room since she's only ever slept on a twin bed.

"Single like no roommates. It can be a crapshoot, trust me." Cicely replies, grimacing at a repressed memory eager for its day in the sun.

"Right, yeah I think I want a single." Janie nods, cool and collected like Cicely.

The hostel is an old brick building, painted to match the deep sand color of everything around it. An old coffee can filled with sand and brimming with spent cigarettes, sits atop patchwork concrete steps. Narrow and deeply inset between two larger buildings, much of the interior is robbed of natural light. Worn to the crux of threadbare, the furnishings are clean and well cared for. Like a visit to grandma's house, if grandma smoked five packs a day, ate from a vending machine and believed old waiting room chairs were the swiss army knives of furniture. An ode to bric-à-brac. Chipped paint scars the hallway, memories of all these walls have seen. Running her finger along the chips, Janie marvels at the colorful paint striations.

A tall man with a messy ponytail checks her in. Cicely handles the details. Their easy rapport lifts Janie's doubts. In a matter of minutes, she has become someone's tenant. Back home, hundreds of miles away, she's someone's child. Their missing child. Their gone astray child. Drawing in a breath deep enough to squeeze out every last molecule of the old air, of the old her, she is not the missing child. She is the enfant terrible, and now a tenant. She hopes not to be a terrible tenant.

Cicely hands the key over, regarding Janie as she surveys her new home in scared shitless awe. Holding the key in her palm, Janie closes her hand around it. Taking another deep breath, she rocks on the balls of her feet. "Thank you...really I was...just thank you."

Pulling her collar snug, Cicely wedges her hands in her coat. "Eh, it was nothin'. Take care greenhorn."

Just like that, the closest thing Janie has to a friend slips off into the night.

Her room's up a flight of saggy stairs, last door down the hall. Janie will come to cherish only sharing a single wall with her hostel cohabitants more than she could have known when Cicely asked for an end room. Parked in the valley of a spongy twin bed slung across a humble honey oak frame, she rests her elbows on her knees, soaking up the scene. Larger than her bedroom, she ventures over to the weathered double-hung window with an expansive view of the alley.

Unpacking proves too much of a commitment for tonight, the security of knowing she can pick up to go with only seconds to spare fortifies her will to stay. Where she'd go is another matter. The bus station? Suppose so.

She could dodge the Tanners till her bus leaves. Feet planted, she lies back on the bed, eyes closed. Too early to sleep and too late to wander.

A growling stomach demands sustenance with impunity, the threat of queasiness brings her to her feet. *What was the clerks name again? Dang it.* She'll settle for the vending machine rather than pass him in the lobby.

Burning through a sugar rush from a dinner of stale donuts, Starburst and bonus pretzels knocked loose by her donuts, Janie susses out her finances. Counting out the cash on her bed, she sits ready to flip her blanket over the cash should she hear so much as a tremble of the door handle. Old habits die hard if ever at all. With thirteen hundred and change to her name, there's time to figure things out at twenty-four bucks a night.

Staring up at the scuffed cream walls, the sounds of life beyond her little corner filter in. Holding her Walkman, she wishes she'd remembered batteries. All the comforts from home, which she never knew were comforting, are glaringly absent. Away from her family, the freedom she anticipated is yet to manifest. In its place doubt spreads like a virus.

A car blaring techno through shitty speakers flies down the alley, drawing her to the window. Leaning on the sill, Janie gawks from her darkened room. Feeling smaller by the minute in this strange place, in her strange room, she's coming to terms with how sheltered life has been. Seeking further shelter in the passing of time, surely the wee hours must be upon her. Her watch swears it's only midnight. Dubious, she agrees to disagree.

Cozying up to the small wooden desk, she nibbles on leftover pretzels which wick the last traces of moisture from her mouth. Poking her head into the hall, Janie listens for movements which might validate her fear some heinous creature's waiting around the corner to eat her up, nothing stirs. Digging for change, Hawaiian Punch wins out over root beer. A battle of wills ensues. An undesirable quarter gets kicked back despite gingerly dropping it in the slot. *Seriously!*

A raspy voice frightens the coin from her hand. Dropping to her knees, Janie strains to catch it before it rolls off.

"She's a crotchety old bitch." Extending his macilent hand, he holds out a quarter. "Trade ya?"

Sizing up his lanky frame hiding under an oversized hooded sweatshirt, Janie obliges. Partly for fear rejection may inspire him to eat her up but mostly because she's thirsty and out of change. "Thanks."

Janie leaves him to peruse the snack machine. Skulking to her room, she presses her ear to the locked door to be sure no one has followed.

What are you doing? You can't stay here. Imagining her letter to Lydia stowed in a mail truck, rife with truths that are no longer true, there's an urgency to set the record right. To assure Lydia and herself, that there remains the possibility of salvaging her life before here.

Tearing a page from her makeshift ledger, Janie checks her ticket stub to ensure she spells Albuquerque correctly, thinking they need a song like Mississippi has.

> *Dear Lydia,*
> *Hello from Albuquerque. There's a letter on its way to you. So much has happened since I wrote it. So much that I wish I could have told you if I'd had another piece of tape. It's a long story and I'm too tired to tell it tonight.*
> *The short version is that I got caught again and had to leave, else I might've been sent away. It's harder on my own than I thought. I'm not sure what to do now, think I'll probably hide out here until things blow over then go home.*
> *Everything happened so fast, I left your address behind. Don't worry, my Mom will never find it. I hid it in my Yaya's Greek mythology book.*
> *Wish I could send this now, but it will have to wait till I get back.*
> *Always,*
> *Janie*

Bored with staring at the wall, three small drawers offer the possibility of relics from past residents. While the top two drawers yield only a few dead termites, the bottom drawer stutters open as tired wooden glides grab for anything that might arrest their movement. The sole inhabitant of the drawer is a dog-eared King James Bible. Giving it a quick sniff, it smells of old paper and ashtray. Romans and Corinthians look to be big hits based on page wear.

Flipping to Timothy, Janie calls to mind Pastor Ignacio's sermon inspired by the verse *For God hath not given us the spirit of fear; but of power, and of love, and of a sound mind.* Most sermons were tuned out like the hum of overhead power lines, not this one. His excitement when speaking of divine love and the hurdles of modern faith was contagious. When all felt lost, Janie thought of his words. Inevitably the less loving experiences of the past year would ride their coattails to the forefront of her consciousness, bursting her biblical bubble. *And so it is.* Closing the text, she kisses the embossed letters in reverence and places it back in the drawer for the next wayward soul seeking a spiritual tincture.

Chapter Seventeen

The days following Janie's arrival meld into a therapeutic blur of living an hour at a time. An hour spent at the library, an hour spent finding food, and so on. Overwhelmed, thinking of yesterday or tomorrow threatens her footing. But an hour at a time is doable.

Absent a genuine desire to celebrate the holidays, Janie forges ahead on principle. Buying a foldout tree with glued on tinsel, she spends Christmas alone in her room with her cardboard tree and a rubbery turkey tv dinner that's defiantly cold in the center. Abstaining from the usual marathon of episodic nostalgia, football wins out in this moment of maverick holiday reverie. Solitary as it may be.

Meticulously tracking every penny, Janie gifts herself the luxury of time. What next will not be allotted a single hour for the rest of the year. Splurging on an 8-pack of AA batteries for her Walkman does wonders to dull the abiding pang of shrinking away from herself little by little since their summer, bathing her memories of everyone back home in a warm gaussian blur the way a country song makes you ache for a time and place you've never known.

Notwithstanding an arsenal of power ballads, her last thought each night is *do they miss me?* Some nights, buckling under the conjured guilt of having made her parents sick with worry, the tears flow until she flips her pillow. Other nights, she imagines their relief at being delivered from their encumbrance. Those are the nights she feels most alone, hiding in her room from the specter of a fate laid flat by a lousy piece of tape.

New Year's Eve arrives quietly for Janie, less so for some of her floormates. Faking left, she swerves right to avoid drunkies in the throes of a giggle fit. *It's the quarter guy.* Cloaked in his massive sweatshirt, he cranes over his companion's shoulder to get a better look. Prominent cheekbones reveal a gaunt beauty that might otherwise pass for sickly were it not for his hauntingly affable blue eyes. With a sly smile, he turns in time to right their course. Pausing on the first step, a need to see that they've made it without a tumble rises within her.

Mighty Burger exists in a universe devoid of holidays, promotions or trends. A lipstick-stained party horn with a chewed mouthpiece offers the lone hint. Grabbing the gnarled end bare handed, the cashier chucks it into the bin. Disturbed, Janie watches his germy mitts clip her receipt up for the line cook, bag a drive thru order and fetch her tray all without ever washing his hands. Pensively staring at her meal, she gambles on the vigor of herd immunity.

Jotting down the cost of her lunch, Janie's weekish long streak of avoiding Cicely ends abruptly.

Dropping down like a sack of potatoes, Cicely nabs the notepad for inspection. Nibbling a fry, Janie waits. Unimpressed, Cicely folds her arms over it. "My lord this is a long shift. Anyway, you gotta get a job." Pointing to Janie's ledger, she slides it back. "Cause this kinda shit right here will drive you nuts."

Janie looks at her book then back at Cicely. "It's called being frugal. Besides, who's gonna hire me without ID?"

Leaning in, Cicely whispers. "Reggie will. He hired me under the table when I was barely 17. Prepare to work your ass off and not get a cut of the tip jar."

"Just like that? Without knowing me?"

Shaking her head, she laughs. "What's to know? You come in every day for lunch, don't cause any trouble and clean up after yourself. I'll vouch for you."

Janie puts her burger down. "How'd you know I eat here?"

"You're the only person I know who orders extra mayo, people notice." Cicely settles back. "Listen. You're not doing the books, just slingin' burgers."

"Yeah, you're right."

"Course I am. Come up after you eat and we'll sort your shit out." She steals a fry before vanishing, lost to the mysteries of all that lies in the walk-in.

Hiring and orientation take all of ten minutes. Reggie's a man of few words, his rules consist of five don'ts and three always. Cicely digs through a laundry sack in the back office, emerging with two uniform shirts and a newish visor. Her name added to the schedule, Janie's first shift is two days out.

Settled in to watch Dick Clark say so long, Janie pulls all the fixings from an old cooler she picked up at the Salvation Army. Crushing some Fritos into her sandwich, an eye level assessment leaves her unsatisfied with the inadequate distribution of crunch. Keenly aware of the sweet spot between prepping and eating the sandwich before it goes soggy, she crams in more Fritos. Giving it a light press with her palm, she goes in for the first bite. The best bite.

An unexpected knock sends an enthusiastic swig careening down the wrong pipe. Janie stifles her cough into sharp nasal squawks, scuttling her go at pretending no one's home. Reluctantly turning the deadbolt, relief washes over when Cicely greets her with a half-hearted blow of a party horn and a bored expression. "Jesus greenhorn, sounded like you were dying. Here, brought you one. Hurrah!"

Janie accepts the gift, reflexively eyeing the mouthpiece with disgust. "Thanks!"

"So?" Cicely asks, looking for a place to sit, settling for the bed. "This is the plan for the night? You and your sandwich?"

Nodding, Janie stammers an explanation while chewing through an oversized bite. "I mean, I don't really know anyone. Ya know?"

"I'm just teasin'." Standing, she plunges her hands into her coat pockets. "I should probably get. Just wanted to check up on you on my way home."

"Wait, so are you goin' somewhere to celebrate?"

"Me? Nah, Nathan doesn't get off till three, so I'll probably head home. You wanna come over?"

Way to put her on the spot. Janie shakes her head. "That's alright."

"Seriously, c'mon. We can be bored together. At least I have a couch to be bored on."

"Yeah, well my bed is my couch," Janie counters.

"Look greenhorn, we can cuddle up on that old ass bed watchin' the ball drop, but I can't guarantee I won't get frisky."

Janie flushes, grabs her coat and shoos Cicely out the door. "Let's go."

A cutting wind blows through them as they step off the stoop. Janie has never been so grateful for a burst of cold air as she is in that moment. Anything to soothe the heat cowling her face.

"Keep up greenhorn! The busses are runnin' slow count of the holiday. We can walk it faster than freezin' our asses off at the stop."

Hustling to catch up, Janie does a walk run till she matches her pace. "It's fine, I like walking."

"Good, cause we got a mile or so left."

Cicely and Nathan live in an old neighborhood forgotten by civic planning and improvements. The blocks are littered with small stucco duplexes and single cottages clad in dry rot addled siding. Small strips of grass stomped flat suffice as sidewalks. Lots with three and four cottages crammed onto them seem to spill their contents out into the yards. Couches lay perched on one end of the porch with heaps of scrap piled on the other. Derelict cars sprout up from the ground with popped hoods and decaying tires, now little more than jetties defining crude boundaries amongst the residents of these communes of crap.

Celebration and fireworks abound as neighbors mill about each other's yards toasting to a new year, a better year. All the while their kids trample dark pathways they've run a hundred times on hot summer evenings and crisp fall afternoons. Cicely shares a wave and a smile here and there as familiar voices call out to her, inviting her to join them.

She and Nathan reside in the sole apartment building on the block. No doubt the work of a 1960s dingbat visionary, certain in their belief that the other lots would eschew their shoebox vintage in favor of the newfangled vernacular. By the time the pragmatic greatest generation aged out of the decision-making process, their kids had missed the bus to offload their bequest of bugs and blight. The market had shifted to new development incentivized by tax breaks and cronyism.

Janie does a two-step down the block avoiding potholes and the occasional dog stealthily body slamming chest height chain-link fences. Cicely knows each of them by name, shushing them with cautionary warnings of frightening her new friend.

"They're harmless. Little riled up with the fireworks and whatever the hell else they're firing off." Trailing off, she devotes her attention to a thorough scratching of scruff. Wiping her hands on the inside of her coat, she coos at her mottled duo. "Shit, I'd bark my ass off too if someone left me out in the cold. Poor bastards."

Following suit, Janie gets in a few chin scratches. "They're pretty cute when they put their teeth away."

"Ain't we all?"

Reading the apartment name aloud, Janie dips into a puddle turning up the drive. "The Sun Belt, fancy." Inspecting her sopping shoe. "Dang, didn't see that one."

"Gave it a name instead of a soul, but it's home. Gotcha huh?"

Janie shakes the excess free. "Just barely, I'm alright."

The apartment's a small second-floor unit up a flight of pebble stone stairs. Cicely disappears to change. Taking it all in, Janie longs for a place of her own. A place for which she holds the only key, where she can stay as long as she likes or leave whenever she wants.

Mistaking wonderment for assessment, Cicely grabs at odds and ends to tidy up. "It's not much I know, but it's mine. Well, mine and Nathan's anyway."

"No, it's great. Gives me hope."

"Well, bring your hope and sit down already. You're making me nervous," she commands, cracking two cans of Natty Light.

Janie takes a sip. "Mmhmm." Painfully conscious of her expression, she smiles like it's her first taste of water after wandering the desert. *Too much.* Doesn't matter, Cicely's already flipping channels to get to *Rockin' New Year's Eve.*

Sunken into the old couch, they make idle chatter about this or that. Never threatening the veneer of good humor and witty banter. Janie babysits her drink, taking shallow sips whenever she catches Cicely checking in. On to her second, Cicely lifts Janie's can, gauging the weight. "You want something else?"

"Oh no, I like it." Janie grabs it, taking back a big swig to demonstrate her okayness with it.

"That's gotta be warm by now. I'll get you something else." Returning, she hands Janie a soda.

Happy to wash the hoppy tinge from her mouth, Janie waits for the dig that never comes.

Slouching, Cicely fights to stay awake after working a double. "My lord, I don't think I've ever seen so many men declare their love of dick in all my life as I've seen in that crowd."

Janie smiles along, blushing when Cicely glances her way with a knowing smirk.

Cicely admires Janie's naïve nature, though she cannot remember a time when she ever knew that kind of guilelessness. Aside from Nathan, she's never felt a kinship with anyone around here. Yet she feels called to look after this stray and somehow happier for it. Life's peculiar that way. "Darrell tell you about the occupancy rule?" Cicely asks, rolling her neck along the couch cushion.

Tearing herself away from Vanessa Williams, "What's that?"

"It's a rule that says you gotta check out every forty-five days. Mark it in that diary you count your pennies in, so it doesn't sneak up on ya."

Mildly offended, Janie sips her drink. "It's not a diary. Will I get my same room back?"

"Well, whatever it is, write it down. Yeah, you leave yer stuff. Just can't sleep there." Cicely pries herself out of her seat, taking her empty to the kitchen.

Cheers and hooting draw Janie back to the screen, they're counting down. "Cicely! Hurry, they're about to drop the ball."

"I'm comin'." She sips the foam from her hurried can.

Toasting at the drop, Cicely takes a long swig before sinking back into her slouch.

A fog of sadness rolls in, her mind drifts to back home. Lucas with Isabel watching the ball drop, not making a move. Matty crashed out like a lead blanket across her father on the couch. Checking her watch as though the hour were a mystery, "I should probably go."

Cicely turns her sleepy gaze from the anti-climactic wind down of celebrities mouthing the words to "Auld Lang Syne." "What? No, stay. I'll have Nathan drive you home."

"I'm sure the last thing he wants after coming home is to go back out to drop me off."

Her can between her knees, Cicely slaps her hands down on her thighs. "Then I'll just have to walk you home. Did I mention I hate walking in the cold?"

"I don't need a chaperone. I'm fine on my own," Janie declares.

Cicely matches Janie's sass. "Greenhorn you're liable to get eaten by someone's yard mutt or a pothole." Waiting for a hint of a smile, she holds steady till she gets it. Patting Janie's leg, she implores her, "Just stay. I'll drop you off myself when he gets home. K?"

Collapsing onto the couch, Janie grabs Cicely's beer and sips it. *Still tastes gross.* "K. Only cause you insist though."

Laughing, she reclaims her beer. "Gimme that."

Not remembering having fallen asleep, Janie awakens to Cicely leaning over her. Flattening her couch hair, a lanky figure silhouetted by the TV's light comes into focus. His curly hair and grizzled stubble are not what Janie expected. Not that she can say why given she was unaware of his existence only hours ago.

"Janie, this is Nathan."

Extending his rough hand, there's a shyness about him up close. "Hey, heard a lot about you lately."

Hearing Cicely call her by her given name sounds strange, almost foreign. "Thanks for having me over."

"C'mon, I'll drive you home." Reaching to her tippy toes, Cicely gives Nathan a peck on the lips. "Be right back."

A drizzle destined to frost over covers everything in a frigid embrace. The drive is silent as the little pickup chugs along one lazy gear at a time. The wipers fall in sync with Janie's blinking. Revelers blotting the bars and sidewalks earlier have ended up wherever they're going to be for the night. Flashing stoplights applaud their reflections on the wet road.

Sticking the clutch a little too hard pulling up to Janie's place, Cicely curses it. "God damnit. Alright greenhorn, you're home."

"Thanks for the ride. Guess I'll see you at work."

"See ya, night." She watches till the lobby door swings shut behind Janie.

Heavy legs carry Janie to the edge of her bed. Dropping her coat and bag, she sleeps in her clothes.

Chapter Eighteen

While her first few shifts are daunting, Janie soon falls into a rhythm. Though there are aberrant days where her purpose pivots around whether someone wants fries or onion rings, she's grateful for any sense of purpose at all. Everyone here has their own story, and they keep it to themselves. A perk over the scuttlebutt of the diner.

The low rung gets the worst shifts, meaning she only sees Cicely a couple times per week. In the home stretch of her first forty-five, checkout day looms. Janie maneuvers herself into a late shift, resolved to check out a few books and spend the wee hours at the bus station.

As inevitable as that one customer a day chucking their tray into the bin, her fabled first shit shift takes the form of a Taz sweatshirt clad customer sent into a fitful rage over charred burgers. Janie watches Taz jerk back and forth with each wag of the finger, wishing he'd leap off her chest and swallow her whole. Reggie offers a refund with one hand and points to the door with the other.

Cicely catches Janie on her way out. "Rough shift?"

Not feeling so chatty, Janie grumbles, "You heard?"

Cicely nods. "They're few and far between, Reggie said you did good."

Janie turns to leave.

"Hey," Cicely calls after her. "Isn't checkout day coming up?"

"Thursday."

"Come stay with us. I'll have Reggie add me to the schedule for your shift."

Lacking the energy to refuse and knowing she'll end up caving to Cicely's aggressive kindness, Janie nods. "Okay, if Nathan doesn't mind."

Victorious, Cicely's a little let down at Janie's lack of fight. "Go home and wash the night off, you'll feel better tomorrow. See you Thursday."

Wandering the plaza in Old Town on her day off, a succession of plaques tell tales of those who sacrificed themselves with no promise of anything beyond the knowledge there was nothing behind them to return to. Getting lost in what was, resets Janie's perspective. She'll let a hiccup be a hiccup instead of a heart attack.

Tapping into the tourist vibe she envied at the diner, Janie pops into one last shop before calling the day good. Wall to wall with trinkets, she imagines what she might buy for everyone back home. Abandoned atop a barrel of polished ore chunks is a small carved slingshot. She easily pictures Matty pummeling bottles and cans alike. Paying the tourist tax, the pleasure of *could be* is worth it.

Thursday arrives on a bed of nerves, only slightly assuaged by Darrell's promise to keep her room key on his person. With a full day to whittle down, today's fixation is making up lost class time. *Wasn't Amy home-schooled? She wasn't too weird.* Resolute, Janie maxes out her checkout privileges with a backpack full of this semester's subjects.

Stumbling upon a hole in the wall with a Greek flag hanging in the window, Janie dives into a gyro so good it tastes like home. At work with time to spare, she crankily ignores Nathan dropping Cicely off. Without reason, she continues pretending not to notice when Cicely saunters through to clock in. Trying to push past the distance she's compelled to put between them, Janie cannot keep tempo with their normal back and forth. Holed up in the bathroom on her break, she splashes water on her face trying to snap out of it.

Rounding out the sixth hour, the staff divide their time between cleaning and shooting the shit while Reggie naps in the back office. The door chime sends them ambling back into position. Janie mans the counter, having earned her stripes facing off with a raging customer.

Hardly recognizing vending machine guy without his sweatshirt, she's doubtful he remembers her or anything else for that matter. Eager to move him along, Janie offers the same amiable grin she wears for every customer. "Can I help you?"

"Yeah, let me get..." Pausing, he studies her. "Don't we live on the same floor?"

Looking upward in contemplative theatrics, "Yeah, think I've seen you."

"Hawaiian Punch?"

"Sorry?"

"You were trying to buy a Hawaiian Punch, we swapped quarters."

Pointing to her name tag, "I'm Janie."

Pleased with his recall, he smiles. "Hey neighbor, I'm Butch."

From the corner of her eye, Janie spies Cicely watching as she refills napkin dispensers. Guiltily self-satisfied, Janie gets on with it. "What can I get you?"

Though he notices Cicely, he betrays not so much as a flick of the eye. "Yeah, I'll get a number eight with swiss instead."

"You got it!" Janie takes his order slip back the long way to avoid Cicely.

Waiting in silence for Nathan, Cicely's deep sigh signals her annoyance at his delay.

"You sure this is alright?" Janie asks.

Between drags off her cig, Cicely counters, "Yeah, why?"

"No reason." Janie blows into the cuffs of her coat to warm her hands. "How come you didn't just drive yourself to work?"

Her eyes go momentarily wide, she draws a breath to settle. "Cause he said I'm gonna burn out the clutch is why. Damn greenhorn."

"Sorry, I didn't mean it like that." Janie looks the other way, again blowing into her cuffs.

Taking one last drag, she stubs out the remnants of her cigarette. "I know." Pulling off her gloves, she tosses them down on the table in front of Janie. "Go on, put em' on."

Pushing them back, Janie abashedly shoves her hands free from her sleeves. "I'm being a baby. I'm not taking your gloves."

Lighting another cig, Cicely stares over the glow of the lighter. "I got another pair at home. Take em'." Shaking the lighter, she speaks with the cigarette perched between her lips. "I always buy them in twos on the count of burning through them eventually. So, I see you met Butch..."

"You know him?" Janie's curiosity piqued.

"Yeah, he was moving in around the time I was moving out. Listen...he's got some substance issues, just so you know."

"Yeah, he and this other guy Alban at the hostel hangout a lot. He's been fine to me though, gave me a quarter for the vending machine when I needed it."

Exhaling to the sky, Cicely sighs her dissatisfaction with Janie's assessment of Butch's character. "Well, don't say I didn't warn you."

Nathan blinds them pulling into the spot. Cicely shields her eyes, hopping off the table. Pulling on the second glove, Janie follows. Scooting into the middle, Cicely kisses him and hands off her smoke.

Taking a quick drag, he hangs his arm out the window. "Sorry babe, that axle was a stubborn sonofabitch." Leaning forward to greet Janie, he gives her a little two finger wave. "Hey there Janie."

Buckling, Janie presses herself against the door and tries not to notice Cicely's hand resting on his thigh.

Already knowing the answer, Cicely continues her line of thought undeterred. "Hope he's payin' you for all this work."

Cracking a little smile at their usual sticking point, he hands the cig back. Cranking his arm on the wheel to the chagrin of the power steering pump, it squeals and submits. "He can't pay me anything if he can't work. He's good for it, you know that."

Agreeing to disagree with a huff, Cicely leans into him.

Nathan swigs on a beer, unwinding while Cicely gathers blankets and pillows. "Checkout night huh? Man, I don't miss that."

"Yeah, thanks for letting me stay." Stealing a good look at him while he's turned to the news, it's hard to believe he's six years older than Cicely. He has that quiet way about him like Lucas' dad. *I wonder if Lucas told anyone.* "So, you stayed at the hostel too?"

"Mmhmm, spent a few months when I landed here. Cicely and I met there."

"Met where?" Cicely inquires, dropping the pillow and blankets onto the couch.

"The hostel babe." Nathan grabs her around the waist, pulling her backward onto his lap.

Pushing his stubbly face aside, Cicely looks over. "You need anything before we turn in?"

Janie shakes her head and pats the blankets. "Think I'm set. Going to read some, then turn in too." Stretching, she forces a yawn.

Pushing up from his lap, Cicely pulls Nathan to his feet. "Night Janie."

Shutting the TV off, Janie lays back on the tired couch. Her mind wanders from the strangeness of the night to wondering how many people have slept over on this couch. Her pressure points settling on the crossbeams, how did she not notice this on New Year's? *Could be a bench at the damn bus station so suck it up.* Wiggling into a comfy spot, she closes her eyes. A low cadence and stifled breathing permeate the attenuated wall dividing them. Staring blankly at the popcorn ceiling, Janie draws a deep breath then bunches her sweatshirt over her ear and rolls over.

First light flits through the window, waking her slowly. Motionless, she listens for movement. Slyly tucking a library receipt thank you note under the ashtray, she checks her watch. Blankets folded and pillow in hand, she freezes at the click of the bedroom door.

A sleepy whisper grows closer. "You leavin'?"

Caught, Janie sets the pillow down. "I didn't want to overstay. Did I wake you?"

Pushing her messy hair back, Cicely drowsily shakes her head. Grabbing her pack of smokes, she taps one free. "You can't check back in till ten."

"Yeah, I know." Janie reaches for her book left atop the blanket stack. "Figure I'll hang out in the common area till then."

Intercepting the book for closer inspection before handing it back, Cicely sighs. "Woman in White? Whatsamatter, not getting enough ghosts and ghouls in your comic books?"

Janie rolls her eyes, tucking it under her arm. "It's more of a who done it. Anyway, I'm not of one mind or another about it yet."

"Hmm. Hand me my lighter, would ya." Struggling to shift Janie's bag out of her way, she lifts the flap. "Jesus, that's a lot of books."

Hefting it onto her shoulder, Janie concurs. "I may have gotten ahead of myself."

Waking up with each drag, Cicely watches Janie intently. "C'mon, don't leave. We'll have breakfast."

Wedging her other arm into the strap, Janie pushes up from the couch. "Go on back to bed. I'll be alright."

Resting her cigarette on the rim of the ashtray, she looks at Janie head on, "I'll drive you. Wait here."

Giving the old rotary ample time to warm up, Cicely harasses the heater knobs to coax out a pittance of warm air. "I know a place not far out with breakfast worth dyin' for."

Apprehensive, Janie cannot help but feel she's putting her out by trying not to put her out. "You sure Nathan won't mind you taking the truck?"

Laughing, she puts it into gear. "Shit, since he likes fixin' stuff for free, he can fix the clutch in this when I get back."

Cracking the window an inch, Cicely taps the ash free and massages her temple. Letting the crevice of cold air edge out the lethargy of this ungodly hour, she takes the temperature in the cab. "We alright greenhorn?"

Emerging from the gloom of a day gone by, Janie warms to her clement tone. "Yeah, we're good boss lady."

Awake as she ever cares to be, Cicely rolls up the window. Grinning, "Boss lady, huh?"

Snickering across the bench, Janie nods. "That's what I said."

Soon thereafter Cicely's bumped to shift manager. Scheduling Janie on all her shifts, it's mostly nights with Reggie's claim to the day shift. Janie doesn't mind, it's lonely in the off hours. Everyone's older and being treated like a kid blows.

Darrell's the outlier. Though he treats her like a kid, his chats seek to elevate instead of nanny. Every so often he calls her over to reception with an old paperback in hand, and a bare bones review. Entire genres of literature open before her, some better than others. She gives the Beats and the Romantics a go, but it doesn't stick. He adjusts, taking her reticence in stride. Always encouraging her to stretch with *What doesn't fit today might be just what you're looking for tomorrow.*

In turn, Janie introduces him to Charley's New Orleans overrun with the legion of the endless night and Bruce Wayne's beloved Gotham besieged by Mutants. Though he's more of a Metropolis man, there's no turning back from *Dream of the Endless.*

Climbing the stairs to put the day behind her, Janie palms an old, yellowed paperback. Unable to resist a whiff, she raises the book as she flips through it again. Darrell's books always smell of old tobacco or perfumed incense, save for the occasional junk store find fallen prey to mold. Butch descends upon the stairs with that sickly fella Alban who moves so much he practically vibrates. They arc around her, Butch gives a quick wave.

Searching for her ledger, a page from her study guide will have to do.

> *Dear Lydia,*
> *Somehow I'm still here, but I'm not alone anymore. I've made some friends and think I'll stick around a while longer. I owe it all to Cicely. She told me about the hostel and got me a job. You'd like her, she's whip smart and has a way of making everything less scary.*
> *The hostel manager Darrell loves books, maybe even more than you do. He's always giving me new stuff to read. He pestered me into reading the Woman in White. It's Victorian but not like what you would expect with all the weird complaining about prissy stuff. It reminds me of Fright Night issue 19, except in the book Laura doesn't stake her dad in the heart since he's already dead. I bet she'd want to if she could though.*
> *You probably already got your license. The only time I miss home is when I think how much closer it is to you than here. Maybe after I'm eighteen we could meet up in McCreary. By then they'd have no say. I guess that leaves me some time to think about it.*
> *Always,*
> *Janie*

Spring brings stuffy afternoons to the upper floors. Exhaust wafting from the alley does its share. Janie claims an overstuffed loveseat in the common area, seesawing her way through library textbooks and Darrell's book club selections. Butch drops down, sighing dramatically in case the full weight of his person free-falling into the wrinkled leather were not enough to announce his presence. Janie briskly raises her eyes, smirking before returning to her studies.

Flipping through magazines, he grows weary of waiting for curiosity to get the better of her. "Whatcha readin'?"

"This? Mostly Greeks and the like. You?"

Holding up the magazine, he offers it over. "You wanna give it a sniff?"

Flushed from sternum to crown, Janie's book slips and lands closed on her lap.

He tosses the magazine over. "You being a history buff, you might like the Smithsonian. There's some crazy stuff stored in those places."

"I just started learning about it. So, is that what you wanna do?"

"What, work in a museum?" Eyeing her curiously, "No. I'm a lil' past the what I wanna do part of life."

Janie nods knowingly, not really understanding considering he looks only a few years older than Cicely.

Chasing a new thought, Butch points to Darrell's book. "Although, I did once aspire to be a psychonaut."

Janie looks at the book, wondering if Darrell has a flair for sci-fi. "Is that like an astronaut?"

"Not exactly. I guess you could say I was interested more in cerebral ether than cosmic ether." Reaching for the book, a flood of memories give rise to a secret smile. "This man right here is one of the greatest psychonauts of all time, Mr. Leary was ahead of his time." Contemplatively, "You know I tried reading the *Book of the Dead*, but I dunno, undisciplined I guess."

Eavesdropping, Darrell recites his mantra. "Well, you know, what doesn't fit today..."

Butch sees it through. "Might fit tomorrow. Truer words man, truer words."

Smiling, Darrell carries on.

Taking them in, Janie surveys the worn cover. "Is this a drug culture thing?"

"Drug culture? What are you, the fuzz?" Scratching his temple, "It's a culture of consciousness."

Janie agrees to disagree, returning to her reading.

Not one to surrender his point, Butch pokes her arm with his pen. "Janie, there are two kinds of psychonauts in this world." Holding up two fingers, he rotates his hand back to front. "Two. Those who chase dragons and those who don't. And once you stop being the latter, you'll always be the former. I'm living proof." He wipes an imaginary tear with feigned solemnity. "A promising career cut short."

Eager to be done with the topic altogether, she tucks the book under her thigh. "Alright, I'll give it a look-see."

"That's the spirit. Welp neighbor, have fun with your Greeks."

Though she mostly skims Darrell's book, it serves as a road map to who Butch was. Who Butch is. An amalgamation held together like stained glass. Radiant in the light, and opaque in the darker expanses.

Chapter Nineteen

S ummer's an arid dream compared to back in the valley. Just the same, hot days get folks griping at work and in the halls at home. *Home. What a weird thought. But what else would I call it? I lay my head there at night, pay rent and if someone's looking for me...well, they know where to find me...at home.*

Accustomed to Cicely and Nathan's lighthearted bickering, Janie feels at home crashing with them on checkout days. Nathan's brooding nature collapses under Cicely's genial prodding, giving way to fanciful tales of childhood adventures in the Boston Mountains. Which, much to Janie's surprise, are nowhere in or about Massachusetts. *Go figure.* Cicely on the other hand is bossy from dawn till lights out, a loving hell as Nathan calls it when she's picked at his last nerve. Back home's never far from Janie's mind, but on these evenings, she lets herself get swallowed up by this home.

Unlike bygone summers, this first one here in Albuquerque seems to come and go. In her old life, summer meant triumph. Respite until the next big step in the fall. There doesn't seem to be any steps in this new life. The start of summer is just another day, only warmer. For Nathan, it means carrying a jug of coolant in the toolbox on the back of his truck, and for Cicely it's a ceaseless battle with the swamp cooler. What with Butch drifting off mid-soliloquy, she's not entirely sure what summer is to him. As for Janie, it's too early to tell so she'll settle for basking in the comfortable days and mild nights for as long as they'll have her.

Dropping off her key with Darrell, Janie scans the common area. "Have you seen Butch?"

"Saw him leave with his laundry. You're a good influence, got him acting like an adult."

"Please, he's probably out of clean underwear." Janie smirks at the thought of making an impression on anyone, let alone Butch. "I gotta go or I'll be late."

"I dunno, either way keep it up." Darrell jokingly shouts from the desk as she clears the door, "Don't talk to strangers."

Janie's greeted by Cicely on the stoop. "What're you doing here?"

Stamping out a butt, she plucks it up and flicks it into the can. "Yer on the way, thought I'd save you the walk."

"Aww," Janie coos, walking to the truck.

"Just a few blocks greenhorn, it ain't flowers," Cicely remarks before hopping into the driver's seat.

Eyeing her predictably prickly companion, Janie tosses her bag to the floor of the cab.

While their shift is unremarkable, Cicely's unusually quiet and secludes herself in the back office with the door closed.

The apartment's dark when they get in. Cicely flicks on the television and disappears to change. Empty beer bottles litter the kitchen counter along with a day's worth of dishes in the sink. *Something's off.* This is not the kitchen of a woman who scrubs the grout beneath the drive thru window at the end of every shift.

Calling from the bedroom, Cicely asks, "Are you hungry? Wanna grab something?"

Looking up from her Roman aquifers article, Janie answers, "Nah, I ate that patty melt Vernon burned."

Brushing her hair in the doorway, Cicely grimaces. "I swear that man burns more food than he doesn't. Shit greenhorn, that thing was charred."

Shrugging, Janie searches for her place. "You wanna get something? Where's Nathan?"

"Workin'." Cracking a beer, she moves Janie's bag to get a peek at what she's reading. "You a history fan greenhorn?"

"Not really. You know, it's a trip to think they built all these complex public works in ancient Rome when I can't even get my chair to sit level."

"It's cause they were aliens, them an' the Egyptians." Cicely lifts and drops each magazine when they fail to interest her until she arrives at an issue unlike the others. "Who in the hell gave you this?"

"High Times?" Janie chuckles at Cicely's inner puritan surfacing. "They're Butch's, must've left it in there on accident."

"Accident my ass," Cicely grumbles. Slamming it down, she shoves them into Janie's bag. "You need to stay away from him. Has he offered you any illegal shit?"

Doggedly exhaling with exasperation, "No, gosh. He's my friend and so are you, so just stop it!"

Resting her head against the back of the couch, she rubs her eyes. "Shit, I'm sorry. Nathan's not working, he's staying at his friend's place."

Janie shifts to face Cicely. "What happened?"

"Ever since I got promoted, it's like he always thinks I'm throwin' it in his face." Still resting against the cushion, she looks over. "It's like he spends his day getting' talked down to by guys who can't frame half as well as him, but with no diploma he's kinda SOL."

Not buying it, Janie holds firm. "I dunno, kinda crappy if you ask me."

"You don't get it, it's macho bullshit but it's real to him. And I get so damn mad, then I get mean." Scooting forward, Cicely wrings her hands. "I should lettem' be. Ya know, my mama picked at my daddy till he hauled off and hit her once. I ain't saying he wasn't a real prick, but he spent a month in county while she sat around on her fat ass. I'm not ending up like that. All's I'm saying is I think I got a touch of that mean streak."

Not wanting to disagree partly due to fear, but mostly out of loyalty, Janie hugs her.

Cicely nods off, spent and a little drunk. Janie discreetly cleans the kitchen, returning the sink and surfaces to a standard worthy of boss lady's approval.

Taking the can wedged between her knees, Janie shakes Cicely to wake her. Groggily stretching for an assist, Janie helps her find her feet.

Cicely gives an off-axis wave walking into her bedroom. "C'mon greenhorn, you can share the bed. I hate sleepin' alone." Stopping at the door, she feels around for the switch. "I ain't gonna bite."

Prudently grabbing her pajamas, Janie throws the bolt on the front door. By the time she changes, Cicely's sound asleep. Hugging the mattress edge, sleep does not come easy. Holding her breath every time Cicely's weight shifts, Janie lies stretched in a rigid tangle.

Morning sneaks past her, Janie awakens to Cicely perched next to her. Lifting a cup from the nightstand, she holds it patiently. Waiting for Janie to push herself up onto her elbows, Cicely smirks. "You drink coffee?"

"Sure." Janie lies, hoping it tastes better than Lucas described. Sipping, it does. Knowing she should scoot back, she doesn't.

Surprisingly chipper for how hungover she feels, Cicely rests against Janie's legs before thinking better of it and shifting her weight back to her knees. "Thank you for cleaning up last night."

With a shrug, Janie swings her legs over the side. "So, what're you gonna do?"

Peering into her mug, Cicely's shoulders settle. "Give him another day to cool off. It'll be alright." Sipping, she gives Janie a cheeky smile. "What are you doin' with your day off?"

"Probably napping. You kinda snore, ya know that?"

Letting out a put upon sigh. "I think it's high time we make your room look like you live there." Waiting, and waiting until she can wait no longer, Cicely looks at Janie wide eyed. "Hello, high time? That was gold."

"Har!" Janie rolls her eyes, finishing her coffee in a gulp.

The day slips away in a whirl of boutiques and thrift shops, netting a blanket, lamp and pillow that doesn't feel like it's stuffed with old socks. Waiting out the afternoon heat, they lounge in the common area. Looking through photos from their trip to Uncle Cliff's amusement park, Cicely lingers on a photo of Nathan holding up his prize. "God, he makes that stupid face every time I take his picture."

Having too much fun to let her wallow, Janie flips the next photo in the stack. Spying Butch chatting with Darrell, he drifts their way. Leaning his lanky frame against the wall, "What're you two up to?"

Oblivious to Cicely's stink eye, Janie excitedly dishes. "Lookin' at photos from Uncle Cliff's. You been?"

"A while back." He glances at Cicely.

"We so have to go, we could all go." Janie nearly catches Cicely, but her wry grin is a step ahead.

Knowing the score, Butch smiles at his young friend. "Yeah, for sure. I gotta run, but I'll see ya around."

"See ya!" Looking back, Cicely's packed up the photos. "Something wrong?"

"I'm starvin' is all. Should probably get outta here."

"We could pick something up. You wanna stay here tonight, till Nathan comes home?" Janie asks without looking up, equal parts hopeful and fearful she will.

Full up on Greek food, they lay shoulder to shoulder beneath Janie's new blanket listening to news reports of a quake somewhere neither of them has ever been. Every channel, another tearful interview with survivors searching for their children among the rubble.

Janie's heart grows heavy wondering if her folks are waiting on her. "Back home, I have a little brother. Probably about the age of the kids they're looking for." Sniffling, "I bought him a slingshot in Old Town."

Plaintively, Cicely asks, "You gonna send it to him?"

"I don't think so." Rolling on her side she faces Cicely, choosing her words carefully. "Why'd you come here?"

Mirroring her, Cicely thinks on it. "Shit, I dunno. I knew what was waitin' for me back home, s'pose anything seemed better than that."

"Why here though?"

Looking past Janie to the window, the itch of proximity closes in. "This was just gonna be a pit stop to make some money, till it wasn't. Kinda got stuck here on my own, then I met Nathan."

Nearly nose to nose, Janie dares not move. The ruckus of heavy machinery grappling with debris and translated foreign news tinny like an AM radio falls into the background. Staring at what could be, Cicely takes a deep breath and reaches for her pack of reds. Sitting up, she pulls her sweater on. "I'm gonna go smoke."

Janie watches her leave and wonders if anything will ever make sense again the way Lydia did. The way stars just make sense to your eyes or how the ocean makes sense to your ears, like home should.

Cicely roosts upon the stoop in Janie's old sweatpants. Not long ago this was her stoop, and she was the one feeling her way around adulthood. Stealing drags from her second cig, she curses herself for breathing life into what shouldn't have amounted to more than a passing curiosity. She looks through Butch and his usual companion stepping around her, taking the steps in twos. Buzzing off adrenaline and nicotine, she stubs it out.

Janie keeps salutations to a minimum as Cicely rushes in disheveled and late for her shift. And when she assigns Janie to inventory the walk-in despite having done so herself last shift, Janie obliges without complaint. Working on next week's schedule, Cicely sends the new kid to work the drive thru as Butch ambles up to the counter.

Looking side to side, confusion blooms. "Where's Janie?"

"Busy. What can I get you?" Her fingers clip the counter in a rolling tap. Unbridled, her contempt rises with every second he dallies. She glimpses the walk-in, assured Janie's out of earshot. "You should know, she's underage. Don't go gettin' her mixed up in your bullshit."

Cockily grinning, Butch leans on the counter to abridge the distance. "I might say the same to you."

Taken aback, Cicely stands speechless and laid bare.

"You wanna chew the fat some more or are you gonna take my order?" Butch asks, masking his annoyance with a clever smile.

"Go on then."

"Number eight with swiss."

"We're out of swiss."

"With whatever then."

Calling back to the cook, "Can I get a number eight with whatever." Looking back at him flatly, "To go."

Nathan takes a few days coming home. Watching their romantic renaissance leaves Janie so bothered, she takes to spending time with Butch. In spite of his free-spirited ways, he's an immovable force with this GED business. Rejecting the exam schedule for reasons she refuses to divulge, they compromise with a pinky promise she'll take it once she turns eighteen.

A week before Halloween and one day till checkout, Janie wonders if her standing invitation with Cicely and Nathan still stands. It's been a few weeks since they've done more than bitch about work during the lulls in their shifts.

Janie watches Butch work his magic sifting through the damaged bins of Halloween odds and ends at Thrift Mart. "Butch?"

Holding up a crayon scrawled hockey mask, he beams with possibility until she gives it a thumbs down. Discarding his find with hesitation, he moves on. "Yes, youngin'?"

"Where do you go on checkout night? I mean like, you're always there." Starting to think he gave her the lousy bin, she grows disheartened one broken prop after another.

Without looking up from a bountiful heap of capes and wigs, "I stay in someone else's room." Draping an auburn wig across his arm to appraise its interaction with his pale skin tone, he looks to her. "Yeah?"

"Oh." Unable to fathom him as a redhead, Janie crinkles her nose and shakes her head.

Sighing in reluctant agreement, he tosses it back. "You wanna stay in my room? All I ask is you bring snacks."

Holding a tattered wedding dress against her frame, the thought of lacing up the corset makes her back ache. "I can do that. Maybe next time around."

Anticipating their unabating lovefest, Janie brings snacks and her GED books.

Digging through the snack stack but coming up empty, Cicely swipes some of Janie's chips. "You taking the GED?"

Laying the opened book on her lap, Janie replies. "Eventually, maybe a year or so."

"Think you'll still remember all this by then?"

"Yeah, I gotta lot to learn so I'm doing it in chunks."

Cicely tamps down a jealous urge to dissuade her. "Good for you."

"What's good for her?" Nathan asks, drifting in fresh from a shower and gnawing on a Slim Jim from the snack stack.

"She's studying for her GED big ears," Cicely laughs. "Drinks? Going once, twice."

"Damn, I should have you tutor me." Turning to the kitchen, "I'll take a beer, babe."

"Nothin' for me." Hesitating, Janie goes for it. "I could tutor you as I go. You can take the test at the library when you're ready."

"Yeah, I dunno. I can't pay you much."

"The homeschooler's gonna homeschool you?" Cicely quips, wishing she could take it back the moment it escapes her lips.

Rolling her eyes, Janie turns to Nathan. "You don't have to pay me. Why don't you just study with me, you're basically teaching yourself."

Janie shows Nathan what she's doing and which books she's read. Cicely puts on a face, but fumes. Knowing herself as well as she does, she heads to bed early lest she say something else she'll regret.

Laid off for the slow season, Nathan throws himself into studying. Janie watches as hope brings out a vestige of the boyish charm that probably left Cicely a gonner. *If you're into that sort of thing.* Slowly but surely tensions ebb with Cicely.

The chill before their thaw brings Janie closer to Butch. A bottomless pit of apt anecdotes, Butch has something to say about most everything. Not like some numbnuts know it all either. Rather, there's a gravitational pull to him. Everywhere they go he knows someone, and each of them knows a distinct flavor of him.

There's a cyclical quality to his erratic orbit in the time they're attached at the hip. Janie discounts the days he falls off the map. She keeps to herself on those days out of deference for who he is when he's with her.

Waking up seventeen isn't so different from going to bed sixteen. Left-over dreams swirl as Janie brushes her teeth, listening for anyone who might toggle the loose latch on the bathroom door. While the particulars evade her, a sentiment of vagabond sadness hangs heavily.

Treating herself to a mopey birthday breakfast, by afternoon Janie's grateful to have shaken the cheesed off mood trailing her all damn day. Nearing the end of their shift, Cicely asks Janie along on a break. "Green-horn you'll never believe it, but Nathan passed his test."

Intent not to siphon her excitement, Janie hugs her and keeps the date to herself. "I knew he would. That's great."

"I know!" Cicely exhales a lungful to the night sky, her tenor settling closer to pensive. "His cousin got him a spot working on eighteen wheelers at a truck stop. We're movin' to Fort Smith."

Stunned, Janie manages to muster a congratulatory smile. "Where?"

"Arkansas." Cicely tries to soften the blow. "Nathan's from there origi-nally, and he finally patched things up with his brother. It'll be a lot easier to make a go there. Ya know?" Flicking the ash with her thumb, she takes another drag. "You don't know yet, but you will greenhorn."

"I get it. I'm happy for you guys." Janie summons her most convincing smile and asks, "So, when are you leavin'?"

"Next week. Gave Reggie my notice today." Smiling ear to ear, Cicely raps her feet on the bench. "Hey, you wanna take over our apartment? We pay cash. You could always get a roommate."

"Nah, my place is kinda starting to feel like home."

Cicely emphatically corrects her. "Don't say that, ever. I may not have much to draw on, but I can sure as shit tell you that's not what home is."

Somewhere between packing, working off shifts and more packing, Janie and Cicely miss each other through moving day. Janie chalks it up to Cicely not being one for goodbyes. Perched on the stoop, Janie draws shapes in the can of sand with an old matchstick. Butch nudges her to knock it off, waving away weightless fragments of stirred up ash. Sighing at his theatrics, she jams the matchstick into the sand. Brushing her hands off, she sniffs the clingy scent and grimaces. "I'm hungry, you wanna eat?"

Shrugging, Butch nods. Giving Janie another nudge, he points to Nathan's tired pickup.

Hauling herself off the stoop, Janie tempers the loss welling up with a squinty grin. "Didn't expect to see you."

Leaning against the door, Cicely takes a drag without taking her eyes off Janie. Punctuating her exhale with a smile, she puts her arms out. "You know I wasn't leavin' without saying goodbye." Hugging Janie tightly, she holds on until she knows she won't cry.

Janie leans down to razz Nathan. "This thing gonna make it?"

Laughing, albeit a little concerned, Nathan pats the dash. "She's always made it home."

Janie gives Cicely a skeptical smile, tucking her hands in her pockets. "You should hit the road. I'll see ya."

"Hold up." Cicely catches Janie before she gets to the stoop. "I meant what I said, don't get lost here. One day at a time, it'll happen. At some point ya gotta start swimmin' greenhorn." She kisses Janie's forehead and turns back to the truck.

Looking to Butch, Janie cannot bear to watch them leave. Cresting the stoop, she hears Nathan in the distance. "Thank you, for everything."

Not meaning to, she watches them disappear into the string of cars bound for the 40.

Janie keeps to herself, letting Cicely's advice marinate, emerging fixed on being the one driving off into the hazy midday sun by this time next year.

Holidays are the hostel's bread and butter, new faces ad infinitum. Which is great if you're looking for a fix of fresh blood. Not so grand if you're trying to lie low. Entertaining herself with the comings and goings, Janie saddles up to the reception desk waxing philosophic with Darrell, readily trading salt and vinegar chips for pearls.

In strolls Butch and Alban. "What's good neighbors?" Glassy eyed, he catches sight of Janie's chips and plunges his hand into the bag. "Ooh chips, may I?" Contorting his face, he drops his next bite's worth back into the bag. "Traitors!"

Undeterred by returned chips, Janie grins between bites. "More for us."

Wiping his hands free of crumbs, he pushes off the counter. "This is how you're bringing in the New Year?"

Janie and Darrell nod in unison. Darrell gets a little squinty at the prospect of Butch stealing his companion for the evening.

Chapter Twenty

After four months of grinding out every shift she can lay her hands upon, Janie feels herself drifting and grabs on to what next. Looking to offload the night shift, Reggie offers her shift manager. She turns it down but puts a bug in his ear for Vernon. While he's terrible on the grill, turns out he has a talent for managing people. Bone tired from working a double, Janie wearily counts her till, mere minutes from being bathed in the brisk evening air that's carried on from winter into spring.

Flashing lights reflecting off catty cornered storefronts signal something dire awaits. Passersby and passers-through gather around the stoop, congesting the narrow path as a paramedic motions for a pair of firemen to follow. Gossiping amongst themselves, onlookers loiter with hopes of witnessing the carnage from a safe distance.

Janie pushes past, she waves to Shorty at the front desk, mouthing "What happened?" All he manages is "Butch" before the officers taking his statement follow his gaze. Stone-faced, Janie holds steady till they lose interest. Dashing up the stairs, she prepares for the worst.

The scene is far more tranquil than one might expect given the fanfare downstairs. Standing outside his room, Butch speaks to a paramedic. Hugging his side, Janie keeps her arm around him. "Are you okay? What happened?"

"I'm still standin'." A thud from the next room draws their attention. "You might not want to see this. How bout I come see ya in a couple minutes."

"See what?" Janie pulls her arm free. "Are they in Alban's room? I'm stayin'."

Another metallic thud fills the corridor, followed by wheels negotiating the old plank floors. A paramedic backs out of the room, guiding a gurney.

Wait, not a paramedic. A coroner. A coroner pulling a gurney with a body bag poking out from beneath an EMT blanket. The little voice which has largely fallen silent this past year, awakens with a start. *Holy shit! is it too late to go to our room? Oh my god they bumped it into the door.* Trying to breathe, Janie clenches her jaw to keep her inner panic from escaping outward. Butch puts his arm around her, as much for his comfort as hers.

Staring straight ahead, he wheels past them to the stair ledge where firemen wait staggered a few steps down to assist. Without a word, Butch and Janie fall into the procession.

Time leaps forward while they're upstairs. The officers and paramedics have gone. All but two of the firemen wait in the truck. Butch and Janie watch them load the van, holding their breath as the doors close. The street is once again as ordinary as it was a few hours ago.

"Bone pickers," Butch hisses under his breath to the remaining rubberneckers, who've now turned their attention to Janie and him, clucking hushed suppositions that they must be involved somehow. All the while wearing looks of tepid sympathy.

Rare is the occasion to draw upon Cicely's repertoire. Janie grumbles loudly, wearing her mother's furrowed brow. "Sad sacks of..." Putting his hand on her shoulder, Butch gives a little shake of the head.

Exhaling heartily at the lackluster sendoff he's given his friend, "Let's get out of here. You hungry?"

Though Janie couldn't be farther from hungry, it's plain he needs to unburden himself in a place with smaller ears and fewer pairs of gawking eyes. "Yeah, I'm always hungry. Haven't you noticed?"

Her stomach in knots, Janie feels like she's ordered a whole corner of Alexi's menu. "What happened?" Janie asks, minding the root-wrecked sidewalks.

"Nothing really worth all the lights and badges. I went to get Alban, hadn't heard from him all day." Handing his takeout to Janie, he lights up. "There he was on the floor, lying against the bed with a fucking needle in his arm."

Janie rubs his back, leaning into his side. "We don't have to talk about it."

Taking a long drag, he breathes out a fog against the damp evening air. "That was it, typical OD I guess. He got some bad shit or hit it too hard. Anyway, I had Shorty call the cops, and that's all she wrote."

"I'm sorry Butch. Does he have anyone here in town?"

"Nah, his folks are in Italy or Germany, somewhere. I think Shorty gave them a copy of his emergency contact. There's a girl, but she'd be more interested in his stash than where to send flowers." Finishing his smoke before casting it astray, he speaks mostly to himself. "Man, if I hadn't stayed in the hall shit could've gone south. Real fucking south."

Walking past reception, something nags at Janie. *Shit, it's checkout night.* Sheepishly handing her key to Shorty, he pushes it back. "Far as I'm concerned, I ain't seen ya. Get some rest kid."

Standing in the hall, they stare at Alban's open door. Exasperated, Butch closes the door decrying Shorty's obliviousness. "You wanna stay in my room tonight? Keep me company and eat some of this food that better be delectable since we damn near walked across town for it."

Telling herself only because it's for him, Janie obliges.

Butch's room looks ransacked. Nervously tidying up, he shoves complementary heaps together and crams them into the armoire. He folds out an old metal card table to dine on. Just as they're about to dig in, he leaps to his feet as though he's forgotten the most important part.

"Don't mind my shitty mix tape, I don't have a turntable so que sera." He races the white noise of the tape leader back to his spot, frenetic strumming and bright drums soar into a sound Janie was just getting into back home with Lucas.

Excited to recognize some of his music, she nearly raises her hand. "Oh I know them. New Order, right?"

Smiling, Butch wavers his hand. "Earlier."

"Earlier?" Janie asks, not convinced she's wrong.

Closing his eyes, he sings along inaudibly with the first verse. Surfacing, he savors a bite or two through the chorus. "They were called Joy Division when they released this song." Off he drifts with the song again.

"They just up and changed their name?" Janie asks between nibbles.

"Not exactly. As I remember it, a member of the band passed so they couldn't exist as they were without him. They honored an oath made before the fame and other shit." Reflecting, he puts his fork down. "Man, I can't think of a better example of brotherhood than that."

A cascade of Smiths, Echo & the Bunnymen and Siouxsie and the Banshees fortify Janie's aural education. They speak little as they listen, grateful for sound absent sirens, hard wheels on old floors and hushed tongue wagging.

His hands no longer occupied with the task of eating, Butch busies himself cleaning. Janie takes over, shooing him, "I got it."

Picking her blanket off the floor, he tosses it onto the bed. "I'll take the floor."

Sinking into bed, Janie listens to Butch expound the deeper meanings, influences and experiences, without whose occurrences, the songs in their present form would have never been possible. Nodding off, a memory of listening to the radio with Lucas in his dad's truck is punctuated by the click of the tape player and subsequent silence.

Butch lays awake, staring at the ceiling and picking mercilessly at his tattered nails while Janie pretends to sleep. The way Butch described Alban having no one in his life to miss him except Butch and his folks, whom he hadn't seen in God knows how long, nags at her. Is this the future she's sowing for herself? Being one misadventure away from being forgotten.

Putting his arms up, Butch swings his body into a crunch formation. "You awake?"

Janie responds without opening her eyes. "Yeah."

"I can't take this anymore, let's go walk off this bad juju." He rocks forward to his feet. Throwing on a sweatshirt, Butch feels around for his shoes.

"Now? Alright." Janie pulls her clothes on over her PJs.

Walking with purpose, he checks over his shoulder here and there to make sure she's keeping up. A cold spring night and the consequences of a marathon shift amplify the stiffness in her lower back.

"Where we goin'?"

"You'll see." Butch points to a dingy gas station ahead, a beacon in an abyss of dark storefronts. "But first, coffee."

"There?" Janie asks, crinkling her nose.

Butch nods, hooking his arm in hers as they cross the parking lot. Deserted, a lone drowsy clerk watches *Tales from the Darkside* reruns on a small portable TV. They pass an open door, exposing the vast nothingness of the dark garage. The smell of old gas and gear oil is omnipresent. Wind whistles through a busted glass pane in the bay door, setting some piece of trim lost to the ages aflutter. A shriek from the TV startles them, Janie's heart stomps to the beat for a moment before falling back into time. The clerk is friendly enough for the hour, switching between the show and the closed-circuit monitor watching them leave.

Cautiously sipping the underrated french roast, they arrive at their destination. Standing before locked wrought-iron gates, Janie waits for an explanation. He gives her a sly smile, setting her coffee with his own atop the brick wall framing the gate. With a good heave ho, he pulls himself up. Straddling it, he extends his hands. Shaking her head, he persists with grabby lobster claw motions. Relenting, Janie grapples the wall with his assistance.

"Did I mention I hate cemeteries?" Janie whispers, stepping over an overgrown grave marker.

Scoffing, Butch pauses. "Why are you whispering? They're all sleeping the big sleep." Rummaging through his pockets, he pulls out a worn soft pack. "There's not a more peaceful place in all the land. I do all my thinking here."

Looking around with eyes open, Janie sees what Butch sees. "You know, I can kinda see it. So, where's your thinkin' spot?"

"See that heap of marble?" He points to just beyond the bend in the small single lane road. "There's a guy buried just to the left up there, poor bastard shares a name with my asshole uncle. I like to sit on his grave, makes me feel like I won since ya know, I'm still alive an all."

Tracing the grave's edge with the toe of her shoe, Janie finds the thin boundary and squeezes in, so as to not impose. The dampness of the earth below goes straight to the bone. Despite knowing she'll be walking home with a damp ass, there's comfort in knowing Butch will too. Some things are more tolerable when you don't have to endure them alone.

Tipping the soft pack, a malnourished joint falls free into his palm. Unimpressed, he gives the soft pack a gentle tap, the little guy is the sum of it. "Wanna hit?"

Putting her arm out, Janie nods. "Sure."

Holding back, Butch processes the shifting paradigm. "Really?"

Frowning, Janie asks, "Are you offering or not?"

Nodding, he hands it over. Taking a puff before he can offer guidance, he mentors her through the next one. Fingertips singed, he drops it in the grass and reclines onto his elbows. "That last bit's for you uncle Gary."

Janie does the same till she feels her sleeve wicking up all the dew. Light and untroubled, she closes her eyes and listens to the breeze flowing through the leaves in the darkness above.

Conversation's sparse walking home. Butch glances at her from time to time, chasing away his guilt. He almost laughs aloud at the little inextricable version of his mother within, badgering him. Always pushing him to be his best self, always disappointed.

Sleepovers ease into a weekly ritual. Janie doesn't mind, the company's uncomplicated and nice. Tiptoeing out of Butch's room in the wee hours for an opening shift, a long timer gawks. His imaginings fail to take hold in the minds of Darrell or anyone else for that matter. Eventually, his focus shifts to the perpetually intoxicated yet exuberant Kiwi who's moved into Alban's room.

Her first day off in twelve days, Janie picks up coffee and donuts. Hoping today won't be an off the map day, she catches Butch rounding the corner. Spilling hotter than hell coffee across the tops of her hands, her sleepy nerves lag. "Shit that's hot!" Shaking off what she can, she wipes the rest on her pants. "Where are you going?"

Maintaining his cadence, he mumbles, "Had some stuff to do. Why don't I meet you back in a bit?"

"What, you got a breakfast date or somethin'?"

Butch grabs the bag to peek inside, savoring a bite of an old fashioned. "I have to tie up some loose ends, just boring stuff."

Disappointed, Janie stops. "You usually visit your friends over by the plaza today. I thought we could hang out. It's fine, I'll catch you later." Trying not to pout, she turns to head back.

Exhaling loudly to the sky, Butch calls back without turning around. "Okay, just come on. You're gonna be bored though."

With stores barely opening in the plaza, Janie waits in the courtyard while Butch sees a friend in one of the old offices behind the bar. Normally, she browses while Butch shoots the shit, today is different. By lunch, Janie's feet ache from trekking all over town and she begins to wonder if Butch is planning to move away too. *Oh God, not another goodbye.*

Lunching at a small Cantonese place Butch reveres as deeply as she adores Alexi's, Janie's convinced he's chosen his favorite place to break the news. *Was he going to sneak outta town? What kind of shit is that?*

Sipping her tea, she grows impatient as he natters on about the second run theater down the way. "Are you leavin'?"

"Leaving? No, why?"

"Then why are we walking all over God's green earth visiting everyone you know, unless you're saying your goodbyes."

"Jesus you're adorable. They're not my friend friends, they're business friends."

"Business friends? I thought you didn't have a job." Pouring more tea, she looks at him willfully obtuse.

"Janie, where did you come from? Okay, listen." He smiles graciously as the waiter places their plates in front of them. "I'm their dealer. Was their dealer. Whatever, I'm closing shop."

Desperately trying not to make the judgy face, Janie nods. "Yeah, that makes a lot of sense now." Changing gears, she lifts her beef chow fun for a long sniff. "Wow, this looks good. Let's eat." She dives into her food, leaving no room for eye contact or conversation.

Butch makes a couple more stops on the way. Janie keeps her distance, feigning fatigue. Wishing he'd sent her home, he sequesters himself, dedicating the afternoon to the good work of drowning it all out.

Sadder than she might've been if he were leaving, Janie's transported back to her diner days thinking she had the whole thing wired only to discover she knew nothing.

After an early shift, Janie spends the afternoon in her pajamas grumbling at trashy talk show guests. Gnawing on stale jerky, she resents the hosts placating them much the way she resents Butch for humoring her illusions of him. Her pride smarts imagining Alban and him laughing at her going on about Butch's uncanny way of making friends. Indignation is laborious. Perhaps a nap to steal away reserves for future rancor.

A solid knock wakes Janie from a deep sleep. Eyes adjusting to the darkness, she rubs the sleep away.

Butch holds up a familiar thank you bag, the smell of gyro awakens her stomach. "Peace?" He picks through his food. "Just so you know, Alban didn't get his stuff from me. I'm a weed man, nothing more."

Relieved and feeling foolish, Janie pushes her hair back, twisting it into a messy ponytail. "I'm sorry. I had no right judging you. You don't need to explain yourself, really."

Looking at her, seeing her perhaps for the first time as an adult, Butch feels closer to Janie than he has anyone in some time.

Uncharacteristically candid, Janie digs deeper. "So why are you done if you didn't have anything to do with Alban?"

Searching for the right words, Butch sips his beer. "Well, it's like this. I don't sell to anyone who has a drug problem, only to hobbyists. Alban had one hell of an itch to scratch, so I only sold to him once."

"But he always looked trashed," Janie prods.

"He was, that was his business though. Free will man. I don't judge and I don't help them dig in. Do no harm, ya know." For once, Butch cares if he's understood. "Problem is, he went over my head when I cut him off. Not that weed was ever really the thorn. My warnings went unheard, and I can't do business with someone that agnostic about their clientele. So fuck it, I'm quitting." Looking away, he laughs nervously. "Sounds like some bullshit, right?"

"No way. You're living your credo."

"Credo, I like that."

Overfull, Janie lies back on the floor. "Don't you need the money?"

"Been broke before, it's alright. I get disability every month so I can get by on the cheap." He swigs the last of his beer. "I could use a smoke tho, wanna keep me company?"

Raising her arm for a lift, Janie laughs. "Sure, but you gotta help me up. God, I'm gonna fit into Yaya's dresses by 18 if I keep eating like this."

The weeks to come reap an unexpected toll on Butch. Janie sets aside extra shift savings as a Butch adjustment fund. Cognizant of his unshakable pride, she looks for ways to take up the slack. Miles ahead as always, he never commits to plans he cannot manage. The cost for which he couldn't prepare is the loss of standing with those whom he thought their relationships transcended commerce. Faces once alight at his approach, now haven't time for more than thin platitudes.

While months later he'll claim to have taken the falling of his star without batting an eye, Janie knows otherwise. She knows it in the days he barely eats a bite, only leaving his room to smoke. Further, she knows the days his hobby falters into the murky depths approaching a problem. Having spent the better part of a decade walking a razor's edge between hobby and habit, Butch knows the linchpin to this fickle equilibrium lies in never allowing murky days to become sequential.

These are the days Janie offers small kindnesses to remind him of who he is now, to remind him he's needed. Never one to miss a shift, she'll miss a few in her efforts to never let a day become a week. When food and libations fail, she resorts to good old fashioned pestering. She imagines it was some good old fashioned pestering on Jonah's part that drove Nineveh to repent. Nagging the whale to the point of hurling was just a warm up.

By the time summer leans hard, life finds balance. Butch rallies, his frequent evening absences pique Janie's curiosity. Particularly curious given that the usual suspects around the hostel are all accounted for. Resisting the urge to pry, Janie takes a counter path into GED prep as the countdown toward government sanctioned adulthood gains steam.

When their paths don't cross, Butch drops in at closing to walk her home and catch up over whatever's left under the heat lamp. Occasionally sharing a smoke, for Janie it's more an act of commiseration. Convinced she's mastered the art of the shallow inhale, Butch pretends not to notice her falling asleep.

Too hot to sleep, they lounge on uncle Gary's place. His prime hilltop real estate boasts a view and the odd passing breeze. Occasionally, an unnervingly chilly breeze bristles their arm hair. Janie grabs a flower or two from newer graves with enough to share, her way of making amends for the wear and tear on his turf.

Butch twists his watch to check the time, an ironically irksome tick grinding Janie's gears. Enamored with the timepiece since she first laid eyes on it, Janie begins using it to gauge how willowy a figure he's amounting to.

"Where you been?" Playing it cool be damned.

Taking a drag, he taps the ash loose into the grass. "I thought you'd be happy to have me out of your hair some."

Making a face, Janie waits for her answer.

"Ran into a couple friends from when I first got here. I'll introduce you some time."

Nodding as though she's not of one mind or another about it, "Are we back in business Dr. Feelgood?"

"Nah, nothing like that. I meant that shit about doing no harm." Picking through the bag for scraps, he pitches the crumpled bag at Janie. "Score!"

Janie picks at tattered blades of grass. "Think I'm gonna take the GED this fall. You wanna be my study buddy?"

"You're turning eighteen, right? When's your birthday?" he asks without really looking at her.

Janie stiffens, wishing she were long past the days of worrying someone might ask about her life before here. "Heh, yeah I'll be eighteen."

"Are you really not going to tell me your birthday?" Seeing fear in her eyes for only the second time since he's known her, Butch eases up. "Ya know, none of my business. It's okay."

"November 8th, my birthday's November 8th." Janie looks down, illogically concerned she's given away a state secret.

Butch grins, "I'm gonna write that in my diary."

Janie reaches for a hit. "Sorry. Kinda got used to living like a spy. Since we're sharing and all, what's your real name?"

"Butch is my real name," he replies, scuffing his heels along the grass.

"Your given name is Butch? Were you raised in the O.K. Corral?"

Granting as close to a real answer as he's willing to part with, Butch replies, "I went in the Army a scrawny little dude with a deep voice, they christened me Butch. Came out of basic a different person, so I guess you could say yeah, it's my given name."

Like a loose thread on an old hem, Janie can't help but pull a little. "Fair enough. How long were you in the army?"

"Two years, signed up for four but shit happens." Not wanting to dip his toes any further into the past, he pivots. "What about you? Your folks lookin' for you?"

"Dunno, but in a few months won't matter much anyway." Janie pushes herself to her feet, content to cut the journey down memory lane short.

Chapter Twenty One

Monsoon season's a dud, save for two good for nothing haboobs that kick up the dirt and leave a pitiful scattering of debris. Memories of sweltering summers in the valley remain fixed in Janie's mind, always keeping her from joining the bellyaching about the heat. However, bleating on about her stuffy room's another matter altogether. There's nothing like the heat of an old brick wall baking in the sun.

A month left in her arsenal, Mother Nature teaches Janie not to count her second summer in Albuquerque dull and done till she says so. What begins as a summer storm progresses to torrential rainfall, flooding streets and knocking out power for blocks at a time. Reggie gets word to shut the place down till they clear the underpass. Darrell puts out a box of tea lights for everyone coming home to darkened halls and pitch-black rooms.

A prep book worth less than the paper it's printed on wedged in the window, Janie tries to cool her humid room. Resting on the sill, she watches massive drops pelt the alleyway. Closing her eyes, she breathes in the smell of the rain and yearns for respite carried on gusts of cool air careening through the narrow passage. Letting herself drift, she can almost hear the chains settle as their swings came to a halt. *She must be eighteen by now. Coulda sworn she said her birthday was in the summer or was it fall.* Janie suspects Lydia's eighteen will be quite different from her own. For a fleeting second, she thinks on heading back west. Thinking again, she'd rather be here tethered to the limerence that keeps her than chance losing hope. Tearing another page from her ledger, Janie moves the tea light closer.

Dear Lydia,
As I write this, the rain is pouring down like it did three years
ago when I had given up on seeing you again. Then there you
were. I wish you were here now. Do you think God gives us
chances like that more than once? I like to think so, but there's
so much risk in finding out.
I'll be 18 in a couple months. Feels like I've been waiting forever,
and now that it's almost here I still don't know what to do.
You're probably picking out colleges and planning your life.
With Cicely gone, I'm just trying not to think about losing
Butch too. Don't know if I told you about him, but he's really
something. Kind of a prism.
Sometimes I think of how much living I've done since I've been
here. Then I remember it's other people who have been living
and sometimes losing, and it's me who's watching.
I'm sweating all over your letter, guess that's as good a reason
as any to end it here.
Always,
Janie

A familiar knock lessens the stirring fear of hearing it while sitting in a dim room, on a dark floor, during a thunderstorm punctuated by sporadic cracks of lightning. Janie hears Butch speaking to someone, he sees her and returns from the stairs. A smaller silhouette descends, too far out to define. Butch's soaked, and from the looks of it high.

"Hey neighbor."

"Hey yourself," Janie responds, glancing back to the stairs to watch for his friend.

"You mind a sleepover? I'm afraid of waking up poached in my room."

A small radio picked up at the Salvation Army plays on low, occasionally threatening to jump stations. They hardly notice against the rain battering the windowpane. Old bottles Butch cut down cradle tea lights to add some desperately needed luminance.

Stretching his lanky frame along the floor, Butch uses his sweatshirt as a pillow. Riding out the last of his buzz, he watches Janie bounce between reading her comic by candlelight and plopping down to make sure he's alright. He was about her age when he asked his folks for permission to enlist, anything to get out from under his brother's shadow. And while he may not know what or whom she's running from, he does know anything that spooks you enough to go against your base instinct of staying with the herd has already gotten under your skin enough to hitch a ride.

"You ever think about going home?" he asks, trailing his fingers in shapes along the ratty patched planks.

"Nope." She finishes the page, dutifully uninterested. "You?"

Sighing, he pushes his messy sun-streaked mane back. "It crosses my mind from time to time."

Dog earing her page, Janie closes the book. "Yeah. What's stopping you?"

Lighting up, Butch moves to the window obediently. "I dunno. This was just meant to be a timeout. Somehow here I am four years later."

"Why here?" Janie asks.

He shrugs, raising his eyebrow ever so slightly as he takes a drag. "Followed a girl till she followed someone else."

Intrigued, Janie drags her chair closer. "Where's she now?"

"Last I heard back home, purged of me and this place."

"You still love her?"

Picking at a piece of tobacco, Butch flicks it out the window. "Sometimes. Sometimes I hate her. It's a mess."

Reflecting on her own messes, Janie lets him say his piece.

"Enough of my tragic tale." Emboldened by a weakened filter, he studies her. "What about you? Why here? Some girl leave you behind?"

Janie lifts her head. "I guess I kinda left her behind. I was aiming for away, and this is definitely away." Taking a drag off his cig, she grimaces. "You think she was the one? The girl back home."

He shakes his head and hands her a warm soda. "I dunno about the one. I don't think everyone gets a one, but she was close enough."

"Let's hear it. How'd you meet?"

Resting his head against the wall, he ponders the toll of stirring what's settled. "Met her at an NA meeting, I was tagging along with my brother. Next thing I knew, they were inside asking God to grant them wisdom and we were making out on the smokers' bench out back."

"How romantic."

"I guess you had to be there. It was us against the world kinda stuff. We were inseparable till I enlisted."

"She waited?"

"Kinda, she did her thing but was there when I got home. We lived together, which caused a bunch of shit with my family. So, I jumped when she wanted to move here."

Hanging on every word, Janie barely notices the storm anymore. "What happened?"

"We got pretty lost here, before we left too I guess. Anyway, she got bored with this life and I wasn't done yet. So, she left with someone in our group who was." Pained, he scratches at the damp hair clinging to his neck. "I used to get lost a lot more than I do now."

"Her loss, but there's still time."

Nodding, Butch smiles. "You've got lots of time. Don't swallow that One daydream."

Janie laughs, wishing she agreed. She grabs her copy of *Hellraiser*, reading her favorite parts aloud to cheer him up. Somewhere around midnight, the rain slows and the air cools enough to sleep. Errant lightning bolts menace the darkness, whipping Janie from one fragmented dream to another. Daybreak brings blue skies, marking an end to their long inclement weekend. And after last night, an end to the line between before and here.

Shuffling in her PJs, Janie returns to the room in a huff. Slumping down on her bed, the springs don't put up much fight. Shifting to avoid being pulled into the crater, Butch longs for the gloominess of yesterday to soothe his squinty eyes.

"Backup went out at work, gotta get all the spoiled stuff out before provisions comes round noon." Sniffing and patting her cheeks, Janie wills herself to her feet. "Gonna be a shit day. You'll be around later?"

Unable to fathom why he's awake, Butch massages his throbbing temples. "Yeah, I'll be around."

October's a revolving door at work, which nudges Janie to keep her eyes on what next. Watching Reggie work double after double, and seeing Vernon burn out one punk kid at a time, she knows her end there is nigh. For now, Halloween spurs her on. She and Butch have planned their night of tramping around the neighborhood. A night culminating in a soiree at the cemetery, complete with a feast of Mighty Burger complemented by a fortified fruit varietal. Butch has taken costume design upon himself while Janie's charged with catering the affair.

Praying the new kid shows up, Janie anxiously collects a few botched orders maturing under the heat lamp. They may or may not also be Butch's favorites. Vernon looks the other way, grateful for her help after Labor Day.

Heeding a tip from a guy on the dayshift, Janie veers a few blocks out of her way for a liquor store that doesn't card so long as you don't expect change. Her mission fulfilled, she nearly skips home cheering on excited kids prowling for candy or mischief. After a week of Butch bragging about his haul from the thrift store, the hype is riding high.

Janie declares her arrival, bursting through the door with a greasy bag in one hand and brown bagging it in the other. "Where's my costume good sir? I come bearing gifts!"

Giggling, Butch claps at her grand entrance. Not one to pregame, a giggling Butch is an indication something went sideways. Setting the bags down, her vision of feasting on fried vittles and drowning in Boons is circling the drain. Seeing his new friend perched like a sentinel, Janie's patience wanes in awaiting an introduction.

On the cusp of chortling, Butch unfurls his hand towards his guest in one fell swoop. "Where are my manners? Janie, meet Reyna. Reyna enjoys curiously strong herb and practical footwear."

Rolling her eyes, Reyna gives Janie a brisk smile.

A fragile truce between amusement and annoyance teeters as Janie struggles to discern whether they're laughing at some unseeable thing or at her caught in the weeds. With no frame of reference, Janie gleans nothing from Reyna's expression. *Is she high too? Shit.* Apprehension bleeds into petulance. If she cannot read her, she'll excise her from the conversation. Nudging Butch's foot, "Are we doing this?"

"Yes, ma'am!" Lighting up, he takes a hit before handing it to Reyna. "But not till you take a little puff. It'll help relax your shoulders."

Janie ignores Reyna passing the joint, casually taking it after a beat. She resolves to stake a claim, to show this interloper she can hang. Taking a long drag, a wall of *what the fuck* pummels her. This is not standard issue Butch stash. Keenly aware she's made a face, Janie commits to another as Butch pinches it away like a firecracker with a spent fuse. "Easy tiger."

Pulling a box from the armoire, it's full of clothes with a dollar store bag tossed on top. "Reyna bought me out, so I had a little extra to throw at it."

Janie swivels to glare at Reyna then back to Butch's big reveal. "Go on, let's see."

Holding a worn out black parade overcoat, he motions for her to try it on. "Might be a little big."

Janie slides into the coat, the satin lining is cool against her skin. Probably two sizes too big, she's unbothered straightening the woolen cadet collar and fastening the tarnished brass buttons. She marvels at how smooth the buttons are against her fingers. Lifting her arms as though she might take flight, she faces Butch to edge Reyna out of her line of sight. "Well?"

Her epaulettes evened out, Butch cuffs the sleeves and grants his approval. He adjusts the shawl collar on his mustard-plaid Pendleton coat. One last tug of the wrists and they fall into place as though it were tailored to him. Giving them a little twirl, Butch strikes a pose. "What do ya think?"

Pretending to gag, Janie smiles wide. "Gaugeous dahling." *Stop giggling, no one said anything funny. Pull yourself together.*

Reyna nods. "Yeah, you look good."

"Thank you ladies, thank you." Lighting up, he smirks at Reyna while speaking to Janie. "Reyna's coming with this evening."

Janie says nothing. Feeling a tad floaty, there's an air of levity suddenly afoot. Initially unaware, she notices her arms have begun a subtle flapping motion within her roomy sleeves. She watches them in bewildered amusement.

Cigarette grafted to the corner of his mouth, Butch takes to the armoire determined. He grabs a faded black car coat and tosses it to Reyna. "Best I can do sister. You'll have to settle for gothic dyke."

Taking off her coat, she pauses long enough to flip him off. "Asshole."

Bear hugging Reyna, Butch kisses her cheek. "You know I love you."

Janie whips her head around. Had she heard what she heard or imagined it? Staring back expectantly, Reyna and Butch watch Janie parse her environment. Rankled at Reyna's delight, Janie shakes it off.

Butch hands off Janie's mask first, a brittle plague doctor beak. "Got this at that junk store on Broadway. Careful, it's old as shit."

Following a brief battle, Janie gets the band over her head. She can hear her breath bouncing off the mask. She doesn't notice them watching until Butch snickers a little. "What?"

Exchanging a knowing glance with Reyna, he tries not to laugh. "Nothing, you kinda got a Mr. Roboto thing going on. So, you like it?"

Self-consciously pushing the mask up, "Yeah, it's great. Where's yours?"

His is an opera mask covered in black inked petroglyphs, with poorly glued fake owl feathers crowning the corners. His prominent bone structure lends an eeriness to the look. "Good, yeah?"

Delivering a little comeuppance, Reyna cocks her head with a cheeky grin. "What are you again?"

Taking her mask from the dollar bag, he tosses it over with a huff. "I'm a skin walker. You know a shapeshifter? Man to animal, that sort of thing."

Giving an unimpressed ahhh, Reyna appraises her crappy printed bunny mask. "Looks like one of the ears snagged on the line." Putting it on, Reyna turns to Butch. "Really?"

Creeped out, Janie stares wide eyed. "Shit. She wins."

Stepping off the stoop, they're underway. The night's grown colder since Janie left work. Fighting her heavy cuff, she gives up trying to see her watch in favor of keeping up. Light on her feet, the walls pull at her. Trick-or-treaters are scarce to none. Janie imagines them all home in bed while their parents loot their candy in the next room.

Crumbs of time drifting away, Janie looks behind them to orient herself. A rent-a-cop is parked by their usual entrance, Butch hooks Janie's arm to keep her moving. Reyna strolls a few paces behind with a cig in one hand and her disguise in the other. Spying the hedges, Butch stops at a utility box. "Here."

Giggling their way over the wall, they set off up the hill and settle by a large fountain beyond the mausoleum. A tree line obscures them from the entrance as they power through tepid burgers and soggy fries, washing it down with lukewarm Strawberry Hill.

Iffy on her place in their novel trio, Janie lingers on the periphery listening to tales of exploits which predate her. Savoring the covert vantage point her mask affords, she studies the way Butch regards Reyna. The way his teasing never rises to the level it does with Reyna. Only a few feet away, Janie feels invisible. There's a familiar sadness in Butch's eyes, the thought of this signaling a stretch of murky days is sobering.

Janie swirls the remnants in her cup before dumping the last drops in the grass. Scooting over next to her, Butch speaks quietly. Asking of her day until assured she's having a good time. Killing off the bottle and a joint, Butch banters back and forth between them.

Her high compounded by a sugar rush, Janie's attention strays from their conversation. Instead of shrinking away when she catches Reyna looking over, she stares back free of the uneasiness plaguing her earlier. Like a graceless Selina Kyle, less the surplus desirability of course, she takes in the scene.

Reyna's unlike anyone she's known back home or here. Her initial impression of detached rudeness expands to a more neutral stance of unaffected confidence. She exudes a sense of self from her cropped dark hair pushed back without fussing to her wardrobe bearing a striking resemblance to the cool boys in her youth group.

Butch takes to singing along with the radio, pulling Janie into his sway. Reyna swats his attempts to bring her in. Losing time, Janie misses him wandering off in a stupor having declared his intent to seek out wandering spirits. Strings of heartfelt lyrics catch the wind here and there.

Feeling someone sit next to her, Janie turns to see Reyna. She wonders if she floated over and asks as much before cracking up. Laughing, Reyna gently lifts Janie's mask. "I think you could use some air."

"Think Butch found his spirits? Do you see him?" Janie asks, surveying the darkness.

"Only spirits he's going to find are the ones he pukes up. Dude was lookin' green."

Realizing how close they are, Janie trails off more from nerves than drunkenness. Without a second thought, Janie leans over and kisses her. Reyna kisses her back, caressing her neck. Janie's head tilted, the axis of the earth shifts.

Goddamn this ground's cold. Murmurs of a hushed conversation disrupt her confusion. Opening her eyes to a purple sky speckled with stars, they peer at her through the sparse canopy. Janie pushes herself onto her elbows as the air falls quiet. They watch as she looks at them and through them. *They're sitting right back where they were before.*

Butch scoots over next to her while Reyna picks up their picnic. Putting his arm around her, he fixes her collar and pulls over the top of her coat. "Think it's past your bedtime." Pausing with uncertainty whether a burp could signal another gastric upheaval, he sighs with passing relief.

Chapter Twenty Two

Waking up half-dressed, even Janie's thoughts hurt. This must be the storied hangover that's had its way with Butch and Cicely time and again. *My God, no wonder they get so crabby.* Looking at the source of this hellish radiance, she wants to punch the curtain for failing in its sole purpose of existing. Janie offers a quick prayer in exchange for an empty restroom. Hopeful that if she looks as bad as she feels, the sight of herself might be sufficient to induce a purging of last night.

Vending machine coffee in hand, she knocks on Butch's door and lets herself in, ready to fetch some aspirin and whatever greasy amalgamation his heart desires. He's stunningly awake, showered and clean shaven. Stacks of clothes sit next to a duffle bag on his bed, he tucks a few folded shirts into the bag before greeting her. "This for me?"

Wriggling in between the small piles, this is all too much. "You got any aspirin?"

Sympathetically, he grabs the small bottle from his ammo can turned man tote. "One or two?" Looking at her, he reconsiders, "Yeah, two."

Downing the aspirin with coffee, she halfheartedly lifts the corner of the stack. "What's going on?"

Breaking stride, he explains. "The pile to the right is yours. I'm not gonna fit into them in a few months so you may as well have them. I'm keeping Oingo and Closer for posterity."

Lifting the little stack of old tee shirts, Janie places them on her lap. Refusing to beg for an explanation, she sips her coffee waiting for his flurry to settle.

Stopping for a sip, Butch moves the duffle to sit down. "My disability ran out, and I found out yesterday my appeal was rejected."

"You wanna stay with me? I could get you a job," Janie offers.

Touched, Butch shakes his head. "I'm going home. I spoke with my mother yesterday." Waving his arm at an imaginary pest, he sighs. "I know, I know how cliché."

Concerned, Janie looks him in the eye trying to gauge where he's at. "Are you sure?"

Forcing a contented smile, "Yeah. I'm gonna make a go of outpatient treatment. Live with my folks while I get my shit together, that kinda thing."

"Where's home?" Janie asks.

"Windhaven, Arizona. It's a suburb outside Flagstaff." He packs the last few items from the armoire.

An ache of impending loneliness builds as it did with Cicely. "When are you leaving?"

"Tonight, 6 o'clock." Surveying the room, he checks the time on his alarm clock and stuffs it in the bag. "I need a haircut. You wanna come? Maybe get some real coffee?"

As days such as these are wont to do, minutes move with the immediacy of seconds. Janie calls out sick with the benefit of actually being sick. The brown bottle flu's not for the faint of heart. They load up at a diner full of old timers and truck drivers. Being both peckish and nauseous, Janie keeps breakfast simple. Butch orders with the tenacity of a man ordering his last meal but ends up picking at it.

Stopping by a curbside florist, Butch buys a bouquet of wildflowers. Satisfied with their quality, he tucks them under his arm. Putting her arms out pageant style, Janie cheeses for an imaginary camera. "For me, no you shouldn't have."

Smirking, he hits her with the bouquet. "Yeah, Miss Hostel USA. They're for uncle Gary."

"Aww, that's really nice of you Butch."

"Nah, I barfed all over his grave last night. Figure I owe him one before I go."

Walking through the open gates, they admire the grounds in the light of day. Passing an elderly woman wiping down her husband's headstone, she slows to watch them go by.

Butch stares down at uncle Gary's grave in disgust. "Damn." Dragging his feet across the grass, he mashes everything into the soil. Looking around, he turns to Janie. "Can I have your water? I'll buy ya another." He empties the bottle across the marker, grabbing a handful of fallen leaves to abrade the surface. Laying the flowers across the marker, he wipes his hands on his pants. "Alright. Peace Gary."

Walking away, Janie glances back at the spot shuffled bare by Butch's feet. "You should've bought roses for that mess."

"Men don't like roses," Butch replies matter of fact.

On their way back, the elderly lady looks up again. They offer a smile, to which she replies in kind. Stiffly getting to her feet, she grabs her bag and crosses their path on the way to her car.

"You have people here?" she asks.

"An uncle." Butch pipes up.

Janie looks on mortified, convinced the little old lady's on to them.

"It's nice to see young people here. It's mostly just us old fogies," she remarks, rifling her purse for keys.

"We try to stop in every week, it's really peaceful." Butch takes her bag so she can get at her purse.

"Oh, I only come once a month. I'm going to be here soon enough. My Earl doesn't mind." She laughs, opening the door to her Granada.

"I'm sure he doesn't. You take care." Butch slows until he sees she's gotten in the car.

While Butch gets his hair cut, Janie dips out of the stuffy little barber shop for some air. When he walks out, she's tempted to salute. Gone are the messy locks he rarely bothered to comb, in their place is a high and tight buttoned up Butch. Running his fingers along the buzzed sides, he's taken back to times before here.

"Are your ears cold?" Janie asks, standing on her tippy toes to touch his hair.

"They are actually," he replies laughing. "New me, ya know."

With a few hours to kill, they head home. Chain smoking on the stoop, Butch pulls a tin of mints from his shirt pocket. Palming it until Janie plants herself next to him, he pops the lid with his thumb and holds them out. Ruefully, Janie takes a mint then two when he shakes the tin while smirking. Her aplomb at having stepped away for a third time to toss her cookies dissolves in a single gesture. Sucking on the mints, she prays there'll not be any further trips, or she'll never hear the end of it.

Beholding the frenetic tapping of Butch's foot, his nervousness edges into contagion. "You gonna smoke the whole pack? Cause I think if you have another, you're gonna have a seizure or somethin'."

Stubbing out the butt on the step, he tosses it into the sand. "I was trying to finish off the pack, but I'm getting anxious. I'll finish them on the road."

"You quittin'?"

"My folks are clean livin', no booze, no smoke and no nothing," he laughs.

"You sure you wanna do this? I've got some money put away," Janie offers, trying to get his eye.

"They're good people. Me and my brother put them through hell but I'm what's left. I owe them this. I owe myself this." Standing, he exaggeratedly pulls her to her feet. "Wanna help me clear out my room?"

"Yeah." Janie follows. "Your brother's gone?"

"Five years in February. It's a long story."

Checking her watch, they round the top step. "I've got quarter past two, time enough for me."

Unlocking his room, Butch takes a pass for anything left in drawers. "Drunk driving, he hit some guy coming off the night shift. Never hit the brakes."

Searching for the right words, nothing feels apt. "I'm sorry. Were you close?"

Shrugging, he tosses a small box of cassettes on the bed. "When I was a kid, yeah. Things were different when he came home from college and I left for basic not long after, so we just drifted, I guess. Ya know on paper, he was really something. Grades, degree, all that. In person, he was a drunk and an addict."

"Is that how you got started? Sorry, that was terrible."

Dismissing her apology, "No, he would've beat my ass. First time I dabbled beyond weed was with Becca, the girl from NA. Dove in head over feet before basic."

Raising her eyebrow, Janie sits riveted. "And..."

"And life on base is lonely. I had trouble staying on my meds, ended up with an adjustment disorder discharge. He found out she and I were using, then told my parents. When shit hit the fan, we moved in together and she introduced me to the healing world of psychedelics. I climbed out from under the suffocating blanket of psychotropic management. It was fucking magical Janie." Butch looks at her imploringly. "My psych contacted my folks, they cut me off till I got back on my meds. All I could see was her, how I felt around her. So, I cut contact."

"What about your brother?"

"That asshole, God rest his soul, that asshole stayed clean but never stopped drinking. He let my parents believe he was sober, never got more than a week or two. Anyway, when he wrecked, they blamed me for challenging his sobriety with my using. So, we left, and here we are. Here I am."

Nodding, Janie shims his cassettes into the duffle. "You can always come back. Just call the front, I'll make sure you get a ticket."

"It'll be alright." Compelled, he searches for how to begin. "Listen Janie, I've got no place givin' advice, but I'm given it anyway. You're too young to get comfortable here. This place is an abstraction. Don't get lost in the in between. That's all this is, the in between."

"Why does everyone keep sayin' that? I'm not getting stuck any-where," Janie replies crossly.

"Good girl." Butch flicks her shoulder before peeling his Freshjive sticker from the window. Pressing it onto his ammo can, he raises it. "Promised it to Shorty. You taking the test next week?"

"Friday."

"Don't mess it up." Slinging his duffle over his shoulder, he hands her a bag. "When Reyna shows up, give her this."

Holding the bag at a distance, Janie sighs put upon like. "What's in it?"

"Nothing illegal, just some stuff I don't need." Lifting a box of odds and ends, he balances it to pull the door shut behind them.

"You better not be giving her your watch. You know I got dibs," Janie declares, only half joking.

Pulling back his cuff, there sits the object of her envy firmly affixed. "I'll will it to you."

They leave the box at the Salvation Army to live on as someone else's find. Butch's ticket is waiting as promised at the station. Looking towards the vending machines, Butch smiles. "One last cruddy coffee for old time's sake?"

Nodding, Janie pulls him to his feet. "Does Reyna know you're leaving?"

"Yeah, told her yesterday. Bitch was supposed to stop by, she's bad about goodbyes."

"By the by, thanks for leaving me with her." Feigning a grudge, Janie sips her coffee sheepishly.

Raising an eyebrow, Butch counters, "You looked like you were doin' alright to me."

Fragments coalesce, leaving her flush. "Shit."

"We've all been there." Leaning back, he leverages the infinite legroom while he has it. "You can't hide from life. It will always find you. Always."

"Okay, okay. I know." Janie would just as soon drop it.

The overhead squawks the call to board. Rolling a twenty around her *Hellraiser* comic, Janie shoves it in the duffle end pocket. "For the long stretches. They'll tide you over on the road."

"That's mighty kind, but I can't take that." Butch curls her fingers around the bill as he pushes her hand back.

"It's twenty bucks. I know you're broke, you gotta eat," Janie contends.

"Inevitably the panic's gonna hit. That twenty bucks might make the difference between me stayin' on the bus and getting lost in some other in between. Just the way it goes." Butch stands. "Walk me to my bus?"

"First, let's get some snacks for the road." Using up her ones and change, she buys all the salty sweet goodness she can.

Butch pulls a repurposed receipt from his pocket. "This is my folks' number and address. Write me when you get wherever you're going. Okay?"

"Okay." Janie stows it away. Standing on her tippy toes to hug him, she holds on tightly. "Let me know you got there."

Watching him board, she waits till his bus clears the station before allowing her forged smile to fall away. Dusk submits to darkness on the walk home. While she could walk the path to her room blindfolded, it's as though she's just gotten off the bus.

Pushing her bed closer to the window, she gazes upon the same moon she had two years and a thousand miles ago. Everything's different, save for her, forlorn and waiting in perpetuity. Winding down, sleep calls first quietly, then adamantly. Then and there, she promises her heart that she'll not hitch her happiness to anyone else so long as she's here.

Chapter Twenty Three

With four days to go, afternoons are spent at the library until her shift. Wallowing in a plate of birthday kabob and spanakopita, Janie thinks of how much she misses her mother's cooking. How one of her meals embraces you in a way she never could. What she would give for a bite of her kataifi and the thrill of waiting for her to lob a barb at Yaya, baiting her father into conversation on a sullen evening.

A knock disrupts her doleful meal. Janie turns the TV up. *What if it's Darrell with a message from Butch?* Opening the door to give him a hard time, Janie's caught off guard.

Averting a standoff, Janie remembers. "The bag. Hold on."

Reyna takes it and speaks to head off the prospect of another standoff. "Thanks. Can I come in?"

Thinking about it longer than she should, Janie pulls the door. "Yeah, sure."

"You're tough to track down, been here twice this week," Reyna remarks, looking around for somewhere to sit.

"Studying, taking the GED Friday," Janie confides, perched on her bed. "So, Butch said to tell you bye."

"Yeah, I got called in to work. Gonna miss that prick." Reyna rests her hands on the bag, unresolved to go or stay. Motioning towards Janie's dinner, "Don't let me interrupt. Special occasion?"

"Nope. I was done anyway." Dying with embarrassment, Janie can bear it no longer. "Listen, I'm sorry about what may or may not have happened on Halloween."

Laughing, Reyna settles into a smirk. "Relax, it's fine."

"Why do you do that?" Janie asks exasperatedly. "It's not funny when someone's uncomfortable."

Straightening up, Reyna's voice takes on an earnest tone. "Sorry, I just meant don't worry. We just kissed and you passed out. End of story."

Simultaneously relieved and disappointed, Janie shifts restlessly. Stammering until she lands on what she wants to say. "I don't usually do stuff like that."

"Kiss girls or get high?" Reyna asks pointedly.

Blushing, Janie weakly replies, "Both." Taking a deep breath, she explains, "I'm not really sure where I am with the girl thing, that's not really true, but..."

Saving them both the pain of continuing, Reyna interjects, "I have a girlfriend."

Tilting her head, Janie haughtily asks, "Did you have a girlfriend Halloween night?"

"We were broken up. We do that a lot. It's complicated."

"I'll say," Janie retorts sulkily. Utterly confused, why is she pissed off when if she's being honest, she's not particularly into her.

Snagging every available shift, Janie's satisfied with her nest egg. Too exhausted to miss Butch except for those nights when she can't sleep, she takes one of their walks. There's been an intangible shift since the night of Halloween. She's more awake, more aware of the world around her. Like new skin, her nerves feel closer to the surface. Paranoia creeps in, and conversations with strangers are no longer innocuous exchanges. Instead, inane soundbites are logged for late-night analysis, a forensic study of what they meant when they remarked on her shoes or asked about her weekend. Janie checks out books on cities within a day's drive to ease her restlessness.

November reaches its median. After two callouts and a fryer on the fritz, Janie fears this may be the shift that finishes her. Keeping her eyes low, she avoids furious glares of hovering fryless customers. Relief abounds when Vernon distributes a tray of fries and pawns off frost-bitten sweet rolls as consolation. He gives her the nod that they're back in business.

Renewed, Janie steps to the register to find Reyna and her perpetual smirk. "What're you doing here?"

"Dinner. You?" Reyna responds glibly.

"The ambiance, can't tear myself away." *Maybe she really did just come to eat.* "Know what you want?"

"I do." Staring her down, Reyna lets Janie squirm. "I'll get the eight with swiss."

"Butch's favorite," Janie remarks.

"Yeah, I turned him on to that," Reyna replies, handing over her cash. "What time do you get off?"

"Ten. Why?"

"You wanna come play pool with my friends?"

"Oh, I'm not twenty-one yet," Janie responds, somewhat impressed with her obvious maturity.

Catching herself before going full smirk, "Yeah, I know. Bartender's a friend. The Wheelhouse, on Central by Yale." Tapping the counter, Reyna leaves without another word.

Farther east than she usually ventures, Janie plays it cool when the landmarks lose familiarity. Bustling streets slow as storefronts closed for the night dominate the landscape. On the brink of giving up, there it is tucked between a machine shop and a video store. Heedful of her surroundings, Janie slips into the wood paneled entryway. A cacophony of sportscasters, cracking pool sticks, and a litany of unintelligible banter form the aural fabric of the room. On the surface, the Wheelhouse is a sports bar collapsing into a dive.

Cliques of clientele coexist in a symbiotic ecosystem of stiff pours and cheap beer. Blue collar trade types clad in company shirts congregate with their girls beneath the big screens, branching out with firm command of the dart boards. Loner office drones too broke to hang with management and lacking the mettle to assert their place among the dirt under the fingernail types, are sprinkled throughout the high tables and peripheries like freckles. Off in the corner, wedged between the pool tables and a wilting plywood stage lie the lesbians. Janie beholds a sea of black cotton, stonewashed denim and light beer for as far as her eyes can see under the glow of tired billiards lights.

Calling upon her courage, Janie draws a deep breath. Noticing the waitress clocking her, she's on course for an intercept. Reyna emerges, signaling the waitress that they're together. With the flick of a finger, the bartender summons them. Certain she's about to be tossed out, Janie closes the gap.

Leaning over the bar, a crunchy curled brunette of indefinite height and infinite cleavage leers down. "How old are you?"

Twenty-one, twenty-one, just say twenty-one. "Eighteen." Janie rests on the bar defeated.

Glaring at Reyna, she throws her hands up. "Fuck man."

Reyna tries haplessly to chat her up. "Come on Gigi, I've been coming here since I was twenty."

"That was like six months ago and you at least had a shitty fake ID." Opening bottles and dressing them in lime wedges, she passes a tray to the waitress. "What, now that you're twenty-one, you go and raid a daycare? She looks sixteen." Looking at Janie, she leans a little further. "You're on soda pop. Got it?"

Nodding vehemently, Janie stays fixed for fear of jinxing her good fortune. Reyna smirks, ready to steal the floor.

"Don't bullshit me. I know you." The bartender wags her finger. "C'mere."

Janie obliges, already lost in the grips of her plunging neckline. The bartender plants a kiss on Janie's cheek, unleashing a peppering of hoots that leave Janie's face burning red as the lipstick staining her.

Satisfied, she waits for Janie to look up. "You're marked kid. No one will serve you. If I see that cheek clean, you're out." Pushing a small stack of quarters across the bar, she calls back for a coke. "Take your pop and go feed the jukebox."

Clawing at the quarters, Janie clasps them in her palm. Sipping her Coke, she smiles at Reyna's attempts to introduce her over tangled conversations. Reaching across the table, Reyna grabs a shot for each of them. "Happy Birthday!"

Caught somewhere between surprise and the weight of Reyna's girlfriend Rita watching her every move, Janie only manages "What?"

"Wasn't your birthday a couple weeks ago?" Reyna asks, keeping the glass low.

"Yeah. How'd you know?" Janie asks. *What else does she know?*

Reyna nudges her to tip it back while the waitress is busy bitching out the kitchen. "Butch told me. I was gonna say something when I came by your place, didn't seem like a good time."

Her throat burning, Janie takes a long swig off her soda. "I'm gonna get thrown out."

"You're fine." Jealousy in her girlfriend's eyes distills to a scowl. "Glad you came. Back in a few."

Janie scopes out the jukebox. An old guy with a stack of quarters, a pack of Pall Malls, and a Coors is stationed an arm's length from the box. Absentmindedly smoking, he half watches the closest big screen and impassively works his way through a pile of scratcher tickets. Squinting at Janie's advance, crow's feet curated from a thousand suspicious gazes crease together in perfect unity.

Prudently lying in wait pays off when his aging bladder gets the better of him. Another old timer in an aged red board shirt watches on in muted delight. Counting her change, she's good for seven songs. While there's nothing new and not much older than mellow gold, what's there is solid. She kicks off her set with "Don't Do Me Like That," then goes for gold with the Divinyls, which garners expected clamoring from the lesbians and a few noteworthy shrieks from the darts region. Janie rounds it out with "Folsom Prison Blues," a peace offering to a noble foe.

Defeat accepted, he gathers his things and saddles up to the bar. The bartender brings him a Coors on the house, throwing Janie a wink for a job well done. Resigned to his fate, he sips his beer looking around with a wistful eye for the good old days before the queers and suburbanites.

Janie makes small talk to spare Reyna the burden of checking in at the expense of her girl's contentment. Hanging in there until midnight, time to cut out.

Thanksgiving fast approaching, the prospect of spending it alone is depressing as hell. Wafting garlic and onions from Vernon's dinner heating in the microwave reminds her of how the whole house smelled on Thanksgiving morning. Reminiscing, she can almost taste the garlic and feta as her father made his mother's potato salad. The way her mother chided there'd be nothing left to serve if they kept picking at it. The sound of Matty crunching on apple scraps their mother couldn't cram into the pie crust. Hell, she even missed listening to Kate sing along with the hymns on the radio. Her voice was always like vinegar to Janie's ears except when she sang, sweet as honey.

Reclaiming herself from the wages of sentimentality on the walk home, Janie thinks of that last year back home. Her silent rebellion at the dinner table as they sat miles away.

Holding up a letter, Darrell flags Janie down as she blows by. "Correspondence!"

"Finally!" She takes the letter, assuming it's from Butch. Tossing her things onto the bed, she looks closer. Settling down at the desk, she twists the lamp to her vantage point. Scratched out in blue ink is a letter written in true Cicely fashion. Dug in and with an alignment all its own.

Greenhorn,
First of all, if you're reading this then let me say I am sorely disappointed. Did you not hear a damn word I said? Anyways, Nathan and I are getting married. Got a bun in the oven and we have to get this show on the road before I can't squeeze into a dress. December 18th if you're interested.
They had a bitty rodeo come through, smelled to high heaven. I was just telling my sis in law about the time we drove out to the rodeo in Santa Fe. We had a right good laugh about you getting stuck under the kiddy mechanical bull. We had a lot of fun didn't we, wish you were here with us.
As much as I want to see you, don't come if it means the difference between leaving and not.
Cicely

Reyna passes by with an invite to Thanksgiving with her friends. Gracious yet firm, Janie declines. The only thing worse than being alone during the holidays is being in a room full of strangers pretending they're not alone during the holidays.

Janie awakens to the second run of the Macy's Day parade. Lazily making her way to the donut shop, she relishes the aroma of fritters. Gripping a carton of milk in her teeth, she digs for her key while navigating the last few steps until she sees Reyna resting against her door. Holding up her bag, "Hungry?"

Holding up her own bag, Reyna counters, "I brought real food. Save the dessert for later."

"Who says it's dessert?"

"I have it on good authority. Am I wrong?" Reyna asks.

"They're breakfast pastries, so yes. What's in the bag?" The smell of savory goodness hastens Janie's surrender.

Eating breakfast burritos and watching the parade, they hope for a rogue balloon. Reyna tries again to convince Janie to join their friendsgiving, she's unmoved.

Ignoring the TV, she reads comics from the local newsstand and eventually Cicely's letter again. Evading the pull to drag herself away from this place, she wanders downstairs to keep Shorty company until Reyna turns up half past seven with eats. An ease emerges as their relationship grows less opaque. She comes to regard Janie much the way Butch had, and herself as a guardian whose wayward ways have met their match.

With Butch on her mind, Janie asks, "You heard anything from Butch?"

"Nope, not really expecting to," Reyna replies dismissively.

"He said he was gonna let us know he got there though."

"It's kinda one of those things people say. Only way he's gonna make it there is to put this place, and us behind him," Reyna explains.

Kinda like how you did Lydia. Saddened, Janie reluctantly agrees with Reyna and her jerk of a conscience.

"I should get back. Get your test results?"

Ruefully, Janie picks at her fingers. "Didn't take it. Turns out you need an ID. I'm so dumb," Janie gripes.

"We're going to have to do something about that then. See ya later."

Waiting till she hears her hit the stairs, Janie inspects her meal. Devouring all of tonight's and some of tomorrow's, she's grateful for a taste of home even if it's not her home.

On the verge of her third Christmas in Albuquerque, Janie watches holiday travelers drift in and out, shifting the hostel's vibe from intentional vagabond to cash strapped crash pad. Coming home to cigarette butts on the stoop inches from the ash can along with loud conversations in the hall, wears on her. Janie helps Darrell pick up the common areas. *How does he stay sane around these slovenly miscreants?* Thinking back to her first year, she remembers the holiday carelessness. While it may not have bothered her then, it goddamn bothers her now.

Counting inventory, Janie notices the calendar. December 18th. Checking her watch, Cicely's probably cursing up a storm getting ready to walk down the aisle. Janie wishes she could be there to celebrate or lend an ear, whichever she needs.

Somehow, without Janie noticing, Reyna becomes a fixture around the hostel. Though she suspects her chumminess with Darrell isn't entirely friend, but more business friend. She gives that one up to the big JC or whoever, so long as she doesn't have to know about it. Like Butch, Reyna edifies Janie about the world as she knows it. Janie shares nothing of life before here while Reyna remains a closed book secured by a comely smirk. They abide by the law of the land in the hostel: live and let live, just keep the bathroom clean.

Disregarding better judgment, Janie spends checkout night on Reyna's couch. The small house is much like the hostel, only gayer. There's more foot traffic, swearing and drinking than she's ever seen, save for when the Kiwi brings friends home from the bar. It doesn't take long to figure out a house full of women is a lot messier than sharing a floor with the guys she calls neighbors. Reyna being the exception, Janie spies a spotless room when she pops her head in to say goodbye.

Moving on up from cardboard trees, Janie springs for a Charlie Brown Christmas tree to combat the post rain mustiness. Everything's flourishing and green like back home this time of year. A few long timers speculate the persistent dampness has inspired mold to flourish in the nooks and crannies of the aged masonry.

Flopped out on her bed after a long shift, the calendar taunts her with its incessant march. No closer to knowing where next than she was a month ago, rows of red X's beckon failure. Crossing out Christmas Eve, the crushed marker felt wages an invisible protest.

Curled up, she picks at day old Christmas cookies and antipasto salad while watching cartoons she's watched countless times snuggled up next to Matty. Sometimes she wished he'd be quiet instead of asking a million questions but now she'd give most anything to hear him ask why the snowman's so angry and what's a yeti, and why isn't he called the abominable yeti.

A knock at the door reels her back, there's little doubt who's calling. Shoving the last of a dismembered Santa cookie into her mouth, Janie knocks the tray under her bed. Chewing with purpose, she brushes crumbs from her chest and invites Reyna in.

Brushing stray sugar crystals from Janie's chin, Reyna hesitates. "You missed some." Setting a paper sack on the table, she unpacks. "You eaten yet?"

"I ate light," Janie replies, moving in to see what she brought.

Handing over a sandwich, Reyna sits on the far end of the bed. When her foot clips the cookie tray, she takes a cookie instead of giving a lecture. "Not bad. I used to love butter cookies when I was a kid."

Janie watches, waiting for her to spill. Reyna clears half her sandwich without a word. "Okay, what's wrong? You gave me zero hassle about the cookies, and you didn't say a word about the pile of laundry by the desk. What gives?"

Scoffing, Reyna retorts, "I'm not your keeper."

Arms crossed, Janie stares.

Never having seen this side of her, Reyna's tempted to let her fume for the sake of it. "Things are kinda messed up right now. You remember Gigi, the bartender?"

Janie nods, waiting patiently.

"So last Tuesday me and my girlfriend Rita got in a fight, then she got one of the roommates in the middle of it talking shit too. I left all pissed off. Anyway, I went to the bar and it was a graveyard. I bought the house a shot for each one I bought myself."

Shaking her head, Janie knows where this is going. "No. Reyna, tell me you didn't."

"No, it's not like that. It's just, well basically I hung out till closing hoping Rita would be asleep by the time I got home. One thing leads to another with Gigi, and we ended up back at hers."

Cocking her head, Janie throws her hands up. "So it is like that."

"Yeah, but no. I mean she said we were over, ya know?" Reyna pleads.

"Did you believe her?" Janie grills.

"No, not really," Reyna concedes.

Sighing, Janie circles back. "Then yeah, it's like that."

"Fine, whatever. Anyhoo, here's the problem. When I woke up, I heard all this yelling. It was Rita and Gigi. Then when I tried to diffuse things, they started screaming at me." Heated, Reyna paces.

"Then what happened?"

"Well, Rita left yesterday to spend Christmas with her folks. Pretty much nuked my life on her way out, so there's that." Reyna leans against the desk, nibbling another cookie. "Rita and I have known each other since I moved here, and she pretty much shook all the skeletons outta my closet."

Taking half of Reyna's cookie, Janie's enthralled. "Are you broken up for good then?"

"I'm pretty much broken up with life here. She told the landlord I slept with her girlfriend while she was in Montana last year settling her father's affairs. We were drunk. One-time thing. And she told my manager Eddie about his younger sister coming around our place to party a while back, and ya know shit happens." Running her fingers through her hair, Reyna puts her face in her hands. "I'm pretty much out of a house and a job."

"You got fired?"

"Not officially, but he hates my guts now. It's such bullshit, guys like him. They love talkin' to you about chasing tail and all that shit, till they find out it's their sister you're chasing."

"You make really bad choices when it comes to girls, really bad," Janie gently chastises.

"You'll learn, it's tough to say no when there's a beautiful girl standing in front of you and you know you can have her. You're only young for a minute and when you're old, no one's gonna want you. Gotta live now."

Feeling that the world has only begun to reveal itself to her, Janie considers the frightening notion of finding her way only to realize it's already the twilight of her youth. Seeing Reyna on the brink of tears is an especially bleak sight. Putting her arm around her, Janie rests her head on her shoulder. "You wanna stay here tonight?"

Lying in bed watching the best of Christmas TV, Reyna wraps her arms around Janie. Both finding comfort in the other without the burden of expectation, sleep comes swiftly.

Morning comes, bringing an unspoken gratitude at not waking up alone. Half asleep, they lay in silence.

"You awake?" Reyna asks softly.

"Yeah," Janie replies, not wanting to hear what comes next.

Reyna continues. "I'm getting out. Like soon."

Though not surprised, Janie's heart still sinks. "Yeah, I figured."

"I've got a friend outside Houston who said he can get me a job in the oil fields. My cousin's moving out the same way, could save on rent."

On the brink of tears, Janie forces a smile and sits up. "That's great. I'm happy for you."

Hugging her, Reyna leans her head on Janie's shoulder. "Come with me."

Frozen, Janie searches for something to compel her to oblige.

"Look around Janie. Nothing here for either of us. May as well stick together. My friend said he'll ask around for somethin' for you."

Crippling fear she hasn't felt since leaving Clayton overtakes her. It's hard to give up the devil you know, no matter how fed up you are. "Reyna that's really sweet and all, but I dunno. I don't have much here, but I know what's comin' when I wake up in the morning. I don't know if I can risk everything for maybe."

"Everything? Janie this is treading water in the shallow end. You gotta put your feet down sometime. So why not with me?"

Pushing her hair out of her face, Janie glances at Reyna before turning her eyes to the marshaling of red x's on the calendar. Fear of being stuck here thins when pitted against the fear of leaving.

Pulling her back towards her, Reyna slumps to meet Janie's gaze. "Come with me." She smiles warmly, hoping Janie will come around.

Taking a deep breath, Janie closes her eyes and nods. "Okay."

"Yeah?" Reyna hugs her. "We're going to have a good time, you'll see." Lying back down, she allows herself to begin planning. "Let's leave in the morning."

Chapter Twenty Four

Reyna's old Blazer takes a beating on the small roads traversing the staked plains of eastern New Mexico. Two-lane highways and county roads branch out like veins bringing vital sustenance to ranches and small towns. Deep canyons rut the flat lands where their crooked fingers have dug into the dry earth. A close call descending the icy Sacramento Mountains leads to Cloudcroft, as good a place as any to service the brakes before continuing into West Texas.

Heeding the mechanic's advice, they check in to a small motor lodge walking distance from the main drag, Burro Avenue. While Reyna's put out by the delay, Janie revels in the old rail depot town's snowy Christmas vibe. Every Christmas thing she's missed is laid out before her, save for her family. She has Reyna though, these days that's close enough. The motel clerk cautions of snow flurries by early evening. Thanking him kindly, they set out.

"There's a café a block over that way. Good eats, wanna?"

"Lets. You been here before?"

Reyna shoves her hands in her coat pockets for warmth. "Yeah, couple times. Long time ago."

The café's small and intentionally rustic, much the way they kept the diner quaint to draw in tourists seeking respite from their chain infested lives in the suburbs. An imagined past sweeps over them in a single row booth with a view. Greeted as though they were old friends, the waitress reminds her of Isabel.

Peeking over the menu, Janie groans. "Everything's got green chile in it. Like everything."

"We're in New Mexico, what do you expect?" Reyna hides her restlessness behind her menu.

Not wanting to go back to the room and less keen to freeze, they settle on a row of shops standing tall against the heedless march of time. Browsing, there's little that would grab Matty's eye.

"Must be a sight in the summer," Janie remarks, leafing through summer festival tees.

"Oh it is, can't hardly see the sidewalk come Memorial Day weekend!" A friendly shopkeeper chimes in, craving interaction more than a sale.

Looking up, Janie welcomes his good cheer. "I dunno, Christmas here's really somethin'."

Adjusting his glasses, he comes halfway around the counter. "Oh it is, nothing like it where I'm from originally, Nevada. Retired here. Love every minute of all the seasons. You from a warm climate too?"

Reyna eyes them conspicuously, staying her distance.

"Yeah, Central Valley, California. It got cold and all, but not all folksy like this. I mean, like in a good way," Janie rambles.

Putting his hand up. "No, that's a good word. Folksy. It's what keeps em comin' every year. How bout you two, just passing thru?"

Ready to move on, Reyna pipes up. "Brakes got dicey by the summit, getting them fixed over at Mac's."

"Well, George is a good man. He'll set you right. Be careful heading out, you'll hit some ice on the way down."

Putting her hand on Janie's back to keep her moving, Reyna smiles and nods. "Thank you, we will."

Halfway across the parking lot, Reyna halts. "Think I'm gonna head back to the room. Wanna meet up later?"

Outpaced by her moods, Janie falls back. "I'll go with you." Pulling on Reyna's arm, her fingers sink into the well-lined coat. "Come on, let's go."

While Reyna naps, Janie watches traffic. Her head plunges into the bygone depths of that which she cannot change. *I could just go home. I'm 18. There's nothing they can do. Nowhere they can send me.* Rattled like the old single pane windows against the distant boom of thunder and rigs descending the grade in their futile push to stay ahead of the weather, Janie's left sadder in knowing any homecoming would likely be tethered to rejection.

Grabbing the small motel pad and pen from the drawer, she knows she'll have to keep it short.

> *Dear Lydia,*
> *I've decided to join the living. This will be my last letter from New Mexico.*
> *Butch went home and I've sort of inherited his friend Reyna. Who's now my friend too. Without them, there's nothing to stay for. Since you're probably getting ready for college, there's not much reason to head west. I'm going with her to Texas.*
> *I've never met anyone like her before. She has this way of getting under your skin but then she's usually right, so I guess it works. Aside from you, she's the only person I'd trust enough to go anywhere with. We're just friends though.*
> *Always,*
> *Janie*

"Snow's starting to fall." Janie pulls back the curtain, motioning for Reyna. "Come see."

"Got dark fast." Weightless flecks floating down, she smiles. "Snowed like this last time I was here."

"When was that?"

"When I was seventeen. Feels like a long time ago. I guess it wasn't all that long ago come to think of it."

"You were with your family?" Janie asks, lost in the night sky.

Nodding, Reyna acquiesces to Janie's curiosity. "Used to come every year with my folks and grandparents, we'd stay here on our way home from the St. Joseph war memorial."

"Your Dad a vet?"

"My grandfather, World War II," Reyna replies, fighting weariness.

"Ahh man, I bet he had some stories," Janie remarks enthusiastically.

"Not really." Reyna begins flipping channels, replying sharply. "He was a mean ass old drunk."

"Sorry." Janie rests her forehead against the cool glass, anything to draw her from the corner she's pressed herself into.

Sighing, which is tantamount to an apology once you know her well enough, Reyna tosses the remote. "Nah, don't be. We had fun when he wasn't bitchin'." Reflecting, she continues. "Got us out of El Paso. Shit, that alone was worth a week of listening to the old man."

The oxidized blue beast is road ready by lunch. Eager to put the great state of New Mexico behind her, Reyna leans on the pedal mercilessly till they hit the state line. Stopping off to fill up and stretch, the sour tang of sulfur creeps up bit by bit until it's all they smell.

Holding her nose, Janie squints. "Smells awful! Must be a leak or somethin' out here."

"Gasses from the fields. My cousin Fernie says folks around here call it the smell of money." Reyna laughs at Janie's disgust, trying to conceal her own aversion. "You'll get used to it."

"Why would I get used to it?" Janie turns to face her. "Whole state doesn't smell like this, does it?"

Turning the dial to circulate the air, Reyna puts the windows up. "No, it doesn't but Odessa does have that West Texas smell. You get used to it, trust me. Just like the stench of cow shit where you're from."

"Doesn't smell like cow shit where I'm from," Janie replies huffily. "Besides, I thought we were going to Houston. I was expecting it to smell like rocket fuel or somethin'."

"Okay, for one it does too smell like cow shit. We drove through one summer going to Yosemite, was enough to make you cry." She laughs at Janie's furrowed brow. "Second, I said outside Houston. Odessa's outside Houston."

"Yeah, almost outside the state it's so far outside," Janie huffs.

Reyna leans into the pedal again. "You've never even been to Texas. You need to just hold your damn horses and give it a chance."

Janie says nothing, staring out the window like days gone by with her mother.

Penitent, Reyna shifts into park waiting on the world's longest freight train. "That was bitchy, I'm sorry. Thing is, the job's in Odessa. So that's where we gotta go. If you hate it come summer, I'll look for something in Houston. Deal?"

Resting on her crumpled coat cuff, the cold of the passenger window transcends the fabric, chilling Janie to the bone. Glancing without reply, she settles into a staunch silence. Mashing the brake pedal on end, Reyna lurches them forward until Janie succumbs with an exasperated giggle. "Okay, fine."

Smiling, she tears around the crossing guard after the last car.

Odessa and Clayton are kindred at first blush. The marrow of it fills Janie with memories of home. Pickups and churches everywhere with the odd dive bar peeking out from the recesses of rowed storefronts keeping a long-brokered veneer of respectability. People going about their business, saving the discussion of your business for the dinner table.

For the first time since Janie's known her, Reyna's nerves best her getting ready to meet her friend Emmett. Rethinking her outfit twice, she settles on a combination of the two. Fitted jeans with a Wrangler black pearl snap button down. Foregoing her usual combed down look, she musses her hair with her fingers, paints her eyes, then leaves the mirror disappointed. Though Janie fidgets with secondhand anxiety, she remains unwavering in her choice of overalls and sneakers.

Walking up to a cantina plucked out of the Alamo, the root of Reyna's nerves leans patiently against an adobe wall adjacent to the entrance. A lanky personification of Texan mystique steps forward to greet them. He hugs Reyna, lifting her with a sway. Intrigued, Janie stares into his soul reaching to shake his hand.

Returning with a round of Shiner Bocks, Emmett smiles slyly as Reyna flattens Janie's hand before she can push her beer away. Stifling the underage disclaimer, Reyna slides the bowl of chips in front of her.

Taking a long swig, Emmett looks across appraisingly. "Been a long time Miss Reyna. Long time."

"Has been. You went and turned into the Sundance Kid," Reyna replies cheekily. "Last time I saw you, I'm pretty sure you were wearing a ratty Def Leppard shirt."

Blushing, he flattens his pressed plaid shirt. "Gotta look the part. It's nice to see you've discovered shirts with sleeves too."

Blushing in like, Reyna raises her beer in honor of being put in her place.

Fixing his napkin on his lap, Emmett looks up one last time before committing to the obliteration of a skillfully charred skirt steak. "You sure you're up for this?"

"Just moved four hundred miles for this job, so yeah I'm ready." Reyna challenges his gaze. "You worried?"

Smiling, his eyes betray him as has always been the case with her. "I got faith in you, you know that. It can be tough out there. You're gonna be the only woman on the crew, and well ya know men can be pigs sometimes."

Nodding, Reyna's undeterred. "I just spent two years working in a machine shop, and before that my uncle's shop. I know all about it." Cutting into her steak, she drags it through a swathe of cuminy jus. "Look, you don't need to worry. You're not gonna have to babysit me or anything."

Taking a pack of smokes from his shirt pocket, Emmett lights up. "I know that. You know that's not what I meant." Taking a drag, he offers Reyna the cig. She obliges, happy to change the subject. Holding the pack toward Janie, he lights another for himself. "You won't have to worry anyhow, I got a good crew. No one fucks with the driller. But a worm's gotta pay their dues, man, woman or beast. Anyone gets outta line, you just tell me and I'll ginsel their ass."

Appreciative, Reyna sips her beer. "I love it when you talk tough Emmett Wheeler."

In watching their friendly verbal jostling, another layer of Reyna emerges beneath the warm glow of the precariously hung iron chandelier. A vulnerability has surfaced, a foregone need to be seen as enough.

Sleepless, Janie turns the TV on to drown out the silence. Reyna's apprehension looms from across the room. "You alright?"

"Yeah, fine," Reyna replies, her back to Janie.

"You and Emmett know each other from way back?" Janie asks matter of fact.

Blinking into the darkness, Reyna's not keen for a heart to heart. "Yup, since we were kids."

"Ya'll ever get together back then?" Janie asks.

"Ya'll? Really?"

"What? I'm trying out my Texan. Trying to look the part, ya know?" Janie replies, a bit of undeclared jealousy elbowing through her teasing.

"We're just friends, Janie. All we were, all we're ever gonna be." She turns to the wall with a sigh that says that's enough now.

Chapter Twenty Five

Fernie gleans what he can from Reyna's scant introduction while he moves in the last of his stuff. Working with Emmett's crew outside Andrews, Reyna's picked up before dawn only to come home ragged well after the dinner bell's rung. Janie and Fernie, unsure of one another, keep to themselves. To stave off being the household wart, Janie sets out on missions of exploration, then retreats to her room until Reyna gets in.

Reading a battered copy of the *Tales of the Watcher* anthology, Janie gets lost in the saga of ancient cosmic beings enduring an eternal post observing man's perpetual folly. A light knock gives her a jolt.

Fernie steps back. "Reyna's gonna be late, they're waiting on some tools getting brought out to them."

Smiling politely as she slips back behind the door, "Okay, thanks."

He speaks up hurriedly. "I made dinner. Wanna join me?"

Aside from being a fantastic cook, Fernie's an easy conversationalist. Janie finds herself swept up in getting to know him, admiring him simply because he makes no effort to seek admiration. Careful not to tell too many tales of Reyna's past, he offers glimpses of a lighter Reyna. Laughing long after the last bite's been eaten, the conversation moves to life in Odessa.

Reyna gets in at half past midnight. Her skin stained in patches, she smells of solvent even after having changed onsite. Exhausted, she stares half asleep with her eyes open. "Can hear you guys down the walk."

Fernie whisks their plates off to the sink. Up close, Reyna's eyes are so tired they're almost blank.

"Let me fix you a plate," Janie offers, taking her lunch sack.

"On it," Fernie calls from the stove.

"I'm alright. I gotta sleep." Taking off her coat, she disappears down the hallway.

Fernie's left by the stove, plate in hand.

Janie reaches, "I'll take it to her."

Averting her eyes, she nudges the door. "You decent?"

"Mmhmm," Reyna replies, shoving laundry into the hamper. Still tender looking, her bare shoulders reveal a deepening olive tone as another sunburn heals over.

Setting dinner on the nightstand, Janie gasps at the sight of her blistered hands. "Oh God, your hands."

Etiquette eschewed, Reyna shovels her food. "Been digging ditches all week, just gotta push through till they move me to the floor."

Already on her way to the bathroom, Janie trails off. "We have to clean that up, yer gonna get infected." Ignoring Reyna's protest, she tends to her raw hands. Wrapping the weeping wounds in gauze, she tapes the bandages. "Don't they give you gloves?"

Setting the fork down harder than intended, Reyna snipes, "Of course they do."

Inspecting her hands again, Janie's unconvinced. "Well, then you should wear two pairs. Gimme your plate. Need anything else?"

Heaving the comforter over her knackered body, Reyna shakes her head. "Almost forgot. Emmett found you a spot in the company offices. Said you can start next week."

Janie curls up on the couch to dozens of channels with nothing on. There'll be no sleep as the gravity of an above board job sends her down a rabbit hole of what if. *What if an ID flags something in the system? Could they just show up on our doorstep?* The thought of facing her folks ties her stomach in knots.

Janie awakens to Reyna squeezing in on the end of the couch. *Who the hell opened the blinds?* Shielding her eyes, she spies a grouch. "Why are you still here?"

"Company man called, one of the gas readings was too high. Gotta wait till it clears and test again later."

"I think this whole town's gotta gas leak, but hey it's a day off." Janie sleepily celebrates with a silent hurrah.

"People drop dead right where they're standing from these leaks. Besides, I don't work, I don't get paid." Reyna pushes Janie's feet over the cushion. "Get showered, we got shit to do."

Throwing some side eye, she rubs the sleep away. "So, what are we doin'?"

"Time to get your ass back on the grid. I'll make breakfast."

Bouncing from one county office to another, it will take two weeks to gather certified copies of the vital documents needed to validate her existence and thus establish herself in Odessa.

The ease of acquiring a copy of Janie's birth certificate is bittersweet. *No one was ever looking for me in the first place, or if they did, it was a short search.*

The first week's hard in an environment that's a far cry from what she's accustomed to. Day in, day out, the hours are the same. The work's the same. And worst of all, the people are the same with no customers to break it up.

After a month of astute observation, Fernie abandons his quest to understand the dynamics of Janie and Reyna's relationship. As his friendship with Janie flourishes, he lets sleeping dogs lie, lest he get bitten for prying. Like any big brother worth his salt, blood or not, Fernie takes it upon himself to see to Janie getting her license. Driving lessons are an easy excuse to explore his Odessa.

Doris the HR manager takes a shine to Janie right off. So much so, she misplaces her hiring packet for thirty days, giving Janie time to take her GED. Swearing Reyna to secrecy, she keeps her studies from Fernie.

By the ides of March, Janie has her diploma and is the holder of a Texas driver's license. This being the closest she'll ever come to an adult card, she embraces all that it affords her. Which as it turns out, is mostly taxes and the expectation to dig into a career. For Fernie, a reversal of fortune is delivered in the form of a torn ACL earned leveraging his body weight against a tipping pallet at work. Recovering from surgery, he restlessly hobbles around on crutches till Janie gets home from work each day.

Life as Janie knows it changes, so subtly she cannot pinpoint when exactly, except to say it has. Telling herself that somewhere in the fray of getting by, she was too caught up to consider what next wilts in the light of the truth. That being, she hadn't tried. In fact, she refused altogether. Even going so far as to deny herself a vision of a future which didn't include Lydia.

With nothing left to hide from or behind, the future bleeds away a day at a time. Nearly four years gone since that first summer at the diner, yet when Janie closes her eyes, there's Lydia smiling back in her poncho. Still, she recoils at the prospect of hitching her future to anything or anyone else. Refusing to sink, and unready to swim, she'll float on a while longer.

Toiling to prove she's worth her salt, Reyna hardly sees them, save for the weekends, which are decidedly dedicated to sleeping and prowling. Notwithstanding her absences, she remains the hub of the household as they wait for their collective lives to resume upon her return from the oil fields each evening.

Janie surveys her office over the span of a few months, parsing all variables to form a navigable path. Working with women of faith, she's under no illusion of their potential to come between her and a paycheck. In time, she learns to deflect personal questions with precision, smiling agreeably when they answer their own questions before she's uttered a word. The matriarchs of the office see her as they wish to, doting accordingly. Janie soaks up the attention, doing her best to hold on to their good favor.

Her efforts pay dividends when she lands a coveted spot in the office bowling league. An invitation from Doris is a seat at the table. Nestled under the protective wings of her office ladies, Janie's kept at a distance from the evils of men and booze. Fortified by one another, she drags Fernie in all his awkward glory to bowling night. There's just enough of an age gap to give them something to gab about, which suits Janie just fine. A little misdirected gossip never hurt anyone, right? After the first evening there'll be no dragging required, Fernie's in his element. Beneath his manicured goatee and burly frame resides the soul of a spinster whose heart beats faster at the sight of an estate sale, and who doesn't mince words when it comes to talking recipes.

By summer, Janie's settled into her quiet little life in Odessa with Reyna, Fernie and the NP Nightingales bowling team. While she was spring's ripple in the pond, Allison's the splash of summer. A transfer from the Gulf Port office, her dossier precedes her. She's the kind that men say they want to be friends with when they want to sleep with her, and with whom women seek friendship when what they're truly after is more akin to espionage. After a week of watching her circumnavigate the office, Janie remains clueless as to what Allison actually does.

Janie's not the only one watching. The Nightingales keep her at arm's length in a bless your heart sort of way. *What the hell do they know? What don't I know?* Janie keeps her distance too, which does nothing to keep her from stealing glances. From a distance of course. Conflicted as all get out, she's no less grateful for Texas summers and the barely conforming hemlines they inspire.

Happy hours laden with a barrage of indiscriminate adulation earn Allison the unofficial but heralded role of planner in chief among the younger associates. While Janie's the belle of the empty nester ball, she's gained little traction with her peers. And until recently, outsider status was of little consequence. Somehow, that inkling of otherness has widened to a crevasse of left out she dearly wants to traverse. Something approaching envy, or is it admiration, has crept in watching Allison carve through the office social stratus with ease. Office pricks who look through underlings in the hall, teeter on the edge of their chairs with Allison's approach. Eager for a few moments of banal banter over the precipice of their cube.

Weeks become months, and so it is that Allison's allure evolves as she deftly moves from one office clique to another. Perhaps it's Janie's unbothered demeanor, or her potential as an entry point to the Nightingales that piques Allison's interest. Whatever the catalyst, the shift is succinct.

Running behind, Janie practically shoves Fernie through the front door. Rushing into the office, she fumbles at her rolled sleeves putting her jacket on. Doris sees all from behind her monitor, including Janie's poor attempt at sneaking in. Dropping into her seat, everyone's working away. Absently tucking her bag under the desk, she nudges an orphaned cup of coffee.

Clutching it, her eyes meet Allison's. She winks at Janie before returning to her call.

Lukewarm and black as a tank bottom, Janie sips away. *Maybe she had an extra cup. That must be it.* Drifting by Doris' office, Janie unburdens herself. "Doris, I'm sorry about being late. I took Fernie to the doctor, and they were running late."

"Janie, I know. He told me about it when he dropped off my embroidery hoop."

Nonplussed, Janie stares off. "Oh. Well, I can stay late to make up the time."

Doris shakes her head. "Nonsense, we all need some time here or there for personal matters."

"Thanks Doris." Janie lingers, an internal battle of should I rages on.

"Was there something else?" Doris inquires, adjusting her bifocals.

Turning, already feeling a fool, "Did everyone get coffee this morning?"

Puzzled, Doris replies, "No. Not that I'm aware of. Why do you ask?"

Shuffling her heels to hasten the sinking process, Janie trails off. "No reason, just wondering. I gotta get, bye."

Rinsing her cup, Janie finds herself elbow to elbow with Allison. "Sorry, taking up the whole sink." *Say thanks. Manners! Manners!* "Thanks for the coffee."

Allison dries her already dry mug. "Was it alright? Probably cold I guess."

Janie pours herself another cup. "It was fine, not cold at all."

Waiting for the carafe, Allison switches places so Janie can dress her coffee. "That's sweet, but you're a terrible liar."

Janie stops stirring. "What?"

Closing some of the gap, Allison leans against the counter. "You got enough milk and sugar in there to make dessert."

Sipping, Janie shrugs. "It was alright. I'm versatile."

A roguish grin glimmers. "Good to know." Without another word, she strolls out to anywhere but her desk.

Much akin to eyeing a colorful bug certain to bite if you pick it up, Janie does so anyway. Loneliness forges a doomed alliance with restlessness. These days, it's her perched on the edge of her chair yearning for a pittance of banal banter over the precipice of her cube. Ditching the Nightingales a couple days a week to eat in the breakroom, she leaves her stuff on the next chair over in case Allison wanders in. And when she does, Janie feels the eyes weighing in as Allison's attention settles on her.

What's a little harmless flirtation? Worked out alright for Samson and old Uriah. Unsure of who asked whom, Allison's in on bowling night. The Nightingales are cordially dismissive, notwithstanding Allison's campaign of flattery and hinting at her bowling prodigy heyday.

Licking their wounds in the wake of being wrecked by a team of CPAs, Fernie and Janie share a look of concern seeing Reyna's truck. Cleaned up for a night out, Reyna's finishing up a call.

"You're home early," Janie asks, without actually asking a question. "You goin' out?"

Fernie mutters from the kitchen, "She ain't dressed up for us."

"You two have fun playing with balls all night?" Reyna asks, as she does whenever she's home before them on bowling night.

Rolling her eyes, Janie stares her down. "So?"

"So, I got promoted to floorhand. Gonna shadow the chainhand, I'll have a shot at that on the next well." Beaming, she declares "Now if one of them bastards calls me a worm, I can tell them to fuck off cause I'm a goddamn roughneck."

Squawking with joy, Janie almost knocks her over hugging her. "I knew you could do it!"

Fernie cheers from the kitchen. "Emmett better watch himself."

Proud, Reyna fixes her shirt. "Emmett's safe. I've got my eye on an engineering gig. Or maybe he's not, driller's a good gig."

"Like the boss?" Janie asks, nibbling on a piece of leftover pizza Fernie's handed her. "Don't you have to go to school for that?"

Taking a bite, Reyna grimaces and hands it back. "It's cold, ugh. Emmett got me into his program. There's a session starting next month. Eventually, I'll gettem to send me to mud school."

"Mud school?" Janie giggles.

"Go on an laugh. That's the shit that gets you out of the muck," Reyna replies willfully.

"Sounds like you got it all figured out." Janie goes back to eating her pizza, a bit gutted.

Headlights shining through the living room window are Reyna's cue. "Don't wait up kids."

Janie and Fernie are caught mid eye roll when she steps back through the door. "I saw that shit. Having some people over tomorrow night. You can bring the old ladies from your league if you want."

Throwing his dish towel at the door, Fernie gasps. "Get out."

Reyna cackles down the stairs.

Watching TV and trying to stay awake, Fernie nudges Janie. "You think Grace would wanna come?"

Half asleep, she asks, "Grace from bowling? I dunno, ask her."

"Thanks." He crosses his arms, working up the energy to go to bed.

Turning off the TV, Janie gets up. "Of course she will. Why would she carry your smelly ass crutches to the car if she didn't like you?"

Fernie's delighted and offended. "They don't smell."

Scoffing, Janie fills a glass from the tap. "Bullshit, they spend all day in your pits. Of course they reek."

A flatness hovers over Janie on the drive to work. A feeling of the world moving around her, a fear that the world will walk right through her if she doesn't find a way to move in kind.

Stepping into Janie's cube, Grace and Allison exchange an awkward hello. Unsure of how to signal Allison she has to get back to work, Janie does nothing. Being older and wiser, Grace gives Allison her back. "I think it's line three that's your troublemaker. You see? Maybe give Brit in accounting a call to verify. Dunno, looks wrong to me."

Dying inside, Janie nods in agreement. Her peripherals spy Allison carrying on a mouthed conversation with one of the guys next cube over. "Yeah, that's probably it. I'll give her a shout."

"Great, let me know when you're done. I'll give it a pass before you submit it." Straightening up, she pauses, "Should I bring something tonight?"

"No, I think Fernie's making a buncha stuff. Lord knows he just called with a list the length of my arm."

"Sounds exciting. Alrighty." Grace side eyes Allison on her way by.

Set on catching up with deadlines, Janie slips off to warm her leftovers. With an empty seat beside her, Allison calls to her from the crowded table. A circle of curiously disinterested eyes track Janie's approach, an unspoken accusation of interloper is hurled as Allison forces them to "Scoot a little so Janie can sit."

Prying her container open, Janie keeps her eyes low to take in the scene. Mostly empty containers and crumpled wrappers. Any minute now they'll fall away one by one.

Allison picks at her last bite, drawing out their time. "You get your big report done?"

Not appreciating the tone, Janie keeps eating and nods.

"It must suck having Grace hovering all the time like you don't know what you're doing."

Putting her fork down, Janie retorts, "Grace was helping me out. I've never done one of those before an she started in my position, so she knows."

Undeterred, Allison continues. "I know, but she doesn't have to be such a know it all."

"She wasn't. Grace is a nice person." Her annoyance simmering, Janie leans into her food.

Letting out a dramatic sigh, Allison snaps the lid on her lunch. "I'm sorry. You're right. It's just, well." She runs her hands through her auburn hair, pulling it back and letting it fall somehow perfectly into place. "Listen, I'm gonna let you eat your lunch in peace."

"Just what?" Janie asks.

Stalling, Allison sits. "It's nothing. It's just one of my roommates is such a flake. Shorted me and my other roommate on rent so now I'm just stuck." Standing, she smiles shyly. "It'll work out though, it's alright."

Guilty over her sullen mood, Janie calls out, "Wait. How much you short?"

"One twenty, but don't worry. I'm gonna figure it out." She leans against the door.

"I can loan it to you until payday if you need it," Janie offers, half wondering if she has that much to offer.

"Are you sure?" She strolls over and hugs Janie. "You're just the sweetest."

Finishing her last bite, Janie tosses everything into her bag to follow Allison. "I can bring it on Monday."

Her face strained, Allison leans closer. "Not to be a pain, but you think I could pick it up tonight? I mean, I don't want to interrupt your get together. No, ya know what, Monday works. I can get by."

"Tonight's fine. Ya wanna come by? My roommates and I are having a few people over," Janie replies.

Perked up, Allison gives her another quick hug. "Of course I'll come! What time?"

"Around 8."

Armed with Fernie's list, Janie hits the grocery store after work. Driving home, she anxiously runs through how this is all going down. *What will she think of them? What will they think of her? Why the hell did I invite her? Did I invite her, or did she invite herself? Oh God, forgot the goddamn chips. Shit.*

Two mud laden half tons parked out front confirm what she already knows, she's late. Marching in, she discards the bags on the dining table en route to the bathroom. "Sorry, had to go back for the chips."

Fernie catches her before she can clear the hallway. "Hey Janie."

"Hold on Fernie. I gotta pee like no one's business," Janie replies, shoving the door closed.

"Your work friend's here." Fernie smiles apologetically.

Peeking into Reyna's room, she doesn't see her. Taking a deep breath, she heads into the kitchen. Grace and Fernie are occupied at the stove while Allison chats with Reyna, Emmett and Doug from the crew.

"There she is." Allison comes over, wrapping her arms around Janie. A thinly striped boat neck top teases a sliver of collarbone, stopping just shy of hip-hugging jeans cascading over chunky camel heels. Her perfume blooms a step ahead, leaving Janie to breathe her in. Janie dizzily fights to shake loose the vision of her fingers tracing all those leading lines.

Staring long enough to get caught, Reyna takes to completely ignoring them altogether.

Stepping aside, Janie shields herself from the stink eye. "Sorry you had to hear that. Let me go grab the..." Realizing Reyna's well within earshot. "...the thing for you before I forget. Want something to drink?"

Lifting her beer, Allison smiles. "One step ahead of ya chica."

Janie counts the cash from her top drawer, the remaining sum of her worldly riches is a couple twenties and a few ones.

"Knock knock," Allison coos, slipping past the door. "Alright if I come in?"

Trying to remember whether she picked up her laundry or if there's food wrappers on her nightstand, Janie offers a redundant okay.

Allison tucks the cash in her pocket and hands off a bottle. "You look like you could use a drink."

Holding the door, Allison places her hand on the small of Janie's back. "After you."

A shiver chases a rush of confusion, diving into her beer's the only logical next step.

"Janie, you have to try this," Fernie calls, holding up an old wooden spoon.

"Mmm, that's good."

"Isn't it?" Grace chimes in.

"This is your best chili verde yet."

Cockily, Reyna quips, "So now you like chili?"

"I said I don't like chiles, not chili," Janie retorts.

Smug, Reyna shares a cheeky glance with Emmett. "And what do you suppose they put in chili?"

Exasperated, Janie turns away. "You know what I meant." Turning to Allison. "You want some? It's like nothing you'll have anywhere else."

"Oh, no thank you." Wiggling her empty bottle, she holds it up. "Mind if I squeeze through for a refill?"

Fernie and Grace clear a path. Grabbing one for herself and Janie, she coyly hands a beer to Janie. "Drink up, can't have you double fisting."

Speaking up from behind, Fernie steps around Allison. "Ya know, Janie it looks like you're still workin' on that one. I'll take that off your hands."

Already fixing a bowl of chili, Grace models the fixings for Janie showroom style. "You sure you don't want some Allison?"

"No, but thank you." She drifts off toward Emmett, Janie follows resisting the urge to tip the bowl back.

"Janie! Long time no see. How's it workin' out for you at NP?" Emmett asks, though his eyes keep finding their way to Allison.

Between bites, Janie extols the virtues of office life. "They're a pretty great bunch of people. We've got a bowling league and everything."

"You work with Janie there?" He asks Allison.

"Yes sir. You an NP man?" Allison replies, holding eye contact while lazily drinking her beer.

Janie seeks sanctuary in the depths of her bowl as Reyna glares at her.

Flirting in kind, Emmett stands a little taller. "As a matter of fact, I am." Pulling Reyna into his side, "We both are."

Reyna forces a smile, making no effort at authenticity.

Pointing playfully, Allison asks "You work in the fields?"

"Yup," Reyna replies flatly, pushing off Emmett.

"Isn't that dangerous? How do the guys on the crew feel about it?" Allison asks, fixed on sparring.

"Who gives a shit what they think? No more dangerous for a woman than a man." Reyna replies, looking through Janie on her way to the fridge.

Allison turns to assuage the offense before looking to Emmett haplessly.

"I get what you're askin', but that's one tough chick let me tell ya," Emmett explains, fishing around his shirt pocket.

"No shit," Comes an echo from the corner. "And she ain't a worm no more. She's a roughneck. Should see her throwin' that damn chain. Makes me wanna tear up." Nudging Reyna, Doug leans against the wall. "Ain't that right Miss Reyna?"

"Doug, get your nasty ass boots off their chair. You got any smokes?" Emmett asks. Looking back to Allison, "Did you used to work out of the Gulf Port office by chance?" His eyes betray a knowing twinkle.

Doug throws the pack over. "Leave me one."

Holding the pack out, Emmett offers. "Smoke?"

Shaking her head, Allison's posture stiffens. Her eyes search the room for Janie.

Tossing the pack to its rightful place, Emmett heads towards the door. "You coming?"

Leveling out his chair, Doug calls to the living room. "Babe I'm gonna smoke with Tex."

"Real nice meeting you," Emmett declares on his way past Allison.

"Yeah, you too. Tex," Allison replies, taking down the last of her drink.

Playing backgammon with Janie, Fernie ignores Allison's approach.

Leaning in close, Allison whispers, "Hon, I'm heading out."

"You sure? You wanna play?" Janie asks, concerned.

Feigning a yawn, Allison slings her bag over her shoulder. "You have fun. I'm just beat."

"I'll walk you down."

Janie longs for the evening's end. Killing time with Emmett and Doug, they tell tales from the rig. Drying the last of the dishes, Janie takes a deep breath to clear the air with Reyna. Rapping lightly, "You got a minute?"

Reyna coldly replies, "Yeah, what?"

"What's your deal?" Janie closes the door over behind her.

"No deal here. You're the one who wants to talk. So talk then, cause I'm going out." Fuming, Reyna never breaks stride.

"Is this about Allison? She didn't mean anything by what she said," Janie replies defensively.

"Like I give a shit what she thinks," Reyna huffs, plopping down to change her shoes. When Janie says nothing, she continues. "Are you really this stupid? That bitch is trouble."

"You don't even know her," Janie protests, resting against the dresser. "You know what I think? I think you're jealous cause I made a friend that has nothin' to do with you."

Laughing, Reyna looks dead in her eyes. "Jealous of what? This shit is going to blow up in your face. When it does, you're on your own." Grabbing her coat, she pushes past Janie.

Staying put until she hears the front door close, Janie turns out the light behind her. Poking her head into the living room, Fernie's heard everything. Holding up his blanket, he summons her to join him in being carried off by a sea of blue light.

A melody of giggles and garbled exclamations wake Janie in the wee hours. Rolling over, she pops Butch's tape into her Walkman to dampen the strange testimony of just how jealous Reyna isn't.

Presuming a plus one at breakfast, Janie gets ready in her room. Intent on mending fences, she prepares to welcome their guest. Somewhere in the bylaws of adulthood there's a clause which states one must swallow their pride at times, even though they're totally in the right and their roommate is being a complete jerk, nonetheless it must be done for the greater good of the domicile. Knotted snores permeate Fernie's door, the kitchen feels empty before she turns the corner. Nothing. No gear. No dishes. No note.

Chapter Twenty Six

eace achieved through atrophy is neither hard won nor gratifying,
it's little more than a mendacious truce. Weeks of silence ease into
a terse rapport. Conversation is casual and vacant when Janie and Reyna
cross paths. Janie remains convinced Fernie's willed his tendons into early
repair out of a pure desire to escape the tremors of their tumultuous
diplomacy.

Despite an 11 a.m. start time, he shuffles out of bed each morning to
drop Janie off. Motioning for him to roll the window down, Janie leans
on the door. "You dressing up tonight?"

"Yeah. You?" Rubbing his eyes, he catches his reflection in the rearview.

"I'll see, dunno." Janie heads in.

Donning a red windbreaker and Hawaiian shirt, Fernie goes as Chunk,
he boasts that everything is sourced from the belly of his closet. Changing
again and again, no matter what Janie tries on, she still feels meh. Pacing,
desperation pushes her to tempt fate by borrowing Reyna's biker jacket.
Surely, she can return her lucky charm unnoticed.

Launching into the kitchen with her hair pulled back and moussed
into a pompadour, Janie tugs at the collar of the jacket. "What do ya
think?" Pitching her head back, she gives Fernie the dude nod.

"What's on your cheek?"

"A teardrop." Janie looks at him plainly.

"Are you like a chola or something?" He asks quizzically.

Gasping, Janie throws her arms up. "I'm Wade Walker! You know, the
movie *Cry Baby*."

Licking his thumb and smudging the eyeliner off her cheek, Fernie ignores her complaints. "Okay, well that teardrop means something else to most people. Let's leave that part out, k?"

"Gross." She wipes away his wiping with the dish towel.

"Janie, you look good, don't worry," he consoles, rubbing the make-up off his thumb.

Pinning back her flaxen hair, Grace pulls off an ingenue Sandy with a red Peter Pan collar blouse peeking over her cream cardigan. "You two look so cute!" She exclaims, motioning for Doris to come see.

"Okay kids, you're gonna have to help me out. Janie, you're Danny?" Eyes wide, expectant. "From *Grease*? And Fernie, a tourist?" Doris stares, feeling more out of touch with each increment of silence.

Granting himself a reprieve, Fernie unzips his jacket. "Close. *Goonies*. I guess it's kind of a kids movie."

Doris pats his arm. "Oh, you're the little pudgy boy. My kids loved that movie. Fernie, you're so funny. Janie, if you'd worn a poodle skirt, we could have had two Sandys." She walks away chuckling at the hilarity of it.

"Wade Walker, actually," Janie trails off looking for any sign of her.

Bowling nights, workdays, and just about any other day when work-mates gather become an excuse to see Allison. Janie sees the stares when they take their breaks together, and the envy from some is appreciable. Having a secret, sans threat of being grounded, is kind of exciting. Janie walks a stealthy line with the Nightingales. As has become custom, they do not ask anything they may not want to hear the answer to.

To her surprise, the Nightingales throw her a nineteenth birth-day party after an all or nothing Saturday bakers match. Frugal with her words, Reyna suffers through the ordeal at Fernie's behest. Janie doesn't mind, taking what she can get. Stealing her away every chance she gets, Allison sequesters Janie in the arcade. While the ladies ap-plaud Judy from HR for her near perfect game and baking such a beautiful cake, Fernie, Grace and Reyna watch from afar.

"This is for you." Allison hands her a small box wrapped in shimmery pink paper.

Blushing, Janie admires the box. "Thanks, you didn't have to."

"I know, it's just a little something." Nudging her, "Go on, open it."

Carefully pulling away the tape, Janie opens the box. Inside's a compact manicure kit and deep rouge nail polish. Calling upon her nine-year-old self after opening a box of socks from Yaya, a big fraudulent smile draws across her face. "Wow, thank you so much."

"You sure you like it?" Leaving no gap, she takes Janie's hand. Fingers splayed she runs her index finger across her nails. "You have such great nails. Thought they might look nice dressed up a bit."

Looking down at Allison's meticulously manicured talons in a matching shade, Janie forgets her misgivings.

Gradually, Reyna becomes a ghost in the house. The extent of their exchanges little more than where she can be found and who owes what for the electric bill.

New year, new season. The Nightingales present Fernie with a league shirt. "You're one of us now," Doris coos.

Clapping along, Janie's ushered into formation. Arms folded, they pose for the team photo. From the corner of her eye, she spies Allison slip off to the arcade. Looking past Fernie and the gals tough talking the competition, her hackles are raised watching Allison flirt with Shawn from accounts payable. Owing her no claim, Janie's left to stew.

Staggering her lunches, Janie avoids Allison for the better part of two weeks. Glad for Janie's return, the ladies cheekily let a few remarks about trouble in bestieland slip. Grace being the great equalizer, swoops in to change the subject.

A step ahead of Janie sneaking off to lunch, Allison stoops cherub like with her chin resting on her folded hands atop the divider. Staring mischievously, "You've been avoiding me Missy."

Caught, Janie rambles, "No, it's just deadlines and stuff."

"It's forgotten. Let's eat." Looking down at Janie's lunch sack, she takes it from her. "You don't need this. We're going out."

Plotting drive thru options, Janie stares back at the parking lot. Allison hits the pavement. "C'mon, there's a little café around the corner." Jeeringly. "They have chili, you'll love it."

"This place looks above my paygrade," Janie quips, regarding the linen napkin tents.

Ignoring her grievance, Allison orders by heart. "Hey darlin', was hoping you were on today. Can we get two merlots, Mondavi if ya got it handy."

The waiter assesses Janie before giving Allison a secret smile.

Avoiding her wine, Janie picks at her lunch, appetite waning.

"It's just a glass of wine Janie, no one's gonna know. Group of us come here once a week, gets ya through the day. Know what I mean?" Holding her glass to her lips, she waits for Janie to join her.

"Okaay." Janie lets it hit her lips and fall away.

"Look at those bare nails, just lettin' my gift go to waste," Allison chides.

Curling her fingers, Janie looks down. "I'll get around to it."

"Let's get around to it then." Drawing her own bottle from her bag, she reaches for Janie's hand. Flicking her fingers, "Give it here."

"Wait, so you just carry nail polish around, like whenever?"

Flattening her fingers, she pats her hand. "Chips happen, and one must be vigilant."

Each swipe of Allison's thumb across the top of Janie's hand sends a chill. Quietly, Janie watches her apply the polish. The wine drowning her grievances a sip at a time, her hands look as though they belong to someone else. She watches as Allison touches up her own.

Holding her hand next to Janie's, "Look at that." Breaking off into a laugh, Allison finishes her second glass.

Smirking, the waiter sets the check down. With a flick of her finger, she motions to give it to Janie. "Hon, can you get this? My nails are still wet."

Obliging, Janie hands off her last two twenties.

Alone in the dark kitchen, Janie rifles through a bag of lunchmeat. Caught in the act of shoving a wadded slice of turkey in her mouth, she freezes with the flip of the switch.

Staring at one another, Janie blinks first. With a mouth full of food, "Hi."

"What are you doing?" Reyna asks, her hand still on the switch.

Closing the bag, Janie chews what she can and swallows the rest. "Nothin'. Didn't hear you come in."

"I'll be at Rachel's. Tell Fernie he left wet clothes in the washer." Flipping the light off, she disappears through the front door.

Tossing the bag in the fridge, Janie leans on the door staring into the shadows. Moving Fernie's clothes to the dryer, she scowls at Reyna's room. Their relationship having devolved to a fickle series of circuits, Janie can't seem to keep from tripping fuses one after another.

Reading a few back issues of The Punisher, the comfort of a mapped out universe is a welcome recess from today's ambiguity. Probably tomorrow's too. Unsure of how long it's been ringing, the phone carries on in the dark. In no mood to chat with one of Reyna's bar friends, Janie lets it cry on. A few minutes later the plaintive cry begins again. Janie sighs, putting her book down. "Hold tight Frank, back in a minute."

Annoyed. "Hello."

"Janie?"

"Yeah? Allison?"

Sniffling, she clears her throat. "Yeah, sorry to call so late. You busy?"

Pulling a length of cord, Janie grabs a seat. "Nah. Everything okay?"

After a drawn-out sigh, Allison speaks lowly. "I hate to ask you, but I just don't know who to call." Sniffling, another exhale. "Our water got turned off and we haven't been able to get another roommate in here. I'm so sorry, I know you've been so generous."

Cutting it short without cutting her off, Janie closes her eyes. "How much do you need?"

"On the count of us not payin' for a while, we owe $300."

"Three hundred?"

"I know, I know. It's a lot. Ya know, it's okay. We get paid next week."

"Wait, wait. I can loan it to you, but I really need it back on payday so I can pay rent."

"You got it. You're such a lifesaver." Pausing, Allison's voice softens. "You think you could drop it off tonight?"

"Tonight?"

"Ya know, so I can pay it on my way to work."

"Fernie's not home yet, but I could stop by after."

"I'll see ya soon hon."

A dial tone punctuates the exchange. Left with ten bucks for a week, Janie cannot look at herself passing the mirror. Staring at the ceiling, the TV drones on about nothing.

"You're still up? Kinda late for a school night," Fernie laughs, giddy from an evening with Grace. Well, Grace, Doris and Judy.

"Can I borrow your car?"

"Tonight?"

"Yeah, just gotta run by Allison's."

Handing over the keys, "Want me to come along?"

"Nah, I'll only be bout a minute or two."

Checking the address, Janie scopes out the house from the car. It's a helluva lot nicer than her house. No wonder their bills are so damned high. Knocking for the second time, someone turns down the music.

Cig perched between her fingers, Allison answers the door in the midst of shouting over her roommate about shutting up cause her friend's here. Resting her arm on Janie's shoulder to keep the smoke out of her face, she pulls her in. "Come in. Wanna beer?"

Allison's roommates look over from the couch, artfully, one pushes the rolling tray aside.

Holding Janie's hand after she gives her the cash, Allison makes a tisk tisk sound. "Girl, you gotta touch up those nails." Hugging Janie, the smell of tobacco's offset by the fleeting weight of her head resting on Janie's shoulder. "What would I do without you?"

Weeks pass, marked only by excuses. Rent increases and one broke down car later Janie's heard it all. Scraping by, she keeps it to herself. So long as her bills are paid, no one will be the wiser. Janie takes to eating on her own as Allison stops by less and less. Another payday closing in, Janie's no longer watching from her seat. In fact, she pays no mind to foot traffic at all these days.

Sliding her spare mug in front of Janie, Doris made it just how she likes it. "Thought you could use a little pick me up."

Appreciative, Janie sips slowly. "I surely could. Thanks Doris."

Giving her a motherly pat on the back, Doris returns to her office pleased with herself.

Washing Doris' cup, Janie swipes to catch it after an ill-timed hip check. Sighing with relief, Janie holds it to her chest as she turns to a giggling Allison.

"Shoot, sorry. Didn't see you had something in your hands."

Tossing the paper towel, Janie manages a half smile. "It's alright."

Doing her victory strut to the ball return, Judy's on fire with back-to-back strikes. Janie likens her to a proud pigeon. Already seated with the younger associates, Allison makes a good hostess seeing to it that no glass lacks beer, nor any plate lacks pizza. Janie keeps to her team, dying a little each time Allison catches her looking over.

Tilting her head, Allison eyeballs Janie confoundedly. "Didn't you see me waving? Phil bought a pitcher. He's such a sweetie." She starts to head back, expecting Janie to follow.

"I'm up next," Janie bemoans.

Unaccustomed to being dismissed, Allison lays it on thick whenever she thinks Janie might look over.

Bypassing the high fives, Janie waits for Fernie by the car. Agitating his limp hurrying across the lot, he massages his leg before getting in the car.

"You alright? Here, let me drive." Taking the keys, she swaps seats.

"Yeah, I think the doc might've been right. Probably no way around another surgery." Wincing as he stretches, "Doris said you forgot your dues for next season."

"Shit. I'll settle up next week."

"You sure you're alright. I can front you."

Stoic, Janie drives with purpose. "Just forgot is all. Lot on my mind with work."

"Work huh." Unacknowledged, he lets it be.

As grateful for payday as the Pope is for Sunday, Janie ardently wakes Fernie. Struggling to move his swollen knee, he pulls the blanket over his head.

A lonely gear bag sits by the door. Janie chuckles at how pissed Reyna will be when she realizes. Down to the last of her food, Janie tucks a stale box of store brand fruit rings under her arm. Approaching desperation, she'd still rather choke down dry cereal than drink that chalky soy stuff Fernie likes.

Maintaining a delicate balance between counting off the seconds with the curling iron and grabbing fistfuls of cereal, Janie can practically feel her teeth sinking into the gyro she's going to buy when she demands Allison pay up.

Startled by Reyna breezing through the hallway, Janie burns her scalp. "Shit." Shaking her half-assed attempt at curling free, she yanks the plug from the reluctant outlet.

Popping her head in, "Looks nice. I thought I threw that box out?"

"Thanks, trying something new." Janie disregards the latter. "How far'd you get?"

"All the way to the county road." Pointing to the box again, "What's up with that?"

"Breakfast!" She cheekily replies, her eyes pleading to leave it at that.

Stretching her arm across the doorway, Reyna cocks her head. "What's going on? You haven't bought groceries in weeks. Fernie said you're skipping meals. You're not even buying that crap at the bowling alley you love so much."

Brow furrowed, Janie leers at Fernie's door.

Reyna gets in Janie's eyeline. "Don't get mad at him for giving a shit about you. We both do. You giving her money? Janie?"

Tossing the curling iron in the cabinet, Janie pushes past Reyna. Punching the bag down in the box, she chucks it onto the counter. Grabbing her barren lunch sack, she heads to the door.

Reyna yells from the kitchen. "Janie. Wait!"

Despite having never met the woman, Reyna's mastered a tone which hits the same obedience trigger Helene could hit from a block away if the wind were just so. Furious, Janie closes the door.

Softer now. "I'll make you breakfast."

Fuming, Janie wrestles her hunger but stubbornness wins out. "Listen, I gotta go."

The tick of the ignitor is akin to a fiddler rosining their bow, music to Janie's ears. Knowing the road to Janie's better nature is paved through her stomach, Reyna lets her brood while the eggs fry.

Setting their plates down, Reyna waits for her to take a bite. "I don't know what you've got going on, an I'm not gonna ask anymore. Whatever, don't go not eating when there's a fridge full of food."

Dragging her bacon through the yoke, Janie shakes her head. "Not gonna eat up you guys' stuff. Don't worry about me."

Putting half her toast onto Janie's plate, Reyna leans back, arms folded. "You going to tell me you haven't lost weight? We know you're good for it. Okay?"

Guiltily savoring every bite, Janie swipes up the remaining yolky bacony goodness. "Thanks."

Janie has it worked out by the time her oxfords step out of the elevator. Adrenaline pumping with nowhere to go, the mission grinds to a halt at Allison's empty cube. Monitor dark, message light blinking, and her mug upside down.

"She called out," Phil volunteers. "Need something?"

Her resolve withered come Monday, Janie ekes through the week avoiding everyone at home while being avoided at work. Cashing in her change, she scrapes together enough to get in the black with Doris by bowling night. Judy and Doris carry the team as always.

Allison threads herself into the group, throwing her arm over Janie's shoulder. "Must be all that pent up...vivacity giving them their focus." A cheeky laugh's cut short when Janie looks on. Resting her head on Janie's shoulder, "I've missed you around the office. You mad at me?"

Loathsome of her wasted spine, Janie dares not spurn her. Tracing her fingers along Allison's slung hand, Janie's posture slackens. "No, not really."

Pulling her arm free, Allison leads them away. "Let's go to the arcade."

The usuals flank the games, Shawn meets Janie's gaze.

"No, you go ahead. It's getting heated over here. Didn't you hear, I'm part of the cheering committee."

"Your loss. Have fun with the biddies."

Grace and Janie act as surrogates for Fernie each time he's up. He teases they're killing his average. Despite their ineptitude, the team secures another win. The Nightingales lead the league for the first time since formation. Ashamed of not pitching in on a round of celebratory loaded skins, Janie begs off after prodding Grace into helping Fernie to his car.

Pinball machines crowned with empty pitchers stick out like thorns. Shawn leans against Area 51 as Allison squeals with delight at each shot fired. Turning a blind eye, he skulks away with his pint when Janie closes the distance.

"Crack shot."

"Suppose I am. Honored you could tear yourself away." Tippy toeing to trace the cabinet ledge, Allison whirls around, "You take my drink you snake?"

Tipping back the last of it, Shawn raises the glass.

"You think I could catch a ride home?"

Sweetly, "Of course darlin'." Half twirling her blue sidearm, Allison holsters it for the next taker.

"Another round Ally?" Shawn asks, with eyes for her only.

Tapping a quarter on the console, Allison raises a victorious arm. "Quitting while I'm ahead. We're gonna head out."

When a chivalrous smoker holds the door, Allison scoots in to clear the gap and slides her hand in Janie's. Afraid to jinx it by breathing, Janie does the only thing she can do. Keep walking. No words. No glances. Letting their hands fall to their sides when they reach the car.

Allison's hand wavers, restlessly shifting through the short gears with ease. Not hazarding to risk the fallout of reaching for her, Janie wedges her hand beneath her thigh. At times like this, breathing's a triumph. Forget about thinking critically.

Pulling up, Allison kills the lights. Unbuckling, Janie hesitates to let the belt go. This isn't the moment, clearly. However, it is a moment. Perhaps the only one they'll have. "Why do you act different in front of Shawn, Phil and the others?"

Wringing her fingers like wispy branches in need of pruning, Allison looks over with peccant eyes. "It's nothing, they just made some colorful remarks. They don't mean anything by it." Her eyes trail from the windshield's abyss to Janie. "People always gotta talk."

Sheepishly, Janie goes in for the kiss. How she's thought about this kiss, those lips, all to be cast down. Is this the apotheosis of her yearning? A blankness imbued with tinges of menthol and mannered reticence. Then Allison kisses her back.

Pulling Janie in, Allison lets the talk drown in the inkiness of anywhere but here. This moment is hers. Theirs.

Drawing a breath, Janie opens her eyes. There's an ache or is it sadness, staring back. Whatever it is, it's sort of beautiful.

Pushing her palms against the steering wheel, Allison reclines against the headrest. "I should get going."

"What are we? Or this?" Janie asks, her hand on the door.

"I don't know."

Climbing out, Janie lets the door fall closed behind her.

Rolling down the passenger window, Allison leans across. "Hey."

Crouching down. "Yeah?"

Allison hands her five folded twenties. "I know that I owe you a helluva lot more."

"Thanks. I'll see you tomorrow?"

"Night Janie."

The hum of an idling engine serenades Janie up the walkway. Almost breathlessly, "Night Ally."

Chapter Twenty Seven

Left to entertain himself on their morning drive, Fernie taps the wheel and mumbles along with "Slip Sliding Away." Weary of waiting for Janie's accompaniment, he breaks out his top shelf ballad squint.

Bowing to the pressure, Janie mumbles in kind.

One odd stare can be dismissed, even two if it's been a long day, but four before you've made it to your desk is an omen of bad things to come. Looking across the aisle for a friendly face, the stained chair and cast aside cables dangling over the ledge can mean only one thing. Allison's been let go or transferred. *No way, she would have told me.* Searching a sea of cubicles for a coppery lifeline, she returns to center with Doris fast approaching.

"I hope you've got coffee!" Sizing up the situation, Janie sees empty hands and Doris' badge clipped to her blazer. *Shit. She only wears her badge when someone's gonna get it.*

Cracking a courtesy smile, Doris is all business. "Janie, can we take a little walk?"

Rising, Janie needn't look up to feel the room shift. "Everything alright? Should I bring my things?"

"No, you can leave em be." Doris, already walking, motions for Janie to follow.

Looking to her fellow Nightingales, they avert Janie's gaze as though the very meeting of their eyes would turn them to stone. She knows that look of sheepish curiosity stamped out by fear of association as sure as she knows her own reflection.

Face strained, Doris looks wounded when they reach the courtyard.

Janie stalls by the coffee cart. "Doris, am I in trouble for something?"

Glancing around for piqued ears, Doris guides them out of earshot. Adjusting the clip on her badge, she pats it into place. "Honey, I don't know how to say this so I'm just gonna say it. Allison filed a complaint with HR."

Janie's heart slams to a halt against her ribs, all's quiet until the *thunk thunk* of it thumping back into the swing of things brings her around to an uneasy Doris waiting for her to say something. "A complaint?"

Taking a seat, Doris pats the concrete bench for Janie to join her. Clearing her throat, she struggles forward. "She suggested that you made advances after bowling last night."

Thunk thunk thunk, pounding away in her ears. Exhaling slowly to stay her voice, Janie looks to Doris. "Listen, this isn't..."

"Let me stop you there, before. Well, thing is she doesn't want this to go on either of your records. She just wants you to keep your distance and we can all forget the whole thing. We moved her over to accounting so, well, should be pretty easy to avoid each other."

Casting a silent prayer for the blood filling her face to find its way to less humiliating regions, Janie finds her feet.

"Can we call this settled then?" Doris asks gently.

Unable to face her, Janie nods. "Mmhmm."

"Let's get a cup of coffee, soothe those nerves before we head up. You sit a minute. I'll be right back."

Steadying herself, Janie reckons if she isn't willing to walk away right this second, then she better pull herself together long enough to get to her desk. Pushing feelings of betrayal away kicking and screaming, she wedges the door shut with the last crumbs of her pride.

Dawdling their way to the lobby, Doris puts a motherly arm around Janie. "It's natural to have bouts of confusion Janie, you're young. There's always a way back to the path. Besides, gossip never lasts. Keep your distance, and this will blow over."

Holding the elevator door, Janie follows. "You really think so?"

"Oh, yes." Stepping aside, Doris speaks barely above a whisper. "I'm not one to proselytize, but I think you could find a home with our congregation. They're good folk who know Jesus redeems all."

Almost to herself, "Book of Isaiah."

Bewildered, Doris stops in her tracks. "Yes. You know it?"

"From a long time ago." Janie hitches herself to the heart of Doris' homily, goodwill. "That's really kind of you Doris. I'll keep it in mind."

"Okay, well, when you're ready."

Watching Doris hurry into her office, Janie gauges the distance to her desk. Hanging her head, she gathers up courage enough to take the first step towards never going to be the same. *This breathing thing isn't taking.* Goodwill be damned, this is going to boil over into an ugly cry...she takes a deep breath, hoping to hold on till she clears the restroom door.

Stooping to check each stall, she fights off renegade sobs. Clearing the last, Janie lets go. Wadding up all the kraft paper the stingy towel dispenser will give, she runs it under the tap and splashes the counter. "Shit." Dabbing her face, she abandons the damp heap into the sink.

A thin, bird-like hand pushes the door open. Janie starts for the nearest stall, falling silent.

"Janie wait. It's just me, Grace."

Cornered between the sink and the stall, Janie backs herself into the paper towel dispenser. "Does everyone know?"

"Afraid so." Bumped by someone pushing the door open, Grace puts her shoulder into turning the lock. "Occupied. Try the third floor."

Embracing Janie, "Anyone who's not half blind knows this is all a bunch a bunk."

Dabbing at her eyes. "I dunno Grace. In my experience this rabbit's not going back in the hat."

"What you gotta do is put your head down and plow through till the next scandal." Helping Janie get a stubborn smudge of mascara, Grace's eyes sparkle with optimism. "You've got me. Anytime you wanna take a break, go to lunch or just hide out." Grabbing the heap from the sink, she flings it into the bin. Giving Janie's puffy eyes a once over, "There, that's better. You ready?"

Sighing, Janie lurches forward.

Head held low, Janie digs in. Checking, rechecking and then checking again, she works through every deadline she can lay her hands on. Only sipping her coffee, she staves off leaving her desk even for bathroom breaks.

The minute hand finally completes its orbit, granting Janie's release. Her famished belly full with anger, she takes the stairs as though the fourth floor were aflame. Seeing Grace crossing the lobby, Janie trots to catch up. "Glad I caught you."

"Everything okay?"

"Yeah, yeah. I just wanted to say thanks for earlier." Craning her neck, there's a UPS truck where Fernie's car should be. "Can I ask, would you mind not telling Fernie about this?"

Reticent, Grace counters, "Not if you don't want me to, but ya know he'd understand."

"I know, I just don't want to talk about it right now."

Grace invokes the sacred scout oath, raising three solemn fingers in salute. "Mums the word."

"What's the word?" Fernie asks, falling in step.

"The bird," Quips Janie.

"What?" Fernie retorts puzzled.

"Never mind, just girl talk. To what do we owe the pleasure?" Grace teases.

"Had to park next door, so I came to wait for Janie, then here you are. Guess it was meant to be." Blushing, he slows to chat with Grace.

Eager to put as much distance between her and work as possible, Janie would gladly give them a mile if she knew where Fernie parked.

Holed up in her room, Janie's grateful for Reyna's trip to Galveston with her girlfriend Rachel. While she can avoid Fernie for stretches, no such feat is possible with Reyna. Janie uses Allison's guilty offering to load up on feel good fare. Beef bologna, always beef cause if they don't label it, means they don't know either, mayo, Wonder bread, Fritos and a pit stop for a gyro. Cautiously watchful, Fernie resolves to be thankful she's eating again while enjoying the pita wrapped morsels of her generosity.

Crawling under her comforter Friday night, Janie emerges once all's quiet to fix a sandwich. Stealthily, she retreats to her fortress of wallowing.

Come Sunday evening, she awakens to Fernie checking in. Gathering her wits, she pushes crumpled chip bags and a stack of dishes aside. "Hold on."

The hall light acts as a spotlight on her sleepy eyes. "What's up?"

"You alright?" Fernie asks, straining to see over her shoulder.

"Yeah, catching up on some sleep. Why?" Janie asks, adjusting her arm to block his view.

"Are those your work clothes from Friday? You wanna get out of the house for a while?" Fernie asks, studying her.

Looking down for confirmation, Janie flattens her wrinkled blouse to no avail. "Think I'll sit this one out. You go have fun."

"If you wanna talk, let me know."

"I know. Night Fernie."

Wearing the best of last week's laundry, merely changing clothes feels an accomplishment. Janie vows to heed Grace's advice. The narrow delineation between casual looks over the shoulder and calculated observation vanishes by midweek. Pretending to proof a production report, Janie stares expectantly into an ink smudge staining the gray fabric of her divider like a Rorschach blot.

Nearly a week has passed since she last saw Allison. Though she's pretty sure she heard her yesterday, either that or someone else has taken to calling Phil darlin'. Each day Grace comes round asking her to lunch, each day she declines. The days of thoughtless trips across the office are behind her. What lies ahead is mirthful smirks, or worse yet mousy flicks of the eye as she passes. A trip to the breakroom has become a plotted maneuver.

As it has before, and undoubtedly will again, Janie's belly harasses her into motion. Eyes ahead, she hurries to heat her lunch only to find Allison and Shawn in the breakroom. Arcing into the supply closet, she grabs a surplus of pens and ducks out. Stocked up and beat down, Janie seethes at another day, let alone another week like this.

Pulling out all the stops, Fernie tosses a hero onto her lap when she climbs in the car. "Aww, you went to Junior's?

"Had some time to kill after the doc."

"What's it gonna be?" Tucking the sub away in her bag.

"You're not hungry?"

"Waiting, don't wanna get dressing on my work clothes. So?"

Tilting his head, Fernie sighs. "Not what I was wantin' to hear. Didn't take. Looks like he's gonna have to go in an fix it."

"I'm sorry Fernie. Are you gonna miss a lot of work?"

"No, I'll just keep hobbling around while I'm on the mend."

Tipping her imaginary hat, "You know I'll be your chauffer."

"I know. You mind if we pick Grace up on the way tonight?"

"I'm gonna sit this one out." Janie rolls down the window, letting the warm breeze envelop her arm.

"You're going to miss bowling?"

Picking at her pilling slacks, Janie shrugs. "Not into it tonight. Tell em I said you can take my turn."

"I'm sure my ortho would love that."

Chapter Twenty Eight

A quiet house makes for a noisy mind. Playing one of Butch's favorite tapes on Fernie's boombox, Janie takes her first shower in days. Settling in for the night with the final issue of *The Punisher*, Janie lets her mind delve into the underbelly of Frank's mobster infested New York. Steering her imagination away from fancifully fruitless pursuits of vengeance, she dissects her stowaway hero for a bite that persevered against sogginess.

When "Love Will Tear Us Apart" comes on, Janie thinks of that night in Butch's room. Putting Frank aside, she leans back, eyes closed. For another verse, she isn't hiding in her room. She's skipping through the headstones, goofing off in the plaza, she's free.

A rattle of the window signals someone's home. Grabbing her watch, too early to be Fernie. Flipping the lamp switch, Janie dives across her bed to turn off the radio. The sound of Reyna's gear bag meeting the kitchen floor confirms her suspicions. Pulling the blanket snug, she closes her eyes.

Pushing the door an inch or two, Reyna peers across the darkened room to Janie cocooned in her comforter. "I know you're awake. Heard you turn off your music. I'm here if you wanna talk."

Waiting for the click of the handle, Janie rolls over. A week of hell wells up. Lying awake, bargaining with herself, she promises to keep it low-key. *No crying, got it? Be a good roommate, ask about her trip, then say goodnight and cry yourself to sleep. I can do that. Definitely.*

"Hi." *Don't cry.* "How was your trip?"

Patting the bed, Reyna calls her over.

Shoulders drooping, Janie sighs. "How much do you know?"

"Grace told Fernie."

Sitting side saddle, Janie pulls her knees up. "Go on, get it over with."

Cupping her ear, "Say it."

After months of resentment, Reyna smiles at Janie without animus. "The sad truth of it is, girls like her are a rite of passage for folks like us. Not to be a downer, but you're gonna meet her again."

Brow furrowed, Janie huffs. "Like hell. I'm not going near her again."

"Not like the actual her, the proverbial her."

Sniffling, Janie blots at fugitive tears with her palm, weighing whether to come clean despite knowing this was coming the minute she set foot in her room. "You know what kills me? Not only did she turn me into some pervy joke, but she borrowed a bunch of money too." Tearing at a crumpled tissue clenched in her hand, a rogue sob fuels her rising ire. "Ya know the worst part?"

Reyna sympathetically smirks, shaking her head.

"I paid for all our lunches. Damn."

Rocking back in a fit of laughter, Reyna catches herself. "Dude, I knew it. I knew you were giving that bitch money."

Laughing along at the absurdity of it all, chuckling gives way to weeping. Trying to find a dry piece of tissue, Janie gives up and stuffs it in her pocket.

Handing her a glass of water, Reyna waits. "Did you love her?"

"No. I mean, up until I kissed her, I thought there might be something there. But it was kind of strange and colorless. A beer and cigarettes kind of empty I guess." Shifting, Janie continues. "Looking back, I'm not even sure if I liked her, like as a person."

Following, Reyna lets her talk it out.

Looking up, on the precipice of shame. "I dunno, I kinda got caught up in the attention. It was nice feeling wanted, by someone everyone wanted. That sounds awful, doesn't it?"

"No, sounds honest. Hell, I've been there," Reyna replies reflectively.

Tearing up again, Janie's frustration overflows with anger. "The way they looked at me. Like some gross thing. Same old shit as back home." Indignantly, "Goddammit! She kissed me back!"

Sliding over, Reyna wraps her arms around her. Laying her head on Reyna's shoulder, Janie closes her eyes, exhausted.

Stroking her hair, Reyna's cadence slows. "The girl's a mess." Resting her chin on Janie's head, she continues. "You're gonna have to learn to look out for girls like her. Infatuation's a blast, but it's a far cry from love."

Sniffling, a sheepish smile flickers. "Wasn't really looking for love. Loneliness is a wretched mistress, let me tell ya."

Wiping an errant tear from Janie's cheek, "Don't waste yourself on someone who sees you as a means to an end. Don't get me wrong, curious girls are a real good time. Thing is, you both gotta know going in it's just for a good time."

Pushing her hair back, Janie takes a deep breath to clear the doldrums. "You're right."

Reaching across, Reyna traces her fingers along Janie's jawline. Leaning in, she kisses her tenderly. "Your first time should be with someone who cares about you." Kissing her neck, "Someone who loves you."

Pulse ticking up, Janie runs her fingers through Reyna's hair. Grabbing at her scruples before they sail off into the ether, "What about Rachel? I'm not trying to be a fool and a harlot all in the same week."

"What I have with Rachel's not this. This is us." Fixed on less talking, "She'll understand, and if she doesn't then that's on me."

Losing herself in the eyes of someone yearning for her, the crushing mass of humiliation and rejection lifts. Less talking is good. Come to think of it, less thinking too.

Running her hands up Janie's sides, lifting her shirt off, Reyna self-consciously bares her palms. "They're kinda rough."

Cradling her hand for closer inspection, Janie kisses her palm. "They're perfect." Entwining their fingers, Janie pulls Reyna to her. Touching her and being held by her is everything being with Allison could never have been.

Nuzzled against Reyna's chest in the wee hours, Janie listens to the cadence of her heartbeat. Unbridled by guilt or fear, something approaching contentment swells. "How old were you when...?"

"I met my first girlfriend?" Reyna laughs.

"Sure."

"Junior year. I played every sport they offered for girls, would've played football if they'd let me."

Interrupting, Janie props herself up. "You were a jock?"

"Hard to believe, it's true though." Sighing as though she's still not fully come to terms with it, "Funny thing is, seems most people knew I was gay before I did. Pretty much skipped the whole coming out thing. Anyway, me and a few of my field hockey teammates were smoking out under the bleachers after practice and one of them brought their sister along."

Grinning, "Lemme guess a cheerleader."

Scoffing, "No. She was kind of a smarty pants. A senior, a very popular senior into ASB an shit. We started hanging out all the time after school. At school we were like strangers. Saw her sister most days for practice, didn't have a clue. Went on like this all year. I didn't care though, she was worth it. Figured after we were out of school, everything would be different. She was my first everything."

Intrigued, Janie waits impatiently. "Then what? What happened?"

"Then nothing, nosy." Reyna pinches her, blocking each retaliatory move with ease.

Surrendering, Janie settles back into her nook. "Me nosy? You can't leave it like that. Why'd you break up?"

"Prom came around. I heard through a friend she was going with a guy on the baseball team, varsity. Gave me this line about being in the court, and her parents expecting her to go. We fought some, then just stopped talking about it. I ended up being asked by Emmett."

Nudging her, "I knew it." Mockingly, "Oh, we're just friends."

"Do you wanna hear the rest or not?"

Clearing her throat, "Go on."

"Prom was at the American Legion. We had a big ol' crappy lodge. We hadn't spoken since Emmett asked me. She spotted me, so we took off to the bathrooms down a dark corridor by the offices. Teenage me thought it was genius." Pensive, Reyna exhales the way you do in the eternity between the alcohol swab and the phlebotomist going in. "One thing leads to another, never heard the door or noticed the footsteps until the sound of heels hitting the tile and the door swinging closed. It's been years and I can still see the panic in her eyes. How quiet she was getting dressed, we both were."

Kissing her shoulder, Janie holds her tighter.

Eyes glistening, Reyna tries to blink it away. "She couldn't even look at me. Could barely look at herself fixin' her hair in the mirror. The hall was empty, she was getting further and further ahead. I kept asking if she was okay. All she'd say is I don't know, I don't know. Then she said she was sorry and shot ahead into the ballroom."

"Did you find out who walked in on you?"

"Not till school. I wasn't sure what I'd walk in to, so I cut out. Heard she didn't place in the court. And the best part, word got around she blew him in the backseat of his mom's Taurus. Can you believe that tacky shit?"

"A week ago, no. Today, you bet. Who was it? That walked in?"

"Oh, so come Monday, her sister comes up to me at practice. Confesses it was her. That her sister was confused, but not anymore. That she forgave me and wasn't going to tell anyone." Vexed all over again. "She forgave me! Thing is, I got with this girl from back home a couple years ago in Burque. Said she knew of two girls smarty pants had messed with."

Offhandedly, Janie remarks, "That's a long experiment."

"Nah, she knew what she was into. Trust me." Rolling onto her side, Reyna rests her hand on Janie's hip. "You kinda met me at the end of my bitter phase."

"At the end?" Janie asks coyly.

"I'm not bitter. Am I?"

"No, you're pretty sweet when you're not being a hard ass." Janie lifts her head, rising to meet her lips.

Hazily, Janie's eyes make sense of Reyna's silhouette flowing in and out of ribbons of first light breaking through the blinds. Watching her dress, Janie reaches for her as she ties her laces.

Stretching across, Reyna kisses her. "You better hurry up, gonna be late."

Slipping into her PJs, Janie makes a dash for her room. Banking off Fernie rounding the corner, she points to some unseen thing. "Overslept, then I had to pee. Okay, ready in a minute."

He watches her disappear behind her bedroom door. Stone-faced, Reyna brushes her teeth with fastidious singularity. Undecided if he wants to know more, Fernie walks away.

Liberated from her morose state, Janie builds a plate worthy of her former self. Fernie looks on as she prepares a plate for Reyna, even remembering a napkin. Eating sporadic bites to look busy, Fernie's eyes dart, expecting Janie to dive in. Instead, she waits for Reyna to join them. No backhanded compliments or criticism, Reyna takes her seat.

The what the fuck hangs heavily in the air. Fernie can bear it no longer. Passing the Tapatio, he points his fork. "Aren't you late?"

Disobediently, Reyna's eyes blaze past Janie and back to Fernie. "Have a meeting at the field office," she replies, matter of fact like. "Janie, I'll drop you off on the way."

Agreeably, Janie avoids eye contact with Fernie. "Mmhmm, great."

Sipping her coffee, Reyna looks across to Fernie. "You know, so you can take your time this morning."

Looking from one to the other, Fernie *tisks*, shaking his head while scraping the last bite from his plate. "Ya'll are a couple kooks." Washing his plate, he ignores their stifled laughter.

The office is no less an exercise in endurance. Everyone in Janie's department except the temps, whom hold only marginally superior social standing, seem to fall into three camps. Those who want to scorn her, made up of younger associates and Phil. Phil's fashion forward sensibilities coupled with his inability to advance have grandfathered him in as a junior associate. A den mother of sorts. Those who want to save her, the Nightingales and a few born agains sprinkled amongst the general population. Lastly, the bottom feeders who want to turn her, which is basically two guys who think their dicks are enchanted wands.

Doris at ten o'clock. *Shit, she's in her Aerosoles and gliding.* Janie watches helplessly, desperate to wrap up a call with an accounting clerk at corporate. Yes, yes, she knows that the fiscal year is not the same as a calendar year. *Jesus, it was one typo.* Fishing around for the cradle, the handset tumbles into place. Unable to get a read, Janie reminds herself she's done nothing wrong.

"Good morning!" Smiling, Doris extends her spare mug. "Noticed you didn't come in with a cup."

Janie scans her lapel for a badge before unclenching. "Running behind. You're the best! Thank you!"

Leaning over, Doris does a cursory check for perked ears. "Between you and me, I'm glad you haven't thrown in the towel. You're one of the strong ones." Tapping the divider for emphasis, "I should know, I am too."

Appreciative of being back in Doris' good graces, Janie beams as she had when her mother made a meal she loved to show the storm had passed. Peeping around Doris to assess the other Nightingales, not so much.

"Don't worry about them. They'll come around," Doris whispers. She pulls a small pamphlet from her coat pocket. "Just a little something about our worship services. If you ever wanna chat or just get away, my office is always open."

"I'm gonna read it on break." Lifting her mug, Janie takes a big sip. "Thanks again."

The thought of another lunch alone with her thoughts is unappetizing. Last night lingers sweetly, a wren song carried on the breeze. A blush rises thinking on any moment for too long. Best not to dwell. Allowing exultation to cultivate the seeds of expectation would surely sow calamity.

Taken aback at Janie's inclination, Grace grabs her keys. Understated in her empathic capacity, she leaves work and home in their respective places. Regaling Janie with tales of life abroad before claiming a swatch of Odessa to call her own, Grace proves to be far more than meets the eye.

"No offense Grace, but I'd never take you for the nomadic type."

No stranger to presumption, Grace knows folks see her as a buttoned up Sunday school type. "It's a long story, but the short end of it is I basically had a crisis of faith. I was midway through discerning, and I don't know, I just woke up one morning asking myself if this is what I really wanted."

"What is that, discerning?" Janie asks, absentmindedly chewing her food.

"It's kind of the baby steps to becoming a nun. Grew up in a devout family and felt a calling since, oh gosh, junior high I guess. I was a sophomore studying theology with aspirancy on the horizon."

"You were going to be a nun? Really?" Smirking, Janie abandons her fork onto her plate. "Don't you go to Doris' church?"

Laughing, Grace nods. "I was, and I do. Started going with my grandma when I moved to Odessa. My daddy converted to marry my mama."

"So, what happened?"

Pulling at the cuffs of her sweater, Grace continues. "I knew I couldn't go further with doubt in my heart. On an ill-received whim, took half of my college fund, told my father I was taking a sabbatical and booked a flight to Paris with a hop over to Lourdes."

Puzzled, Janie tries to follow. "Were you like a backpacker or something?"

"Not exactly. I wanted to feel other people's faith, if that makes sense. A shrine was about the best place I could think of to do that." Sensing Janie's polite agreement, Grace explains. "Think about how much belief it takes to save for so long, to make a pilgrimage to somewhere just so you can touch a statue or slip a note in a wall. I wanted that."

"You lost your faith then?" Janie's eyes betray a knowing kinship.

"Yeah, I guess I did," Replies Grace, keeping watch of the time. "It really was something, you could feel it all around you when they held prayer services at the shrine. Even more at times, when I was alone praying, before the tours began."

Gathering her bag, Janie walks alongside Grace. "Was it not enough? I mean, here you are at NP."

Slowing to a stroll, Grace searches for how to put her experience into words. "I was gone for almost two years. I worked where I could, then moved on to the next place. After Lourdes, I went to Fatima then Lichen. Eventually made it to Jerusalem. Anyway, at some point what I was looking for changed."

"Maybe you grew up some. Didn't need the same stuff you needed back home," Janie offers or perhaps projects.

"Yeah, maybe. It's hard to explain."

"Sorry, I'm always the queen of why."

"No, it's fine. I've never really talked much about it. I went to have my faith validated, which I guess is a little at odds with the concept of faith to start with. When I was around these people who were so filled with peace and hope, it was almost intoxicating. Then there were the ones seeking a miracle for themselves or someone they loved. The desperation was tangible. I could feel their sorrow. It was heavy."

Janie nods.

"Point is, I was there to transmute my faith from dubious to devout on the steam of others. Which was good and fine when I was selling relics in the shop. However, I was an empty vessel when it came to those who remained steadfast at their weakest moments."

Thinking back to her last Christmas at home, Janie can still feel that communal light for those brief moments when the congregation rose above their everyday pettiness. In retrospect, it made the ostracism to come all the more painful. Knowing little of how Catholics operate, Janie finds herself envious of Grace's experience. "For what it's worth, I think you're being kinda hard on yourself. I'm glad things ended up how they did, bet Fernie is too!"

"Taken a while to get here, but It's just plain honesty. I would've kept bouncing round if I hadn't come home to look after my grandpa. He was at the end with emphysema, and my grandma needed some respite. I dug deep, and it just wasn't there. Proof's in the pudding as they say." No longer keen to walk this forgotten path, Grace laughs away an impending cry. "You know, meeting you and Fernie has changed my life. Don't tell him, but I kinda love that man."

Janie relishes her secret. "God, you two are so cute it makes me wanna barf. Happy barf though."

Greeted by the aroma of barbecue wafting down the walkway, a rare temperate evening settles across West Texas. A perfect night for grilling, Reyna declares from the back patio. Each doing their part, the three share a meal in high spirits. Passing around the ribeyes, Reyna cracks open her second Shiner. "I met with Leland today. You remember him Fernie? I think he was a rig manager when you were on."

Painting a bite of meat with sauce, Fernie savors the mouthful. "Sounds familiar. Man, we never saw the boss unless they came to chew us out if someone got hurt."

Laughing, a shit eating grin emerges. "He remembers you."

"Why?" He asks, knowing it's going to be a good one.

"He said when you were on Brady's crew, you got so sick of them talking shit about your Mom that you threw away all the dirty magazines and put up a crucifix in the doghouse."

Clapping, Fernie roars with laughter. "They told him about that?"

"He said that he's never gotten so many complaints from one crew at the same time."

"Funny thing was, none of them would take the cross down. They all baked in the sun just to crack a cold one."

Chiming in, Janie asks, "Why wouldn't they take it down?"

"You wanna be the dude who denies Christ?" Fernie replies, Reyna nodding in firm agreement.

"He says hi. Told him you were all hobbled and shit right now." With a crooked grin, Reyna toasts him.

Having always thought of Fernie as being too clean cut for the fields, Janie's learned heaps about assumptions today. "How long did you work in the fields?"

"Not long, six months or so. Needed a job, and a buddy brought me along," Fernie replies. "It's not for everyone, not for me anyway."

"Leland was telling me there's a gopher spot opening up soon. Told him I might know someone." Looking to Janie with a raised eyebrow, "What do ya think?"

Janie wraps her head around it, ignoring Fernie's snickering. "What's a gopher?"

Shrugging, Reyna's nonchalant. "You know, like dropping off parts, running around between rigs, like..."

"The company bitch. Sorry for being crude, but it's true," Fernie interjects.

Descriptions aside, Janie's not entirely put off. "Do I need experience?"

"You basically just have to be a warm body that can read a map." Smiling, "I think you're perfect. Gets you out of that shithole office. And I can probably get you on a crew after a while."

"Reyna, no," Fernie counters. "C'mon, look at her."

"What? She's probably stronger than I am. She can do it."

"I know she's not like a little thing," Fernie argues.

"Jesus, I'm right here," Janie butts in.

Patting her back, "You're beautiful, you know that." Fernie turns to Reyna. "Do you remember when the commode backed up into the tub? She squawked and ran into the yard." Gesturing towards Janie, he continues. "What do you think is going to happen when she has to deal with the smell kicking off the bowels of an old rig?"

Laughing at the memory, Reyna remains vigilant. "Janie?"

"You're both assholes, for the record. Can I think about it over the weekend?"

"Yeah. Let me know when I get home on Sunday."

"You leavin'?" Janie asks.

Carrying her plate to the sink, Reyna doesn't turn around. "Going to Rachels."

"Have fun." Janie leaves off her dishes, disappearing to her room.

There will be no discussion of what they are to one another. No promises made or implied. An unambiguous, unspoken entente is forged.

The notion of driving around in the heat, swatting at bugs and lifting filthy parts all day is marginally more appealing than being the office predator. Contemplating Doris' rose-colored theory of time healing all wounds versus a fresh start in the mucky muck, Janie decides to sleep on it.

Come Sunday, Fernie gets an early start in his Sunday best. Sweating through the back of his shirt, he's nervous to meet Grace's church friends. Pacing, Janie weighs the ethical implications of breaching her promise to Grace. Surely benevolent candor warrants absolution. Not to mention, Grace did give Fernie the scoop on work.

Turning the fan toward Fernie, Janie leans on the dining table. "Can I tell ya somethin'?"

Sniffing his shirt with fear laden eyes, "What?"

"She loves you." Nodding with a self-satisfied smirk, "Told me so herself. Don't say anything, you'll ruin it."

Standing taller, Fernie's eyes search Janie's expression for any hint of a merciful lie. "I am kind of a catch." Popping his collar, he falls out laughing.

"You're good my friend. Besides, if it doesn't work out with Grace, I'm pretty sure half the Nightingales would line up to take her place."

"Those women are way too high maintenance. And the ego on Judy. Phew, friends is all I can handle."

"It amuses and disturbs me that you've thought about this," Janie remarks, departing with a precariously cradled bowl of frosted flakes.

When he isn't home for dinner, Janie assumes all went well. Wavering between driving across town for some passable pastitsio or compiling the contents of her fridge shelf under a blanket of cheese to help it go down easier, laziness prevails until her throat declares an embargo. Holding a takeout menu, Janie hangs up mid-dial as someone comes in.

"Looks good, and I don't say that often about your cooking. What is it?" Fork in hand, Reyna gathers a hearty bite. Reyna expels it back into the bowl, "Fuck, that's rank. What is it?"

"Leftovers gone wrong I reckon."

Emptying the contents into the trash, Reyna ties up the bag and tosses it to Janie. "Let's go out for dinner."

Lying in bed, the heat of an August night stakes its claim. The fan's no match. An unwilling accomplice, it distributes the sweltering air with the fortitude of an oven left ajar. Rolling over to face Janie, Reyna takes her in before speaking. The way her eyes look a little sad when she doesn't think anyone's watching. How the hair around her crown goes its own way in wispy rebellious curls under the influence of sweat and heat. "Have you thought about the transfer?"

"Yeah, still thinking I guess." Reaching, Janie pulls Reyna close.

Reyna fidgets with the crumpled sheet edge. "Listen, I gotta lettem' know. If you don't want it, no sweat but they're not gonna hold it."

Flipping over, Janie chews at her thumbnail unheedingly. Closing her eyes, she jumps into the foggy abyss of Reyna's world. "Tellem' I said yeah." Flattening the sheet at her side, Janie gives it a chop. "I gotta get out of there. I mean, how hard could it be?"

Reyna, throwing her head back, laughs to the edge of a cackle. "You have no idea. But I know you can do it."

Chapter Twenty Nine

Mustering the courage to give notice to a manager you adore is akin to breaking up with someone you want to stay friends with. The moment's never right. As the fates would have it, they start making plans. The longer you wait, the harder they'll take the news.

Handing over two bowling shirts, one a shade of magenta and the other teal with a gray stripe, Doris doesn't take a breath. "I have to place the order tomorrow, so take them home to see which one we like. We'll vote in the morning. Goodness, what a great way to celebrate last season. Oh, and don't forget to see which one Fernie likes too. You know Janie..."

"Doris, I requested a transfer. I'm sorry," Janie blurts in a panic.

"Oh." Petting the shirts, she pauses. "Where?"

Unable to meet her eyes, "I'm taking a gopher job out near Andrews."

Aghast, Doris gives a motherly sigh, wringing her hands. "Janie, that isn't work fit for a girl. Has someone been giving you a hard time? Honestly, you just tell me."

Adamantly shaking her head, Janie puffs herself up. "No, no, it's just that, well Doris, there's no comin' back from what happened. And you don't have to worry about me. Reyna works on the crew, she's gonna look after me."

Studying her hands, Doris acquiesces to her perception of what's lured Janie away. "I see. I know you're an adult, so I'll just say one last bit before I hold my tongue. Janie, those people that work in the field are rough folk. If you have trouble, you can call me, and I'll find a spot for you here. Okay, hon?"

"Thank you, really, thank you Doris!" Scooping up the shirts, Janie slings them over her arm. "I'll run these by Fernie."

Looking up with an afterthought, Doris peeks over her glasses. "Far as I'm concerned, you're still a Nightingale. Even if you're too busy wandering around nature's backside to make the games, you still get a shirt."

The insufferable waxes tolerable when you're a short timer. As her two weeks draw to a close, Janie leans into what little time she has left. Freed from the constraints of perpetual judgment, she doesn't shy away from eating lunch where she pleases or taking breaks when she pleases. Holding her head midway between scrutinizing her shoes and provocation, Janie walks through the office eyes ahead. There'll be no mending of fences among she and a few of the Nightingales nor anyone else for that matter. Appeasement was never the design, merely a burgeoning desire to gather the crumbs of self-respect they'd fed upon these last weeks.

Friday arrives quietly, there'll be no farewell cupcakes in the breakroom or see ya around happy hour. A collective anticipatory lightness hovers. Much to her relief, Janie's called in for her exit interview before lunch. Playing her part, she answers as expected. Painting the image of a contented young woman who's heavy hearted leaving her fulfilling job in pursuit of new opportunities. Her only suggestion for management...*keep up the solid leadership.* Is there anything else she would like to add? *Yes, yes there is, she's going to miss the close-knit culture. Almost feels like family.*

Tucking the interview form under a file, Doris comes around for her hug. "I'm going to miss you. I hope to see you at bowling from time to time, and I mean that."

Drawing in as much breath as she can while engulfed by Doris, Janie laughs. "I'm going to miss your coffee."

Hurrying back around her desk, Doris rummages through the cavernous bottom drawer. "Here it is. Something to remember us by."

Heartened, Janie admires the salvation she's often leaned on. "Your spare? I love this cup. Thanks." Turning to see Grace in the doorway, Janie holds up the mug.

"You ladies after some lunch?"

Frowny faced, Doris begrudgingly holds up a clipped stack of spread-sheets striped with highlighter and rumpled edges. "Don't I wish. I have a budget meeting. You two go on."

"I'll bring ya something. Janie, I'm gonna grab my purse. Right back."

Brushing past, Doris checks her watch. "I gotta skedaddle. You two have fun."

While hanging out alone in Doris' office feels weird, loitering in the doorway is somehow a lesser oddity. Evading Judy's stare, Janie shifts her gaze to the breakroom. The sight of Allison unassumingly sipping tea stirs a streak of panic. The allure of seeing while unseen forbids her to look away. And when their eyes meet, Janie bears down. Tinged with shame, Allison's gaze hints at remorse. Only then does it occur to Janie she's alone. No Shawn and the gang, no one. The anger stowed all these weeks, a mere slip of the tongue from the surface, falls away. Pity is all that remains.

At times like those, Janie's left with why. Why are some people so damned hard to see when they're standing right in front of you? Why are moments we daydream of, nay, fantasize about, so dispiriting on the rare occasion they intersect with reality? One would think after having lived the reverie of righting a wrong a hundred times in our mind, the physical manifestation would be more noteworthy.

Begging off from bowling and stewing over Reyna splitting to Rachel's before she got home, Janie fetches her shoebox from the closet. Scribbling on the lid to see if her motel pen's any good, she thinks of a better use for her transfer form. Flipping the page, she absently picks at the staple.

Dear Lydia,

It's been a long while since I've written. Time gets away from you when you're trying to keep up with the living. We've settled in Odessa, which is not all that close to Houston if you were wondering. It's becoming home, it's where Fernie, Grace and Reyna are. Grace and Fernie are like the older siblings I always thought I'd be to Matty. Guess I'll never know.

You must be halfway through college by now. I'll bet your prospects are pretty good. I'm fixing to go from an office to oil field work. Sort of terrified I'm going to fail and disappoint Reyna. I think I could love her if she loved her. Sometimes I think I do anyway, but she's not you. An abiding obstacle I suppose.

For all I know, you're not you anymore either. I don't think that's true though. Even as a kid, seems like you knew who you were. Even more, you somehow knew who I was when I didn't. I wonder now if that part of me, the part that you knew, is all that's left from before. Do you think it's too late to find out?
Always,
Janie

A dream, defying recall, withers one rut at a time as the tired Blazer's suspension heaves off the road, creakily threatening to bottom out. Yet another threat the old girl will have to pack away for the ride home. A hazy sunrise greets Janie's sleepy stupor.

Watching Reyna's every move, Janie stays in step. Men's voices wax and wane as the rig groans to life in the distance. Tipping back the last of the morning's first cup, Gil smiles warmly. "This the new blood?"

"Yessir," Reyna confirms, grinning in anticipation of his are you ready speech.

Removing his glove to shake Janie's hand, Gil reads her trepidation. "You ready to be a roustabout?"

"Is that like a gopher?" Janie asks, eying his thermos.

"Gopher? No, I don't train no gophers. They're undignified critters I pick off with my rifle. No ma'am, I train roustabouts." Pausing, he unscrews his thermos for round two. "So let me ask you again. You ready to be a roustabout?"

Harnessing the paucity of enthusiasm available to her, Janie affirms her intentions. "Absolutely!"

"That's what I like to hear. You'll shadow me before we throw ya overboard." Pointing to an old GMC utility truck, "See that? That right there will be yours once you're on your own. Can ya drive a stick?"

Reyna interrupts, "She's a little rusty, but I'll work with her." Pivoting, she gives Janie a look to go with it. "The clutch drags on that thing, but you'll get used to it."

"Ain't nothing wrong with that clutch. I just said that to keep ya from getting pissy." Ignoring Reyna's bristling, Gil looks to Janie. "I don't care if you can or you can't, cause you'll surely know how in two weeks. Cause after that, I'll dock ya if ya burn out my clutch."

Nodding emphatically, Janie dares not look over at Reyna.

Motioning to Reyna, "Go on, get over there or one of them's gonna climb up and steal your spot." Grabbing his thermos, he's off. Waving his arm, Janie double-steps to follow.

Feeling every bump, Janie lets little groans escape as they clear the dirt road heading for the highway.

"You think you're gonna stick around?" Reyna asks, equal parts sympathetic and amused.

"Yeah, the clutch lived to grind another day, so I guess I will too," Janie laments, trying not to think about the smell of the clutch after stalling for the third time.

Smiling, Reyna pats her leg. "You're doing good. Gil likes you. Trust me, you could be stuck with Randy."

"Yeah, I like him alright. Who's Randy?" Janie asks.

"Randy's the motorman. He's the one always kickin' the dirt and bitchin' over by the doghouse. Gil's the pusher. He's old school, likes to show the newbies the ropes to get a feel for whether he likes ya or not. He likes you, otherwise you'd been digging drainage ditches while they were loading the truck."

Sleepy, Janie slumps back a bit. "Reminds me of my Dad some, kinda cranky and sweet."

Fears abated, Janie takes to her work with ease, save for the heavy lifting. Always watching, and assessing her resources, she arms herself with tools to circumvent the ceaseless expectation and subsequent commiseration among the boys that she'll always need a hand. Amassing a trio of a hand truck, furniture dolly and an old banged up loading ramp, Janie proudly gets most anything off the truck. At least anything one of the guys could manage on their own without calling for help. A rough patch of brusquely telling them to back off whenever they try to sidestep her unloading ritual earns her the nickname Back Off Betty, which eventually fades to Betty.

Watching the sun come up on a particularly cold October morning, Gil shares one of his wife's fried blackberry pies. "Lord, I could eat a dozen of these things left to my own."

Wiping blackberry from the corner of her mouth, Janie nods. "I can see why." Wrapping half her pie, she tucks it next to her knee. "Reyna'll kill me if I don't save her some."

"Go on, finish it. I'll fetch her another when she finishes her primping in the doghouse." Sharing a laugh, Gil shushes them. "Don't tell her I said that. Gotta be nice to them when they're up on that monkey board."

Janie makes a zipping motion and tosses back the last bite of pie.

"You plannin' to follow her up to the derrick?" Gil asks earnestly.

"Dunno. Haven't thought much about it," Janie replies, staring ahead.

"Ya know, you could do pretty well as a mud logger if this is what you really wanna do. Wouldn't have to break yer back every day either."

"Mud logger huh. Kinda seems like the company man's bitch, pardon my language. I know I can't lift as much as the guys, but I try to pull my weight."

"Janie it's not that." Gil chews on his words. "Don't take this the wrong way, but if you were my daughter, there's no way in hell I'd let you run around on a rig. You're young enough to go get an education, do something else. We're all dug in out here, don't know nothin' else."

Brushing away crumbs, Janie smiles at Gil. "I dunno, got you a pretty nice house and your truck ain't exactly starved for comfort."

"I'll grant you that. You know what else it got me? My knees are shot, my wife has to shout at me from a few feet away and I've missed more of my kids' birthdays than I care to say." Gil bemoans, sipping from his piping hot thermos.

Squinting against the sun, Janie wishes Reyna would hurry up already. "I hear ya, but Reyna's still here."

Gil raises an eyebrow. "Reyna's still here cuz she's like one of them little guys who make up what they lack in muscle with angst and stubbornness. Some of them got a lifetime supply, come a few years they'll be in jail or working up on the monkey board. Most of 'em burn out. I dunno if she's a lifer but she's definitely got reserves." Laughing, he readies himself to get up. "Got her eye on driller, so ya never know."

"Didn't know that. Huh," Janie remarks, mostly to herself.

Nudging Janie, he smiles. "What do I know. Hell, what do you know, you're just a kid." Grabbing his coffee, they head to the doghouse.

Grinding down the clock on another year, life settles into a new routine. Janie celebrates her twentieth birthday among friends and the crew. The line between the two grows indistinguishable. Driving home on a frigid December evening, the heater on the old gal cuts out. Receding into her coat, Janie fidgets with the knobs. "We gotta get this thing fixed or it's gonna be an icebox in here for the next two months."

Reyna turns the dial. "It's no good, the whole thing's fucked."

Turning the dial a quarter of the way back, Janie counters, "How do you know? Can't hurt to get it looked at."

Reyna twists it back. "Cause I know. Anyway. I was talking to Emmett, and he's moving in with his girl. Said we could take over his lease. Wouldn't be but a fifteen-minute ride out to the rig. What d'ya think?"

Surly and shivery, Janie's in no mood to be agreeable no matter how sick of the drive she is. "So we get to freeze for fifteen minutes instead of forty-five. Golly, sign me up."

Twisting her neck to see if the face matches the tune, it surely does. Reyna takes a breath to let the first thing that crosses her mind keep going, making room for something nicer. "Would you like to go car shopping? Cause so far as I can see, I'm the one haulin' your ass around. Drivin' Miss Janie over here."

A chuckle averted renders a nasal contraction best left without comment lest Reyna were looking to kick the hornet's nest. "You wanna move all the way to Andrews rather than fix the heater? I'll pay for the damn thing."

"Oh my God! What?" Pulling over hastily, the tail catches and skips a little on the loose dirt. "Janie, this isn't about the heater."

Huffily, Janie concedes. "Fine. Christ, no need to yell about it."

Reyna tries a calmer approach. "I'm tired of drivin' so far every goddamn day. Aren't you?"

"Yeah." Shifting in her seat with her back to the window, "What about Fernie? Is he coming too?"

"No. Grace is pretty much living with us, they'll probably just make it official and move in together."

"I dunno. Grace is pretty churchy."

"They can call themselves roommates, whatever. I mean who cares, she ain't that churchy. She stays over a lot."

A crack appears in the salty veneer. "What about Rachel?"

"What about her?" Reyna retorts, putting the truck back in gear.

Grabbing the oh shit handle as Reyna tears onto the blacktop, Janie knows the answer before she asks. "Is she gonna move?"

Staring dead ahead, "That's not gonna workout. Never was. Janie, what's the word?"

"Yeah, fine." Settling into her seat, Janie pulls at her collar to get the flaps as close to her ears as she can.

Chapter Thirty

Two years in a dry county is enough to turn anyone into a teeto-taler. Almost anyone. For the sauce loving souls who toil away in the shadows of towering drilling rigs and relentless pumpjacks, highway 385 just across Ector County line is their road to salvation. If the itch in need of scratching is greater than the pulpit can relieve, West Odessa can set the spirit right. At least for a week or so, till a memory will no longer do.

Much like falling in love, turns out we grow up when we're looking the other way too. Reyna, whom Janie thought of as a grown up, has somehow managed to become even more adult like. She and a few guys from the crew gave her beloved old gal a five-gun sendoff before surrendering her to the wrecker. Dressing to impress, she's joined the ranks of roughnecks driving Dearborn's finest three-quarter ton trucks.

Her sights fixed on driller, Reyna bides her time on the derrick under Emmett. She, Emmett and Janie are all that remain of the original crew. Gil took a job with the company men once his last kid started college. Roustabouts come and go with the breeze, some more worm like than others. Despite having threatened to quit twice in the heat of the moment, Janie's still on the floor and training with Reyna. Loving life on the platform when she gets the chance, aspirations of moving up have yet to escape the abstract.

Traces of Reyna's perfume billow in the cross breeze of their bungalow. A sure sign she'll be laying on the horn in five minutes time if Janie's not ready. She scrambles to get her new boots on, a status purchase at the urging of one of the other floor hands. Walking like she forgot to take the stuffing out of the toes, Janie climbs into the truck. "Think I'm gonna change."

Already pulling away from the curb, Reyna's having none of it. "If you go back to change, we'll miss Fernie."

Sighing, Janie stretches for one last look. "Fine. Can't dance in these."

"You can't dance anyway." Alone in her merriment. "What's wrong with em'?"

"They're just, they're hard. I dunno," Janie pouts.

"You wear boots to work every day. How's this any different?"

"Those are work boots. I'm over it." Shifting to find a nook in the cold leather seats, Janie pulls a flask from her bag. Taking a nip, she passes it. "You think that girl from last week will be there?"

Handing it back, Reyna keeps her eyes to the road. A road they've driven weekly since their move. A road she could drive blindfolded if she had to. "Dunno. Should've made your move. Waste not want not."

Taking a last nip before screwing the cap on, Janie lets the burn settle into her belly. "That friend of hers was hoverin'. If they're there, might call on you to run interference."

"That's one I won't take for the team, but I'll buy her a drink for sisterhood." A wicked grin cresting, Reyna takes in the smoky horizon.

And so it goes. Another Saturday night at the Hangout, where leaving alone is a choice. While there's been occasion when a girl's made the trip back to Andrews with one of them, Reyna avoids the complication of flings whenever and wherever she can. Hell, half the time neither of them can be assed to cozy up to anyone at all, so they leave together. Letting pretense shield them from that being the plan all along. Janie finds it easy enough to tell early on who's local, and who's taking the tour. The ultimate wingman, Fernie leaves a couch open for one or both if the evening gets away from them.

A pretty brunette, the type who ends up a bank teller or pharmacy rep, eases up beside Janie at the bar. Leaning a smidge farther than she needs to, she calls out her order. Handing off a beer to Janie when the bartender brings their rounds over, "You look like a Coors kinda girl."

Content to be whatever type of girl earns a beer from her, Janie takes back a swig. "As a matter of fact, I am. I'm Janie."

"Lisa," she replies, glancing at the round of Bud Lights perched between Janie's fingers. "You need a hand?"

"Maybe later," Janie replies coyly. "Wanna play some pool?"

Janie watches Lisa survey the room with caution stepping away from the crowded bar. The way a woman takes in the scene is a good tell of who they are. Regulars like Janie and Reyna look around in blithe anticipation of a familiar face, a genesis for a knowing nod. Tourists, real and rare in these parts, steal glances. Cloaked in insecurity, they rifle through true crime tales of pickups gone wrong. Conversation is guarded and banal, unless they're from the city. In which case, they're the ones bored by a bunch of West Texas queers who couldn't give two shits about much of anything beyond who's up next at the table.

Then there are the Lisas. They almost always have a man at home, maybe a kid. Even when they don't, there's no room for this in their lives. Lisas are here for the same reason most everyone else is, to fuck or get fucked. Push aside the small talk, the flirty competition over a game or two, or the building tension of dancing to Hal Ketchum followed by slow dancing to "I Swear," every goddamn week. The only way they could make their intent any clearer is if they grabbed you by the collar and whispered it in your ear. Reyna has a fondness for Lisas, and they for her.

Janie figures with a little time under her belt she'll come to appreciate them too, the way one develops a palate for whiskey. For now, it's akin to kerosene shots from the well. Don't search for nuance, and before long, your head will float just the same.

Come tomorrow, you'll feel a bit shitty. You'll tell yourself it's the cheap booze reaping its due. Not the modest indent you felt on her ring finger as her hand gripped yours while you had her on her back. Afternoon will come, pulling you out of your head, bringing you good company, and cheap beer to soothe the ache. You'll wake up tomorrow to break your body in the heat or the cold until you're too tired for the luxury of regret. By the end of the week, you're so antsy to lay your eyes on something prettier than coveralls and mud, all you can think about is that little sign perched along a dark highway.

Not looking to spend another evening waiting on Reyna finishing her shift, Janie picks up a used Jetta from a company intern heading back east. Taking all the diesel jokes the boys can dish out, she fires back with inquiries about their sisters, which is always a safer topic than their mothers.

"Hey, you wanna drive tonight?" Reyna asks, peeking around the door.

Already in her PJs, Janie looks up from her newly procured copy of *Crimson Mist*. "Think I'm staying in." Regretfully, "Sorry, should've said somethin'."

Leaning on the door jamb, "You want me to stay? We could rent some videos, have a night in."

"That's alright. Go on and have fun. I'm just gonna read." Janie rests the open book across her knees.

"What's it about?" Reyna asks, dragging her thumbnail across a loose paint chip.

"Ya know Batman? Well, in an alternate universe he basically becomes a vampire. So far, seems like he's gonna kick some ass."

"Only you would pass up getting laid for a zombie," Reyna scoffs, turning to leave.

"Vampire, they're not the same thing ya know. You wanna take my car?"

Already at the door, Reyna calls back, "I do not but thank you. Don't wait up."

Listening to the hum of the super duty firing up, she'll soon be alone in the silence of her room, the house and a block made up of families turned in for the night. It all feels woefully quiet.

Lately thoughts of Arkansas nag at her, more precisely Cicely. Janie marks her spot, coming up for air from the bitey bloodbath. Brushing dust and cobwebs from her old Red Wing box, she takes out her trusty Walkman, long put away since she traded up for a Discman. Leafing through an orphaned stack of letters she's never meant to send and sparse remnants of days past brings her to a yellowed envelope stained with what she can faintly sniff out as tzatziki.

She can hear Cicely's matter of fact sass clear as day when she reads those words again. Unsettled for the last month or so, Janie's reaching for something to put the ground back where it ought to be.

Dear Cicely,
First order of business, I'm truly sorry for missing your
wedding. You will be pleased to know I have gotten on with
it, all the way to Texas with a good friend. I think you'd like
her a lot if you ever got to meet her. I hope this letter finds
you after all this time, and that you'll be inclined to write
me back about your life. What shall I call the bun? Well,
give Nathan and the bun a squeeze from me.
Greenhorn

Denying herself the misery of scrutinizing her thoughts until they're molded into trite iterations of have a great summer or other dull musings, Janie seals the envelope and scurries to the mailbox. Wrestling the warped flag into an upright position, the deed's done.

Discord between the company shirts and the rig contractor makes for a long week. Tension building among the crew, Reyna grows broodingly quiet by midweek. Janie rides along to keep her company. "Let's stop for some coffee while it's still cool enough to drink it."

"Yeah, gotta get gas anyway." Growing her hair out, Reyna pulls it back with an inch to spare, tucking an obstinate wave behind her ear.

"Almost forgot, Fernie called. They're barbecuing Saturday an want us to come. You up for it?" Janie asks.

"Sure, if I'm not stuck out on the rig watching the wind blow."

Rubbing Reyna's back, Janie feels the stress knotted up to her shoulders. "If'n that happens, then we'll watch it together. Otherwise, it's brisket and all the fixins'. I'll get the coffee, you get the gas."

Tank full, coffee tall and hot, and two buttered biscuits later, they're underway. Livened if only slightly, Reyna grumbles. "I dunno if I want to do this anymore. Gettin' to be a whole lotta horseshit."

"Like work on a rig or what?" Janie asks casually, having heard some variation of this diatribe once every month or two for the last year.

"No, here. Working on a rig is damn near all I know at this point. Thinkin' it's time to try it somewhere else." Reyna's eyes wander long enough to survey Janie's reaction.

"Where? Are you really thinking about this or is this on the count of you havin' a shit week?" Janie asks anxiously.

"I dunno where, maybe give offshore a try." Her words ring in Janie's ear for the day's remainder.

In an absurd fit of temper, the company man walks off the job. Emmett calls Friday early, sending everyone home. While Reyna washes their work clothes at the laundromat, Janie stocks up for the barbecue. Easing their boredom with wild speculation, they wager the barbecue's a rouse to announce an engagement.

Having not seen them in months, Janie grapples them in bear hugs. Their notion falls flat when Fernie announces Grace's promotion before the screen door swings shut. Keen to catch up, Janie helps prep while Reyna and Doug make a beer run.

"Janie, your hair's getting long like when you first moved here. Reyna too, look at ya'll." Snacking while she makes the snacks, Grace works around Fernie's indecisive pauses with an elegant choreography.

"Don't I know it. Kinda like it actually. Alright Grace, dish on the promotion, let's hear it."

"Moved up to senior financial analyst. Got a nice little raise and lost a manager, just reporting to Judy now. Lord am I glad to be done dealin' with Phil. One little promotion really went to his head." Rolling her eyes, she rebounds with a bite of deviled egg.

Grabbing one for herself, Janie's mood is lifted with secondhand joy. "Grace, you make them look so good, I'm gonna eat them all before anyone gets here."

Fernie motions for Janie to grab the cutting board. "You should've been here last weekend. Reyna made some with hatch chiles we roasted, *Dios mio* those were good."

"Wait, Reyna was here last weekend?" Janie inquires, nearly losing her cargo to the screen door snapping back.

Fernie focuses on the imperative task of grill alignment. "Yeah, said you were being a homebody. You two have a fight or something?"

"No, I was just reading. Didn't feel like going out is all."

"Guess she didn't either." Catching a glare from Grace, Fernie trails off. "Forgot the foil, right back."

In the company of three great cooks, Janie fills up. Catching up with Doug from Reyna's old crew keeps the evening lively. Sated in belly and soul, Janie falters for fear of setting the evening askew.

Her eyes, seeking form in the darkness along the vast stretches of highway, conspire against her in the glare of oncoming headlights. Fatigue tames time, a blink threatens to stretch out to the length of a nap were it not for the rough shoulder.

"You okay? Want me to drive?" Reyna asks, shaking her arm.

"I got it." Cracking the window, the balmy air lulls her all the more. Nothing like the third degree to awaken the senses. "How come you didn't tell me you were goin' to Fernie's last weekend?"

"Wasn't planning on it, just went."

"You didn't go out then?" Sitting up, Janie makes herself uncomfortable enough against the rigid seat to stay awake.

"You're falling asleep. Pull over. I don't wanna die in an import." Walking around, she opens the driver's door. "Scoot over."

Clumsily climbing over the shifter to the passenger seat, Janie wishes she'd walked around. "Jesus, that was graceful. Careful, I think I knocked it into first gear. So?"

Leaning across, Reyna closes the distance. "I felt like going out, then I didn't. That's it, so I crashed at Fernie's." Staring into Janie's eyes until her gaze is less auger like, Reyna kisses her. "Yeah?"

Sleepily smiling, Janie pulls her in for one more kiss. "Yeah."

Sharing her glass of water, Janie crawls back into bed. "How come we always end up in your bed?"

Scooting down, Reyna bunches her pillow. "My pillows are better."

Nuzzling her head against the feathery cloud, she can hardly argue. Nor could she stay awake if she wanted to.

Chapter Thirty One

S howing the new company man the ropes makes for longer shifts for Reyna, Emmett and the new driller Mitch. Never one to ask, Emmett doesn't need to. Reyna knows the rig better than anyone, save for himself. Knowing Emmett has a kid on the way, she volunteers at any chance to free him up. Though the drive's short, and they rarely say much, Janie misses the company.

August brings heat and a letter from Arkansas.

> *Greenhorn,*
> *How the hell are you? Your letter was very timely, like getting the baby in a king cake. The buns are Hailey and Silas, and they, like their mother, are in need of a break. I reckon we'll be in your neck of the woods in a couple weeks.*
> *Cici*

Breaking for a cold one, Janie rereads the letter. Feeling like she has to tell her Mom that she broke a piece of Yaya's china, Janie's on the edge of her seat when Reyna gets in. Pouring her two fingers of Glenfiddich, Janie takes Reyna's gear.

"Should I be worried?" Reyna asks, sinking into the sofa.

Dropping the bag on the floor next to the dining table, Janie grabs another lager. "No." Flopping down, Janie lays her head on Reyna's lap.

Brushing loose strands of hair from her eyes, Reyna smiles down suspiciously. "Spill."

"It's nothing." Pulling herself up, Janie folds her legs over. "You remember Cicely from Mighty's back in Albuquerque?"

Crossing her legs, Reyna looks past Janie. "Butch mighta mentioned her."

Janie puts a finger up to wait a minute. "To be fair, they did not get on well, at all. She's good people though."

"And?"

"Oh, so she's coming to visit," Janie says in an overdone unceremonious manner.

"Here? Why?" Reyna asks, now keenly interested. "I didn't know you kept in touch."

"Well, we didn't, actually." Shifting, she picks at a piece of lint on the blanket draped over the couch. "She'd written a while back an I never answered, so I finally answered." Throwing her arms up in an ain't life crazy kind of way. "Next thing I know, I got a letter saying she's coming to visit."

Nodding, Reyna remains neutral. "Huh, have fun with that."

Embracing the words over the spirit of Reyna's response, Janie scoots closer. "I can't wait for you to meet her!"

The week comes and goes like any other. Despite his greenness, the new company man's sympathetic to the harsh and unpredictable elements of working on a rig. Nervously anticipating her arrival, Janie scrambles for distractions.

Unbeknownst to Janie, Cicely arrives Saturday morning on the 10:15 Greyhound fresh from a stopover in Dallas. Catching a cab from the station, they check into a small motor lodge on Andrews Highway. Pragmatic comfort abounds. Everything they need with little of what she wants. Which lately matters less since what she wants is an ongoing process of elimination based upon what she doesn't. Showering while Silas sleeps in a pillow fort atop a bed pushed against the wall as a redundancy measure, Cicely tries to remember how Janie looked when they last saw one another. What she herself looked like for that matter.

Anxiously instructing the cab driver to circle the block once more, she needs time to pull herself together. Climbing out, Silas gallops to the farthest reach of his tethered backpack. Four feet to be precise, though it may as well be a mile if he's beyond an arm's length. "Silas please try not to make an ass of mama."

Flapping his arms, he hops alongside until the weight of her palm grounds him. "K mama."

Pulling at her hem, Cicely knocks on the door. Giving Silas' hand a little squeeze to help him focus, they wait. Glancing back to the curb, the cab's gone. *Christ, what if she's not home. Knock again.*

Pulling the door open, Janie crams a week's worth of wondering into a few seconds of appraisal. Cicely's bone straight blonde hair has gone wavy brunette, floating down to the small of her back. She's thinner than Janie remembers, tired even. Tired and beautiful. Before Janie can question whether the ornery soul of her has fizzled out in motherhood, the mischievous glint in her eyes comes alight.

"Christ greenhorn, you went and became a woman on me. Quit eyeballing me and give me a hug."

Wrapping her arms around her, Janie feels a lot more points than she remembers. "It's been a long time." Kneeling, "You must be Silas?"

Nodding, he holds tighter to his mother's leg.

"Where's Hailey?" Noticing a bare ring finger, Janie doesn't linger.

"With her daddy, she starts school next week." Cicely strokes Silas' hair, fidgeting again with her dress.

An unfamiliar voice calls from the background. "Janie are you gonna invite them in or what?"

Whispering, Cicely asks, "Who's that?"

"Reyna. C'mon, you gotta meet her." Janie ushers them in. Hurrying into the kitchen, Janie pulls Reyna along. "Reyna this is Cicely and Silas."

Shaking Cicely's hand firmly, Reyna gives Silas a little nod. "Hey buddy. How old are you?"

Holding up two then three fingers, a grin confirms his final answer. He returns Reyna's praise with a high five.

Reyna takes her leave to the kitchen at the first opportunity. Strangers for an afternoon, gives way to old jokes and familiar turns of phrase. In true Cicely fashion, she recounts their day-long journey limping across the expanse of the great state of Texas with feeble ventilation in an old bus worthy of condemnation, if busses were eligible for such things. Tales of those in need of a fix, a bath or both are told as only Cicely can tell them.

Short on things to do with a small child, Janie takes them through the preserves out by Midland. People in these parts often give you a once over as a female roughneck. If they're old school, they may even wonder what your husband thinks about it or wonder about him altogether for allowing you to get out there with the men. What with all the qualifying, they'll never doubt your character for putting in a hard day's work. Someone from the outside, say someone like Cicely, has this image of *Five Easy Pieces* or similar tales of men using brute strength to buckle the earth to their will. And no matter how hard you try, you can't seem to elbow yourself into that vision.

Work is only hours away, yet Janie has no notion of Cicely's plans. For short spells she's as vivacious as she ever was. Longer stretches reveal a pensiveness alien to the Cicely whom Janie remembers. Attributing the transmutation to the toll of motherhood, Janie refuses to dwell on what amounts to none of her business.

Bailing last minute on their barbecue, Reyna leaves dressed for a date. Wanting to believe she's off to Fernie's, Janie knows better. Her shirt's fresh from the cleaners, and she was buffing her boots when they arrived. An aloofness Janie knows all too well is the deadest of dead giveaways. Reyna's out for distraction in the only form which tempers the restlessness stirring in her lately.

As Silas rolls his firetruck along the planter's edge, Janie lights citronella candles. Cicely having commandeered the grill, manages a comforting meal of chicken, corn and potatoes. Slowing to watch Janie grab up Silas, Cicely says nothing as Janie helps him tear into his dinner. In some ways it's as though they're meeting anew. Gone is the soft baby-faced girl unsure of the world, in her place is a lean and tenacious young woman trying to outrun the girl she was.

Letting herself hang onto the moment for a spell, she whisks through the sweltering living room in pursuit of refills. Handing off a beaded bottle of Shiner, Cicely shakes off a sly laugh as Janie tips the bottle back. "How times have changed. I remember when you'd babysit your drink all night like you was afraid your mama was about to come bursting through the door. Now look at you."

"Now look at me what?" Janie asks, meeting her challenge head on.

Intrigued, Cicely leans in to hold onto the reins. Drawing a slow sip from her bottle, she rests upon her elbows. "So, are you two a couple or somethin'?"

"Reyna and me? We're friends. Been through a lot together," Janie replies. "Why? What would make you think I'm into girls?"

"Good lord. I don't know, lucky guess I suppose," Cicely replies.

"I mean I am." Janie shores herself up. "Anyway. Not to change the subject, but I gotta work tomorrow. You wanna take my car?"

Cicely adjusts to having to go along. "We're alright. Mind if I smoke?" Turning her chair downwind of Silas, she lights up with an approving nod. Taking all the time the first long drag affords, Cicely catches Janie staring at her hand. Giving the pack a tap, "Want one?"

Shaking her head, Janie leans back. Holding up her left hand, she wriggles her fingers. "Is there anything you wanna tell me?"

Cicely gives a princess wave. "What, this?"

Janie reads the uncertainty in her eyes and is through with their exchange of provocations. She sees the same Cicely from afar. Propped up with southern bohemian swagger, lesser friends wouldn't know she's barely hanging on. "What happened?"

"Nothin' really, who the hell knows." Staring down at her son, "Can I tell ya later?"

"Yeah, sorry. Let me drive you home. I'll get my keys." Janie heads in, grabbing their dishes.

Tucked away on the far side of their springy queen bed, Silas cuddles his funky Tarzan doll. With her chair backed against the open door, Cicely trades sips on Janie's flask between cigs. Certain Silas will hear little more than the hum of pipes running the length of the wall, she gives Janie a woeful stare. Where to begin, for God's sake just ask.

"So, are you getting divorced?"

Flicking ash from her smoke, Cicely looks away. "No. I don't know. I just needed out. I was suffocating there with him, with his family. Hell, the whole thing." Pulling a strand of hair as an example, Cicely looks at

Janie exasperated. "See this? All his sisters, his mama, even his granny, all blondes. Some by nature. Some by nurture. Looked like a damn bunch of daisies everywhere we went."

Curbing her laughter, Janie treads carefully. "Can I ask, how do they feel about your colorful way with words?"

Reaching with a flick of the hand for the flask, Cicely takes a long swig. "Smiles, then talk shit behind my back all proper like." Leaning back, a stifled laugh flies free. "You know I can't be bothered to care about that bullshit."

Fidgeting with her keys, Janie keeps her eyes low for fear of losing her nerve. "What are you gonna do? Does Nathan feel the same?"

Stretching her legs across the doorway, Cicely pushes her palm against the edge of her chair. "You know Nathan. Love him to death but he's fixed to walk through his whole life asleep."

Sitting up, Janie searches for eye contact. "Cicely, what are you doing?"

Sighing, Cicely swallows a spark of indignation before it flashes into a fit of temper. "Janie you don't know anything about my life. Do you? You up and started over, now you'd deny me the same?"

"Starting over?"

"I told him I needed to breathe, and I couldn't do it there." She hangs on every shift in Janie's expression. "Thinking I might stay around here for a while, get a job. I don't know, something."

"What about your Hailey?" Janie asks more accusingly than intended.

"I'll send for her when I'm settled. Do not presume to judge me." Quieter now, Cicely caves under the burden of her compunction. "She's alright, always been a daddy's girl anyhow. Besides, Nathan's mama will love another excuse to try and put her stamp on her." Jettisoning her cig to the dark parking lot, Cicely drags her chair away from the door.

In and out of sleep, crickets serenade Janie with summer harmonies. Contemplating her next move, she thinks of the day Cicely sat down across from her for no other reason than offering a kindness to a stranger. In her heart, Janie knows this is her opportunity to return the favor.

Psyching herself up all morning, Janie launches into it before Reyna clears their block. "I think Cicely's left her husband. I wanna let her stay with us till she figures herself out."

Impassive, Reyna responds sparingly. "She's just gonna leave one kid behind? You really wanna get in the middle of this?" Trailing off, "Shit's gonna get ugly."

"Said she's gonna send for her. I think it's just a timeout. Prolly go on home when she gets homesick." Appealing to her sympathetic nature, Janie implores Reyna to hear her out. "Reyna, she was there for me when I didn't know a soul. I feel like I gotta be there now."

Reluctantly agreeing, Reyna lets her frustrations out on the gas pedal. "Do what you have to do. I don't want the house looking like some kind of daycare though."

"Thank you. Won't be for long, promise." Janie looks out across the horizon victoriously, uncertain of what she's won.

Happy Meal in hand, Janie interrupts an epic Hot Wheels race to the mini fridge. Mouthing her sorry to Cicely, Janie treads lightly. "How far ahead you paid up here?"

"End of the week. Why? You tryin' to figure out when we'll be outta your hair?" Cicely replies sullenly.

Chomping away at her fries, Janie lets it roll off. "I thought you and Silas' might come stay with us till...for as long as you need."

Slowing, Cicely takes a seat. "I dunno. That's awful sweet of you. Ya know having a kid runnin' around's not for everyone. How does Reyna feel about this?"

"Fine, she feels fine about it." Running her palm across the small table baring warped scars earned through years of careless spills and retributive scrubbing, Janie leans closer. "I must warn you, I can't promise finishes as fine as this white oak peel and stick or that freezing pool out there. So, go on and take some time to think on it."

Cicely nods along. "I suppose we could manage in your shack of an abode." Hugging Janie, she finds herself genuinely smiling for the first time in a good while.

Giving it an honest go, Reyna helps toddler proof the house. Which mostly consists of removing anything she's remotely fond of from their shared living space. Figuring she'll leave Cicely off with her car most days, Janie buys Silas a car seat. A lightly used pack and play from the second-hand store will suffice as a bed. Sheets changed, personals put away and a stuffed Batman plush awaits.

Relishing the first blanket worthy evening in September, Janie wraps herself up on the couch. Remote in hand with a Dos Equis in waiting, she's on track to crash before the *JAG* credits roll. The *clackety clack* of Reyna's boots draws near. Stopping short, she hovers in the hall until she can play it convincingly loose. "Hey, let's go out."

Admiring her couch potato splendor, Janie ponders the effort required to get dressed. "Think I'm in for the night."

An anomalous persistence drives Reyna. In spite of herself, she's inching toward grief. "This time tomorrow there'll be a kid tearing through the house. Your friend's gonna be here and it'll take a pry bar to peel you off that couch. C'mon, I don't want to go alone."

Theorizing there may be an ex, or a...*what does one call a former one-night stand? An acquaintance? No, that doesn't feel right either. Whatever, one might be getting weird.* Showing up a cozy couple usually leaves them chastened enough to ditch the Saturday night crowd for the Sunday afternoon patio crew. Janie shudders at the thought of showing up on a Sunday. *That'd be like Charley Brewster walking into the Hangout if Sundays were Legion day.*

Janie slams her beer and dresses with a quickness. Pitch-black while the moon's off to better things, the arc of their headlights casts out to the outer margin of the highway.

Deader than usual, a smattering of tourists mingle among the regulars. Janie's theory evaporates faster than the ink on her handstamp. A wing woman in waiting, she points out girls only to have them dismissed without even a turn of the head. Chatting up the girl from a while back, Janie watches for her covetous friend. Reyna puts an end to it, stepping between them to tell Janie she's up.

Dutifully throwing back a dram of Makers when Reyna sinks the 8 ball, Janie sees the friend slither up from afar. *There goes that.*

Having lost two rounds, Janie's an equal measure deep in Maker's shots. Not to mention the one, maybe two, beers she had along the way. Spinning a wilted coaster, she waits on the bartender wading through last call. The indecisive or unintelligible are handed a can of Falstaff with consolation that first call's a mere five hours away. Leaning on the bar, she squints to sharpen nebulous forms into singular silhouettes. One belongs to the girl and the other, her friend.

Emboldened by the synergy of the second shot joining forces with what might have been a third beer, Janie jumps queue calling out her order. Hopping off her barstool, she's cutoff at the pass. Reyna stands before her with a foam coffee cup. Peering around, the girl's lost in a pack of Lisas huddled by the door. Uncommitted to leaving and unwilling to concede there's no one left worth staying for, they smoke and cackle their way through last call, milking every ounce of joy from Saturday night.

Chagrined, Janie pokes the cup. "What's that?"

"What'dya think it is? Need to sober up or I'm gonna fall asleep. You aren't gonna get sloppy on me, are you?" Reyna asks. Her posture taking on a tilt. "You wanna go? We can sit in the lot till I finish this."

Bracing her elbow against the bar, it may in fact be Janie who's tilting. "In a minute, just ordered a beer. Want one?" Goadingly. "Oh wait, you have coffee."

Reyna saddles up to the bar, encouraging Janie to do the same by patting the barstool. "You sure about that?" Pointing to a guy looking to have struck out hard, Reyna counters, "That guy looks like he could use a beer. You could give it to him."

Sneering, "Let him buy his own then."

Sliding her coffee in front of Janie, Reyna calls for another. "Easy tiger. Drink that while you wait."

Heedlessly, a Falstaff's pushed in front of her sans consolation speech. "What's this shit?" Spurned, Janie holds up the can for closer inspection before passing it to the thirsty fella down the bar.

Slipping forward in time, Janie's head rests upon her arm. Window rolled down, cool air rushes through her hair and down the back of her shirt. Sobering, a cohesive timeline sets about reconstructing itself.

Teetering on tippy toes, Janie drags her fingers along the fridge ledge. "It's gone," Reyna remarks, shaking aspirin loose from the bottle.

"You smoke it all by yourself?" Pouring herself a tall glass of water, Janie takes the pills.

Reyna takes some too for good measure. "Gave it to Doug. Don't want the kid finding it if he or mama go snooping."

Shrugging, Janie tips back the rest of her water.

Putting her hand on Janie's waist, Reyna draws her close and nuzzles into her shoulder. "Stay with me tonight."

Janie wraps her arms around her.

Struggling to pull her boots off, Janie steadies herself against Reyna. Boozy giggles carry them gracelessly to the foot of the bed. Stumbling over a discarded boot, Reyna pitches it with a mocking display of strength. Pulling her shirt over her head, Janie casts it out to parts unknown. Looking up at Reyna, there's a marked intensity in lieu of the usual comely cheekiness. Reaching, Janie brings Reyna down to her. An aura of sorrow nags at her. Whispering, "You alright?"

Feigning a grin, Reyna holds steady. "Peachy." Janie lays beneath her, floating on a sea of bourbon and cheap beer. Reyna silently takes her in. Her fingers trace a memory across Janie's jawline, along where her neck betrays the quickening of her pulse. Reyna pokes at her comically furrowed brow deepening with impatience. "You're so serious."

Avidly, Janie lifts her head to kiss her. Be it inebriate fixation or reluctant candor gathering in Reyna's gaze, such desire is intoxicating. Letting out a weighty breath as Reyna kisses her neck, Janie cannot resist a last jab in the face of certain surrender. "So, this is why you blew off them girls tonight?"

Daylight creeps in, a thorny thicket stabbing at Janie's puffy eyelids. Tangled in the sheet, she takes most of it with her rolling over to the nightstand. Straining to see her watch, her aching head answers the burdensome request with a throbbing spear to the temple. "Damnit."

Heaving her share of sheet back, a gravelly voiced Reyna asks, "What's wrong?" When she really means please shut up and go back to sleep.

Sitting up, a wave of nausea permeates her entire being. "Oh God." Janie bails for the bathroom. Last night's indulgences expelled, she limps into the shower to rest against the wall until her axis realigns. Clean, fresh breathed and feeling like hell, she laboriously pulls on a pair of clean jeans and a wrinkled tee. Grabbing last night's clothes from the floor, Janie tidies a mess in the kitchen she doesn't remember making.

Setting a cup of coffee on Reyna's nightstand, she kisses her bare shoulder. "Going to pick up Cicely and Silas. Back in a bit."

An unintelligible reply from the depths of her pillow suffices to say thanks for the coffee, drive safe and your ass looks fantastic in those jeans. Janie's flattered.

Chapter Thirty Two

A congenial routine of Cicely looking after the house and preparing dinner each evening emerges. While Reyna bristles, Janie readily warms to someone waiting for her. From time to time amid the daily grind, she catches herself wondering what Silas is up to and thinking how he reminds her of Matty.

Without explanation, Reyna takes to cutting out after work. A registration packet from a local college spurs unease. Coming in late, Reyna beelines to her room, occasionally returning an orphaned toy. Quick to apologize, Cicely maunders on about him sneaking off while she was doing this or that. Rueful, Janie knows Reyna tolerates the intrusion for her.

Weekends eaten up knotting the loose ends of daily living, Janie and Reyna hardly see each other outside of work. A mutually amiable tension sets in.

Finishing off Silas' Batman costume, Janie fits his mask. Enthralled, she doesn't notice Reyna watching. "Hi, didn't hear you come in."

"Where's Cicely?" Reyna smiles down at Silas. "Hey Batman!"

"Went out for candy." Standing, she adjusts her wrist brace. "You like? I'm an expert bowler."

"You love all this don't you?" Reyna asks, putting on her coat.

Checking the flashlight batteries, Janie flicks the switch. "I think Halloween may just be the best day of the year."

"No, I mean all of this," sweeping her arm in Silas' direction.

There's that look again. Smiling warmly, Janie gathers costume scraps. "Yeah, I guess I do. Why don't you come trick or treating with us. I'll give you my chocolates."

"Got a date," Reyna replies, passing Cicely on her way out. "Night all."

Emmett calls everyone together outside the doghouse. Hardly a good sign on a Monday morning, it's a lousy sign on a Tuesday. Spontaneous morning huddles scream of crisis in an office somewhere their dirty boots will never be welcome.

Emmett lays out the gig. The company wants to bring a rig out in Lynn County back online after it was shut down due to an accident that left two dead. None of the local rig contractors are interested, so NP's taking it on. A Hail Mary contract before they pull the whole thing down. Story goes, they brought in a new geologist who claims it's not a sunk cost situation. They want an experienced crew plus a fifth hand for parts runs. Due to the distance, it'll be seven days on, two off. Twelve-hour shifts. Company will put them up locally. Doug's stepping in as toolpusher here in Andrews. "If we're gonna do this, then I say we do this as a crew. Now with that said, I know it ain't so easy for family folk. Chew on it some and let me know."

Reyna pulls Emmett aside. "You really think it's worth the risk?"

Emmett sighs. "Here's what I think. I think it's getting awful slow out there, they're shuttin' down rigs left and right. All the big boys are pulling out. NP's tryin' to do right by us. Keep us busy, keep us on the books."

"I appreciate that, but I'd be lying if I said it didn't concern me being out in the boonies with an ornery well."

"I know, I know. Word is, it was more operator error than anything." Emmett runs his hands through his hair. "Listen, they're on the tail end of a lease that hasn't paid shit. We're going to be outta work if we don't take it. They ain't expecting the Santa Rita or anything close. If we get out there and that shale bitch doesn't wanna give it up, then we break it down and get. Deal?"

Nodding reluctantly, Reyna concedes.

To no surprise, the whole crew goes along. Randy brings his nephew on as a roustabout.

By the time their boots hit the ground in Lynn, the entire crew has the skinny on the kid. How Randy's trying to help his sister out, keep him out of trouble and all. Rounding out his uncle of the year campaign, he allays their fears by sharing that Chet is three months clean. Meaning, he'll have no call to swipe their shit for smack. The irony of Randy, a bona fide connoisseur of hookers and narcotics, being charged with the sobriety of another is not lost on anyone. Just the same, a motorhand like him doesn't come along every day. While he may grate on you after a long shift, he speaks machine like no one Emmett's ever worked with.

Second day in, Chet's accused of lifting a wallet. No stranger to the corrosive potential of conclusions drawn through reputation, Reyna steps in as Ricky the floor hand readies to lay him out. Sending the kid on a run while Janie helps retrace his steps, the wallet turns up wedged in the seat of Ricky's truck. A curt apology issued, and a nickname's born.

The first stretch nearing its end inspires dreams of home-cooked meals, good water pressure and sleeping past dawn. Silas spots them coming up the walk, chants of "Janie's home" greet them. Nudging her, Reyna asks, "How come you never did that when I got home?"

Swaying into her, Janie puts her arm around her. "Never say never."

Packing an overnight bag, Reyna's off to catch up with an old friend.

Nervously, Cicely pulls a piping casserole from the oven. "I'm not one for fancy cooking, but I wanted to try my hand at something. I remember you always dragged us to that little Greek place for your moussaka. Anyway, I tried."

"Alexi's! My God they had good gyro." Cutting in before it's found a form, her piece spreads across the plate. "Cicely, this smells like heaven."

"Well, let's hope it don't taste like hell." Cutting a piece for herself, she sets it aside while trimming the crust from Silas' grilled cheese. "Has his daddy's picky taste buds."

Comparing the dish to Yaya's would be reprehensibly unfair. Janie puts her sulking over Reyna's old friend away and savors each bite with plans to lay siege to the rest before they head back out.

Ordinarily dedicated to the business of laundry and lounging, these mild autumn weekends are best spent outside grilling and watching Cicely chase Silas round and round in the sprinklers. An eye to the street, Janie hopes Reyna might come home early but doesn't suppose she will.

Packed, Janie rides out Sunday on the steam of Cicely and Silas' whim. Cutting up veggies who've lost their luster, they make a seed stop at the feed store. Silas shrieks with delight suspended over the pond. Reaching for a duck playing hard to get, he scares all save for a goose who's marked him a worthy adversary.

A picnic of salami and provolone sandwiches complemented by coldish Shiners do not disappoint. Laying on the blanket, they watch Silas chase bugs and nothing at all through the tall grass. "What's it like back home?" Janie asks.

"It's nice, I guess. Decent people. Big enough, we got malls and plenty of things to do. Shit, I live there but I don't know I've ever called it home. Christ, the weather's fickle."

"Home's just a word, that's all. Can't be much hotter than it is here."

"It's not just a word, and you know it as well as I do." Sitting up to keep an eye on Silas, Cicely picks at the remnants of her sandwich. "We're in what they call tornado alley. Had a bad one tear through in the night a while back. Killed a little boy not much older than Silas." Flicking an encroaching ant off the blanket, she fixes it flat. "You know the pisser of it? Nathan's sister was beside herself over the damage to downtown, then goes an changes the channel when it came on about that poor little boy. I loathe that heifer sometimes."

"She why you left?"

"No, wouldn't give'er the pleasure. Besides, there's no love lost so we don't see much of one another. You know about fight or flight? Well, I didn't know who to fight, so I chose flight." Cicely gets to her feet. "Silas, too far. Come with mama. Let's eat."

Gobbling up PB&J, Silas falls asleep playing with his cars. Enjoying another beer in the clement afternoon, Cicely insists Janie tell her about rig life and everything in between. Janie tells tales of Butch and their midnight walks less his avocation and Alban's demise. She shares a similarly redacted tale of Texas, cleaving Allison and the weltering path she and Reyna have walked from the recital.

Janie speaks of how hard rig work can be, and how amazing it is too. Days you want to cry from your back hurting so bad or when you can't get the tongs to bite just right. Then once you've put more time in, there're days sitting up on the derrick. Sky goes on forever, peppered with clouds telling you how hot it's going to be like you didn't already know. Perched up above the smells of the rig after a rain spell, the scent of creosote comes up. "Man, when it gets hot and all that metal's kicking off like a furnace, I just go huntin' for some creosote shrubs. Smells like a rainy day when I was a kid."

"You've really made a life here for yourself. I'm happy for you."

"I don't know where I'd be if it weren't for you. Reckon I would've turned tail and caught the next bus home. I'm glad you're here." Checking her watch, Janie brushes crumbs from around Silas till she hits a swath of jam concealed in a blanket fold. Wiping her hand across the grass for lack of a better choice. "We'll just wash that, maybe throw him in too."

Packing, Cicely watches Silas. "He's not gonna sleep tonight if I don't wake his cranky ass up."

"I've heard. I'll wake him while you pack." Janie strokes his hair. Through grumbles and groans, they stop to dispense the remnants of the duck picnic. Janie slings a howling Silas over her shoulder.

Reaching a standoff at the driver's side, Cicely takes Silas, soothing his ire. "Sorry, guess I've gotten used to driving your car."

Rummaging for her keys, Janie follows the jangle. "Swear, I'm always leaving stuff down one place or another."

Cicely holds onto the keys before releasing them to Janie's hand, giving her a peck on the lips. Reclining, she locks her seatbelt in place.

Over-cranking the ignition, Janie nervously shoves the car in gear. "You didn't have to do that."

"I know," Cicely rests her hand on Janie's.

A sleepless night on the couch leaves Janie brimming with gratitude for a long hitch to seek an ounce of perspective. Training Chet proves an uphill battle that Janie feels ill-equipped for. At every turn he disregards instructions, despite warnings from senior crew that he'll earn himself a licking from Betty if he keeps it up. Emmett and Reyna have grown closer, often chatting the evening away in the motel bar. Janie catches wind of Randy and the fruit of his warped family tree murmuring tales of a crew romance.

Sharing a room with someone doing their best to steer clear of you has a way of sowing anxiousness, harkening back to days of falling out with her mother. No argument to latch onto, or dig your heels in for, just a fuzzy timeout.

With Emmett meeting the company man for drinks, Reyna brings food back to the room. "Fried chicken, mash and green beans. Ricky said they're the shit."

"No rendezvous with Emmett tonight?" Janie laughs. Peeling the foil container, she breathes in the delicious aroma.

"Givin' the old boy a rest, think he threw his back out last night." Grimacing gives way to the wicked laugh Janie's come to adore.

"Gross. I guess Ricky told you about Randy and his shitbird nephew." Tearing off a piece of chicken, she savors it. "Damn, this is good."

"Yeah it is. That woman in the restaurant looks like she's been making it for about a hundred years." Taking a swig, Reyna relaxes in her chair. "That worm's done soon as we finish this hitch. Too hard to get someone out this far on the fly or he'd be kicking rocks."

"He don't listen for shit either. Left the hose laying out half running, nearly broke my damn neck," Janie grouses.

Sitting up, Reyna's more serious now. "Why didn't you tell me? He pulls anymore shit like that, he's gone. Someone gets hurt out here, we got a drive ahead of us."

"I told Randy. He said he'd work with him." Janie continues eating, wishing she'd kept it to herself.

Reyna bags the trash and wipes down the table. "You wanna go to the bar for a drink?"

Stiff from the long day, Janie stretches. "Yeah, maybe one to wind down."

Reyna keeps Emmett in her line of sight. The logistics are not lost on Janie, she's rendered a living prop. "Why don't you join them already, then I can go to bed."

Caught, Reyna smirks. "What? I thought you'd enjoy a drink. Homesick?"

Janie sits back, folding her arms skeptically. "Eavesdrop more like. And yes, at this moment, I'd rather be home."

"With Cicely?" Reyna asks coldly.

"No, just home. To hell with this, I'm tired." Draining her jack and coke, Janie pushes her chair in and leaves.

Rolled in her blanket when Reyna comes in, Janie lays awake for longer than she'll ever admit.

Day three's off to a rocky start. Chet shows up hungover, puking in the shrubs and unable to remember where he put the frickin' walkie. Tensions swelling, the crew waits on everything getting going.

"C'mon Chet goddammit. Pull yer shit together. Reyna said something seems off. Let's take a look or she'll have Emmett on my ass." Building a case to keep Chet on, Randy takes him up on the derrick to fuss with the drill line.

"Yeah well I guess that's what fucking the boss gets ya, special treatment." Following his uncle, Chet's stomach churns as they go.

Fighting to catch his breath and every other word, Randy intends to put an end to talk that'll only get them on the pusher's bad side. "Hoss, I think yer barkin' up the wrong tree. I hear she and Betty is a thing. Don't mean Emmett ain't sweet on her though."

"Ain't they all once they get out here. What choice they got when oilfield trash won't even look at them?" Gripping his harness, he hits his knees once they're up top.

Red with rage and exhaustion, Randy speaks through gritted teeth. "Shut it! You hear me?" Braced on the rail, he stoops with an afterthought. "And from what I've seen, you been doin' plenty a lookin'. Put yer eyes down an do your job or I'll drop you on your mama's porch myself."

"Yessir," Chet replies meekly. Muttering, he tunes out Randy's rig whispering. White knuckle gripping the rail, he pulls at the tools clipped to his belt. Setting the hammer and pry bar down, he turns to climb down. Calling to Randy between heaves, he works up courage enough to crawl onto the ladder. "Unc I gotta get down, gonna be sick."

"Gimme a minute," Randy snaps, looking over his shoulder to make sure he's not leaving. "What the shit is that? Pick those up!" Randy yells, already moving as fast as his harness will allow.

Grabbing at the pry bar, Chet's knee clips the hammer, sending it over. Lunging, Randy screams down to the floor. Slipping, Chet swings off. Suspended by his harness, he frantically claws to pull himself in.

"You alright?" Randy asks, pale as can be.

Chet nods, eyes full of panic and tears.

"Don't say nothin' when we get down there," Randy cautions before climbing down the ladder at such speed he slides the last ten feet.

Heading for the floor, Randy's met midway by Emmett. "You may wanna stay back a minute."

"It hit anyone?" Randy asks, trying to see over Emmett's shoulder.

"Clipped the tong. Knocked Ricky back and swung him into Janie. They're alright, shook up some." Emmett grips Randy's shoulder. "He's gotta go. If one of the suits had been onsite, we'd be shut down."

Their gaze turns to Chet, heaving next to the ladder. Wiping his mouth with the back of his hand, he walks past them without saying a word. Reyna beats him to the doghouse. Planting both palms firmly on his chest, she shoves him with all she's got. "What kind of idiot takes a five-pound hammer up on the monkey board, without a fucking lanyard to boot?"

Refusing to look at her, he tries to push past.

"You almost killed them you piece of shit! You think you're walkin' away from this?" Reyna holds her ground, blind to Emmett and Randy fast approaching.

Drawing back with an inclination to knock her on her ass, Chet thinks better seeing them not more than a few yards out. Spitting in her face, he leans in close. "Fuck you." Shoving her out of his way, he takes the stairs in twos heading to the clearing.

Handing Reyna his handkerchief, Emmett looks to Randy. "Get him outta here. You take the night off and come back fresh tomorrow."

Nodding, Randy touches Reyna's shoulder only to have his hand swatted away. "Reyna, I'm real sorry."

Ricky pacing, a slew of obscenities fly from his God fearing mouth while Janie tells Mitch for the tenth time, she's okay. A trail of dust follows the company truck off toward the county road. "You two sure you don't wanna go into town and get checked out?" Emmett asks.

Pointing at Mitch, Reyna fumes. "I told you that kid was no good. You should've handled that shit."

Stepping between them, Emmett looks Reyna square in the eye. "Go cool off before you say something I'm gonna have to write you up for. I mean it, go on." Emmett turns to Mitch. "She's worked up, doesn't mean no disrespect."

Massaging his temples, Mitch sighs. "She's right, he's a liability. You and I let Randy talk us into a hole. Are we calling this in or what?"

"And get shut down?" Ricky argues. "I can't afford to be outta work. None of us can. I'm good. Janie, you good?"

Nodding, Janie concurs. "Yup, ready to go."

"You're a good manager Emmett, but there ain't nothin' to report but a worm dropping a tool. He's gone now, so I don't see a problem." Ricky looks to Janie again for a nod of solidarity.

Reluctantly, Emmett goes along. "Alright. Let's shutdown till we get the tongs checked out. I'll write it up as maintenance. Go find some shade."

The coolers brought out early for lunch, everyone knocks off to wind down. Holed up in the bed of her truck, Reyna's too spent to hassle Janie when she climbs up. "Want some company?"

"C'mon. You sure you're okay?"

"Hard hat did its job. I'm fine. You alright?" Janie unwraps her sandwich, keeping her hands low to conceal their trembling.

"I shouldn't have gotten so angry and shoved him," Reyna replies regretfully. "Shit's not professional. I have to set an example, not live up to their bullshit philosophy of women ragging."

"Are you kidding? I've seen Emmett and Mitch yell their asses off plenty of times. Hell, Ricky had him by the collar second day in. He had it coming."

Shaking her head, "You don't get it, it's not the same. When a dude does it, he's putting his foot down. When a woman goes off, she's a crazy bitch. Watch, you'll see." Crumpling her wrapper, Reyna tosses it aside. "Whatever, fuck it."

"God, I'm gonna be glad to have a couple days off," Janie counters, resting against the cab.

"We're going to be so behind." Reyna eyes Janie soaking up the afternoon sun. Assured they're alone, she leans to kiss her and is met with a turn of the head. Hurt and embarrassment flow where only a blink ago lived yearning. "It's like that?"

Wishing for a do-over, Janie's caught in the currents of leftover adrenaline. "Like what? I don't think we should go there right now."

"Go there? That's hilarious. Are you sleeping with her?" Reyna asks, assuming the answer but wanting to hear it leave her lips.

Straightening up, Janie pulls her knees in. "No. This isn't about her."

Reyna's intent on hearing her say it. "But you're going to. Right?"

Pulling at unruly wisps of hair nagging her peripherals, Janie looks on. "I don't know."

"You're a fuckin' fool, you know that?" Reyna seethes as she hops down.

"Fuck you and your priggish judgment. Don't tell me how to live my life," Janie retorts, hardly able to believe the words leaving her mouth.

Smiling condescendingly, Reyna rests on the tailgate. "Wouldn't dream of it. You know what, have fun playing make believe with someone else's wife till she gets bored."

Janie stares dumbfounded.

Boiling over, Reyna comes back for another go. "You know why you fall for chicks like Cicely and Allison? Cause they'll never look past themselves to see you. They'll never notice you're too afraid to give anything real. Shit, maybe that's all there is to you. The empty space and the surface."

Staying ahead of tears that will surely flow, Janie shores up her nerves. "That's really something coming from someone who's still running around trying to fuck away the misery of getting dumped in high school."

Mutually wounded, they fall silent. Janie turns away from Reyna.

The mud and the mess of the afternoon carry Janie to a vacuous state. Act, react, rinse and repeat until the spinning stops for the night. Reyna stays with Emmett, which does nothing to quell the desperate speculation of Randy and whomever he's corralled into conversation.

Being down a hand makes the work harder than it already is. Fifth day out, they pick up a seasoned roughneck on the morning fill up. His face weathered from years of rig life, a net of burst blood vessels tells the tale of how he ended up hustling for grunt work at dawn in the middle of nowhere. A hard worker who prefers being paid by the day, he goes by Smitty. Janie will come to swear she can predict him coming off a bender, knowing he'll show up at the station to wait on her pulling in before the coyotes have gone to bed.

If only the boys knew the strife between she and Reyna, their illusions of emotional fragility would up and vanish. Through gritted teeth, they work in perfect sync. Ricky and Janie running the floor, Reyna staying in step with them at every change.

A caravan of taillights falls away from the looming silhouette of the derrick. Uncertain about what home brings, Janie knows in the end she'll forfeit someone's good favor. While the days have done well to occupy her thoughts, nights alone have eaten her up. "I'm sorry bout what I said. I dunno why I said it, but I didn't mean it."

Lighter, Reyna keeps her eyes to the road. "I'm sorry too. I was out of line. I don't think you're empty. I was just being mean."

"No, you made some good points. Mean, but good." Janie laughs, more at ease. "It was a shit tour, let's leave it back there."

Their grievances butterflied, an agreement to ignore what will not heal is forged. Fragments of interstate radio crackle over local stations. Janie muses how some nights the weather carries the same station for miles then there are nights like tonight, when the airwaves are as frenetic as her thoughts. The evening DJ leads ominously with warnings of dropping barometric pressure. Spying dark clouds stacking way up high, it's plain to see what lies ahead.

With Reyna off to that old friend of hers, Janie's barely able to stand herself for the streak of jealously needling her to the bone. She wonders what her name is, this old friend smitten enough to pay no mind to her coming round after a day on a drilling rig.

The fragrance of onions, garlic and skirt steak grilling greets Janie ahead of Silas. Setting her gear down, she itches for a few minutes alone to shake this mood.

"You two have a fight?" Cicely asks, setting the table.

"No, nothing like that. Just tired is all." Stretching, Janie forces a yawn.

Cicely runs her thumb across Janie's dewy lashes. "Alright then, go on and have your shower. Dinner should be done soon."

Janie chases Silas down the hallway till his mother calls after him.

Asleep on the floor, Silas lays crumpled amongst his toys. Her bones creaking, Janie pushes off to fetch him. Cicely pats her knee, "I got him." Scooping him up, she coos along with sleepy mumbles. Sinking into the sofa, Janie longs for her blankets perched upon the chair. Sipping her lager, she rests her eyes.

Cicely settles in next to Janie, slipping her loosely grasped beer free. "You mind?" She asks. Taking a long swig, she sets it down. Leaning in, she kisses Janie. "This alright?"

Without hesitation, Janie kisses her back. Scooting down to bring her near, an old ache lost to time surfaces. A want she felt before she knew what it would feel like to be with a woman, when such desire was cumbersome. Reyna's words echo in her ears. Defiantly, she pushes them aside. She wants the warmth of being missed, of someone to come home to, even if for only a little while. *Not now, Goddammit!* Unable to drown Reyna out, Janie pulls back. "Are you sure you wanna do this? What about Nathan?"

"Janie, it's over between me and him." Cicely kisses her deeply, drawing Janie's hands to her. A cry comes from Janie's room. Gathering herself, Cicely fixes her night shirt. "Give me a minute to get him back to sleep."

Sleeping like the dead, Janie's arm hangs listlessly over the couch. Grabbing the blanket, Cicely works herself in next to her.

Operating under the haze of fatigue and whiskey, Reyna drifts in somewhere past two. Bent on waking Janie for a heart to heart, she stops cold at the sight of them wrapped up on the couch. Unable to say how long she's been standing there, Cicely stirring and settling brings the realization it's been long enough. Absent recourse, she'll sleep it off for a few hours.

Janie awakens to faint rumblings of Reyna's dawn departure. Afternoon brings a curt call, she's with Fernie and will come round for her at 5 a.m. day after next.

On her last night home, Janie and Cicely find their way around to one another. Always the student in her most intimate moments, sleeping with Cicely is in particular contrast to the equilibrium of their friendship. From its inception, there was a given ascendancy with Cicely at the helm. However, in matters of the heart, she's staggered by the ease with which Cicely gives over her hand of rule.

Satisfied she could walk this thin line for a good while, Janie feels no less obliged to fess up. Stalling through the next stint, Reyna's left to figure it out. Sick with cowardice in front of Cicely, attempts to clear the air on the next ride out prove too little too late.

Chapter Thirty Three

B ringing Cicely to Fernie's New Year's thing leaves Janie anxious that Reyna's penchant of late towards the irascible may spill over into contempt. Alone in the bathroom getting ready, she catches sight of her reflection and feels a pang of guilt. *She made her choices and I made mine. And it's for damn sure, she's not showing up alone either.* Closing her eyes, she calls upon Butch's wisdom from darker days. *Life is mostly pain sprinkled with halcyon days.*

Silas bounces with excitement walking into the party. Never one to wilt into the wallpaper, Cicely makes fast friends with another couple who brought their young ones. Heeding the gravitational pull of the cooler, Janie adjusts her path. Chatting with Fernie, Reyna's cozied up to a tall blonde that Janie's never laid eyes on. Watching Reyna blithely carry on with her hand resting between some stranger's knees lands on Janie like a lead balloon.

Interrupting, she introduces herself. "I'm Janie. Reyna's roommate."

With a knowing aplomb, she shakes Janie's hand. "Paula. It's nice to finally meet you."

"That's cool Janie, don't say hi to us," Fernie teases.

Hugging Fernie, Janie looks to Reyna but says nothing. Edging in, Cicely slides her arm around Janie's waist. "Shiner alright?" Janie asks.

"Hell yes," Cicely affirms.

Fernie waves at Silas. "What's up little dude? Nice to meet ya."

Full up on barbecue and all the fixings, folks cast anchor among their social islands. Laboring to keep a crabby Silas from catapulting himself onto the patio in a show stopping tantrum, Cicely pins him to her side.

"He looks tired, wanna put him down in Fernie's room?" Grace offers.

"You know, I think I might. That's sweet of ya'll." Cicely lets Grace lead the way, insisting Janie enjoy the fire pit and catch up.

Tipping back her beer, Janie retrieves another. "And how'd you two meet? Reyna's been keeping you a secret."

"No secret. Didn't wanna interrupt family time," Reyna retorts, ignoring a subtle elbow from Paula.

"We met in line at Newman's, if you can believe that. I was buying a twelver of Falstaff. She started giving me a hard time about my peasant tastes. We got to talking, and she promised me some of her Glenfiddich." Laughing at Janie's raised eyebrow, "She's smooth, right?" She kisses Reyna's cheek.

Fetching all the pillows she can find, Grace helps Cicely build a buffer. "Janie said you've known each other since Albuquerque. Isn't timing funny like that? Brings you back together when it's good and ready."

Taking off Silas' shoes, Cicely fixes a blanket over him. "Well, I was with Silas' father back then, we're separated. Janie got in touch last summer and I guess here we are."

Turning the dimmer, Grace sits to finish chasing a wild hare. "Sorry, we kinda assumed you were together before Silas' daddy." Grace shakes her head. "Janie can be an enigma, like she's always worried about being found out. Take she and Reyna, they were the worst kept secret in West Texas. We figured moving to Andrews, they'd settle down some. It wasn't their time. Then you and Silas come along. The Lord works in mysterious ways."

Cicely leans on the bedpost for the sake of sufferance alone. "Yeah, she can be a real head scratcher. I know what ya'll are thinkin', I see the looks when her boys from the crew are over. I don't give a rat's ass about labels. Some folks look at me and all they see is a dropout spitting shits and motherfuckers, but not her. She lets me be. That girl'd do anything for me, and I for her. Can't ask for more than that."

Helping herself to the cooler, Cicely squeezes in with Janie. "Miss me?"

"Always. He givin' you a hard time?" Janie asks, checking her watch.

"Somethin' like that. Let's go inside, swear I saw some Jack."

Tipsy, Cicely kisses on Janie as they settle into bed. Running her hand along Janie's waistband, she pulls the drawstring loose. Janie tenderly kisses her hand. "That drive did me in. Could we pick this up in the morning?"

Life develops a certain duality in the weeks to come.

There's her comfortable life with Cicely and Silas, she no longer looks for signs of the end. When she was still small enough to feel more than she understood, Janie recalls how her father's eyes lit up his whole face. Knowing what she knows now, Janie reckons that twinkle was fulfillment. No matter how shit his day was, his family was enough for him. And it can be enough for her too, she just knows it.

Then there's life in Lynn, work's a different animal since New Year's. Reyna makes no mention of Cicely, nor does she speak of Paula when the guys talk about their wives or girlfriends. Truth be told, this is fine by Janie. She doesn't much want to hear about it. They live together marooned in a motel as two people whose pasts are so intertwined, it's simply easier to carry on as acquaintances.

Winding down, Emmett treats the crew to dinner. They're wrapping operations in two weeks' time. The well's been nothing but trouble from the get-go and the company's pulling the plug. The geologist's singing a new tune about telltale signs of instability.

Two more tours and it's back to Andrews. Relief washes over their road weary faces. They raise their glasses to hard work and bad luck.

After being called into the doghouse leaves Reyna uncharacteristically distracted, Janie finds herself adjusting to keep in step. She and Ricky keep it to themselves.

Pensive, Reyna fidgets against the steering wheel. Catching sight of a roadside smokehouse, she wavers. "You wanna stop for dinner?"

Distant, Janie doesn't much want to talk. Keeping quiet's easier than talking about nothing. "Cicely prolly made dinner. You wanna get takeout?"

"Right, no that's alright." The old cinderblock and stucco building shrinks away in the rearview. Thinking on it a while longer, the tension's making Reyna ill. "We need to talk."

Janie holds her course. "Yeah, what do you wanna talk about?"

"You know how I started taking some classes last summer?" Reyna asks, digging for something that won't come across as retribution.

"Well, you never actually told me, but I saw the mail."

"I told you. Anyway, I got the last of my certs a month back."

"You don't wanna be a derrickhand anymore?" Janie asks, unease mounting.

"You know damn well I've had my eye on driller. This slump ain't slowing and I'm aiming to be worth keeping around." Her nerves withering, "I took a job offshore in Louisiana, they're gonna send me to mud school. It's a small firm, Emmett knows one of the engineers. I've done my time in the dirt."

Fighting her seatbelt lock, Janie slumps defeated. "When?"

"Three weeks. I'll finish out the contract then use the last week to move." Fussing with the radio, Reyna continues. "I'm going to leave you an extra month of rent. There's a guy on Doug's crew looking to move out closer to work."

"I don't care about the rent," Janie interrupts, getting worked up despite herself.

"You will come next month being the only income and all," Reyna quips.

Looking out the window to get her bearings, Janie motions to exit. "Let's stop off for a drink."

"Thought you had to get home," Reyna replies, pulling off the highway. "You wanna go in?" She asks halfheartedly, knowing they'll not make it past the parking lot.

"How long have you known?" With no grounds for her scolding, Janie's too overwrought to turn back. "I can't believe you kept this from me."

"Like you kept Cicely from me? You know what, never mind." Stretching, Reyna's on the precipice of coming undone herself. "Got word two days ago. Applied back when we first started in Lynn."

Shamed, Janie picks at a frayed nail edge. "I didn't know what to say. I'm sorry, I know it was shitty."

Reyna dabs at obstinate tears. "I can't do this anymore. I've got no claim to you, I know that, but watching you with someone else is messing me up." Daring to look over, she sees Janie's eyes welling. "Look, I know you don't feel the same."

Thrown, Janie tussles with the trappings of willful denial and the murkiness of emotional abstention. "Why didn't you say something?"

Floored, Reyna sighs through a pained smile. "I have. I mean not literally, but c'mon. I thought it was pretty fucking obvious. Janie, I begged Emmett to get you on the crew, he did it as a favor. Andrews was a chance to start over, together."

Pinching the bridge of her nose, Janie breathes deeply. "You made it damn clear things were casual. Hell Reyna, you're the one who taught me to chase girls."

Sighing through streaming tears, Reyna wicks at them. "What can I say, I'm fucked up and you're blind."

"I may be, but I'm not a mind reader," Janie counters. "I mean seriously, we spent our Saturday nights chatting up girls together. And somehow I should've known?"

"That was just sex. I don't give a fuck about that. We were more than that, and you know it." Facing her, Reyna draws a long breath the way you do going after a dug in splinter. "I see the way she makes you happy, the way I used to make you happy. Jealousy sucks. Look, if I can't have you, and I know I can't, then I've gotta walk away."

Through tears, Janie cusses and fights the buckle release to scoot closer. "Have me? You've had me, many times. I never even let myself consider the possibility of you and I because you're too cool for love and shit."

Her burden lifting, Reyna responds neutrally. "Thing is, it's easy to put something out of your mind when you've got nothing riding on it. I don't want to fight about it." Letting out a low breath of surrender, "We are who we are."

Her voice staggered by sniffles, Janie blots at her eyes. "I guess that's it then? Shit." Resigned, Janie lets memory guide her to Reyna's lips. A simple kiss the coda to their wren song. "I do love you, whether you believe it or not."

"I know, but sometimes I think our love's made up of oil and water. But who knows, maybe now I'll get my shit in order, for once in my life."

As they sit at the far end of the lot, the sun gradually drops below the horizon, leaving a dusky sky to hide what last light laid bare. Sitting quietly, neither's ready for the change that pulling onto the highway will bring. After a spell, they agree it's time.

"Paula going with you?" Janie asks, her heart breaking thinking of her going alone.

Half smiling, Reyna shakes her head. "We're just having fun, she knows about it. She's got a good thing going on here."

The night before their last tour, Janie scrapes together the mettle to come clean. Not only about Reyna leaving, but about everything. While Reyna's departure's unforeseen, the nature of their relationship is not. Cicely confides she knew long before ol' scuttlebutt Grace gave it away, and only half believes it's over.

Rig shutdown is smoother than working it ever was, and so it is she'll send them home whole. Beset with watered-down regret, Janie curses the spiteful sun for rising and the moon for having the gall to bring her that much closer to the next she never wanted.

In a matter of hours, they'll leave Lynn County behind. Eventually the particulars will fade, but years from now they'll talk of that damned good fried chicken whenever the old crew gets together. Come Sunday, Reyna will leave Janie behind. With a stroke of luck, the particulars of why she left will fade too and heal over enough to come back.

All the nuances, whose sum have invariably drawn Janie to Reyna, conspire to subvert her will. There's a patent, equal longing from Reyna. *A lingering look could do it, a drink for old times' sake surely would.*

A small imprudent part of Janie is indifferent to Cicely, Paula or the implications of one more night, even in knowing Reyna would turn her life on its head for her. A cynical satisfaction in their union ending as it began, at the expense of another, rises in her. Nights like these, Janie wonders if life is anything more than a ceaseless cycle of loss and leaving. Holding her drink to a minimum, she stays on her side of the room and reads a Thomas Hardy novel Darrell had given her ages ago.

Fernie calls with news they've made it to Shreveport. Reyna having made no promise of keeping in touch, Janie figures the least she can do is honor what Reyna would never ask of her. Bereft, she settles into a crowded solitude in the downtime between hitches. Reyna's absence steals the joy from the life she thought she wanted.

Ignoring what she refuses to consider, Janie works hard to prove Emmett a wise man for promoting her. The answer is always yes. While Cicely's embrace has grown chaste, and the space between them expansive, Janie stays the course. And when Cicely looks as though she'd rather be alone, as she did when it was Nathan wanting to share her space, Janie withdraws to the sanctum of her own sadness. *This is the inevitable slowdown. Patience, let the rising tide come to you.*

With all the sunlight they could want for on a late summer afternoon, Janie and Silas throw on their grubbies after her company picnic. Cicely hides from a headache stalking her for the better part of two days. Tearing up a muddy patch with his RC truck, Silas sprays them. Dislodging it, Janie clears the gunk. "Remember, you gotta keep 'em clean or it'll stop working."

"When my daddy gets me one, I'm gonna keep it super shiny," Silas replies, running off grappling the truck with both arms.

Looking to the house, Janie struggles to think of the last time Silas mentioned Nathan. Must have been not more than a few weeks after they arrived.

Sitting a while in Reyna's old room, Janie reads *Going on a Bear Hunt* to Silas for about the hundredth time. Matty loved it too, it was always again and again with the bear book. Already gone to bed, Cicely leaves Janie an icy beer on the table. Sipping, she supposes she'll stew some then let it go. Except she can't, or she won't. *What's the difference? Goddammit.*

Without an ear to bend, Janie turns to her eternal confidant. Not God, the other one.

> *Dear Lydia,*
> *I've lost count of how long it's been since I last wrote or who I'm even writing to anymore. I've spent years thinking of what I might say if we met again. All it's gotten me is a box of unsent letters. An orphan box of my own. I'm over a thousand miles away and still becoming my mother. Go figure.*
> *My gut tells me it's better to pine for the idea of you rather than mourn losing the real you. Take it on faith, proof is setting up house in Shreveport. Further proof is sleeping in the next room, she'll be gone soon enough I reckon.*
> *Life among the living is kind of a two-step, and I'm beginning to think I'm not much of a dancer. Sure I can keep up for a Saturday night, or out in the field where I know what to do and when to do it, but the rest of the time I'd rather get lost in my comics. As of late, my stash has run dry so I've been spending time in Wessex hypocritically judging Gabriel for toiling in the friend zone.*
> *Wherever you are tonight, I hope you're not sitting around writing letters to ghosts.*
> *Always,*
> *Janie*

Climbing into bed, Cicely's pressed to the far reaches of her side. Janie imagines her fingers curled over the edge seam. The answer a given, she asks out of courtesy. "You awake?"

Shoulders sinking, Cicely turns wearily. "I am now."

Ask her. Go on, say it. Say something. "Thanks for the beer."

"You're welcome. You get Silas to bed alright?"

"Yeah, ran himself ragged. Your head still hurtin' ya?"

Cicely turns into her blankets, nuzzling her pillow. "I guess, just need to get some sleep."

"Are you happy? I mean with me, here?" Janie asks, certain she doesn't want to hear the answer.

"Happy's kind of a relative term, ain't it? I'm not unhappy if that's what you're asking." Indignance set alight by silence flickers in Cicely's eyes. She'd give anything for a smoke right now over this trifling bullshit. "Janie, what do you want? Spit it out already, goddamn!"

"Have you been talkin' to Nathan?"

Glancing toward Silas' room, she rests against the headboard. "He wants to see Silas. He's his father, I can't very well deny him."

"Who asked you to?" Janie retorts, battering her pillow into place.

"You may not be saying it, but you're gonna tell me you woke me cause you're happy about it?"

Lacking the grit to go on, Janie sets her alarm and turns over. "Night."

"You're going to bed, just like that?" Huffily putting on her slippers, Cicely fishes through her sweater pockets. "Christ on a goddamn cracker, where are my smokes." Shaking a soft pack free, she snatches it and walks out.

Temper allayed, Cicely comes to bed by and by. Snuggling up, she rests on Janie's chest. "I know you're not sleepin'. I should've told you. Nathan's coming to see Silas once Hailey's back at school."

"I like to think you'd tell me if you were unhappy. You can ya know." Stroking her hair, Janie goes along to get along.

Holding her tighter, Cicely replies, "I know."

The rig will be at its busiest come September. Be it premonition or paranoia, a fear of coming home to an empty house plagues Janie. With less than two weeks left, she's determined to bring to mind the life they're building together.

Down to the night before, Janie stops at a Memphis barbecue joint that Cicely loves. There's a sweetness to her that Janie had given up for lost. Bringing Silas a sticker sheet for his truck, they spend the evening applying decals. Reminiscing over a bottle of wine, Janie wonders if she had it all wrong. They make love as they did the night their friendship blossomed into something more.

Waking in the wee hours, Janie reaches for Cicely, whose folded body again straddles the far edge of the mattress. The gap feels infinite, and in that moment, Janie accepts it to be unbridgeable. *Cicely's going to leave tomorrow. She's going home, and that's a fact. You'll be alright, and that's a fact too.*

Rousing to the snaps of Cicely's duffle, Janie knows the sound before opening her eyes. Without moving, she watches Cicely find her feet. "Were you even gonna say goodbye?" Janie asks groggily.

Slinging the strap over her shoulder, she slumps under the weight of her bag and what she's about to do. "I'm going back home."

"No shit," Janie replies sharply, righting herself.

Setting her bag down, Cicely sits next to her. Demure for perhaps the first time in her life, she cradles her hands on her lap. "I didn't know how to tell you."

Laying her head on Janie's shoulder, Cicely's touch is met with retreat. Standing to dress, Janie's eyes brim with choler. Sniffling, Cicely brushes away tears. "Someday I hope that you might forgive me. At the end of the day, we're gettin' too old to be runaways. It's time to go home." Weary of waiting, she snaps. "Can you please look at me?"

Pulling her shirt on, Janie looks at her, through her.

"I've been running from one thing or another since I was a kid. Hell, I don't even know what from anymore. It's time to stop, for Silas' sake. He belongs with his daddy and his sister. And I've gotta learn to live with who I am. Cause I'm still her no matter where I go, even here. You're no different, eventually you're gonna have to go home too."

Her contempt rising, Janie's on the brink of shouting. "I am nothing like you. I'm not a coward."

Wounded, but unwavering, Cicely scoffs. "You're not? I think Reyna might beg to differ."

"Reyna's none of your business. It's completely different," Janie snaps.

"Don't I know it. You've never once looked at me the way you look at her." Settling, Cicely continues mournfully. "You and I, we were just having a good time keeping each other company. Maybe that's as close to love as either of us is gonna get."

Storming into the room, Silas leaps onto the bed proclaiming Daddy just pulled up. With the wind out of her sails, Janie lifts him onto her lap. Looking at her weepy eyes, he snuggles her. Insisting she come meet his daddy, Janie lets him lead the way. "I'll get Silas ready while you take your bags out."

Fixing his RockHounds hat, she stuffs the truck and controller into his backpack. "Remember, keep it shiny." Without looking at her, Janie hands off Silas to Cicely at the threshold. "I'll grab his car seat."

His messy hair cropped close, flecks of untimely gray span Nathan's crown. Fumbling for his sunglasses, he shields his eyes meeting her halfway. Taking the seat and toys, he sets them in the backseat. "I'm sorry about this Janie. I know you didn't ask for any of it."

Janie offers a penitent smile in lieu of an apology for her complicity. "Take care Nathan. You got a good kid there."

Janie busies herself cleaning the kitchen from the night before. Though she hears Cicely come in, she refuses to look over. Hugging her, Cicely doesn't let her pull away. "I hope that when you finally find your way home, you'll let me know you made it." Without looking back, she closes the door behind her. Absentmindedly washing the same cup till she hears his truck pull out, Janie pitches it to the wall.

Calling out sick, the next few days slip through her fingers. There are no tears, no wistful thoughts of if they'd stayed or maybe they'll come back. Janie lets herself go cold, for if she allowed herself to feel this, then the tears would flow so freely, she may well drown.

With no one to fill in tomorrow, Janie drags herself into the shower. Pulled together, she settles for an evening of low lights and even lower expectations. Making the drive to the Hangout, she breaks their cardinal rule. Unable to remember her new friend's name, stumbling up the path she leans into the anonymity.

Tapping into Reyna's castoff bottle of scotch, they prattle on in drunke-nese. A dance of emphatic confessions lacking even a modicum of sincerity lapses into a lackadaisical make out session. Janie's eyes blearily fix upon mislaid mementos of bygone happiness.

Diving deeper, Janie sprints to outpace the lugubrious voice in her head. When the booze has given its all, she aims to lose herself in the girl. Leading her by the hand, the scent of Cicely's perfume and hair products linger in the stuffy room. Her hands numb and mind sharp, Janie clumsily knocks over Silas' Batman figure which brings the evening to an end.

In a few hours, as dawn prepares to wipe their slate clean, Janie pretends to be fast asleep on the couch as last evening's friend slows by the door.

Chapter Thirty Four

Low spirits having laid claim to Halloween and Janie's twenty-third birthday, the scourge would've taken the holidays too were it not for Fernie keeping vigil on her couch. Months removed, Memorial Day's as good as any to declare her mourning period over, or at least adjourned.

Levi, a motorhand from Doug's crew, moves into Reyna's old room. He works fourteen on, fourteen off, which suits Janie fine on the on and not so much on the off. While different in all the ways housemates could differ, they make it work.

At war with Cicely's imprint, Janie's bent on proving she's not running from anything, least of all herself. Home's just a word, and she'll say it as many times as it takes to believe it.

Conscripted into the ranks of the technological revolution as a consequence of enrolling at the local community college, Janie purchases a personal computer she uses as sparingly as possible. After Levi's first fourteen off, Janie's taught the value of anti-virus software by a mortified computer repair tech. Like that, the next year's mapped out. All roads lead to mud school. *These are not the actions of some runaway.*

Devoted to staying away from girls, Janie swears off the bars which have a way of making her forget she's staying away from girls. Trading nights out for beers with Emmett and the boys, savings begin to accumulate for the first time since moving to Andrews. A relic of foregone golden days, Silas' Batman witnesses all from the living room shelf.

While night classes consume her evenings, Janie grows into her role of derrickhand by day. Summer and fall amount to little more than session beginnings and endings, save for seeing more of Fernie when Grace works late. Though the looming technological apocalypse batters Grace's team one software patch at a time, the fuss about Y2K fizzles as the 20th century cedes its rank to the aughts. Walking home with her Sunday coffee and glazed buttermilk bar, Janie watches crowded church parking lots thin out by the week as those hedging their bets return to business as usual. *God's providence isn't for everyone.*

A new year brings a leave from the rig to complete a condensed petroleum geology course at a local technical school. Itching to feel the sun on her back and the monkey board beneath her feet, Janie takes a breather before surrendering her savings and a couple months of her life to mud school. Being back in the field feels like home. Word of a summer opening in Galveston comes down the line, Emmett reckons she's got a good shot if she's willing to relocate.

Called down from the platform, Janie slogs into the doghouse expecting to hear Levi bellyaching over being locked out of the computer. "Hello," she declares brusquely.

"Janie?" While there's a vague familiarity to the voice on the other end of the line, the inflection's unmistakable. A chill runs down her spine. "Do you know who this is?"

Nodding, Janie catches herself. "I do. Matty? You sound so grown up."

"I don't know if you care or whatever, but I thought you should know. Dad's been diagnosed with lung cancer and they're saying he doesn't have too long."

Covering her mouth, Janie freezes. She can hear him breathing, waiting for her reply. Yet she cannot get herself to say anything. *Speak, say anything goddammit.* The words will not come.

Clearing his throat, Matty swallows hard. "Anyway, so now you know."

Holding the receiver for another ten seconds or so, Janie returns it to the cradle.

Not in the mood to suffer Levi's musings, she gives him the password with a stern warning not to defile her computer. Sequestered in her room with a bottle of scotch, a fresh to her copy of *Strange Tales* and a gyro worthy of a pitchfork, she plans to get lost after letting the dead bury the dead.

Dear Lydia,

You'd think after reading as many comics as I have, I might have known that almost no one who isn't already an orphan escapes the twist that calls them home. In our parting, Cicely said that going home was inevitable. Years of choked down anger spilled off my tongue. She was right and leaving me behind for the second time, I could bear neither.

When I was completing my compulsory penitence, there was an underlined passage I came across in Proverbs. In the margin, my Dad had written the word destiny. Seeing that gave me hope there was something greater ahead. When your brother gave me your letter, I knew it was you.

I knew it when Butch and I listened to Rush on lazy days in the common area. Whenever Bravado came on, I imagined it the soundtrack to our reunion. Over time, it spoke to me less as a rad ballad and more as an ode to what could have been. I wanted to believe that love remains but wondered if I hadn't chosen pride over trying to find you.

In a few days I'll make the drive to Clayton for the first time in nine years. If they'll have me, I'll say goodbye to my Dad who only has months left. If not, I'll say goodbye anyway and curse myself for going in the first place.

Living with ghosts doesn't leave much room for the living. I think I need to let the idea of you go if too much time has passed to find you here among the living.

Always,

Janie

Morning brings a headache of the stabby sort, pungent gyro breath and the realization she's going home. *Not for good though. Christ, not for good.* Propped up with Excedrin and a red eye with a five second pour of cane sugar, Janie hauls herself into the doghouse. Half an hour later her request for leave is filed. Two days later her car's packed.

"Tell your brother to stay out of my room," Janie cautions. Salty as she may be about Levi's creepy brother staying on the couch, she's grateful to have a third of the rent covered.

Dirty boots resting on her coffee table, Levi giggles like he's counting down till his parents leave town. "You got it boss."

Palming a paper sack, Janie tosses it onto his lap. "Try out the nostalgia of the printed page." Pointing at her computer, vulnerable and at his mercy. "You fuck up my computer with your crappy Usenet porn and I'll tell the guys about the weird shit you're into."

Beet red, Levi clutches the bag to his chest. "I can roll with this."

Disgusted, Janie grabs her bag. "Be good. Stay out of my room. Seriously."

"For sure. Hope you and your Dad kick cancer's ass."

Rolling her eyes, Janie pulls the door closed behind her.

At times, the road home feels a pilgrimage to regression. Pulling off the interstate, Janie passes a bus offloading passengers. Though the truck stop's gray stucco walls have faded to a milky beige and the forgettable fast-food joint has been swapped for a Subway, the red neon glow still carries Millie's clear across to the highway. Walking the aisles, it reeks of proofing bread and the noxious funk brought into being by a litany of preserved meats chilling side by side.

Crossing the fuel island, Janie tears into a bag of jerky. Night gathering all around her, she watches the Greyhound driver stamp out his cigarette beneath the white-lettered radiance of Albuquerque.

Part III

Spring 2000

For there we loved, and where we love is home,
Home that our feet may leave, but not our hearts.
- Oliver Wendell Holmes, *Homesick In Heaven*

Chapter Thirty Five

S leeping the morning away in a Grand Canyon overflow lot, Janie awakens to the afternoon sun baking the remains of a burrito exiled to the dash somewhere around Winslow. Persevering, she freshens up at a push button faucet. Teeth brushed, pits camouflaged and one eye stinging from curiously pink soap, Janie's road ready. Stopping twice for gas, she rolls into town on fumes shy of midnight. Parking down the street, the allure of resting her eyes proves irresistible.

You know that moment when you wake with an intense feeling of being watched despite being alone? For Janie, it's just like that. Except she's not alone, she's sleeping in her car at 6 a.m. on her childhood street. And she is being watched, by her father. Ray's expression, a vestige of disgust, blooms to amusement at her bewilderment. Janie stiffly climbs out, wiping a partially dried drool streak.

As they regard one another, Janie appraises him. Before her stands the gray, gaunt, ghost of the man she last saw a lifetime ago. *Christ, why didn't Matty call sooner?* Not knowing whether to hug him or cry, she croaks out "How long have you been standin' there?"

His voice thinner than memory would have her believe, he doesn't miss a beat. "Long enough to know you're not some highway rat casing the neighborhood. You're just the daughter I haven't seen in, what, about a decade." Ray slackens the leash of an adorably overweight bulldog. "I guess that's that then."

Wanting to pet the dog, Janie sticks to the matter at hand. "What's what?"

Shifting his weight, he's ready to resume his walk. "If you're here, then I must really be dying."

Bursting into tears, Janie hugs her father. Pulling away only when it occurs to her how frail he is. She can hate herself later, there's always time for that. Checking her watch, it's as early as it feels. "What're you doing out so early?"

"Clyde here doesn't give a shit about chemo. He's gonna get his morning walk come hell or high water." Motioning to Clyde, he smirks. "Guess it gives him something to look forward to."

Janie crouches to greet Clyde. "Seems like you kinda look forward to it too."

"Eh." Ray nods halfheartedly.

Amid the bustle, Janie hadn't considered that the world she left behind had changed too. In her mind's eye, everything had stayed the same. Those she loved were spared the curse of aging, the haunts she sought solace in continued to thrive and in spite of nine years' worth of living, she was still the girl afraid of what they thought of her. Who they thought she ought to be. Whom they decided she was.

Most timely of her oversights, she hadn't thought of where she'd stay. Well, that's not entirely true. If she's being honest, like cleanse my soul honest, then she had to admit some part of her imagined showing up and crashing in her old room. Any residual enmity would be swept away in a torrent of joyous reunion, in knowing she had forgiven them. Only she hadn't and nor had they, it would seem.

Her childhood home a stone's throw from where they stand, she watches her father barter with himself, calculating the toll of her mother's wrath should he invite her to stay. Her mouth swifter than her wits, Janie stammers, "I should go check in." Flipping through sleepy snippets of roadside signs, Janie calls out the first she can make out. "Best Western. The one by the highway."

He looks at her puzzled. "If you've got a hotel, what're you doing sleepin' in your car like a vagrant?"

"Made good time, got in ahead of my reservation." She stretches, faking a yawn. "I'm thinkin' I'll come by around noon? Gonna freshen' up, maybe take a nap."

"Alright, I'll tell your mother." Giving the house a last look, he wants to remember it as it was before Janie came home. "C'mon Clyde."

Griping over the rate, if only she had recalled the Super 8 next door. Showering till the water runs cold, Janie sits wrapped in a waifish towel. *It's not too late to get in the car and go home.* Then as it is wont to do, the wise and oft shrewish voice adds to the fray. *Go home to what? Levi? An empty bed? Cicely had it right all along.* Huffing, she kicks over her suitcase. "She doesn't know shit, not a goddamn thing."

An olive branch to her mother, Janie wears the one pastel item she owns. The periwinkle blouse creeps up under her armpits with every breath.

Parking a few doors down to take in the scene unseen, the short walk lends time to fuss over whether to ring the bell or walk right in. Sparing further agony, Ray meets her at the door. The house a juxtaposition of elements frozen in time yet rearranged, family photos hang neatly on the living room wall where she remembers them. Though the room itself has become a hospital suite. Yaya's ugly couch and her mother's pristine sofa table have been exiled to the den.

Ray puts his arm around Janie when her eyes settle on an IV pole tucked in the corner of the dining room. His breath a minty acrid, she pretends not to notice. A sparse layer of stubble grazes her cheek. Running her fingertips across his jaw, she marvels.

Massaging his chin, Ray smirks. "I know, my whiskers came in white. Can't shave 'em either. Your mother ordered me an electric razor from Sears."

"Keep 'em. It's rugged." They bust up at the idea of him being called rugged. Inadvertently, Janie locks eyes with her mother.

Stirred at their banter, a chill fills the room. Shame comes over Ray as she looks to him wounded before leaving. Some things never change, seems like some folks don't either. Janie settles for a muzzled chat. "Matty home?"

Rubbing his temple, Ray takes a seat. "At work. Works for Frank Bishop. You remember his son, Kenny?"

Sensing strain, Janie worries she's stayed too long.

"No, you wouldn't. Right. His folks moved to town when Matty was in middle school."

"You've got to be kidding me," Kate barks from the doorway, sent to finish her mother's good work. "You're a stranger."

Janie stands confounded at how Kate's managed to look like a younger version of their mother rather than an older version of herself. A rage wells across her chest like mercury in an old thermometer.

Unfit for battle, Ray's unwilling to referee. "Anyone seen Clyde?"

Pulling the cord, Janie pats his shoulder. "Give me a shout if you need anything. I'll stop in tomorrow."

Kate retorts, "He's gone ten years without you, think he'll be fine."

"If you'd pass my number along to Matty, I'd be grateful." Denying Kate so much as a passing glance, Janie lets herself out.

Drawing the shades, Janie pines for sleep. *It's been nine years, not ten. Nine.* Minutes crawl into hours, doubt prying through the darkness. Leaping from her cocoon, she sweeps her things into the suitcase. *What was I thinking? Don't ya know when you're not wanted.* Crumbling, she yields to sleep.

A dream of her father knocking relentlessly on the car window gives way to a bluish dimness and the sounds of closing doors and beeping car alarm transponders. A sharp knock rattles her awake.

Easing the door open, Matty walks in before she can get a word out. Crossing his arms to ward off a hug, he stays his distance. Rustling her hair free from a rat's nest, Janie smiles cautiously. "That's quite a mustache, very Tom Selleck. I know some guys on the rig who'd kill for that. I dunno if you know, but I work out in the oil fields..." *That's cool, I too like to stare at the floor.* "Ya know, we can talk about that later. Hungry?"

Taking a shrug for an affirmative response, Janie pulls it together in the cramped bathroom. *Give him space. Don't crowd him.*

In silent agreement, they drive to a bar and grill frequented by tourists and families living in the new subdivision a few exits down. While he may be all grown up, there are traits as innate to Matty as breathing. The way he fidgets with straw wrappers, twisting them into knots to ease his boredom or settle his nerves. How his brown eyes darken or lighten is a steadfast barometer of his mood. These are the lifelines Janie clings to as she feels around for where to begin. Looking anywhere but at her, small talk's a wash.

Ordering iced tea when she wants something stronger, Janie uses his lightness toward the waitress as a starting point. "I meant to ask, how'd you come across my number?"

"Internet search. Your name came up on your company's website, had pictures from a barbecue. Who's that kid? You got a kid?"

"No, he belongs to a friend." Trailing off, she waits for his interest to drift from a game blaring overhead. "Can you tell me more about Dad?"

Matty sighs into an explanation he doesn't care to give. "Had this nasty cough he couldn't get rid of. Mom thought he had pneumonia, so she nagged him till he went in. They sent him to Fresno for scans. Turns out, wasn't a cold."

"But Dad never smoked. Least not that we know of," Janie says, mostly to herself.

"Yeah well, doc says you can get it from all kinds of stuff, not just smoking." Voice cracking, he masks it by clearing his throat. "It's in his bones. Crossed from one lung to the other. It freakin' sucks."

Reaching to comfort him, Janie mirrors his recoil. "I'm sorry Matty."

Looking through her, he continues. "Last visit they said months with chemo. Months. I told him not to let them pump him full of that crap, for what, a few more lousy months? But Kate won, like always."

"Months? Shit, sorry. I just, I dunno, that's so fast."

"Fast?" Matty's brow furrows. "He's been fighting this thing for two years."

"Right. Yeah, I just assumed, right." Her every breath an offense, Janie pulls back. "Matty, how's Mom doing with all this?"

"You know Mom, keeping up a good front. Kate's pretty much running things if you hadn't guessed."

"How are Kate and Greg doing? Didn't see them settling in Clayton."

Leaning back, Matty hesitates. "Greg had an affair with an intern, got her pregnant. I think Kate was more upset about getting left for a fat theology major, like he could've done better."

"No shit?" Janie covers her mouth. "Sorry."

"Stop. I'm not eight years old. Anyway, Kate and the kids moved in with us." Eating his fries in twos, he finishes his soda. "They were miserable. Still sucks, but I don't think they were built for the long haul like Mom and Dad."

"God, no wonder she was such a bitch today."

Cracking half a smile, he moves his glass for a refill. "Yeah, that's it."

Janie listens to the scant specs of Matty's life he's willing to share. He asks nothing about her, which she takes as judgment at worst and retribution at best. Still, a question burns through her. *Leave it be.* "Can I ask you something Matty? If no one wants me here, why'd you call?"

He tosses his crumpled napkin atop his empty plate. "Sorry we didn't throw you a parade. You prolly gotten used to them by now." Sliding out of the booth, he zips his coat. "Go home Janie."

Watching the world go by from her small balcony, everyone's going somewhere, anywhere but here. Climbing under the covers, her resurrected Walkman picks up where she left off. "Never Let Me Down Again" pulls her back in time. She feels the weight of someone lying next to her, of Reyna's arms wrapping around her and pulling her close.

Morning brings hunger pangs and the resolve to pursue closure until she gets it, or the pursuit proves more painful than its absence.

Procrastinating, Janie extends her leave through summer's end. Six months is a stretch, but Emmett promises he'll find her a spot somewhere. Though odds are, it won't be Galveston.

Cozied up to the counter at the donut shop, Janie crawls the emaciated classifieds. A bungalow over on Gentry comes up priced right.

No matter how small your town is, there's always that block you avoid for one reason or another. Gentry Road's that place in Clayton. One of the oldest roads in town, it hearkens back to days when Clayton was little more than a junction between the old highway and a handful of ranches. In Janie's time, it was where those who had fallen on hard times converged with those who had known only hard times. Together, they tottered along among relics of the ranch era living out their days on the crumbs of family land they still held claim to.

Driving slow, Janie strains to see any addresses at all. *5201? Where the hell are ya? Shit, doesn't anyone believe in addresses round here?* The little voice, who's become quite lively since returning to Clayton, chimes in. *Why should they? No one's looking for them and they know it. You'll fit right in, no one's looking for you either.* Janie's eyes dart from her scribbled notes to a red cottage. *Shit, there it is.*

Three, no four little cottages sit crammed onto a skinny lot just like Albuquerque. Walking up the gravel drive, something rings familiar. Tattered window screens, warped trims chock full of rotting finishing nails and crooked screen doors cry out in unison "Only those elements time cannot wear, were made before, and beyond time we stand."

Startled by a slamming car hood, Janie halts. Looking over, she spies a shirtless shade tree mechanic taking a long swig. Wiping his brow, he offers a kind smile before retreating to the mysteries of an old tool shed.

"Janie?" Calls a voice from up the driveway. "I thought it might be you."

Matching the voice with the face is a gut punch from the past. "Wendy. Been a long time."

"I'll say. Guess Monica called it right after all. C'mon, I'll show you around." Pushing through the rickety door, Wendy waits for Janie.

Though she didn't think it possible, the cottage is smaller inside than it appears from the outside. "Cozy."

"Uh huh, it's all original. Vintage guess you could say," Wendy declares.

To think all this splendor could be mine if I play my cards right. Ancient carpet walked flat, scuffed plaster walls and mint-tiled counters with hairline cracks running through them like cobwebs. Making no effort at sincerity, Janie blithely remarks, "Sorta shabby chic."

Letting Wendy's lazy voice trail off to the bedroom. Janie thinks back to a blisteringly hot Sunday service, recalling Wendy bragging how her daddy was evicting those Okies from one of his properties. Saying it loud enough for the target of her taunt to hear, a lanky boy from bible study looked down in shame as she shared a laugh with her friends. Ray had been following along too. Cross, he spoke plainly. *Hal Fisher's nothing but a slum lord taking advantage of folks down on their luck. From the looks of it, that apple didn't fall too far at all.*

"So?" Wendy asks impatiently.

Don't put pride above your means. "Okay. I'll take it."

A slow grin crests Wendy's cherubic cheeks. "See that's the thing, I didn't offer it to you yet." Chuckling, her smile falls away. "I know you don't have a job here in town. How are you plannin' on paying rent? Can't use a co-signer."

Stepping over a pile of abandoned toys, Janie slows at the door. In an instant she's taken back to the days of Wendy staring her down in the rearview, daring her to challenge her. Looking out over erosion worn ruts running the length of the driveway like a fault line, she swallows her pride bitterly. Pulling a folded wad of bills from her front pocket, she slaps it against her palm. "I'll pay six months up front whether I stay that long or not. Take it or leave it. If you're gonna take it, then hurry up cause I got other places to see."

Wendy stands in a lonely stalemate, her hand on her matronly hip. "Wait! Don't be so gee dee sulky." Following only as far as the door, she waits. "Get me a cashier's check for the six months and another three hundred for the deposit."

Pocketing the cash, Janie turns back. "When do you want it?"

Looking to the sky for inspiration, "Tell you what, I'll do you a solid and skip the cleaning so you can have it sooner. Let's say Saturday. Drop the check at my office this afternoon."

"Your dad's place by the theater?"

"My place. Daddy retired to focus on ministry. I leave by four." Clobbering the handle, she shakes the key loose from the blunted cylinder.

Letting Matty cool off, Janie does her reconnaissance, which consists of driving past the house looking for her mother's car then sneaking quick visits when she's out. Each visit's less awkward than the last until she runs into Helene and Kate, which sets her back to square one.

Minding her promise, Janie checks in with Fernie. Reassured her found family's waiting for her when all this is done, she can do this.

Saturday arrives on the heels of a spring storm. With nothing more than a suitcase and K-Mart bags of essentials, the move-in's seamless and solitary.

Wendy having generously left the previous tenants' furnishings, Sunday is devoted to sorting her gifts into two sides of the room. The dumpster side and the not dumpster side. While it's a bit worse for wear, not more than a few hundred square feet, and even a little swampy after a good rain, this little red shed is hers.

Chapter Thirty Six

Having stewed for the weekend, Janie prepares for whatever will come. Be that getting shunned, or worse getting pulled back into the fold. A morning's worth of fretting fizzles when no one answers. His car in the driveway, they're not getting off this easy. *You want me gone, you're gonna have to say it to my face.*

Tippy toeing to peer over the fence, something's rustling across the yard. The latch comes free on the second jump slap. Expecting Matty wrestling a dried-out shrub, the figure's too slight. Upon closer inspection, it's her father. "Hey! Be careful. What are you doing?"

Ray stands, exhausted. "So now you're going to tell me what I can and can't do?"

Sacked out on a pile of leaves, Clyde rouses to assess whether she's come bearing snacks and returns to his slumber with a snort. Her raised arm a white flag, Janie kneels to give Clyde some scritches. "Have at it. I'm just gonna visit with Clyde here."

Pacing his breath and on the losing end of a fight with an overgrown bramble, Ray laments, "I've had just about enough nannying from your mother and sister."

Fighting an urge to help drag the debris into the pile, Janie tries to ignore him struggling to get his breath. "Yeah, I hear ya."

Too tired to go on, Ray tosses his gloves next to the pile. "Thirsty? Let's have some lemonade."

Taking an enthusiastic gulp, Janie squints at the reminder of how tart he likes it. Sadness overtakes her as he dilutes his glass.

"Doctor's orders." Patting his stomach, he musters a half-hearted laugh. "Can't tolerate much acid these days."

Sipping their drinks, Ray savors the last sip. Setting his glass down, he taps the rim, eyeing Janie in a way reserved for appraising folks he doesn't believe to be on the level. Pained at being sized up like some backslider, her eyes yield.

Breaking the standoff, Ray folds his hands. "So why are you here? What are you after? Closure? Absolution? Morbid curiosity? Wanted to see me get my comeuppance for however I must have failed you as a father?"

While the bluntness is refreshing, the delivery's no less infuriating. And perhaps too, Janie's unsure if any one of them is the whole of it. No longer retreating, she digs her heels in. "Matty called me. Trust me, this is the last place I ever saw myself coming back to."

Ray huffs, scooting his chair until Janie places her hand over his. "But I'm glad I did. I just want to be here for you in any way that I can, if that's what you want. Say the word, I'll hug you goodbye and keep going."

Ray admires how she resembles her mother in their no muss, no fuss way. Smirking ever so slightly as the arc of her furrowed brow softens, "How do you feel about tagging along to chemo?"

"Yeah, I could do that. What about Kate?"

"Might give her a little break. She hasn't had an easy time. I love your sister but being a captive audience while she goes on about how hard her life is, has a way of wearin' on you. Know what I mean kiddo?"

Nodding, Janie steers clear of commentary. "Anything I can do to help."

Wearing his tired on his face, Ray leaves his glass in the sink. "Think a nap's calling my name. C'mon Clyde, keep this old man company."

Gathering her things, "I'm heading out. When should I pick you up?"

"Stay, I'll be back at 'em in 20 minutes. Make yourself something to eat." Ray disappears to the living room.

Closing in on an hour, hunger creeps up. Rummaging through her father's hiding spot yields bologna and cheese along with a fresh loaf of bread calling from the counter. Frying bologna draws Ray to the kitchen with Clyde on his heels. Quietly, they wait. Letting the American cheese get nice and melty, Janie adds tomato and lettuce before capping it with a fluffy mayo slathered slice of toasted bread. Ray's eyes fill with delight.

"Still your favorite?"

"Always. Haven't had one in ages," Ray replies with eyes only for his sandwich.

"The bologna was in your spot. Under the bacon and jalapeños."

"Oh, that's Matty's now since I can't eat anything worth hiding any-more."

A car door closes in the distance, then another. Janie notices an uptick in her father's pace. "You allowed to have this?"

Not one to speak with a mouthful, he makes an exception. "Not gonna hurt me any, may as well have it." Licking his fingers, he polishes off half.

Going in for that first bite, they're interrupted before she can sink her teeth in. Helene goes the long way to avoid Janie. Kate swoops through, shoulder checking Janie and snatching what's left from his hand. Sand-wich flapping in her hand, she demands an explanation. Cautiously ap-proaching, Janie speaks softly and avoids eye contact. "I was just making him some lunch."

"Were you trying to kill him?" Kate shouts over her.

Tracking Kate's gesturing, Ray throws caution to the wind and reaches for his sandwich.

"Dad!" Kate chides, tossing it in the trash. "What are you doing? You know better."

While Ray suffers a lecture, Janie tidies up. Twisting the bread tie, the room grows quiet.

"And you! Dad's on a low-carb diet. No sugar. None!" Swiping her arms in an x formation, she mimes the globally understood symbol for none.

Tossing the bread on the counter, Janie cops a lean. "Well then what the hell do you feed him? That's not living."

Pushed off the thin ledge of her patience, Kate closes half the distance between she and Janie. Her eyes seek out Helene's location. Whisper shouting, "You have no idea what not living looks like. You've never seen him after a rough chemo session." Kate looks back and forth between them. "You know what, why don't you take him tomorrow."

"We all get it Kate," Helene remarks. Barely looking at Janie, she straightens the jeweled lanyard on her glasses. "Pick your father up at nine tomorrow. Bring something to read."

Furious, Kate says nothing.

After a near miss at the market, Janie settles in with the fixings for a proper dinner. Marinated flank steak, onions, peppers and fingerling potatoes for roasting. She's watched Fernie make this a dozen times or more. A pack of spent matches later, the oven's cold and the kitchen smells of gas. Cozied up to an open window, Janie enjoys a bowl of frosted flakes.

Pulling up at 9 a.m. sharp, Janie spies Ray and Kate through the kitchen window. Coat in hand, he reluctantly holds the door for Kate to catch up. "All set?" He asks Janie.

As though he hadn't said a word, Kate launches into a litany of instructions. Pulling on his seatbelt shoulder strap, she looks at him pensively.

"Ready Dad?" Janie asks, shifting into reverse.

Gently pulling at the door, Ray smiles warmly at Kate. Giving her a little wave, he holds the smile as she watches them back out.

Straining to reach the back seat, a paper bag crinkles under Janie's fingers. She hands it to her father. "Shh! She'll run me outta town."

Opening the bag like a kid on Christmas morning, "No, not a word."

Satisfied, Janie teases, "I'm only doing this on the count of you being so skinny."

"Mmhmm," Ray agrees, peeling a corner of cheese from the wrapper.

Expecting a solemn suite of long-faced folks basking in the perpetual compassion of sympathetic staff, the reality is a stark contrast. Patients in various stages of their treatment journey wait like any other doctor's office. Sure, there's a lot less hair to go around and a more liberal distribution of masks, but for them it's just another day in this new life of theirs.

Infusion stations sit side by side, a curtain between pays homage to privacy. A welcome gesture, though everyone knows the notion of privacy is but a wistful memory at this point. The whole room is a living thing full of moving parts, all dependent upon one another to keep going. Chatty nurses gather their supplies from wheeled carts. Patients sit in high-backed chairs, their arms trained to lay still. If not for the ports and IVs, they could all be there for mani-pedis.

Some are too scared to pay any mind to anyone else or what they're there for, as if there's need to wonder. Young or old, they've been dealt different lengths of the same shitty short straw. The regulars pass the time amongst themselves, most are on their own for one reason or another. So, they make small talk to let the reason they're there fall into the background.

Janie reaches for the curtain until Ray waves it off. "It's just chemo, not a prostate exam."

Snickering from across the aisle bolsters Janie's blushing.

Speaking up, Ray motions to Janie. "June, Martin, this is my other daughter Janie. The prodigal one."

They laugh but say nothing, best not to incriminate themselves.

"Don't tell Helene I said that." Ray smiles over at Janie, a collective secret. "This your last week June?"

She nods, Martin's sad eyes answer questions Ray would never ask.

Ray's nurse lays everything out, cheerily asking of his week. "Your line flushed already hon?"

"Yes ma'am." Remembering his manners, Ray pulls his watch cap and tucks it under his leg. Wisps of gray hair are all that remain, even less than last week when Janie wondered where it had all gone.

Ray closes his eyes as she depresses the plunger. His dominant hand reflexively stretching. "It doesn't hurt. Feels a little funny is all."

Tears stream down Janie's face. The chemo nurse flits her eyes away, asking Ray about his garden plans. Appreciative, he nods it's alright. Giving Janie a cursory glance, she drops her gloves in the trash and reminds Ray to call her if he needs anything.

"You're going to have to stop that or go wait in the car," Ray tells Janie through a pained smirk.

Sniffling, Janie wipes away her tears and flings them for effect. "Done. I swear."

Pulling out her tattered bargain bin copy of *Dark Claw*, Janie pretends to read while stealing glances of her father pretending to read an old issue of *Time* magazine. Little does she know, he's too distracted by fatigue and disinterest to follow so much as the police blotter these days.

The weight and reach of guilt over time missed is an animal unlike any other. It cannot be starved into submission, nor can it be passed on, it's a loyal companion.

Quiet on the ride home, Ray nods off here and there. A few stray hairs framing his temple begin to cling, taking on a silvery matte. Waiting for the light, Janie notices his clamminess.

"Kiddo, I appreciate you taking me, but I can't let you take me anymore if you're going to keep looking at me like that."

Punching the gas after a courtesy honk, Janie asks, "Look at you like what?"

"Like I'm dying. I know I'm dying, but I rather enjoyed that you're the only one who never looks at me like I am."

Pulling up, Kate's waiting at the top of the driveway. "You're late. Did you go the way I told you?"

"Sure did," Janie replies, helping Ray out of the car. She didn't.

Ray's collar damp from a cold sweat, he grasps Kate's arm to steady himself. "Honey, I need the restroom."

Leaving off her father's things, Janie makes for the door while Kate's distracted.

"Janie, a word please," Helene calls from the den.

Her mother motions for her to sit on Yaya's couch, the stranger's seat. Where many a naïve Mormon has sat ensnared for lengthy interrogations of their faith, followed by lunch and a bridge to the way.

"How did he do?" Helene asks, when she's really asking how Janie did.

Casually swallowing hard, Janie shrugs. "Fine."

"Janie!" Squawks an incredulous Kate. "Did you feed him egg mcmuffin?"

Sinking, Janie opens her mouth hoping an explanation will manifest.

Kate wags her finger. "He's up there puking it up. I warned you." Turning to her mother, who's already rising from her seat, "I told you we shouldn't have let her take him."

"But I wanna take him!" Janie protests.

Helene squeezes by to see to Ray. Blocking the doorway, Kate presses. "What's the plan for next week? Ice cream?"

"I won't feed him anything not on your list. Nothing."

"Forget it!" Kate dismisses her to check on their father.

Following, Janie pleads. "C'mon Kate, I'm really trying here."

"Bring a pocket calendar to write down your father's appointments," Helene decrees, stepping around them. Turning to Kate, "Go on and pick up the kids. I'll see to your father."

Waiting till she hears the screen bounce against the jamb, Helene looks narrowly at Janie. "Is there anything else?"

Janie shakes her head, and like that she's alone again. For a second anyway. A blaring horn calls from the driveway. *Shit, blocked her in.*

Letting yesterday go, a drive out to the lake is just the medicine. Spring fends off the sun, hanging on to her cool mornings. Janie's hands gratefully cradle her coffee. Not a soul in sight. This is the closest to the fields, to home, she's felt since turning onto the 40. By noon a baleful curiosity lures her to the diner for lunch.

Though there are a few new faces, all the original ladies are there, save for one. Some a little wiser for wear; otherwise, everything's the same. The once new vinyl booths have softened under years of the sun's unyielding attention, embracing impressions of their springs pressing through tired batting.

Janie garners little more than a passing glance. *My hair's darker than it used to be, that must be it.* Settling her check, she spots a framed photo of Mrs. Maple above the register. Decades younger than when Janie knew her. "She was something, beautiful."

The young hostess turns to admire the photo. "Wasn't she! You knew her?"

Looking down, Janie nods and takes her change.

A sneaky sunburn shows itself to the sun beating through the windshield. Handcart hooped over her arm, a bottle of aloe sits atop the heap of coffee, donettes and a box of matches.

"Excuse me, Miss, do you know where I might find Charley Brewster?"

Janie turns slowly, "Ya know, I think he ran off with this girl Natalia. Family's real shady."

"I knew that was you I saw at the market." Lucas hugs her and kisses her cheek. "I'm sorry about your dad. How's he doing?"

"Thanks. He's hangin' in there."

Seeing that she's almost up, he crams his unfinished shopping list in his shirt pocket and piles his stuff on the belt. "What're you doing after this?"

"Is that kinda like, you come here often?" Janie asks cheekily before holding up the aloe. "Drove out to the lake this morning."

"Yeah, you're a little red there." He nervously adjusts his hat. "You wanna grab a beer?"

Saddling up to the bar at Rusty's is surreal. "You remember how we used to ride our bikes past here?"

Nodding, Lucas laughs at the irony. "Now I guess we're the boozers hanging out in the middle of the day."

Savoring the first sip of an ice cold draft, Janie lets the cool burn settle. "God, we were judgmental little shits." Her feet dangling, they're still the youngest by a decade. Looking over at Lucas with his grin that she'd missed so, Janie's back at Luigi's sucking down sodas while waiting on their pizza. They're the imprints of their younger selves leaped forward into adulthood.

Tattering his napkin, Lucas takes the dive. "So, where ya been? I mean, where'd you go?"

Tipping her half empty pint, Janie takes a big swallow. "That tale would take longer than a beer to tell, but mostly Texas."

"I'd a thought you would've picked something more, uh..."

"Gay?" Janie finishes.

"I was gonna say coastal, but yeah less like Clayton I guess."

"Texas is nothing like Clayton. And for my line of work, there's no place like it."

Wadding up his napkin, Lucas is intrigued. "What line of work is that?"

Janie takes back the last of her pint. "I work on an oil rig as a roughneck, well derrickhand actually."

A chuckle escaping, Lucas stares down the bar in embarrassment. "Wow, that's a lot. You're out there with all the equipment and stuff?"

Sitting tall, Janie does her best not to take exception. "Well Lucas, I'm stronger than I look. Not as strong as most of the guys, but I get it done just the same."

Enthusiastically, Lucas agrees. "Heck yeah, of course. You like it?"

Beaming, Janie continues. "Love it. Especially being up top, feels like I can see the world."

"That sounds nice. You always liked a view," Lucas replies, staring into the depths of his second pint.

Keen to keep up, Janie motions for another. "And you?"

Lifting his Department of Fish and Game hat, he bashfully scratches his head. "Suppose you might've guessed. Honestly though, couldn't imagine doing anything else."

Giving him that I told you so look she dealt out wholesale when they were kids, Janie greets her heady pint with patience.

Sipping, Lucas works up his nerve. "You got a girl back in Texas?"

Not meeting his eyes, Janie shakes her head before a pity sip.

"But you still prefer the fairer sex I take it?" Lucas asks clumsily.

"Some are fairer than others, but yeah I'm still a homo,." Janie laughs. She points to his ring finger and asks, "Who's the lucky girl?"

Flashing a sly grin, "I think you know her."

Giddy with drink, Janie hugs him. "Isabel? Man, I knew you guys were forever. How long?"

"Almost six years, got married after college."

"You went to college together? That's so sweet."

"Hell yes, I wasn't gonna risk losing her to the world." Digging through his wallet, he pulls out a photo. "This is our little dude, Jacob. Speaking of which, I better get."

Trading numbers and a promise of dinner at their place, Janie stays on to finish her beer.

A blankness converges in the coming days. Rueful of time lost, she reminds herself of all she has in its place. Bitter and sweet, it's more than she would've had staying here.

A blanket of morning light swallows Janie's hand despite a weak attempt to block it. Staring down a spent bottle of Jack, her saliva's a tide pulling out to sea. A shot or two would've been enough to coax sleep. *Shit.*

Sweating out last night's whiskey and paranoid her father will pick up on the scent, she pops into the drug store for something to confuse the senses. Having never worn any, Janie racks her brain for what Reyna or Cicely wore. Getting close makes her want to weep, and maybe barf again too. That's probably the booze though. Grabbing a bottle of Curve, it's cheap and there's only a couple left. *So, it must be good!* Spraying herself generously in the parking lot, it wafts through the car like a marine layer. *Sniff, sniff. Yes, drunken flower. That'll do fine.*

Leaning over their father, Kate shoves a bag into Janie's arms. "Snacks. And he's already had breakfast." Giving him a hurried kiss on the forehead, Kate rushes to her car only to give Janie daggers in the rearview. Even the idle of her car cycles impatiently.

Sighing, Ray smacks his lips in a *tisk tisk* display of displeasure. "You sure you're alright to drive?"

"What?" Janie asks, "Why would you ask me that?"

Giving her side eye, his voice is tinged with disapproval. "Can smell the drink comin' off you, even with the air freshener."

"Air freshener?" Janie asks incredulously. "I had a little nip before bed to help me sleep."

"A nip huh?" Staring out the window, Ray replies coldly, "Used to smell the gin coming off my father every morning. Spent his whole God forsaken life buried in a bottle."

Not feeling particularly charitable of spirit, Janie lands a blow rather than continue assuaging. "Yeah, well I can smell the chemo comin' off you, but you don't see me making a fuss about it."

Ray's neck swivels, his jaw long. A slow grin creeps across his face. He shares a piece of the flourless cookie thing that Kate made.

The next few weeks ease into a routine. Tuned in, Janie senses whether it'll be a decent day or a lousy one. She comes to cherish the decent days, spending the whole of it seeking as much adventure as he can tolerate. While she hates to admit it, there's forgotten comfort in her mother's presence when she visits.

Kowtowing over her car running low on oil, Matty's on to Janie before the hood's popped. Still, it's nudge enough. Renting everything released in the last five years, they work through a stack of takeout menus. Matty still asks nothing of Janie's life, leaving her loathing herself for every crumb she drops in hopes he'll ask anything. *Hell, just ask if the barbecue in Texas is as good as they say like everyone else does.*

Riding the levity of the evening, Janie seizes an opportunity to tank it. "Matty, don't get upset, but did Mom and Dad ever look for me?" On the sharp end of a cutting look, Janie wonders if she hasn't blown it.

"When you didn't come home, Mom called Isabel's Mom. They finally got it out of them that they dropped you off by the bus station but didn't know where you went. We filed a missing person's report. Cops said since you were almost of age and clearly ran away, there wasn't much we could do but wait for you to get homesick. They basically did nothing."

"I went to New Mexico," Janie volunteers.

"Word spread, people talked. Some folks felt bad for Mom having a kid like you, but some blamed her. It was hard on her. You really hurt her, it was like you died. We mourned you."

"Matty, leaving was my only option," Janie pleads.

"If you say so," Matty replies. "You may think you were punishing her, but you punished all of us."

"Punish Mom? Are you fucking serious?" Janie barks. "Believe whatever suits you. I'm going to bed."

The panicked pitch of an infomercial shrieks from the living room, casting an engulfing glow into the bedroom. Half past one, Matty's sound asleep on the couch. Unwilling to risk her mother's ire, Janie sends him home.

Chapter Thirty Seven

No one ever notices the first day of summer in the valley. They complain come early May it's too damn hot for spring, and by July it's too damn humid. Except in the waiting room of the imaging center, where folks talk about anything and everything to avoid talking about why they're there. To avoid the pensive loners going it with no one to numb them with banal banter about the weather and how frickin' hot it is.

"First day of summer and we're sitting here waiting to get irradiated," Ray grumbles.

"I dunno, it's kinda cool you finished another round and now you're getting a scan on the summer solstice. Maybe it's a good omen," Janie suggests, trying to temper his sour mood.

"Don't tell me you're into that hippy dippy shit."

Janie stares at her father, waiting for confirmation he's looking to spar. "Ya know, you've kinda developed a potty mouth."

A hint of a smile looms, someone's finally had the guts to say it. "I figure if God's alright with me gettin' eaten up by cancer then he can look past a few sons a bitches. And if he can't, tough shit. He'll be seeing me soon enough, we can hash it out upstairs."

Janie laughs along but wants to cry hearing him speak of such things. His eyes aren't laughing either. *Saying it or not saying it won't change a goddamn thing, so let him say it.*

An early morning call brings news of an interview with the outfit in Galveston. If they like her, they'll spring for mud school in the fall. Janie promises to be back in time for the oncologist.

Counting as she walks, yes, Lucas lives a whopping five houses down from his parents. Isabel steps onto the porch, she went and became a womanly version of herself. Janie supposes she's done the same. Her embrace is so tight, it takes Janie's breath away. Lucas looks woolier than their last meeting. "I like the scruff," Janie remarks.

"I told him he should've waited till fall." Isabel laughs at Lucas massaging his jaw. Discreetly dabbing at her eyes, she hugs Janie again. "Ignore me, really. We worried about you so much." She looks to Lucas for agreement. "We paid for one of those white pages searches a few years back, it didn't come up with anything."

Jacob steals the show, he's a little Lucas. Goofing around, she misses Silas dearly. Over a bottle of wine, Janie's brought to speed on who married who, who left the church and who dove headfirst. "And what about you?" Janie asks. "Still among the saved?"

"We came back to Clayton after college but not to the church." Isabel explains with Lucas nodding along. "Good thing too. Got so ugly after Pastor Mike."

The very mention of his name makes Janie's breath catch in her throat. Flummoxed, she awaits an explanation.

"I thought your folks would've told you." Taking a hearty sip, "There was an accident at the Fathers in Faith retreat about five years back."

Her stomach in knots, Janie leans in. "What happened?"

"They were out over Easter break. It was the last day of the retreat. Pastor Mike and one of the other dads went for a dawn hike. I think it was Emily's husband, Sean. You remember Emily? She was the choir director when we were kids. Still is I think."

Janie nods, hanging on every word.

"They were trying to get to the summit by dawn, so I guess it was pretty dark out still. Somewhere near the top they hit a loose patch and tumbled. Pastor Mike went over, and Sean grabbed onto the brush. Somehow pulled himself up and hiked back for help."

"Couldn't have happened to a nicer guy. Asshole." Lucas takes down the last of his glass. "I'm switching to beer. Ladies?"

Isabel declines, Janie takes him up on the offer.

The remainder of the evening's a blur. All those years, imagining what she might say if their paths crossed. The guilt over those who ended up in his office after her, all of it was for naught. In the end his body's as rotten as his soul.

Thanking God for in-flight beverage service, Fernie's a sight for sore eyes. Everything about being home feels right. Even the heat kicking off the asphalt doesn't bother her. Janie only wishes Reyna were here to greet her, to embrace her and tell her what she should do next.

Last night gnaws at her. He's gone, has been for a long time. Where's the relief? Where's the forgiveness? Janie pushes it to the back of her mind as best she can. She's only home for a few days. *I'll be goddamned if he's going to take that from me too.*

The first Shiner goes down easy, complementing the basket of brisket bark she and Emmett devour. By evening's end, she's sated with good food and enough wisdom to convince the hiring manager she's worth the tuition.

Though the hiring manager cautions it could be a month before she hears back, Janie takes comfort in the lack of telltale signs he'll round-file her application the minute she leaves. The thought of applying with Reyna's outfit dances in her mind, drawing her away from the muss of here and now.

Spending the weekend with Fernie and Grace, Janie admires their life together. Hoping for something akin, she wonders if she hasn't missed her chance at as close as she'll ever get with Reyna. Embracing candor, she speaks freely of where she's from. Grace shares words of wisdom born of her own experience, the breadth of which still manages to surprise Janie after years of knowing her.

In some ways it's as though she's telling someone else's story until she gets to her father. The pain of that is too severe to be borrowed. Sparing them the details and herself the shame, Janie glosses over precisely why she left home. That bastard's death is all the proof she needs to understand closure's an empty promise pushing us forward till we're able to bear the burden of knowing some things will never be done. They can only be buried deep enough to occasionally forget they're there.

Janie flirts with the immense pull to stay, to avoid the pain to come. Fernie playfully toggles the locks until she promises to be home in time for his wedding. Curbside, Janie watches the path of least resistance disappear into a haze of heat waves.

Diverting to Phoenix, the pilot mumbles about summer storms, leaving all 116 souls to wait out the weather. Beyond the tarmac, Janie pictures Butch's life here. Wishing they could disembark for a stretch, her nerves tingle with anticipation at the thought. She could look Butch up. *Shit, does anyone even use phonebooks anymore?* She could get lost here if she wanted to. With a lurch and creak, they're moving again. Non-stop to what's next.

A moonless muggy night greets her flight, the last of the evening. Searching arrivals, she calls Matty to no avail. Her stomach churning on empty, it's a race against time. A familiar pair of Etnies with red lettered soles lay perched atop a backrest in the distance. Deeply engrossed in a game of *Snake*, he didn't notice her call coming in. A lone neon sign beckons from the darkened food court. Sipping a cup of stale coffee, Janie passes the time idly watching Matty chat up the cashier.

Tugging at her twice fried chicken tender, it's ravenously swept through ranch to ease the eating. "Looks like you made a friend."

Blushing, Matty looks over. "Yeah, had lunch here. Then came back a couple of hours ago for an apple pie. She gave me a free coffee."

Raising an eyebrow like a detective on the brink of tying it all together, she waits.

"Shut up, it's not like that. She just felt sorry for me."

"You are pretty pitiful. Sorta like an adorable puppy," Janie muses. "Hey, have you noticed Dad's kinda gotten a mouth on him?"

In between bites, "You mean the cussing?"

Nodding.

"Oh yeah," Matty laughs with a mouthful. "Kate thinks it's a sign of brain mets."

"And you?" Janie asks, watching intently over the brim of her cup.

"Me? I dunno, I think it's a natural reaction to finding out you're dying after spending the last thirty years holding your tongue."

"Amen to that."

A good night's sleep notwithstanding, Janie wakes dog tired and irrevocably absent of hope. Her chest tight, she wears a mask of optimism. Insistent they ride together, Kate multitasks between criticizing other drivers and questioning Janie's inability to assess whether her interview was a success.

Squeezing into the doctor's office, Janie worries he'll feel outnumbered. Kate counts on it. Impassive, his lean frame slips around the desk. Having met a multitude of her father's doctors, Janie's observed an invisible membrane between oncologists and everyone else, specifically their patients. She chalks it up to a means of survival for them and a nerve wrecking barrier for patients trying to get a read on whether making plans for the holidays is time well spent.

The CT scan shows no signs of progression, which is as close to hitting it out of the park as fate will allow. Still, the ache of something awful gnaws at Janie. A hue of what can only be described as elation washes over Kate. The feeling's contagious. In Kate allowing herself a glimmer of hope, she's allowed all of them to bask in it too.

Ray's doctor tempers exultation with a dose of reality, a bleak reminder that slowing progression is the height of their potential. There's no room for complacency. Vigilance is the only course with this marathon of a disease. A plan's set to resume chemo next week, the cycles will continue until they cease to be of benefit, or the side effects are no longer tolerable.

Janie pieces together this is the first true halt in progression since diagnosis. Making the most of their silver lining, Ray and Helene allow themselves the luxury of living. Driving out to the lake as they did when the kids were young, they now pile the grandkids in the car. Though he lacks the patience he once had, Ray attends church for no other reason than the happiness it brings Helene to walk through those doors arm in arm as they always have.

Kate finds herself free to prioritize motherhood. Her son and daughter soak her up like the valley during the first rains of early autumn. Watching them play in the backyard, Janie sees her sister anew, as her highest self in the company of her children. Bursting through the door, Kate and Janie exchange an easy laugh as the kids excitedly pull her along.

Chapter Thirty Eight

T he weekend brings blistering heat, an oppressive uneasiness steals away Janie's appetite. Desperate to crawl out from under the dread, she seeks reassurance and AC with her folks.

A familiar melody dances in the air beyond the kitchen window. Last time she heard "How Far is Heaven" was in an old bar in nowhere West Texas. True as a compass pointing north, it signals they're in a good place. Gingerly blotting her brow as the AC struggles to compete, Helene's always baked in times of bliss. Seasons be damned. "Your sister's at the park with the kids."

Failing to imagine a scenario where she'd come to the house looking for Kate, Janie smiles in acknowledgment. "Matty at work?"

"I should hope so," Helene replies singsong like. Sliding a delicious smelling Pyrex into the oven, she pauses to adjust cookies cooling on the rack.

Reclined in his lazy boy, Ray snores softly. Janie watches intently for signs of distress, Helene motions for her to sit. Looking to her mother for affirmation, Helene pats Janie's hand. "He's fine. We went for a long walk after breakfast, he needed a rest. I have something for you."

Don't get excited, it's probably another of Kate's lists. Or maybe not. Using a footstool, her mother retrieves a dog-eared stack of envelopes.

"I'm sure you can guess who these are from," Helene remarks.

Following, Janie hangs back at the threshold fixed on the stack.

"I'd prefer you read them elsewhere." Helene glances over, satisfied she's been heard. "I'll pack you some cookies."

Her heart rate swelling with an old melody all its own, Janie imagines stomping off with the door swinging behind her. She doesn't. She doesn't do or say anything. Instead, she stands with the parcel tucked under her arm, watching her father sleep.

Helene hands her a small sack of goddamned delicious smelling cookies. "Will we see you on Monday?"

"Of course," Janie replies, wounded.

Her name written in refined teenage loops, the petite stack casts an ominous shadow. Laying waste to neglected chores, Janie's dehydrated and fresh out of means to stall. *One more thing.* She returns a few generous swigs into her beer with a second for efficiency's sake.

Brittle from many summers tucked away, the rubber band snaps against Janie's knuckles. There are five letters, two of which have been opened. The distinct mustiness of the orphan mail bin lifts off with handling. Removing the letter from the first envelope, Janie hesitates. *Shit, here we go again.* The paper's crisp with a faint air of Lydia's hand lotion. Inspecting the envelope, the postmark can't be but a couple weeks after she left.

> *Dearest Janie,*
> *Sorry about the dearest thing, I've been reading a lot of Jane Austen lately. You read any of her stuff? Was starting to think I wouldn't hear from you, but I know how Moms can be. I hope this letter doesn't get you in trouble. I was thinking, can't you tell your Mom we're pen pals? I don't think god would have a problem with that.*
> *I think about the swings too. Couldn't wait for you to write again because I have good news. If Ethan goes to camp next summer, I'm tagging along when my Mom drops him off. We could see each other then. If not, I'll wait as long as it takes. When I read how Captain Wentworth wrote to Anne that she pierces his soul, I thought of you. That's how I feel missing you. Write back when you can.*
> *Yours always,*
> *Lydia*
> *P.S. I heard there's going to be a Fright Night 3D special edition. So excited!*

The second envelope bears a smudged postmark that upon closer inspection over the table lamp suggests sometime in February.

> *Dear Janie,*
> *I was hoping to hear from you. I guess holiday stuff can be crazy so it's all good. We go to my Aunt Barbara's every Christmas. She makes a casserole that my Mom says would gag a maggot. My Mom brings a ziploc bag in her purse and we dump it at the gas station on the way home. That sounds weird, but it s really gross.*
> *My Mom says tradition is important even when it's not any fun. I disagree. Who says we can't make new traditions? Do you have a weird aunt Barbara?*
> *I hope my letters are reaching you instead of being intercepted by inquiring minds. What do you say we come up with a code language? My brother Peter knows a little Klingon, I'll ask him to teach me.*
> *Anyway, write back! I taped a stamp on the back cause I'm a big spender.*
> *Yours always,*
> *Lydia*

Turning the letter, Janie runs her finger along the scalloped edges of an old stamp long since having become one with the parched paper. Envisioning her mother caught red-handed like ol' Madame Fosco warms Janie's heart. The third letter, postmarked in May, is shorter.

Dear Janie,
It's official, I got my license and my Mom's old Saab!
Are you getting these letters? I don't understand why you haven't answered, but you can tell me about it this summer.
I'm going to be a junior counselor at camp, they let my late application slide.
I convinced my Mom to let Ethan and me drive up with Peter. He goes to college in Chico.
Camp starts first week of July. You can call me at the camp or stop by the camp office and they'll come get me. I can't believe we're finally going to see each other!
Yours always,
Lydia

The fourth bearing crumpled corners, has a crease down the middle. It's postmarked from August in McCreary. *Damn, she must have sent it before she left.* The writing's cramped, if not a bit messy. Earning a break, Janie moves on to two fingers worth of Jack.

Hi Janie,
I was really hoping I'd hear from you this summer. Thought maybe I said something wrong, so I passed by the diner a couple of times, but you weren't there.
I went back today and saw your friend Monica. She said you're volunteering at your church this summer with your boyfriend. Is that true?
My Mom's picking us up and we're driving home. Not sure if you're allowed or whatever, but you can call me. We'll be home Monday.
Sincerely,
Lydia

Fuming, Janie squints to transcribe the marginally legible phone number. *My friend Monica. What the actual fuck, that treacherous bitch.* A well-nourished dram drowns her fury.

The whiskey tacitly persuading her to track down Monica's number, she reads the last letter instead. Postmarked the following July, the penmanship's grown up. Carefree loops have squared up, forming an invisible line between them.

> *Janie,*
> *This is my last letter. I'm leaving for college next month. Got into my first choice, looks like I'll be a duck.*
> *I was hurt when you cut off contact, but I'm not mad anymore. Just as Monsieur Paul thought Lucy was born under his star, I convinced myself you were born under mine. I realize now we were dumb kids caught up in a moment.*
> *I mostly blame Victorian literature for clouding my mind. Anyway, seems like you're not confused anymore. I'm glad you patched things up with your Mom.*
> *I wish you a good life friend.*
> *Lydia*

Friend, that's it? I may be a lousy pen pal but tell me please, who could rise to the heights of pierced souls and guiding stars? Surely not me. I need a girl who swoons when I remember to take my boots off and do the laundry. Dizzy from drink and the weight of emotional exhaustion, her stomach flips. Night falls and eventually dawn follows.

Sunday promises to be a bear. While the past wrestles the heat, Janie enjoys a few quiet minutes in the shade. Trading hellos with the mechanic, his peace is short-lived when his wife comes to fetch him.

Cornered by the shifting sun, Janie abandons her stoop. Determined to throw the letters away, she gets no farther than the kitchen counter. *Shit.*

I swear Mother, you couldn't have taken these to your grave? Thinking on it some, Janie chews on whether Lydia's silver-tongued phrasings are so different from her plainly written odes to destiny. Do they not speak of the same primrose path they set out upon years ago?

Kidless for the afternoon, Lucas and Isabel coax Janie from her misery with half-off pool and stale Chex Mix at Rusty's. Hungover and going through the motions, Janie mulls over what to do.

Tucked in a corner booth, a man with a brick of a laptop catches Janie's eye through the bottom of her pint. Limply slapping Lucas' arm, he recovers from a near scratch with a messy break. "Yes, Janie?"

"You have a computer, right?"

Handing off his cue to Isabel, he replies slowly. "Not with me."

"Do you think I could use it?" Digging through her bag, Janie retrieves the letters. "I want to look someone up."

Isabel lights up, "Is it her?"

Nodding. "My Mom had them all this time."

"What a bitch," Isabel mutters. "Sorry."

Inspecting her empty glass, Janie concedes. "No, it's true."

"Well, it's not like she could forward them to ya," Lucas adds, only to be ignored. "Welp, I'm gonna get another round."

Moving to a booth, she tells of mailing her last letter at the bus station. When Janie gets to the bit about Lydia working at Camp Mariposa, Isabel hits the brakes. "Wait, she came to McCreary?"

"Letter says she went to the diner."

"I wonder if I saw her?" Isabel contemplates. "What'd she look like?"

"Doubt it. Monica told her I went full fundie, with a boyfriend to boot." Janie pauses ruefully. "God, she must hate me."

Isabel scoots closer. "No honey, she wouldn't have kept writing if she did. Oh, you just wait till I see Monica. Go on, what else did she say?"

"Wrote one letter after that. Pretty much wished me well before college." Janie shrugs, more defeated with every word.

"I dunno, still think it's worth a try," Isabel counters, checking her watch. "Shoot. We gotta get home. You coming?"

While Lucas walks his mother out, Isabel pours some iced tea. Taking a long swig, Janie holds the glass up. "Just like the diner."

"It's Mrs. Maple's recipe," Isabel replies. "Man, she was a good cook. Taught me how to make a lemon icebox pie that's pretty much an unspoken demand with every invitation we get."

Logging on, Lucas is cautious. "You sure you wanna do this? I mean, there must be some reason you never wrote again."

"I was scared and carrying around a shit load of shame. Till yesterday, I thought Lydia had forgotten about me. That you all had forgotten about me." Taking a deep breath, just saying her name aloud brings her nearer. "I guess I need to know she's okay. Makes me ill thinking of the grief I caused."

A search yields no results, Janie fumbles through the letters. "Hold up. Here's her number, it's kinda smudged."

"I gotta tell you something." Lucas' finger twitches typing the numbers. "I saw her at the docks. She was with a bunch of campers and I wasn't for certain it was her."

Isabel presses him when Janie says nothing. "Lucas, you never told me about that. Did you speak to her?"

Shaking his head, Lucas can't look at either of them. "I was a teenage boy with lots of competing emotions, I didn't really pay it too much mind after the fact. Here, why don't you give it a go. I gotta check on Jacob."

Index finger typing her searches, a few old college projects come up. Discouraged, Janie tells Isabel, "I think this is a sign. Might be time to let it be."

"Don't give up," Isabel consoles. "You could always try the number."

"I dunno. I'm a shitty pen pal and somehow even worse on the phone. It's hopeless." Laughing, her eyes plead to let it go.

Conversation scarce, Blockbuster rentals take up the empty space. Scaring herself awake, Isabel's the first to call it a night.

Letting the car warm up, Janie watches Lucas linger how he used to when he was holding out for a goodnight kiss. Patting the passenger seat, she tosses her bag into the back.

Leaning against the headrest, he wears a pained smile. "I recognized her at the docks."

Nodding, Janie hides her disappointment. "I figured as much."

"I was so mad. Felt like I lost my best friend over her."

Slouching, Janie fidgets with the shifter. "Lucas, you never lost me."

Tearing up, he looks away. "That's just it. We did lose you. I've worried about where you ended up."

"I landed on my feet. It's been okay, really."

"You gave me your word we'd hear from you. It's been nine years Janie. Would you have come back were it not for your Dad?"

Guiltily, Janie replies lowly. "Probably not. Once I started running, I didn't know how to do anything else. Honestly, I don't have the energy for it anymore. I'm done."

"Good." With a knowing nod, Lucas opens the door. "Cause we're not letting you go again."

"Goodnight," Janie calls after him.

"Be good Janie," he replies without turning back.

Chapter Thirty Nine

The week is consumed by lab appointments, an oncologist touch base, and the first session of the new round. Worry fills the spaces in between. Janie fights to stay mad at her mother, as she always has. In the same way Helene's displeasure lays siege to all, so too does her equanimity.

Chemo pulls no punches leveling Ray. Reassured all's well, Janie again tamps down the dread poking away at her resolve. *Simmer down damnit. If Kate's not raising the alarm, there's nothing to fear.*

Resigned to his bed for the better part of a week, Ray reads scripture with Helene and lets her bend his ear with church stuff. Poor in time but rich in spirit, they're living for each good day. From the outside in, it can only be described as an acceptance of what will be, without trying to control whatever that is. Though they all know what it is, whether they speak of it or not.

Helene assuming a primary role in Ray's care ripples through the lives of her children. Guilt loosening its grip, Kate nurtures in her children the seeds of faith. When not working, Matty's generally wherever Janie is. While it's not what it once was, which it could never be, Janie comes to believe the expression of their bond is stronger than mere familial ties capable of strangling you with obligation and the fruitless pursuit of approval.

Lydia's letters languish on the counter, ensuring residency in Janie's mind. Exhausted from running the greenbelt, she's too tired to think of her father's labs or why she hasn't heard from Galveston.

Lusting after something to drink, her throat goes cold with icy Powerade. Waiting out the ache, Janie contemplates how to best combine as many calories as possible between two slices of bread.

"Got one for me?"

Slamming the fridge shut, Janie whirls around. "Shit Matty! I nearly pissed myself."

Stretching, he flattens his hair beneath his cap. "Sorry, fell asleep waiting on you."

Handing him a soda, Janie plops down. "Went for a run. How'd you get in?"

"You exercise?" He asks, bracing for a shove. "Your door handle's broken. I'll replace it for ya."

"Thanks." Pushing off the couch, "I'll make lunch?"

Pensively, Matty asks, "Are you gonna call her or what?"

Without reply, she sets sandwiches piled high with the Italian trinity of lunchmeats in front of them.

"Number's probably disconnected, only one way to know for sure." He slides her notepad across.

Chewing, Janie looks the paper over as though she hasn't already committed the number to memory. "Mmhmm."

"Want me to dial for you?" Grabbing her phone, Matty pretends to reach for the pad. "Hey, your battery's almost dead."

"Course it is. Don't know why I let Levi talk me into this piece of junk, doesn't hold a charge for shit. Let's get it over with." Dialing, waiting for the call to connect is eternal. "I think you're right. Wait, it's ringing."

"They tend to do that." Matty gives her a thumbs up for encouragement.

From frowning to freezing, Janie grimaces and emphatically nods. "I see. That's okay." Trying to make out what Matty's scribbling, she reads aloud. "Email?" It clicks. "Sorry. Yes. Does Lydia by chance have an email address? We're putting together an alumni list. Yeah it's nice to, um, keep in touch."

Summoning a pen, they stare at each other in silence once the call ends.

"You wanna go to the movies? I'll call Lucas, see if they wanna go too. Okay, sounds good, let's go."

Courting sleep with a nip, she leaves it at one for fear her father will smell it off her. Wearily eyeing her notepad, the email address burns a hole through the darkness. *You can do this. Just a quick note. Hi Lydia, I'm alive. Glad you are too. Have a happy life. See it through. See it all through, then go home.*

The house quiet, her mother sips coffee in the den listening to hymns playing on the console. Expunged of guilt in turning over the letters, whether Janie concurs is as irrelevant now as it was in her childhood when life resumed once that week's sanctions were lifted. Ray perks up upon hearing Janie, his exhausted smile more pained than gleeful.

"You look tired. You alright?" Janie asks, scooting his shoes closer to save him from reaching.

Refusing to be fussed over, he shoves his feet into his shoes. "Don't know how anyone gets a decent night's sleep with this heat." Pushing off his chair, he's determined to get moving.

Martin and June are conspicuously absent, Janie nor her father speak of it. Ray puts on a good show, exchanging barbs with regulars for the benefit of a few scared newbies. Each exchange grimmer than the last, though she cannot say why.

Unable to shake it, Janie passes time chatting with the son of one such newcomer. More frightened than his mother, he cups his hand over the thumbnail he's picked bloody. By the looks of it, he's got a rotation going. How do you comfort someone when you feel none yourself? You don't. How can you? You help them accept what is, so much as one can.

While her father's caught up in baseball talk, Janie invites her new friend for coffee. At his mother's urging, he reluctantly agrees. Popping the lid to cool his coffee, he sips cautiously. "You sure your pops won't miss you?"

"He's in his element, baseball, not the rest." *Shit, this kid's buzzing with anxiety. Be sympathetic, be like Grace, be kind.* "How about you? You were lookin' a little green up there."

Embarrassed, he flashes a shaky smile. "Turns my stomach when they flush the line. It's so hard to look at. How do you get yourself to keep coming back?"

Scalding her lip, Janie sets her cup down. "You just do. And when you find yourself thinking of excuses, pinch yourself as hard as you can. Then remember that no matter how much it hurts or how shitty the whole situation is, and it really is pretty fucking unfair, this is nothing compared to what they feel every minute of their day. It's natural to feel lousy about it, but you gotta put a cork in it when you're around her. Cry in your car or whatever, just don't make your pain her pain, cause she sure as shit has enough of her own."

Not quite the pep talk she was aiming for, he digests it without reply. *That was not very Grace like, let's try again with less reprimand.* "Believe it or not, this gets less scary after a few visits." Raising an eyebrow, she sips her coffee. "You'll see."

Sitting quietly at odds, they're endowed with views from different stations on the same awful trip. Breathing deeply, he puts the top on. "I should get back."

Stepping off the elevator, Janie holds the door, "You coming?"

"Thank you. I think I needed to hear that." Sniffling, "I'm gonna take a minute. Will you tell my Mom I went to the restroom?"

While her father consults with the pharmacist, Janie leaves a message for Lucas. Ray's quiet on the drive home. Janie lets him be rather than corner him into a benevolent lie. No sooner through the door, and he excuses himself. Some days end in vomit no matter what you do.

Helene calls to Ray that she'll be right up, adding one last bin to a myriad of boxes. Slowing, Janie debates whether she should offer to help. The little voice nudges her to keep going. *Don't say it. Don't.* "You need help? Want me to stay with Dad?"

Pausing, Helene's silence pointedly asks Janie how it's possible she's so vastly missed the point. "I'm going to stay with your father. You need to take these boxes to your sister. She's waiting."

Pissed at her mother and herself, Janie loads the car with a low grumble. *Told you. You give that woman an inch and she takes a mile. A goddamn country mile.*

Turning onto the old access road leading to the church, Janie bears witness to the transformation of the modest grounds she remembers. Empty lots have been bought up clear to the road. Once chain linked and littered, they're landscaped into lush knolls and paved in soft arcs leading to a wide crescent parking lot. A vibrant sign rotates images of happy families in their Sunday best, welcoming Janie to Christianity 2.0.

The divide clear, the original hall and humble chapel sit nestled on the back end of the remapped property. A scattering of old ranch trucks and sedans whose only sin is being out of fashion, flank the old church. The new wing greets you with a paneled glass façade reaching at least thirty feet. A handful of spendy looking imports line the front under the shade of exotic trees, the likes of which Janie's never seen in the valley.

Kate's whereabouts unknown, Janie's curiosity draws her to the monument of glass and concrete. As magnificent as the outside is, the inside's even more so. The center amphitheater reminds her of a place Fernie took her to in Dallas. Stacking the boxes, Janie awaits further instruction.

"Don't put them here. There, over in the storage room. Go get the rest." Grabbing boxes, Kate leads the way.

"That's all of it." Tempted to slip out, Janie stays in case she's to ferry anything back. "How'd they afford to build this thing?"

"This thing's paid for itself five times over. Look up there in the rafters. See all that?" She waits impatiently for Janie to nod. "We broadcast our services. Our congregation's all over the country now."

"Shit," Janie mutters.

"Nice. I don't know who's worse, you or dad," Kate replies, on the move again.

"Sorry. What about the old church?"

"Mostly used for functions and school events now. Hey, grab that box so we can take it down to the stage."

Wanting to go anywhere except the stage, Janie follows. Choir robes abound, Emily spots Janie from a distance.

"Don't be rude. You remember Emily, say hi," Kate scolds.

"No, no, it's okay. I was trying to remember your name. Janie, you look all grown up. So nice to see you."

"You too," Janie replies. With one last glance, she's had enough closure. "I gotta get going."

"You're leaving?" Kate calls after her. "You should come help more often, might do you some good you know."

The last piece falls into place. *This whole damn thing was a setup.* They presumed her desperation so acute she'd conform in any manner prescribed in exchange for acceptance. Who knows, maybe they would've been spot on before the letters.

Stopping, Janie returns with purpose. "Last time this place did anything for me, I had to run a thousand miles to wash myself clean of it."

Kate's face twists in disgust. "Go on, stay lost then. It was you who turned your back on God and your family. You're the architect of your sorrows Janie. And our parents' sorrows too, for that matter."

Onlookers slow, Janie will give them nothing to cluck about. "I'll be round to see Dad on Thursday."

The day's young and well suited for a burger with some day-drinking. After shooting the shit with a couple barflies, Janie walks home to the heat stifled little red shed. Killing the last beer, she cries her way through a cool shower before a much needed nap.

Laid out on the couch, her ringing cell keeps time with her throbbing head. With Kate banished to voicemail, Janie invites herself to Lucas and Isabel's for dinner, bringing a Luigi's pie as an offering.

Staring the cursor down, Janie prays for inspiration. Lucas offers prompts until Isabel leads him away. Ten minutes of blink blink blink, and all she can muster is the truth.

Dear Lydia,

First, I'm sorry about fibbing to your Mom. She's probably told you about a call from a strange woman with the alumni association. That was me. I confess.

The night I mailed my last letter, I boarded a bus for Albuquerque with my backpack and nothing even close to a plan. I never knew of your letters till a week ago when my Mom gave them to me. I'm back in Clayton because my father has terminal cancer. How's that for a lot?

I know we were just kids, and this is years too late. Maybe you don't remember me or maybe you hate me, I'd understand either way. I didn't ignore you on purpose, but I regret the pain it caused you all the same. I don't expect a response. If nothing else, hope this brings closure if you need it.

Always your friend,

Janie

P.S. That last part's a lie. I'd love to hear from you.

Doubling back, Janie puts her full name and address in the subject line. Had Ms. Post lived to see the age of email, she'd surely approve. Send. Putting yourself out there only to wait on a response which might never come is wholly unfulfilling. Were she in Lydia's shoes, Janie's not sure she'd answer. *Who are you fooling? Of course you would, you just did.*

Chapter Forty

Drained from chemo, Ray blames a cold he picked up somewhere. Hearing him refer to his doctor by her childhood pediatrician's name then bristle at being corrected, Janie suggests a break till he gets over this *cold* of his. No one shares her urgency. Passing time with Matty takes her mind off waiting. Waiting for an email. Waiting on Galveston. Worst of all, waiting for the origin of the malaise rooting itself amongst her nerves to show itself.

A week in, Ray's cold is neither better nor worse. Janie and Matty conspire to lure him out to eat, he accuses the heat of absconding with his appetite. Spurned by Janie's refusal to sign on as a pity project, Helene and Kate return to a state of indifference.

When a hacking cough joins the ensemble of symptoms, treatment is halted pending tests. A diagnosis of pneumonia brings hospitalization orders. Helene refuses, insisting the inevitability of this day was the entire point of turning her living room into a hospital suite. As a compromise, a home care nurse to visit twice per day.

With no desire to sit home, lunch at the docks with Lucas is just the salve. She once read or maybe Butch told her, who knows, the best way to rid yourself of thoughts you want no part of is to let them pass right on through. Miles of trying behind her, she's left with a chorus of rumination. *Whoever came up with that crap must've had a mind like a goddamn sieve.*

Loathsome of such a selfish notion taking root in her mind, Janie wonders how long they might go on this way. Her well sure to run dry come September, she'll eventually have to do the right thing. Go home or give Emmett the go ahead to fill her place. Suppose it's a good thing Galveston hasn't come calling.

Drawing out one timorous hour at a time, mornings are spent at her father's bedside awaiting the nurse at noon. Light with hope of convincing Matty to play hooky, Janie stops in to grab her swimsuit. Fighting the doorknob for her key, someone's coming up the drive. Lankier than Janie recollects, everything else is unmistakably Lydia. "I can't believe it's you. You're here," Janie remarks, her hand mindlessly tugging at the key.

Folding something and stuffing it in her back pocket, Lydia explains, "Got your email."

"I gather," Janie replies, yanking her key loose. "Can I buy you lunch?"

The drive to the café is a syncopated rhythm of stolen glances and small talk, they're unwittingly swept up in volant familiarity despite knowing little of what the other's life has become. Life stats are traded in turn. Lydia's a teacher in Woodland Hills, somewhere down around LA Janie supposes. High school of all things. She likes it alright.

Lunch becomes a walk around town leading to Sunderland Park. The old metal playset has been swapped for a brightly colored plastic contraption and the merry-go-round is now a fiberglass pirate ship with its bow to the enormous old oak tree scarred with initials predating the park itself. *What kind of asshole puts the bow in front of a tree when there's open field in every other direction?*

Her mind working to align all she remembers with all she sees, Lydia loses her place in the story of Mom and Janet from the alumni committee. Roosting atop the cobalt slide, she wrestles with what to say. "It's such a paradox. You look different but the same, all at once."

"I could say the same of you. Except instead of slowly growing to resemble your Yaya, you've gone and scaled up since I last saw you."

"Late growth spurt," Lydia laughs. Cued by the shifting light, she checks her watch, rotating the band to better ignore the afternoon passing.

"Now who's the clock-watcher. You need to get going?" Janie asks genially, leaping from the doomed brigantine.

"Checked my nephew in at camp this morning, supposed to be on the road to Tahoe. Sort of a tradition amongst a few of us from college. Teaching, I have summers off, so I drop Hani at camp on my way."

"Right. C'mon then, let's get you on the road while it's still light out."

Time remains the callous arbiter of their fate. A galvanic uneasiness stirs spying Janie's car in the distance. Slowing to a stroll, Lydia's content to push off goodbye. "Tell me about Texas. I'm kinda impressed. Do you really get out there with the guys?" Stature aside, it's not so hard to imagine Janie with a physical job. Even relaxed, the tone of her arms trailing upward betrays hard earned strength. Her skin a sun-kissed golden hue from day after day of doing whatever it is that she does out in the oil fields.

Doing her best Rosie the Riveter, "I do."

A tinge of concern rides the edge of Lydia's voice. "That must be challenging. I mean, I played coed beach volleyball for a few seasons and it was tough keeping up, to put it mildly."

Nodding, Janie prepares her usual hard work triumphs all speech but loses steam. "It has its moments. Shit, I can't throw chain half as well as some of the guys. Most of 'em can wrestle the tongs better than me too. But ya know what? I'm reliable and get it done with fewer errors than a lot of 'em."

"Yeah, that makes sense." More confused than before, Lydia takes it on faith.

Unlocking the car, Janie hesitates, venturing to rest her arms on the sunbaked roof. "Sorry. It's just, I get asked that question a lot but you're the first person who really seemed like you wanted to know."

"I did, I mean I do want to know," Lydia adds, rolling down her window for relief.

"I'm lucky to be on a crew that values those sorts of things, safety over strutting." Janie trails off, plunging a cassette into the deck. "You still into Siouxsie and the Banshees?"

Settling into her seat, "Absolutely."

Neither broach the prickly topics of family or relationships, no sense in spoiling a beautiful summer afternoon by picking at old scars. Walking Janie to her door, Lydia goes no further than the first step. "Let's keep in touch. I'll email you."

Friends beats nothing at all, now smile like you mean it. "For sure. It was good to see you."

Sharing a cordial embrace, the scent of honeysuckle clings to Lydia's caramel locks like an aura. It dawns on Janie that being friends may in fact be the death of her.

Splashing water on her face does little to cool the heat or quiet the pounding in her chest. *That's it? You're going to be email pen pals now? Really?* Seeking a cold one to soothe her brooding, Janie cranks the radio. A knock pierces her solace. "Damnit Matty. I'm gonna get you a key already."

Lydia leans in and kisses her. Almost forgetting to breathe, Janie mumbles "Matty's my brother."

"I remember," Lydia replies in kind. "I'll be back in two weeks. Can I see you again?"

Casually bracing herself against the jamb, "Mmhmm."

Stealing another peck, she hands Janie a sunflower sticky note. "Here's my cell. Two weeks. Don't lose it!"

Gone are Lydia's stone washed shorts and hyper-colored tees, but standing there, Janie feels fourteen again just the same. Matty's not far behind, letting himself in to save her a trip to the door.

Hell bent on keeping Lydia to herself, Janie prattles on about going to the lake even though it's kind of late already. "What is that face?" *Oh fuck it.* "You'll never guess who showed today."

Scratching his nose, he picks up the sticky note. "I might have one guess."

"Whatever, let me tell you what happened." Sticking the sunflower to the fridge, Janie grabs a soda.

Even as a small child, Matty was never satisfied with how his bedtime stories ended. There had to be more. The loose ends had to be tied up. If she were to hazard a guess, it's why he never got into comics.

"Is she gonna move to Texas with you?"

"What? No, of course not," Janie exclaims, laughing at the ridiculous notion. "We're adults. We've got lives, careers and shit. It's not like you can drop everything cause someone makes your heart beat faster and slower at the same time. Right? Move to Texas? Please, I mean we hardly know each other, Matty." Janie argues, her voice higher as she goes. *Jeezus, breathe Janie, breathe.*

"You're my sister so it's kinda my duty to tell you the truth, and the truth is you're chickenshit."

Put off by his language, she retreats to the couch. "Matty it'll never work. Besides, you bring up airport girl all the frickin' time. I don't see you doing anything about that."

"Her name's Myra and I bring her up because I want you to ask about her. Been seeing a lot of each other." Flopping down, "You're really thick sometimes."

"Yeah, well you're kind of snappy sometimes." Jettisoning the remote. "She met Mom and Dad?"

"Mom and Dad know diddly." His neck flushing, "Told Mom I've been crashing here when I work late."

Janie foresees calamity. "Lying to that woman is dangerous territory. Careful."

"I guess I could always run off and join the circus if she gives me a hard time." Matty remarks flippantly.

Forcing a smirk, Janie's eyes betray the sting.

"That was crappy, I didn't mean it." Regretfully, Matty squeezes her into a firm side hug.

Thanks to the helping hand of antibiotics, Ray's cleared to resume treatment. Snagging any chance to feel the sun on her face, Janie helps garden under his direction. Who knew there was an order of operations for weeding?

Doesn't matter much. Wherever she is, whatever she's doing, her thoughts veer to Lydia. Each day crawls out towards eternity, much the way it did summers ago when the future felt less like an endless round of whack a mole. Matty's of no help, having been devoured by the gravitational pull of young love. A perpetual third wheel, Janie keeps close company with Lucas and Isabel. Anything to keep from calling.

When the weekend hits, her resolve is renewed. *Time to give them a break, be a big girl and exercise some willpower.* When Lucas calls with an invite to the movies, of course she's free.

Fantastically gory, it's improved only by Isabel's squirming. For a couple of hours, all's forgotten. Mercifully passing on a nightcap, she leaves them at the theater. While adorable, their cooing amplifies her loneliness.

Humming the score, Janie's voice goes quiet when she catches sight of Lydia reading on her steps. Stopping short of her stoop, "You're early."

"Is that bad?" Lydia asks, getting to her feet.

Unlocking the door, Janie resists every muscle's impulse to leap. "No, early's good. Whatcha reading?"

"*Persuasion*, haven't read it since, well it's been a long time. Probably not your speed, huh?" Lydia watches her approach.

"Depends, are you sour or sweet Wentworth?" Janie asks.

"You've read it?" Lydia asks, delighted.

"I had some time on my hands. Besides, your letters inspired a reading list." Moving closer, Janie takes Lydia's book and kisses her. "Still prefer comics, but Jane's alright for a Victorian."

"She actually wrote in the Regency period, which was a little before the... nevermind. Doesn't matter." Easing back, Lydia stares at her steadily. "Did you mean what you wrote about us just being kids?"

"No," Janie answers softly. "I've imagined this, here with you, more times than I can count."

Her hands around Janie's waist, Lydia pulls her close. Whispering as she leans in to kiss her, "You have no idea."

Taking her hand, Janie leads Lydia to her room. Her touch an elixir, each kiss is a beacon calling Janie home. Tangled up in one another, they make love.

Twisting tendrils of Lydia's hair in her fingers, Janie admires all that the light of day reveals. Amber flecks in Lydia's hazel eyes are set alight by the morning sun. She could stare into them for the rest of her days without bending to whim's sway. "What made you come back?"

"My friends basically shoved me out the door. I kept checking my phone, you were all I could think about." Entwining her fingers in Janie's, delicate kisses give way to a passionate morning.

Waking famished, they put off getting out of bed until the wall has the sun's full attention. Lydia slips into her clothes. Basking in the afterglow,

Janie much prefers this to whiskey for the business of chasing away meddlesome thoughts.

Lydia calls from the kitchen, "You don't have any food in your fridge. Don't cook much?"

I have food. Janie mumbles, pulling on shorts and a tee. Wrapping her arms around Lydia, she kisses her neck. "I'll go pick something up. Whatcha thinkin'?"

Blissfully, "Let's go out. I can be ready in like ten, maybe fifteen minutes."

An ancient fear rises, choking her. Mantling her reticence in affability, they both know it for what it is. Pulling her hair into a messy ponytail, she slides into her sandals. "There's a place just down the road. Take your time, I'll be back before you know it."

Sadness creeps into Lydia's eyes. "Sure, if you want."

Kissing her cheek, Janie avoids what she cannot quell. Ignoring her phone in favor of sustaining this reverie, Janie wishes this could stretch out into forever.

Her father growing stronger eases Janie's conscience at stealing away every minute she can. Much like her parents, they live each day without paying heed to the transience of their situation. Though Lydia's a hit with Lucas and Isabel, Matty proves her biggest fan, inviting himself and Myra along to most everything. Convinced it's best not to roil the waters for the sake of her father's health, this will be the extent of the introductions.

A call from Galveston comes late in the week, she's a go for mud school in October and onsite training thereafter. Wanting to hold on to this for a while longer, Janie keeps it to herself.

In the quiet moments, they work their way around to loves won and lost. Lydia speaks of rebuking the flakey LA dating scene while indulging in occasional blind dates at the behest of well-intentioned friends. Raising the ante to goad Janie into something resembling vulnerability, she confesses to trying out the closet during college. Two boys too many considering nothing could come of it. How could it when she already knew the sublime ardor of falling head over feet.

"I always thought your folks were alright with it," Janie prods.

"They were, knew about you and everything." Lydia's eyes search Janie without resolve. "Think I wanted that college experience like everyone else. It's hard enough getting to know people without having to wonder if they'd be disgusted by you. Reverse experimentation I suppose."

"What were they like, the guys?" Janie asks, practiced at the art of side-stepping through quibbling.

"Really? You want to know about boys I dated in college?" Mildly rankled, "I sense evasion."

"Hogwash!" Kissing her, Janie reclines onto her lap. "I wanna know you, warts and all as they say."

"One was a drunken freshman year mistake, and the other ended up a good friend. He and his partner live in Denver." Sighing, fear of disapproval edges into her periphery. "Typical college scene stuff, a tale too boring to tell. Out with it!"

"No guys for me, unless you count leading on poor Lucas in high school," Janie muses.

"That's all you got? I give you drunken rendezvous and you give me Lucas?" Stifling what she wants to say, Lydia dresses up long buried rancor as sass. "I swear, you're like a closed book I spend all my time trying to pry open."

"Not much to tell. I'd say I'm a flare that burns bright for straight chicks and the emotionally unavailable." Smiling, Janie gives her a peck on the cheek. "Present company excepted."

Edging closer, "I don't know about that. You're hardly lacking in experience so far as I can tell."

Tracing her fingers along Lydia's jawline, Janie can think of nothing but kissing her. "I had a complicated friendship with someone I took for granted. Went and messed that up for someone who didn't end up sticking around. How's that?"

"Bad breakup?" Lydia asks sympathetically.

"I had some feelings about it. I'm not entirely sure she preferred women so much as she liked me a whole lot and tried to work with that. Sort of like you and Denver, I reckon." Janie instigates a wrestling match rather than a feud.

Days morph into weeks as the end of camp closes in. Another round of chemo nears its end with a scan on the horizon. Heeding Dr. Keil's advice of managing expectations, Helene and Kate analyze what in the world that's supposed to mean. Loss looms, Janie accepts the bittersweet nature of her time with Lydia and her father. One date more malleable than the other.

Reflecting upon her summer with Lydia in contrast to past relationships spurs a shift in perspective. Janie's desire for Lydia, the idea of it anyway, was the yardstick against which all others were measured. Manifest, it's more gratifying than ever imagined. In denying what she had with Reyna the credence owed, Janie preserved the story she'd clung to all these years. Only now did she realize that Reyna had seen her, as Lydia sees her, with a frightening clarity that sent her running, whereas Cicely was a confluence of excitement and conquest masquerading as romantic love. While Janie missed the illusion of their little family, she hardly missed intimacy with someone who was also barricaded behind their own story.

Her stash of secrets piling into a heap, Janie forbids her mind to conjure an image of life here once Lydia's gone. For family day, Lydia tasks her with assembling a care package. Dedicated to inspiring a love of comics, she lines the box with standards guaranteed to hook the uninitiated.

Strolling through town, they AC hop from shop to shop. Raiding cassettes at the back of the Salvation Army, Janie snubs the CDs much to Lydia's amusement. Rounding the home goods aisle, they're face to face with Monica and her mother. Janie's grasp tightening, the cassette cases creak their surrender. An urge to pummel Monica with an ugly gravy boat a mere arm's reach away grows to a taunt within.

Letting her hand go slack, Lydia won't be the harbinger of more conflict than Janie already has headed her way. *Play it off, she gave you an out. Don't make this the hill.* Too tired to run, Janie weaves her fingers through Lydia's. Leaning into her, Janie grins. "Hey there Mrs. Whitley, Monica.

Sure is nice seeing you two." Staring them down, she lets them squirm. "Where are my manners? This is my girlfriend, Lydia. Monica, I think you met at the diner some years back?"

Paler than her JC Penney pearls, Mrs. Whitley dawns a weak smile. "Yes, well, please tell your mother I was asking about her."

In Lydia's eyes, there's nothing quite as fetching as small braveries. Dragging Janie to the register, she can hardly keep her hands to herself till they get to the car.

Acting the fool, they swim under the afternoon sun. Laying out on the old dock, the toasty planks ward off breeze driven goosebumps. Close enough to feel Lydia's body heat, Janie wonders how anything will ever be enough again once summer calls their time together done. Dancing around the inevitable reaches the height of impossible. Night falling, they race the horizon collecting wood from abandoned fire rings. Sipping Glenfiddich fireside, the weight's more than Janie can bear. "You heading home when camp's done?"

Nestled in her blanket, Lydia nods. "I have a planning conference next week and Hani needs to get ready for school. I was thinking I'd come back for a long weekend before school starts."

Irresolute of what she was expecting to hear, this wasn't it. Janie falls quiet. Shifting the wood around, she throws on another log.

Holding her blanket like a cape, Lydia envelops Janie to preserve their elysian day a while longer. Not in the mood to talk, Janie traces the delicate tourmaline necklace resting upon Lydia's collarbone. "I don't wanna think about you leaving."

Kissing Janie's forehead, Lydia speaks emphatically. A thought gone over a hundred times, breathed into being. "So don't. Drive down with me for the conference. Your Dad's doing better, isn't he on break next week?"

Sighing, Janie holds her tight. "Wish I could, can't take a chance on things taking a turn. Just a feeling, I dunno. I'm sorry."

"No, don't be. Honor your gut. It's not that far, we'll manage," Lydia consoles.

"For now." Janie rests her head, sleepy with drink. Watching Lydia stare out into nothing, the glint from moments ago gets lost in the motion of her thoughts. Sipping, Janie settles into her nook and waits for the warmth. "They ever teach you about stars when you went to camp?"

"We learned the constellations but hell if I can remember them now. Besides, don't think we're going to see them with the smoke coming off that damp log you threw on the fire." Lydia nudges her, laughing at Janie trying to ignore the smoke.

Uttering a faint denial from beneath the blanket, Janie kicks the offending piece from its seat atop the pile. As the fire dulls to a glow, the stars make themselves seen.

"Wait, I know that one. It's Cygnus. See there?" Lydia points. "I recall our counselor saying If you see the Milky Way then you'll see it too."

"For the stars of heaven and their constellations will not give their light, the sun will be dark at its rising, and the moon will not shed its light." Laughing charily, Janie keeps her eyes to the heavens. "Isaiah, I think. Funny what you remember."

"That it is. Paints a scene though, I'll give them that," Lydia remarks, turning her gaze upward.

"Moonless nights scared the bejeezus out of me when I was a kid." Janie pulls at her coat cuffs. "Gettin' cold."

Wrapping them tighter, Lydia shakes her head. "I don't think I'd have an ounce of faith left in me if I'd been through what you...well, I'm not sure I do anyway."

"I don't have a lick of faith in the pulpit. I dunno though, sometimes I think God's in those gray spaces between what we know and what we think we know. Sitting there all quiet like, prodding us to try harder at being our higher selves. Always hoping, often disappointed. Then other times, I think we're about as interesting to him as an ant farm a month in." Fidgety, Janie tosses another piece on the fire. "Either way, I like thinking when it's all said and done, maybe there's something more waiting for us."

"You sound like my Mom." Lydia sips, resting her head against Janie. "Devout atheists, she and my Dad. Then she was in a wreck that she had no business walking away from, but she did. She took it as proof of the divine, my Dad likes to tease it's only proof of a head injury."

"For some folks that'd be the definition of irreconcilable differences. She's alright though?"

"It was a couple of years ago, she's good. They're both good. Suppose you could say sarcasm's their love language. My Dad has golf, and she has spirituality."

Dabbing at his nose with a crumpled tissue, Ray looks to be in the throes of a full-blown flu. Listening to him wheeze, Janie can hold her tongue no longer. "What d'ya say we drop in on Dr. Keil today? I'm not sure they'll think you're well enough for treatment anyhow."

Coughing into his tissue, it falls from his hand. Grabbing at it, he reluctantly swaps with Janie for a fresh one. "My labs were fine, I'm fine. Honey, this is all part of it. I'm going to eventually get sicker."

Each time he speaks of what's to come, an anvil of ache presses the breath out of her. *Shit, he must be down twenty pounds. Push harder.*

"Now don't look at me like that. Don't make this more than it is," Ray cautions, weakly finding his feet when they're called.

Helene nor Kate make mention of Mrs. Whitley. They needn't bother, the taciturn cold front they've forged is proof enough. Defeated, Janie dives into her last few days with Lydia. Bending layers of dough and butter to her will, Lydia drops the dumplings into a fragrant blueberry concoction bubbling on the stove. Lid in place, they leave them to their business, settling in for a lazy afternoon. The easy closeness, the way her skin smells of sunblock and perfume after a day in the sun, these are the things she'll miss when Lydia goes back to her life. "You ready for the new school year?"

"Yeah, definitely," Lydia replies blandly.

Stroking her hair, Janie pulls back a strand to better see her. "Sure about that? You get along with the other teachers?"

"It's not that. I guess teaching isn't what I thought going in. Idealism wanes when the rubber meets the road. It's not that I thought I'd be all Michelle Pfeiffer or anything, but I truly believed I'd make a difference."

Rubbing her shoulders, Janie reasons, "I bet there are plenty of kids who'd beg to differ. You're being too hard on yourself."

Sitting up, Lydia shakes her head. "So much has changed. High school's a nightmare. Back in the day, the worst our teachers could expect was the stoners getting baked in shop. Not these little shits. They're crushing their parents' pills in the bathroom. Fourteen-year-old kids. Fourteen. On top of that, it's an endless parade of tests to validate the school's existence but somehow in all of it, we don't teach the kids a thing. I mean, I basically just teach them to memorize stuff."

"Yeah, Matty's said as much about here."

"On top of that, they vetoed three of the books on my reading list. My folks rave about their students. Sometimes I wonder how what I deal with every day turns into a bibliophile by college." Lydia massages her temples. "Sorry, it's not that bad."

"Not everyone goes to college, kind of apples and oranges I'm thinking."

"What about you? Counting down till you're back in the field?"

Tell her about Galveston, go on. "I am, I love it. No one seems to believe me, but I do."

"I believe you, but it's a dangerous way to earn a living," Lydia persists.

"You were an English lit major, so you probably read *Far from the Madding Crowd*, right? Well, Bethesda proved them all wrong and I'm fixing to do the same," Janie counters, glad one of Darrell's books has earned its keep in her memory.

Charmed, Lydia's unmoved in her greater desire to have her message heard. "Point taken, but she mostly gave orders sidesaddle. You can't do this kind of work forever, I mean physically."

"No one wants to, but you gotta do your time. I'm not aimin' to break my back year in, year out, all to come home smelling of drilling fluids. Technology's gonna level the playing field, and I'm gonna be there looking down from the platform when it does."

Gripping Janie's forearms, Lydia squeezes. "I don't know, think you've been away too long. Feeling a little soft."

"Yeah?" Janie grips Lydia's arms, pinning her. "Challenge accepted. You're going down."

Sunday arrives, indifferent to their refusal to greet it. While Lydia picks up Hani, Janie looks in on her dad. He's still in his pajamas, a fierce cough carries clear through to the door. "Should we call his doctor?" Janie asks, baffled at her mother and sister sitting idle.

"It's under control, he's on his way." Helene stares through Janie. "Go on home to your guest."

"You two are unreal." Blood roused to boiling, Janie hugs her father. "Call me if anything changes."

Picking at her lunch, Janie rallies to be a good host to Lydia and Hani. Hiding behind her sunglasses, "Call me when you get home."

"I will." Lydia kisses her goodbye, holding on until she feels the tension in her shoulders give way. "I'll be back next weekend."

Chapter Forty One

All's quiet at the Harris household Monday morning. Deafeningly quiet. Ray's bed unmade, his sheets are a cast aside jumble. A cup of coffee sits untouched on the end table. Janie takes out her phone to call Matty. *Shit.*

Talking herself down, nothing settles the frantic discord racing her mind down the highway. Stomach in knots waiting on an ancient pair double-parked in the drop-off lane, her better nature prevails when they look over blissfully unaware of their impedance to traffic.

Searching the floor for her bag, she looks up in time to spot Matty crossing an aisle over. Hollering, she runs across the lot.

"Where were you? I've been calling all morning." Shaken up, relief at her arrival outpaces his panic.

Janie holds up her phone as evidence of its culpability. "Goddamn battery keeps dying."

"Room 5838. Kate and Mom are up there. I'm going to get Myra."

Kate barrels towards the entrance with sights set on Janie. Veering to the edge, Janie hopes to contain the scene. "Before you start, my phone died."

"It's always something with you, isn't it?" She seethes. "There's always some reason you're not quite responsible, isn't there?"

Her hair's flat and her eyes are red from crying. *Christ, how long have they been here?. Be like Grace.* Janie tries to temper her response till she sees the loathing in her sister's gaze. "Responsible? What responsibility am I avoiding Kate?"

"Lower your voice," Kate whisper shouts, shielding her profile from passersby.

"Fuck what they think. What responsibility?" Janie presses, intent on dragging it out of her.

"Your responsibility to being here. You drop in from nowhere to ease your conscience and then when Dad's gone, you're going to just disappear while I'm still stuck here." She shouts at Janie, no longer capable of being concerned about what people think. "You selfish bitch!"

Janie folds her arms. "Please. You love this whole dutiful daughter bit. You could leave but you won't cause you love being miserable. Admit it, you're right where you wanna be."

Shrieking before she catches herself, Kate steps closer. Janie fears for a split second that Kate's going to haul off and slap her. "Is that what you think?" Kate's voice cracking, she sinks into a nearby chair. "You know, if you ever care about anyone enough to stick around, you'll see. One day you'll look up and realize years have passed. And you won't recognize yourself anymore, or even remember what it feels like to be happy. You'll be empty, and no one will care. No one."

"Kate, I care," Janie replies, softer now, sitting next to her.

Wiping away tears, Kate rebuffs her attempt at mending this. "Dad's going to die Janie. When he does, Mom's going to suck me into her vacuum of church and whatever else today's bee in the bonnet is. And you're going back to your little life with all your friends who probably abandoned their families too."

"You know Kate, you don't know shit about my life." Unable to cultivate another drop of angst, "No one's forcing you to stay."

Hand to her temple, Kate's rage rises again. "Yeah, and where would I go? I'm divorced, haven't used my degree in years. My kids barely know me cause every moment's been about Dad. I'm not like you. I can't just run off when I don't like how things are going."

With nothing left to say, Janie stares ahead listening to her sister fight to stifle a cry that she reckons has been coming for some time. "I'm going to see Dad."

Standing at his bedside, Janie rubs her father's hand. Ray manages a little smile. When glaring does nothing, Helene *tisks* to get her attention. Shushing her mother, Janie sits beside him, paying no mind to her mother skulking out of the room. "They fed you anything yet?" Janie asks, her eyes following the length of wires tethering him to the various apparatus surrounding his bed.

"Not too hungry kiddo," he replies pleadingly, and she knows there's nothing left to argue.

Swallowing hard, Janie holds on. "You let me know. McDonalds, whatever you want. Okay?"

Ray nods, his eyes fighting to stay open. He pats her hand before drifting off.

Janie and Matty take turns with their mother and sister throughout the day. Chatting with Myra where she can, Janie appreciates her being there. Thirst and hunger getting the better of them, they make a break for the vending machines. Seeing Dr. Keil head into their dad's room, they hurry to catch up.

With Ray's white cell count leveling out, Dr. Keil's guardedly optimistic. Answering questions, he introduces his colleague taking over for the night, and like that he's gone.

Helene sleeps on a foldout in the room while everyone else camps in the waiting room. Kate leaves to see the kids off to bed, calling Matty every twenty minutes while she's gone. The sickening ache from months ago cuts through Janie's back curled up on the squat bench.

Tuesday morning washes away their optimism when treatment efforts plateau. The first signs of his end have begun showing themselves. Pastors and elders stream in and out, armed with blessings and promises of the glory of the kingdom to come for brother Ray.

Though unable to respond, Janie has no doubt that the father she's come to know would roll his eyes if he could. Matty and Myra are tasked with sneaking Clyde into the hospital by whatever means necessary. Within an hour they're wheeling in a snorting rucksack, refusing to pay notice to concerned stares in the elevator.

Kate gasps when Clyde pops his head out. "What're you doing?"

"Dad loves him. It's only for a few minutes," Janie declares, dead serious and daring her to argue.

With Matty's help, they hoist Clyde onto the bed. Whining, he licks Ray's hand and nuzzles under his palm for scritches. Ray's heart rate rises and settles.

Gliding in, the night nurse stops midway into putting her gloves on. "I didn't see this. They're coming up at 7:30 to start removing the support. I'll be back then. I trust that I won't see our visitor." Smiling sympathetically, she leaves.

Somewhere around ten, Janie sneaks into the room, careful not to wake her mother. Only thing more unnerving than the incessant cadence of beeps and alarms, is their absence. The great surrender. An admission of our fragility in the face of an unwinnable battle.

Holding his hand, Janie watches over him. Speaking softly, wondering if he hears any of it. The muscles in his palm flutter, surely a sign. Opening his eyes halfway, he looks through her. Massaging his hand, she carries on. *He's in there.* Looking intently into his eyes, she waits for him to tell her to knock it off. He doesn't. Breathing deeply, she rests her head at his side.

Minutes or perhaps an hour passes when Matty comes to trade places. In times such as these, minutes and hours are a mere suggestion but carry little meaning. There amongst her sister, Myra and a smattering of close family friends, Janie's alone. Her thoughts drift to her father's eyes. Closing her own, she sees them. She'll be haunted by the grief of those eyes and him there in that bed. The summation of a disease that's picked away at him little by little.

Don't make your pain their pain. Seeking respite in the restroom, Janie washes up. *Why is it so fucking quiet in this place?* Leaning on the sink, she again looks to the mirror. Closer this time. It takes little imagination to see how her own hands will one day lack the strength or acuity to grasp anything. The way her stalwart legs will slowly atrophy, trembling in protest as they bear her weight until they no longer dare. And when the color leaves her eyes as her soul steps one foot into the other side, a steely blankness will assume its place. Even now, she can see how small a shift in the iris it would take for her eyes to be her father's.

"I'm glad Matty brought you around. It's important." Resting her head in her hands, Janie chats with Myra. "I should've brought Lydia around. He should've known her."

Putting her arm around Janie, Myra stiffens at Matty's approach. "Janie, you should probably go."

Janie beats the dawn by an hour or so. Numbness gives way to a pressure in her head and chest so immense, it makes her sick to her stomach. Sitting in her car, she watches the sunrise. The tears come too, in great heaping sobs. A breathless agony void of thought or memory.

Just past nine, Kate calls. Janie races to her charger, catching it on the last ring.

Speaking barely above a whisper, "We're going to have the service on Friday."

Janie wishes for the words to tell her it will be okay, but nothing comes. It's all jammed up. "Can I help with anything?"

A few hours pass before she's composed enough to call Lydia, only to fall to pieces at the sound of her voice. At Janie's behest, she'll leave Thursday afternoon as planned.

Keeping close tabs with Matty, Janie shows up uninvited, prepared to help or be turned away. There's little to be done except wait, his final affairs were seen to months ago.

Chapter Forty Two

Operating in a state of grief deferred, a murky now holds its place. Everywhere Janie goes, people are carrying on with their lives and she's trudging through mud trying to remember if she ate this morning. A sinkhole overtakes the center of her parent's living room where the pushed aside hospital bed once sat. The home care staff charged with collecting the equipment, wear the same woeful faces as the staff at the hospital in those final hours.

Only when Lydia arrives late in the evening does the grief seep through the cracks. Janie chews through a few bites of pasta to please Lydia before crying herself to sleep in her arms. Two days' worth of fatigue chases away any possibility of dreams or terrors.

From a great distance, the alarm sounds. Reaching over, she runs her hand along Lydia's side for reassurance that she's actually there. "We need to get ready. You wanna shower first?"

"We?" Lydia creaks, sleepily sitting up.

Already gathering her towel, Janie's resolute. "I want you with me."

As compassionately as she can, knowing Janie as she does, Lydia watches her flit about before responding. "You sure you're going to feel that way tomorrow?"

Sitting next to her, Janie brushes the hair out of Lydia's face. "I'm done humoring them."

Unprepared, Lydia wears the navy pencil skirt and black cardigan set from yesterday. Nerves failing her hands, it takes three tries to get her eyeliner right. Her eyes may be red from remover, but her liner's even damnit.

The service is impeccably organized and sadder for the patent divide between Janie and the other mourners. A silent accusation of trespass is implicit in each greeting. Janie stays close to Lydia's side, insisting she stand with the family as Myra stands with Matty.

Old friends and distant family members tell tales of Ray as they knew him, tales of mischief and mirth. A clement morning under blue skies and cottony clouds shelters them at the graveside. All things considered, Janie supposes he would've heartily approved of such a sendoff.

Pastor Ignacio steps to the front with the assistance of a youth pastor. Slower now, he thumbs through the pages of a text older than him. While his voice no longer carries as it once did, it's as kind as it ever was. "I knew Brother Ray since he and Helene first joined our congregation. There were only two of us then, Pastor Malcom and me. One of my greatest pleasures was chatting with Brother Ray after services. I knew he caught every word of the sermon because he always had something to say about it. I looked forward to folks like him the most. They didn't just listen to me preaching the word of God. They heard it."

Adjusting his glasses, he searches for his place on the page. "But time has made an old man of me, so I'll leave the preaching to the young men. In parting, there's a verse from Timothy that comes to mind when I think of your father." Looking to Kate, Matty and Janie, "Timothy 4:7 says, I have fought the good fight, I have finished the race, I have kept the faith. Henceforth there is laid up for me the crown of righteousness, which the Lord, the righteous judge, will award to me on that Day, and not only to me but also to all who have loved his appearing. Our brother Ray fought hard, but his labors are done now. Let us rejoice in knowing he's with the Lord. Amen."

A younger pastor with a tailored suit and capped teeth delivers the sermon and closing remarks. Janie listens unmoved, certain her father would have walked out rather than listen to another word. Kate slips away early to carve out a few moments for herself. Guests mill about the grounds, leaving a respectful gap before caravanning over.

"What a fraud!" Janie declares, blustering about the pastor's showmanship. "Should have left it with Pastor Ignacio, Dad liked him."

Holding Janie's hand in hers, Lydia worries she may come undone. "Maybe I should drop you off at your folks. I can pick you up later."

"No way! I need you there with me. Matty and Myra were the only ones who spoke to us." Toggling between anger and hurt, "They didn't even ask me to speak."

"Kate and Matty spoke beautifully." Kissing Janie's hand, "Your father loved you. He knew how you felt."

"I know he loved me." Fidgeting with the hem of her dress, Janie turns her attention to the window. "But he didn't know me. It is what it is, and it's done now."

Matty's sent to set up chairs in the backyard for any overflow. Myra does her best to disappear into the background, Lydia joins her. Janie and Helene go round and round with Janie picking up a tray of something or another only to have Helene lift it from her with the disclaimer, "You really needn't bother."

With her eye on a tray of drinks too heavy for her mother, Janie's intercepted by Kate. "Mom wants to speak with you."

"Gimme a minute." Janie approaches Lydia and Myra discreetly, "Go ahead and go. I'll call you."

Myra swallows hard, and Lydia utters a barely audible, "Oh God."

"It's fine," Janie mutters. "Myra, now's a good time to go help Matty." Glancing over her shoulder, Kate's staring them down.

Lydia squeezes Janie's hand. "I'm gonna go out the back door. C'mon Myra."

Walking past Kate into the den, Janie shrugs, her patience eroded.

Dabbing the corners of her eyes with a wilted tissue, Helene's livid. "How dare you bring that person into our home?"

Making no effort to constrain her voice, Janie studies them before replying. "Her name's Lydia and banning her won't change the nature of our relationship."

Kate tries fruitlessly to shush her.

Throwing her hands up in disbelief, Helene looks at Janie like a stranger. "Haven't you shamed your father enough?"

"Shamed him or you?" Janie backs closer to the kitchen, intent on bringing it all to the surface. She sweeps her arm across the room. "He's not here. This isn't for him."

All movement in the kitchen grinds to a halt, guests look to anywhere but the den.

Janie labors to rein in her rancor. "If there's a heaven, which I hope there is for the record, he's there. Not stuck here in hell with a pair of shitty lungs taking on fluid faster than the doctors can bail it out. Say what you want, but don't you for one minute think you're going to put this on him."

Stepping closer, Helene's beyond appearances. "You're as vile now as you ever were."

Guests trickle into the yard seeking refuge and refreshments.

Years upon years of rage pour out of Janie, trailing down her cheeks and onto her collar. "I forgave you the past. Misguided as it was, I wanted to believe you did the best you could. But this right now, I will never forgive. One day, that's all I wanted."

Wagging her finger, Kate admonishes Janie's flagrant deviance. She takes a step back as Janie abruptly turns her attention to her. "Ya know Kate, you might still be married if you'd shut up once in a while."

Helene gasps and Kate bursts into tears, running upstairs. Mortified, Helene motions for Janie to follow. "Look we're all upset. Let's talk about this in the den."

Having none of it, Janie couldn't stop now if she wanted to. "It's too late! You've always put what people at church thought ahead of everything."

"That's not true. Stop this now."

Eerily calm, Janie's voice settles. "It is. If you'd been paying attention, you'd have seen the true face of who you were handing your daughter off to every week." Guilt mars Helene's usually flawless glare, which only fuels Janie's fury. "I'm leaving Monday. If you can't find a way to accept me, all of me, not just the bits you can tolerate, then this will be the last time we see each other."

Drawing a deep breath, Helene flattens her dress and again finds the resolve to carry on. "Do what you want. You always have."

Adrenaline spent, a surge of emotion overtakes Janie. Sobbing, she covers her mouth and hurries through the back door. Guests flee inside at her approach. Making her way to Matty, he hugs her and tells her he's sorry.

Kneeling, she hugs Clyde. Forlorn, he rests against Matty's leg. Laughing through tears, Janie blots at her eyes with Matty's handkerchief. "I'm gonna go, think I've worn out my welcome."

"Where's Lydia?" Searching his pockets, "You wanna take my car?"

"She's on her way to my place. I'm gonna start walking and call her." More serious now, Janie puts her bag over her shoulder. "I'm leaving Monday. Come by, I wanna see you guys before I go."

Running her hand along her father's car, Janie sees her mother standing at the kitchen window. Helene stares through her before turning away.

Once she clears the block, Janie follows the greenbelt. Satisfied she's put enough distance between them, she pulls out her phone. *Fuck!* Pitching it into the field, she stomps another few yards before retrieving it.

Brambles shred her nylons, feeling around blindly a thorny branch catches her arm. Wrestling the brick back into her bag, she rolls her ankle on the way up. Crying on the side of the road, she walks with her nylons bunched in one hand and heels in the other.

Sweaty and significantly calmer by the time she gets home, Janie goes straight to the fridge. Closing the front door, Lydia hurries over. "I've been calling."

Taking down half a beer in one swig, Janie surfaces to draw a breath. "Battery's dead."

Lifting Janie's arm for a closer look, Lydia takes in the scene. "That bad?"

Nodding, Janie finishes off the bottle. "Goddamn it's hot out there."

Drawing a bath, Lydia helps Janie undress and joins her. Resting against her chest, Janie tells Lydia of seeing her mother as she left. Caressing Janie's hair, she searches for the wisdom to set it right. "Give it some time."

Taking great offense, Janie sits up, turning to face her. "I can't believe you're defending her." Stepping out of the bath, she grabs her towel, leaving a trail of water in her wake.

Closing her eyes, Lydia lies back for a last moment of solitude. Mopping the floor with a hand towel, Lydia's led to the kitchen. Wrapped in her towel, Janie's cozied up to a bottle of jack and a repurposed jam jar.

Twisting her hair up in a towel, Lydia looks at the bottle then back to Janie. "You left half the tub on your floor."

Hurting, Janie sets her glass down. "Sorry." Backing Lydia against the counter, Janie kisses her. Closing her eyes, she lets the thought of losing herself in Lydia dull her misery.

Easing back, Lydia rests her head against Janie's. "You want to talk about today?"

"No," Janie replies, running her hands beneath Lydia's shorts to the apex of her thighs until she stops her.

Holding Janie close, Lydia tries to reach her. "You really want to do this now?"

Pulling away, a scowl fills her expression. "Not anymore." Taking another glass from the cabinet, Janie pours a round.

Lydia waves the glass away, to which Janie pours it into her own.

"If you're going to honor your father with a drink, at least pour some of the good stuff."

Holding up the bottle, she smirks. "This has nothin' to do with him. See, Jack here's like picking up a stray at the bar. It's not about the taste, it's about getting to the point." Her eyes watering, Janie throws back the shot.

Lydia grabs the bottle. "You're an asshole and you've had enough."

"I'm an asshole? What, cause I don't wanna talk, I'm an asshole?" Janie beelines to her room.

Lydia calls after her. "No, you're an asshole cause you responded to getting turned down by comparing getting laid to whiskey." When she doesn't answer, Lydia takes a beat to quiet her own rising ire.

Whiskey gaining on her, Janie clumsily makes the bed and grows frustrated with a stubborn corner. "Talk, talk, talk. Everyone wants to talk when they feel like it, but no one wants to talk when I want to. You all suck."

Leaning against the wall, Lydia's exasperation settles into exhaustion. "What do you want to talk about?"

Paying no mind to the heat, she crawls beneath the blankets of her freshly made bed. Lying beside her, Lydia wraps her arms around Janie. Sleeping off the afternoon, the sounds of neighbor kids playing in the street under the reprieve of nightfall wakes Janie. Her head splitting, she reaches for the aspirin on the nightstand. Hopeful Lydia's still here, the sounds of cookware moving about sets her at ease.

"Your plate's on the coffee table." Without turning around, "You should eat something."

Food is far from Janie's mind, but she makes an effort. Eating in silence, she chews her last bite with vigilance. "I am an asshole. But if you knew how many times I turned the other cheek with that woman, you'd understand."

"You get a pass. This time." Swaying into her, Lydia sighs. "I wasn't defending her. You lost your dad, and at some point, you're going to go home to the life you've built for yourself. Your Mom just lost her husband. He is the life she built for herself, and she buried him today. Maybe someday she'll choose to hold on to the rest of the life she's built, and she'll regret letting you fall away. But if she doesn't, the loss is hers."

Though dubious, Janie concedes. "Time will tell I suppose."

Flattening the peak of Janie's furrowed brow, Lydia smiles. "That's better." Growing serious, she says aloud what she's thought more times than she cares to recall. "I love you, always have."

Wishing it weren't on the heels of a fight, Janie kisses her. "I love you too. From the minute you stole my *Fright Night*, I knew you were a keeper."

"Stole it, ha!" Pulling Janie into her arms, Lydia tells the tale as she remembers it.

Doggedly intent on one more good day with Lydia, Janie lures her from bed with coffee. "I'll make breakfast."

"Stick to the coffee, I'll make breakfast," Lydia replies in an end of discussion sort of way. "Do you have any lemons? Could make benedicts."

"Let's make giant omelets," Janie suggests, searching the fridge for fillings.

"Omelets it is. Woke up hungry, huh?"

"May as well eat it all so I don't have to throw it out," Janie replies flippantly, catching her slip of the tongue too late. "Shit. I was planning to tell you. I'm going home Monday."

Cracking an egg, Lydia studies her. "When were you planning to tell me?"

"After the funeral." Janie's words are punctuated by the sound of eggs cracking. "You knew I was gonna have to go eventually."

"It's not the when," Lydia replies curtly. "You and your secrets, one big clandestine mess." Tossing the shells, she dresses Janie down with her eyes. Turning away, she whisks vigorously.

"There's nothing here for me anymore." Moving closer, Janie waits for Lydia to look up. "I should've told you sooner. That's a lot of eggs."

Pausing, Lydia sets the bowl aside. "You could come back with me. We could leave here together."

Taking plates down, an ache in the pit of Janie's stomach sets in. She knows the next part by heart, so may as well get on with it. "And what, throw my whole career away?"

"You don't have to. Port Hueneme's a stone's throw from me, there's all kinds of oil stuff there. There has to be something."

"Thing of it is, the rigs I work on are not the same as wherever that is you said. I'm starting a new job in Galveston that I busted my ass to get. I can't walk away from that."

"Right." Lydia's vexed laugh trails off, gripping the whisk she returns to her labor. "I wouldn't want you to walk away from something you love. How insensitive of me."

"That's not what I meant." Choosing her words carefully, "I need a couple more years, there'll be opportunity to move around after that."

Rapping the whisk against the bowl's edge, she tosses it into the sink. "A couple of years," Lydia repeats, pouring the mixture into a hissing pan.

Janie edges Lydia's coffee towards her. "You could always move to Texas. There's lots of schools."

Sliding the pan from the heat, it grinds against the grates. "Do you know how hard it was to get hired in my district? Or how much red tape I'd have to go through to start over in a new state?" More cross as she goes, Lydia drops the spatula in the pan. "I was on a waitlist and temping for a year before I got an interview."

"You don't even like your job," Janie protests, wishing she'd given the thought a whirl before letting it roll off her tongue.

Clutching her coffee, "I never said that. I've spent my whole adult life getting to this point."

"Doesn't mean you can't change your mind. You said you're happiest when you're baking. Why not give that a go?"

"Janie, I don't hate my job. I was just bitching," Lydia reasons. Tucking her hair behind her ear, she's running out of mettle. "Haven't you ever vented about your job?"

Janie backs off, acutely aware things are going off the rails. "We could visit each other. You could spend the summers with me till one of us can make the move."

Adamantly shaking her head, Lydia sets her cup in the sink. "No, I can't do that. I'm selfish, impatient and tired."

"In the grand scheme of things, what's a year or two?" Janie reaches for her, Lydia stays the distance.

"A couple of years? I waited years for you already. I won't do it again."

"This is different," Janie argues.

"Just because you feel differently about it, doesn't make it different." Moving the pan to the sink, Lydia grips the ledge. Willing herself to swallow long-sown resentment, it demands to be unfettered. "You have no idea how humiliating it was driving up here and getting treated like the fucking devil incarnate at that diner. You could have written me from Albuquerque. I would have gone anywhere with you."

"It was stupid, I don't know why I didn't. Deep down I thought it was gonna blow over. They'd come looking for me and I'd come home, but they never did. I dunno Lydia, I don't fucking know. I was scared of being sent away. Then some time passed, and it felt like it was too late, so I let it alone." Janie leans into her line of sight but thinks better of it. "We wouldn't be who we are if you'd come with me. I couldn't be responsible for taking you from your family."

"I guess we're at an impasse then." Drawing a deep breath, Lydia wipes an errant tear. "I should get ready." Folding her clothes, Lydia gives up and shoves them into her bag when Janie sits down beside her. "I think it's better we go our separate ways. Who knows, maybe somewhere down the road things might be different."

Taking her hand, Janie tries to persuade her. "You're really leaving like this?"

Kissing Janie's hand, Lydia slips hers free. "I'm not set up for Monday. What's the point of wallowing together? You've got a lot of packing to do."

Wanting to scream, Janie instead pulls her hair back and leaves the room. Lydia briskly packs her car, returning to say goodbye. When she leaves, all the air in the room goes with her.

Knocking the lid off the trash bin, Janie drags it through the kitchen. Clearing the counter, dishes and all go tumbling in. Shaking the contents of her bag onto the counter, she snatches her phone and adds it to the heap. Grabbing the bottle of Jack, she settles onto the couch. Staring at it, Janie huffs to the kitchen and wedges it into the bin. *Goddamnit!*

By Monday morning the business of goodbye is attended to. The key to the little red shed's left under the mat and her nearest and dearest have standing invitations.

Chapter Forty Three

A pristine copy of *Forever Now* is the first of the Salvation Army cassette haul thrust into rotation on the drive down the 99. "Love My Way" serenades Janie away from second thoughts of that which would be best forgotten. Her mind wanders to memories of happier times. A vision of Butch shimmying across her room as he sang along brings a mightily needed grin.

Janie holes up at a small Greek diner in Bakersfield, wishing she were hungrier. Laid out next to her meal is a small truck stop atlas. Tapping her finger on Flagstaff, her desire for an empathetic ear usurps her fear of finding that Butch has fallen off the map without anyone to right him.

The phone ringing, Janie practices asking for Butch. *Shit, I bet they hate that name.* There's a long silence. Wanting to believe she got the number wrong, she knows better.

Dropping down to the 40, Janie spends the night in a Mohave town full of truckers and tract homes. A nip or three gets her underway to a dreamless night. Rolling into town early, she kills time dodging Route 66 tourists downtown.

Nestled in the hills beyond the interstate noise and bustle of campus life, the community of Windhaven is a study in course timber and bountiful evergreens at every turn. Driving through the neighborhood, Janie imagines Butch growing up here. The adventures he and his brother must have had as kids. Deceivingly large cedar-shake houses sit back on expansive lots, camouflaged among the mature tree line. All the better for looking out than in.

While her body knows it's pushing 90 degrees, her senses swear the first snowfall could come at any time. Constrained wild gardens adorn a winding sidewalk leading to the house. Nothing like some casual birding from your rustic deck, all with the convenience of popping down the hill to Sam's Club if you run low on seed.

Standing before an immense door, Janie thinks of Butch walking through this entryway after so long adrift. Until now she could compartmentalize the devastating news delivered by a faceless voice over the phone. Her grief was her own, and theirs belonged to only them. When this door draws open, she'll have to face the end of a story that should have gone on much longer. *Damnit Butch. Why didn't you send up a flare? Something, anything but this shit.*

"You must be Janie. I'm Russell, Henry's father." Shaking her hand, "Please come in."

Henry. Maybe Hank, but never Henry. "Thank you." Stepping down into the living room, Janie sees his mom. Must be, they're a mirror image of one another. "My condolences. You have a beautiful home."

"You're very kind. I'm Rosalyn, Henry's mother." She rises long enough to shake Janie's hand, there's a frailty about her. Studying Janie, she makes small talk about traffic and construction down the hill. All the while searching for answers to questions decorum forbids her to ask. Perhaps he and Janie were lovers, or she was complicit in his addiction. Rooting about for a hint of guilt to serve as proof it was something from those missing years that played havoc with him, anything for it to be something beyond their reach, their help, their fault. "You'll have to excuse me. I don't feel quite myself today."

Watching her disappear down the hall, Russell smiles apologetically. "She has a hard time talking about Henry. It's remarkable, you're just as he described. He spoke about you and Reyna often. I think he was happiest during that time with you two."

Tell 'em something nice that Butch said about them, go on. Shit. Nothing feels a worthy response. "He was a good friend, the best."

Patting a slumbering yellow lab, "This is Buttercup. Henry's dog originally. She was upstairs barking when Rosalyn came home. He left a note on the banister to wait for dad, but she went up anyway. She and Henry were always so close...sensitive souls have a hard time in this world." Adjusting his glasses, he clears his throat. "He was already gone. Near as we can tell, the bar in his closet gave way. Being as tall as he was, he chose the rafters in the attic." His voice cracking, he swipes his knuckle under the rim of his glasses. "Never gets easier."

"I don't imagine it does, I'm so sorry." Believing Butch had overdosed, the truth leaves her yearning for numbness. A bankers' box peeks out next to the sofa. *Is that it? Give him time.*

"Can you tell me anything about his life in New Mexico?" Russell asks, seeking reassurance his son was the man whom he knew he could be.

Janie shares sanitized tales of their adventures, his love of reading and guidance in her studies. "I don't know where I'd be if it weren't for him. We looked out for each other, but mostly he looked out for me."

"He was always that way, tenderhearted." Setting the box next to her, he lifts the lid. "He stuffed the shirts in a sack, burst the seam. We moved them to the box." Pulling out a padded envelope with Reyna's name in Butch's handwriting, "Do you still see Reyna?"

"She moved for work, but I'll see she gets this." Fixing the lid, Janie overflows with loss. "Would you mind if I went to see Butch, I mean Henry, to pay my respects."

"That's alright, he's Butch to you. He's at Evergreen, I'll write down the address."

Driving around until she finds a craft store, Janie buys a few ghoulish trinkets because Halloween's always in season in the craft world. Pulling up to the curb in Butch's section, Janie stares out across the expanse. Wondering if some young fool with idle time will someday hop the fence and find their way to Butch, she misses those nights. She misses him. Pushing the lid askew, the top tee is his Oingo Boingo tour shirt. Breathing it in, the smell of his aftershave and cologne clings to the fabric, hugging her in the only way he can.

Damn, would you look at that, he got his view. Sitting graveside, the sod's greener and softer than the adjacent turf. Tracing her fingers along the letters of his name, the edges are yet to be dulled by the sedulous breeze whose touch is so pale that it can only be felt by a measure of years.

The pumpkin pinwheel and stocky raven sink into the soil. Wiping her hands on her pants, Janie sniffles but sees no point in fighting back the tears. They never listen anyhow. "Well Henry, I hope you're not expecting me to sit here chatting with you all night. I'm not sure either of us are convinced anyone's listening anyway."

Plucking a few blades of grass, she guiltily collects them. Sighing, she returns the clippings to the earth with a gust of breath across her palm. "Just in case you're somewhere in the ether creepin' on your own grave, cause I know you're vain like that, you should know I'm gonna miss you. Your folks miss the hell outta ya." Adjusting the pinwheel, she sets it spinning with a light blow. "I apologize for not embellishing with additional décor, but it's early September. You were always the one with the magic touch for this shit. Anyway, I should get. I think you'd like this spot Butch, it's a good one."

Dusting herself off, Janie takes one last look before leaving him behind.

Chapter Forty Four

D riving into the night, Janie reaches her limit a few hours from home. Pulling off at a truck stop in Tucumcari, New Mexico for a sneaky nap, she awakens to the sounds of metal skidding across the lot and wind screaming in the darkness. The power's out in all directions. Soon the rain comes in great dense sheets, given shape by random flashes of lightning. Scantly able to make out the parking lights of big rigs huddled across from her, their cargo groans as it's battered by the storm. Hunkered low in the backseat, Janie prays it doesn't get worse. Dawn quells the tempest, drawing out folks from hiding. Janie witnesses the aftermath heading to the highway. Radio towers bent like tin, shopkeepers corral broken glass and downed trees resting where they fell.

Arriving home mid-morning, Janie's greeted by a freckled back, wide as the panhandle, sprawled across her bed. Astoundingly, the house looks as though she just stepped out.

Knocking on Levi's door, "I'm home. Taking a shower."

Resting against the cool tile, lukewarm water runs interference between her and the rest of the world. Dulling the ache of her tired body, her only want is to sleep.

"I'm not looking, I swear," Levi announces, poking his head through the door. "I'll get Caleb outta yer room. Hell, I'll even wash yer sheets for ya."

Too weary to move or open her eyes, Janie cuts him off. "Lettem stay, he's alright. We'll talk when I get out. You did good Levi."

"Shoot, thank you. Ok, well enjoy your shower. By the way, you shoulda seen the derecho that rolled through last night all the way down from the

Dakotas. Thought it was gonna blow the damn roof off." He rambles, closing the door when she gives no reply.

While she may be home, this place doesn't feel like her home anymore. Signing over the lease, she'll take the couch till she leaves for mud school. Besotted, every other thought is of Lydia. A want to call her. A need to tell her about Butch. To ask her to reconsider, to come lift her from these doldrums. Knowing she'll buckle at the sound of Lydia's voice, the thought of her touch, Janie refuses to beguile herself into thinking otherwise. Not If splitting the difference means starting over, even with Lydia, the cost is too unwieldy. While that might make her a hypocrite, she reckons she's been called worse.

Taking only what she can cram in her car, Janie gives her computer to Levi. Who in turn, trades with Caleb for a hand-blown bong. A neutral gesture since they'll continue to use each of them at will. After a thinning of her material life, all that remains is Butch's box. Aside from sleeping in his *Good for Your Soul* shirt, she hasn't ventured deeper. He was a curator of cool, a fact not lost on him. She never imagined that their running gag of listing things she wanted willed to her was being stowed away. Wrapped in his faded Stussy tee is a bulging cassette, a folded note falls free upon opening the case.

Dear Janie,

You're as nosy as I hoped. Sorry I never called, had to give that clean slate a shot. Turns out some hungers never leave you, and no amount of rehab will change that.

Been listening to a lot of early 70s stuff, think of the tape as an anthology. Of all the odes to dragons, Neil Young probably had the niftiest way of saying we'll go by our own hand eventually. I've been doing a lot of thinking, and I think he's right. I'm afraid I'll end up like Alban. Can't say how much will be too much, but I can say when. Please don't carry this around, you carried me long enough.

In closing, I leave you and Reyna all my worldly treasures. The ring and watch are hers. She saw them first. You get the unwashed shirt for your sniffing pleasure. One last pearl no one ever told me, secrets are a betrayal so cross your t's and say what you need to while anyone still cares to hear it. All in all, I'm ready to move on to that other groove.

Butch

As it turns out, staying away from girls is easier than expected when you're persona non grata in the one gay bar in town. Who would've thought that what's her name from over a year ago would end up dating one of the bartenders?

Crashing with Fernie and Grace, she and Fernie booze it up while Grace hands out Halloween candy. A perfect intermission from training, which so far is more about unlearning what Janie's spent years learning.

There are procedures for everything with a larger firm. Shit, they'd have you believe that without them you'll never make it through your first hitch with a full set of fingers. Way back when she was a scared little worm, Emmett told her rule number one of rig wisdom is never put your fingers where you wouldn't put your junk. A five-hundred-page manual encapsulated in a single crude idiom. She'll hold tight to her rootsy philosophy until the first time she sets foot on a large commercial rig. Her instructor will liken it to a small city full of moving people and parts, whose successes and safety depend upon one another knowing what they're doing. Standing before it, Janie will think his assertion an understatement.

Hungover and driving out to Andrews, Janie isn't keen for chit chat. Levi sheepishly hands over a package that came about two weeks back. It's from Lydia. Giving it a shake, it's solid. Tearing through the tape with her keys, there's a new cell phone with a note. Taking a cursory sniff more out of habit, it smells of new plastic and cardboard.

> *I programmed my number and highlighted the charging instructions. For what it's worth, I love teaching but I'm not sure if being a teacher is for me. It's not easy admitting you miscalculated the trajectory of your life, let alone where to go from here. I don't want to end things this way, please call me.*

Waiting till she has the house to herself, Janie admires the fancy Nokia. It's like the ones the instructors use at school. Staring at her lone contact, excuses flow in league with her fear. *Too much time has passed, she's probably pissed. I'll call after training. What's a couple more weeks?*

Her reasoning falls flat when Fernie and Grace's looks of relief turn to confusion. Even the chatty turned taciturn voice within tears at her shoddy excuses. Still, she won't budge.

Drying dishes while Janie puts away leftovers, Fernie admires her phone. "Man, I shoulda waited for the new model, this is way sleeker."

Popping the tops off their bottles, Janie sighs. "Yeah, it gets the job done."

"Does it?" Fernie asks. "A girl straight up sends you a phone to call her and you still don't. You're either over her or scared. Someone at the bar got you swooning?"

"I'm not either of those things, and no one goes to the bar to swoon. No one." He'll get side eye from here on out. "It's just not a good time is all."

"You're not over her, got it. When's a good time? When it's too late? So you can say you tried. You're lying to yourself my friend." Fernie follows Janie to the deck, bolstered by a sly wink from Grace.

Shit, what happened to the Fernie who let things go. On the defensive, "How am I lying?"

Pulling his shorts to knee height, Fernie juts out his leg. "You see this scar? Best thing that ever happened to me. You know why?"

"Because chicks dig scars?" Janie asks flippantly.

Sighing, Fernie laughs despite himself. "If it weren't for that scar, I woulda never met Grace. I thank God every day for that pallet falling."

Tuning him out, Janie turns her gaze to the setting sun.

"So, you're gonna ignore me?" Leaning on the railing, he'll settle for her profile. "You're like my little sister so I'm going to give you some brotherly advice then shut up. You were meant to make peace with your pops, but maybe you were meant to see her again too. Put some skin in the game or you'll lose her for good."

Janie replies solemnly, "Thanks Fernie."

Chapter Forty Five

Three days, a trip to the bank and two trips around town later, Janie's mulishly leaping on her terms.

> *Dear Lydia,*
> *In the spirit of tradition, a letter felt fitting. You said I was a closed book you had to pry open. That's fair but leaving with the belief that I never wrote to you all those years is not entirely true. While I never sent them, I wrote to keep you close in the only way I could manage. You might think me a coward for that, but I'd rather that than have you think me bloodless. As such, I have enclosed the letters. Think of them as the book of Janie, which is more of an abridged archive I reckon.*
> *My friends Fernie and Grace are getting married on New Year's Eve because they're sickeningly sentimental. I'm staying with them for a bit. You'll love them. I've listed you as my plus one, please don't make me look like a lonely loser who made up a girlfriend.*
> *I suppose you noticed the culinary brochure, licensure applications and checks. Choose your adventure. Teaching or starting over, I don't care so long as it's what you want. Wherever it is you're going is where I want to go from here.*
> *Always,*
> *Janie*

A stragglers Thanksgiving marks the end of mud school and two weeks with no word from Lydia. Janie navigates the guilt of keeping Reyna from coming home until Fernie lets her off the hook. Reyna's girl took her home to meet the folks. Hollowed out envy borne of habit lays down its arms at the amusing thought of Reyna smitten enough to endure a family holiday.

Gazing into her cereal as a clairvoyant does their looking glass, *Lead Me On* builds through the fourth track.

Pushing Janie's phone in front of her, Fernie pleads, "Would you call her already. You're breaking my heart."

"Can't do it." Janie pushes it away. "At this point, doesn't much matter anymore."

Giving a nod, Fernie asks, "Since when are you into Amy Grant?"

Giving the tape deck a cursory glance, Janie smirks. "Bought that with my first paycheck."

"Woulda thought your first album would be more British, ya know mopey. But seriously, Grace loves her. Especially the Christmas stuff."

"Yeah, she's great. Kinda wish I could have heard it then, how I hear it now." Dipping to meet her overflowing spoon, Janie slurps her cereal.

Closing his lunch sack, Fernie pats her back. "Grace got you some bologna and Fritos. See you tonight."

Shadowing a junior engineer grants Janie periphery access to an insular social circle, afterthought invites to happy hours and all. The dues to be paid are more akin to fitting in among the Nightingales than proving you're worth your salt.

Each day the cafeteria cashier watches Janie toss her lunch in the bin then raid the premade case. After a few days, she jokes that Janie reminds her of her son. Lacking the heart to explain that biting into a bologna sandwich makes her relive her father's death, she laughs along at the affable comparison to a second grader and rejoices in finishing off the container this morning. She's only begun to learn the extent to which our memories haunt us like the dead never could.

Laying out her clothes, Janie turns her phone on and off again. She accepts that there are no missed calls lodged in there, that's that.

Fernie trims down twenty-three pounds for the big day, while Grace is uncharacteristically filled in around the middle. No one speaks of it. Judy crochets a shawl of ivory linen, proclaiming "No one's arms should be bare for a winter wedding."

An empty seat her companion, Janie's less hopeful with each swing of the doors. Hugs and kisses abound among long-removed friends and family. Excusing herself to wait in the lobby, she wonders if her pride isn't off hiding somewhere behind a vase or locked in the coat closet.

Naturally, Reyna and her girlfriend come through the door that Janie's stalking. Her girlfriend's anything but Reyna's usual type. Instead of young and attention seeking, she's a grounded and self-assured woman.

Hugging Reyna for perhaps longer than she should, Janie would rather ask for forgiveness later. "I can't believe how long it's been. It's good to see you."

"Janie, this is Marla."

Prepared for a bit of arguably earned scorn, there's none. Only compassion. "I'm sorry about your daddy, darlin." Marla pulls Janie in for a hug.

Reyna eyes Fernie, cornered by another cousin at the bar. "Going to the bar, old fashioned?"

"I'll take a Shiner, ol' glen and jack are out to pasture for a minute." Janie laughs, shrinking at what Reyna might have to say about it.

Throwing her arm around Janie, Marla gives her an affirming squeeze. "Good girl. I like to cleanse my palate every so often too."

Dinner's a wonderful distraction, filled with stories of yesteryear. Janie sits in an empty spot next to Reyna and Marla. "I have something for you. You guys wanna walk me to my car?"

Fifteen minutes of circular goodbyes later, they cross the dark lot. Janie's heart sinks with each step.

"You're still driving this thing?" Reyna asks.

Patting the oxidized roof, "She's a beast alright. We made it halfway across the country and back together, figure I owe her some loyalty in turn."

"Lucky her." Reyna's eyes glisten with mollified aggrievement.

Lifting an envelope from the passenger seat, Janie falls silent.

Immediately recognizing the handwriting, Reyna steps back into Marla. "When? Did he OD?"

"Last summer." Her eyes low, "I guess he'd had enough. He left this for you."

"Goddamnit Butch," Reyna laments, emptying the contents into her palm. The humble Wittnauer watch, and a gold ring are the sum of it. Pressing it to her chest, she leans into Marla weeping.

Leaving the note tucked in her bag, Janie makes no mention of it given how gutted she is. Reyna was always the one with her emotions on a tight leash. A little too tight if you had asked Fernie or Janie, though no one ever did, least of all Reyna. Her seeking comfort in someone else is a bittersweet cleaving of who they are from what they were. Reyna runs her thumb over the ring's insignia, and his loss deftly cuts through Janie all over again.

Laughing through tears, Janie asks, "Is that his class ring?"

Sliding the ring onto her thumb, Reyna admires it. "I gave him so much shit about it, he said he'd leave it to me with that damn watch we fought over at the flea market. I guess he made good."

In that, Janie lets go of her diluted umbrage over Butch promising her a watch that was already promised to Reyna.

"We should get going." Wiping her eyes, "We're having lunch with my Mom before the wedding."

Taking in Marla's excitement and Reyna's apprehension, Janie gives a knowing nod. "Fernie said they were coming. You'll do fine."

"Should've said it earlier, I'm sorry about your Dad." Reyna wraps her arms around Janie, and when she pulls back traces of that old look endure.

Awake and coming to terms with the likelihood Lydia's not coming, Janie tiptoes out. Somehow or another, she'll get through tomorrow with bells on. She'll smile big for her dear friends, slip some ginger chews in Grace's bag, and send them on their Belizean honeymoon. When she's done with that, she'll stitch herself up and find a way to get on with it.

Driving a desolate highway, she's bound for the first rig she ever worked on. Stopping for gas and coffee, she half expects to see Reyna staring back at her, judging how much sugar she's adding as she drowns her own in creamer. Those days are gone, they have to be. The omniscient crackle of AM radio is her only companion this evening.

Squeezing between the chain bound fence, her vision settles into the darkness. Years decommissioned, Dessa No. 4 sits massive, lurking imposingly in the shadows. Glimpses of the derrick are betrayed only by the moon shining brightly through vagabond clouds. All is eerily still, save for the occasional creaking of supports challenged by the breeze.

The cold stings Janie's nose and manifests her breath as she climbs onto the floor. The breeze comes up, whipping her cheeks with frigid lashes. *Janie Harris, you're going to sit your ass up here in the cold till you make some peace with this life.*

Even in the dark, Janie can picture the whole crew working the rig. The way her shoulders ached in those early days of loading the truck. Thinking her arm would snap when she threw all she had into the tongs. Looking up, she can still see Reyna watching from the derrick the way she always did. Believing Janie would hang in there well before Janie believed it. Shame wells in knowing a minuscule part of her would indulge the whim of denying Reyna what she could never give her if it meant not being alone.

It was out here that she grew up with her ragtag family. Where she fell on her face but learned to dust herself off. Not because no one was there. On the contrary, they taught her to trust herself enough to get up on her own. In kind, Janie leaned into occasions where she could lend a hand or an ear. Be it shooting the shit over a cold Shiner after a long shift or hearing an uneasy truth she'd turned her face from. She came away with all she needed to operate in the adult world.

It took going back to Clayton to suss out how far she'd come. To realize our lives are made up of eras, still, decades have a way of deceiving our senses. For folks like Fernie and Grace they pass stealthily with little more than the hinting of crow's feet or Lucas wearing out his favorite hat. For others like Kate, they render familiar topography alien. And for most everyone, at some point, the loved ones who signaled home will fade to memories staining our cheeks when our hearts strain to see them again.

Zipping her coat, Janie slouches into her collar. There's serenity in accepting what she cannot forgive or forget. Not in burying it to fester, but in letting it be, absent the wherewithal to let it go. She can only hope this is but one step on the path to forgiving and being forgiven.

Sleeping for a few hours, she hurries to iron her dress, get ready, and pitch in.

Wandering the church grounds, Janie breaks. Her call goes straight to voicemail. "It's ten till. I'm guessin' you're not coming. That's fair." Staring up, again the words hang just out of reach. "My God, this is so stupid. If you don't wanna live in Texas, fine. I'll come to you. I just want to be with you. You asked me to call and I didn't, but I'm calling now. Ya know what else, fuck the Victorians and their goddamned letters. That sounded sorta angry, but I'm not. Think it's adrenaline or somethin'. Anyway, thank you for the phone and I hope to talk to you soon."

First-rate, that wasn't incoherent at all. Janie resigns to an evening of wearing a preacher's smile and eating her feelings like everyone else without a date. Heading to the chapel, she catches sight of Reyna darting by with a garment bag. She hurries to catch up. "Where's Marla?"

Holding her pace, "Parking."

"Listen, there's something I need to say. I owed you way more. I'm sorry." Heading her off, Janie presses, "Reyna, I need you to hear me."

Ready to move around her, Reyna stops. "It's forgotten, you owe me nothing."

"Clearly it's not and I do. You're my family. We belong in each other's lives."

"And you're mine. We're okay, really. There are things I wish I could change, but it's hard when you're in it. I'm one state away, I'll be around." Reyna's smirk has ambitions of grinning. "Can we start walking now?"

Grappling her with a brisk hug, Janie throws a lighthearted glare. "Marla's kind of great. Happy's a good look on you, don't mess it up."

"I won't." Reyna hands the bag off to a groomsman. "She can out drink me, out cook me, and tells me at least once a week that I'm an asshole. When she gets goin' with that Louisiana French, it's all over."

"That sounds like the makings of a great love story," Janie concedes.

"Well, it's an easy love. We hardly fight and she doesn't make me wanna pull my hair out. So, it works." Reyna waves to Marla. "You think your girl's gonna show? Fernie mentioned you were bringing someone."

Shoulders slumping, Janie sighs. "He told you everything, didn't he?"

With a shrug and a grin, Reyna gives him up. "Yeah, he's kept me in the know since I left. Someone's gotta be there to pull you outta your head."

"Nice." Letting out a half laugh, Janie tugs at her sweater. "I don't think that's gonna work out."

Putting her hands in her pockets, Reyna offers the only encouragement she can. "Take it from me, don't give up so easy. Some people are worth waiting for. Fight for it, if it's what you want." Clearing her throat, she smiles warmly at Janie. "I should catch up with Marla, see you inside."

Chatting idly with Doris and Judy, Janie stalls till she's on her own. Falling back as everyone heads in, Janie stops at the chapel steps. "I didn't think you were coming."

"Sorry I'm late, lost track of time unpacking." Lydia tucks her clutch under her arm, "It's a long drive from Galveston."

Extending her hand, "Should we take our seats?"

Weaving her fingers in Janie's, "I'd like that."

The wedding march swelling, they rise in the pew. Lydia whispers in Janie's ear, "I gave it some thought, and I agree."

"About?" Janie asks, turned to the procession.

Kissing Janie's cheek, she whispers "Fuck the Victorians."

Fin

About the author

Meghan Sorley writes fiction that is cinema for the mind's eye. She also believes music is only marginally less requisite than oxygen for a fulfilling life. Meghan's characters are not bound by genre, mostly likeable except for a couple, and she's not ashamed to admit that she sometimes wonders what they're up to.

Meghan has written since childhood. Her family used to say she could write about anything. After years as an instructional designer, she agrees. She shares an old Victorian house in San Diego with her lovely wife, cheeky children, dogs, cats, and various vagabond creatures who wander into the yard. When she's not playing with her kids or avoiding yard work, she's getting to know the characters in her next novel. Visit meghansorley.com to see what she's up to.

www.ingramcontent.com/pod-product-compliance
Lightning Source LLC
Chambersburg PA
CBHW010652100726
47901CB00012B/2524